PENGUIN MODERN CLASSICS

THE DRAGON AND OTHER STORIES

Clearly too individualistic to live in any kind of Russia, Yevgeny Zamyatin was imprisoned at St Petersburg after the abortive rising in 1905, and later banished. He graduated as a marine architect, spent a year in England, and in 1917 only half-heartedly supported the Bolshevik revolution. He published *The Islanders* (about Britain) in 1918 and wrote *We* in 1920. In 1931, with Gorky's help, he left Communist Russia and died in Paris in 1937.

G000243555

YEVGENY ZAMYATIN

The Dragon

AND OTHER STORIES

Translated and edited by
Mirra Ginsburg

PENGUIN BOOKS

Penguin Books Ltd, Harmondsworth, Middlesex, England
Penguin Books Australia Ltd, Ringwood, Victoria, Australia
Penguin Books (N.Z.) Ltd, 182–190 Wairau Road, Auckland 10, New Zealand

—

First published in the U.S.A. 1966
Published in Great Britain by Victor Gollancz 1972
Published in Penguin Books 1975

—

—

Made and printed in Great Britain by
Cox & Wyman Ltd,
London, Reading and Fakenham
Set in Intertype Times

CONTENTS

TRANSLATOR'S INTRODUCTION

YEVGENY ZAMYATIN
(1884–1937)

We need writers who fear nothing
'Our Goal'

Heretics are the only [bitter] remedy
against the entropy of human thought.
'Literature, Revolution, and Entropy'*

One of the most brilliant Russian writers of the twentieth century, Yevgeny Zamyatin belongs to the tradition in Russian literature represented by Gogol, Leskov, Bely, Remizov, and, in certain aspects of their work, also by Babel and Bugakov. It is a tradition, paradoxically, of experimenters and innovators. Perhaps the principal quality that unites them is their approach to reality and its uses in art – the refusal to be bound by literal fact, the interweaving of reality and fantasy, the transmutation of fact into poetry, often grotesque, oblique, playful, but always expressive of the writer's unique vision of life in his own, unique terms.

It is essentially also a tradition of 'oral' literature, of the 'told' rather than 'written' tale. Its works are alive with the rhythms of Russian speech in all its richness and variety, often elaborated, ornamented, and stylized, but always at its best true to its folk origin.

Wit, imagination, stylistic inventiveness, and great verbal mastery are the hallmarks of this school, and Zamyatin's work was richly endowed with all these.

Zamyatin was born in Lebedyan, Tambov Province, in the

* This essay appears in English translation in *Dissonant Voices in Soviet Literature*, edited by Patricia Blake and May Hayward (New York: Pantheon, 1962).

heartland of Russia's fertile black earth belt. It was a region of rye fields, apple orchards, squat ancient churches, peasants, gypsies, horse fairs, merchants, tavern-keepers, monks, and ample-bodied Russian beauties – and the most vivid Russian speech, which Zamyatin absorbed and later used with such extraordinary virtuosity in his work.

Poet and satirist, Zamyatin reserved to himself at all times the right to mock and to question. His first major published work was 'A Provincial Tale', which appeared in 1913. In 1914 he wrote a novella, 'At the World's End', in which he satirized the life of army officers in a remote garrison town. The magazine in which the novella appeared was confiscated, and Zamyatin was brought to trial for 'maligning the officer corps'. He was ultimately acquitted. This was not his first conflict with Tsarist law. As a member of the Bolshevik faction of the Social Democratic Party during his student days, he had been arrested, kept in solitary confinement for some months, and twice exiled from Petersburg.

A naval architect by training, Zamyatin spent two years during World War I in England, designing and supervising the building of icebreakers for Russia. In 1917 he returned to Petersburg and plunged into the seething literary activity that was one of the most astonishing by-products of the revolution in ruined, ravaged, hungry, and epidemic-ridden Russia. He wrote stories, plays, and criticism; he lectured on literature and the writer's craft; he participated in various literary projects and committees – many of them initiated and presided over by Maxim Gorky – and served on various editorial boards, with Gorky, Blok, Korney Chukovsky, Gumilev, Shklovsky, and other leading writers, poets, critics, and linguists. And very soon he came under fire from the newly 'orthodox' – the 'proletarian' writers who sought to impose on all art the sole criterion of 'usefulness to the revolution'.

While he accepted the revolution, Zamyatin chose the long perspective. He chose to examine the assumptions of Bolshevik orthodoxy which were already becoming requisite during the relatively free first post-revolutionary decade and which were to dominate Russian life and literature for years to come. In

1919–20 he wrote in an impassioned appeal, 'Tomorrow': 'He who has found his ideal today is, like Lot's wife, already turned into a pillar of salt, has already sunk into the earth and does not move ahead. The world is kept alive only by heretics: the heretic Christ, the heretic Copernicus, the heretic Tolstoy. Our symbol of faith is heresy.' A few years later he wrote: 'The most effective way of destroying art is the canonization of one given form and one philosophy.' No wonder he was among the first to become the target of concerted hounding by the Party critics and writers.

In 1920 he wrote his prophetic utopian novel *We* – a projection into the distant future of the totalitarian, mechanized, dehumanized state he saw emerging as the end result of the tenets being forced upon society by the Communist rulers. This novel, which anticipated and probably influenced both Huxley's *Brave New World* and Orwell's *1984*, never appeared in Russia. Its subsequent unauthorized publication abroad and translation into many languages, including English, added fuel to the campaign against its author.

Instead of idealized eulogies to the revolution, Zamyatin wrote stories like 'The Dragon', 'The Cave', and 'A Story About the Most Important Thing', reflecting the starkness and the terror of the time: the little man lost in his uniform, transformed into a dragon with a gun; the starving, frozen intellectual reduced to stealing a few logs of wood; the city turned into a barren prehistoric landscape – a desert of caves and cliffs and roaring mammoths; fratricide and destruction and blood. In 'The Church of God' he questions the Bolshevik tenet that the end justifies the means. In 'The Flood' he gives the central place to individual passions against a background that reflects the vast changes of the time as marginally and obliquely as they were reflected in the consciousness of the characters – residents of an outlying suburb, whose knowledge of the history around them is limited to such facts as the deteriorating quality of coal, the silent machines, the lack of bread.

A merciless and outspoken critic, Zamyatin mocked the 'slice of life' school (in this case, 'slice of revolutionary life') as a throwback to the naïve radical realism of the 1860s. How was it, he asked, that the most vociferously revolutionary proletarian writers were the most retrograde in their work? He preached heresy again and again. If we have no heretics, he wrote, we must invent them, for heresy is essential to health and growth. He rejected realism, whether socialist or bourgeois, as an outworn, reactionary form incapable of meeting the demands of a time when both science and revolution had exploded the solid, familiar world. He urged the use of the familiar only as a springboard – from 'real life' to the realities of being, to philosophy, to the fantastic. 'Life itself', he wrote in an essay on 'The New Russian Prose' (1923), 'has lost its plane reality: it is projected, not along the old fixed points, but along the dynamic coordinates of Einstein, of revolution. In this new projection, the best-known formulas and objects become displaced, fantastic, familiar-unfamiliar. This is why it is so logical for literature today to be drawn to the fantastic plot, or to the amalgam of reality and fantasy.'

In 'Literature, Revolution, and Entropy' (1923), he wrote: 'What we need in literature today are vast philosophic horizons; we need the most ultimate, the most fearsome, the most fearless "Why?" and "What next?" '

Zamyatin was the guiding spirit of the 'Serapion Brethren', a group that included some of the most talented and original young writers (Fedin, Kaverin, Zoshchenko, Vsevolod Ivanov, Lev Lunts, and others). In the face of demands for ideology in art and the cry, 'Whoever is not with us is against us', the Serapion Brethren resisted regimentation and were dedicated to stylistic experiment, variety, and the artist's freedom to express his own vision of life regardless of the dictates of political functionaries. Among the principal credos of the group was Zamyatin's statement that 'true literature can exist only where it is produced by madmen, hermits, heretics, visionaries, rebels, and sceptics'.

A most meticulous craftsman, Zamyatin always remained true to his formulation that 'literature is painting, architecture, and music'. With his prophetic vision and remarkable sense of history he combined a rare sense of form. His stories are built as strictly as poems, with complex groups of interrelated themes and persistent images, echoed and re-echoed like refrains.

Zamyatin was a master of many themes and many styles. Some of his stories, 'In Old Russia', 'The Flood', and 'The North', read like ballads. Others, like 'A Story About the Most Important Thing', are many-faceted, ironic commentaries on contemporary life. Still others, like 'The Healing of the Novice Erasmus' and 'The Miracle of Ash Wednesday', are ribald, tongue-in-cheek inventions. Throughout them all runs a profound concern and profound mockery of his own special kind.

Zamyatin's vision was too large, too far-reaching, too non-conformist, and too openly expressed to be tolerated by the purveyors of official and compulsory dogma. Very early he was branded by Trotsky as 'an internal émigré'. He was repeatedly attacked as a 'bourgeois intellectual', out of tune with the revolution. When the Party-line Association of Proletarian Writers (R.A.P.P.) gained full sway in the latter 1920s, with the end of the New Economic Policy and the introduction of the first Five Year Plan, it set out systematically to crush all originality and independence in the arts. Art had to serve the ends of the Party, or it had no right to exist.

All the instruments of power were brought into use in the campaign for conformity. Faced with grim alternatives, most of Zamyatin's erstwhile pupils and colleagues yielded to pressure, recanted publicly, in many instances rewrote their works, and devoted themselves to turning out the grey eulogies to Communist construction demanded by the dictatorship. Other writers, like Babel and Olesha, chose silence. Many committed suicide. Zamyatin's destruction took another form. One of the most active and influential figures in the All-Russian Writers' Union, which included a variety of literary schools, he became the object of a frenzied campaign of vilification. He was dismissed from his editorial posts; magazines and publishing houses closed their doors to him; those which ventured to publish his work were persecuted; his plays were withdrawn from the stage. Under the pressure of the Party inquisitors, his friends began to be afraid to see him and many of his comrades in the Writers' Union denounced him. He was, in effect, presented with the choice of repudiating his work and his views, or total expulsion from literature. A man of incorruptible and uncompromising courage, Zamyatin resigned from the Writers' Union. In 1929, in his letter of resignation, he wrote that it was impossible for him to remain in a literary organization which, even indirectly, took part in the persecution of its members.* The only thing that remained to him was to lecture on technical subjects at the Polytechnical Institute.

In 1931 Zamyatin wrote to Stalin, requesting permission to go abroad with his wife, with the right to return 'as soon as it becomes possible in Russia to serve great ideas in literature without cringing before little men'. † With the aid of Gorky's intercession he was, surprisingly, allowed to leave Russia. He settled in Paris, where he lived until his death in 1937.

Zamyatin's last years in Paris were years of great material hardship and loneliness. As Remizov wrote, 'He came with sealed lips and a sealed heart.' He found little in common with most of the émigrés who had left Russia a decade earlier. He wrote some articles for French magazines and worked on a novel, *The Scourge of God*. Its central character was Attila, whose epoch, he felt, paralleled our own. The novel was never finished. Zamyatin was buried in a cemetery outside Paris. His funeral was attended only by a small group of friends, and his death went unmentioned in the Soviet press.

Like Bulgakov and like Babel, Zamyatin gives us a glimpse into what post-revolutionary Russian literature might have become had independence, daring, and individuality not been stamped out so thoroughly by the dictatorship. The Russian reader – and by the same token, the Russian writer – was deprived for years of the work of these rich and germinal writers, and the effects, alas, are sadly evident.

Unlike Bulgakov, Babel, and some others, Zamyatin has not yet been granted even partial rehabilitation. His name is occasionally mentioned in recent memoirs, but his works remain virtually unknown in Russia today.

* The full text of this letter appears in English translation in Max Eastman's *Artists in Uniform* (New York: Alfred A. Knopf, 1934), p. 87.

† See pp. 13–17 for the full text of Zamyatin's letter to Stalin.

LETTER TO STALIN

Dear Yosif Vissarionovich,

The author of the present letter, condemned to the highest penalty, appeals to you with the request for the substitution of this penalty by another.

My name is probably known to you. To me as a writer, being deprived of the opportunity to write is nothing less than a death sentence. Yet the situation that has come about is such that I cannot continue my work, because no creative activity is possible in an atmosphere of systematic persecution that increases in intensity from year to year.

I have no intention of presenting myself as a picture of injured innocence. I know that among the works I wrote during the first three or four years after the revolution there were some that might provide a pretext for attacks. I know that I have a highly inconvenient habit of speaking what I consider to be the truth rather than saying what may be expedient at the moment. Specifically, I have never concealed my attitude towards literary servility, fawning, and chameleon changes of colour: I have felt – and I still feel – that this is equally degrading both to the writer and to the revolution. I raised this problem in one of my articles (published in the journal *Dom Iskusstv*, No. 1, 1920) in a form that many people found to be sharp and offensive, and this served as a signal at the time for the launching of a newspaper and magazine campaign against me.

This campaign has continued, on different pretexts, to this day, and it has finally resulted in a situation that I would describe as a sort of fetishism. Just as the Christians had created the devil as a convenient personification of all evil, so the critics have transformed me into the devil of Soviet literature. Spitting at the devil is regarded as a good deed, and everyone spat to the best of his ability. In each of my published works, these critics have inevitably discovered some diabolical intent. In order to seek it out, they have even gone to the length of investing me with prophetic gifts: thus, in one of my tales ('God'), published in the journal *Letopis* in 1916, one critic has managed to find . . . 'a travesty of the revolution in connection with the transition to the N.E.P. [New Economic Policy],' in the story 'The Healing of the Novice Erasmus', written in 1920, another critic (Mashbits-Verov) has discerned 'a parable about leaders who had grown wise after the N.E.P.' Regardless of the content of the given work, the very fact of my signature has become a sufficient reason for declaring the work criminal. Last March the Leningrad *Oblit* [Regional Literary Office] took steps to eliminate any remaining doubts of this. I had edited Sheridan's comedy *The School for Scandal* and written an article about his life and work for the Academy Publishing House. Needless to say, there was nothing of a scandalous nature that I said or could have said in this article. Nevertheless, the *Oblit* not only banned the article, but even forbade the publisher to mention my name as editor of the translation. It was only after I complained to Moscow, and after the *Glavlit* [Chief Literary Office] had evidently suggested that such naïvely open actions are, after all, inadmissible, that permission was granted to publish the article and even my criminal name.

I have cited this fact because it shows the attitude towards me in a completely exposed, so to speak, chemically pure form. Of a long array of similar facts, I shall mention only one more, involving, not a chance article, but a full-length play that I have worked on for almost three years. I felt confident that this play – the tragedy *Attila* – would finally silence those who were intent on turning me into some sort of an obscurantist. I seemed to have every reason for such confidence. My play had been read at a meeting of the Artistic Council of the Leningrad Bolshoi Dramatic Theatre. Among those present at this meeting were representatives of eighteen Leningrad factories. Here are excerpts from their comments (taken from the minutes of the meeting of 15 May, 1928).

The representative of the Volodarsky Plant said: 'This is a

play by a contemporary author, treating the subject of the class struggle in ancient times, analogous to that of our own era ... Ideologically, the play is quite acceptable ... It creates a strong impression and eliminates the reproach that contemporary playwrights do not produce good plays ...'

The representative of the Lenin Factory noted the revolutionary character of the play and said that 'in its artistic level, the play reminds us of Shakespeare's works ... It is tragic, full of action, and will capture the viewer's attention.'

The representative of the Hydro-Mechanical Plant found 'every moment in the play strong and absorbing', and recommended its opening on the theatre's anniversary.

Let us say that the comrade workers overdid it in regard to Shakespeare. Nevertheless, Maxim Gorky has written that he considers the play 'highly valuable both in a literary and social sense', and that 'its heroic tone and heroic plot are most useful for our time'. The play was accepted for production by the theatre; it was passed by the *Glavrepertkom* [Chief Repertory Committee]; and after that ... Was it shown to the audience of workers who had rated it so highly? No. After that the play, already half-rehearsed by the theatre, already announced in posters, was banned at the insistence of the Leningrad *Oblit*.

The death of my tragedy *Attila* was a genuine tragedy to me. It made entirely clear to me the futility of any attempt to alter my situation, especially in view of the well-known affair involving my novel *We* and Pilnyak's *Mahogany,* which followed soon after. Of course, any falsification is permissible in fighting the devil. And so, the novel, written nine years earlier, in 1920, was set side by side with *Mahogany* and treated as my latest, newest work. The manhunt organized at the time was unprecedented in Soviet literature and even drew notice in the foreign press. Everything possible was done to close to me all avenues for further work. I became an object of fear to my former friends, publishing houses and theatres. My books were banned from the libraries. My play (*The Flea*), presented with invariable success by the Second Studio of the Moscow Art Theatre for four seasons, was withdrawn from the repertory. The publication of my collected works by the Federation

Publishing House was halted. Every publishing house which attempted to issue my works was immediately placed under fire; this happened to *Federatsya* ['Federation'], *Zemlya i Fabrika* ['Land and Factory'], and particularly to the Publishing House of Leningrad Writers. This latter took the risk of retaining me on its editorial board for another year and ventured to make use of my literary experience by entrusting me with the stylistic editing of works by young writers – including Communists. Last spring the Leningrad branch of the R.A.P.P. [Association of Proletarian Writers] succeeded in forcing me out of the board and putting an end to this work. The *Literary Gazette* triumphantly announced this accomplishment, adding quite unequivocally: '. . . the publishing house must be preserved, but not for Zamyatins'. The last door to the reader was closed to Zamyatin. The writer's death sentence was pronounced and published.

In the Soviet Criminal Code the penalty second to death is deportation of the criminal from the country. If I am in truth a criminal deserving punishment, I nevertheless do not think that I merit so grave a penalty as literary death. I therefore ask that this sentence be changed to deportation from the U.S.S.R. – and that my wife be allowed to accompany me. But if I am not a criminal, I beg to be permitted to go abroad with my wife temporarily, for at least one year, with the right to return as soon as it becomes possible in our country to serve great ideas in literature without cringing before little men, as soon as there is at least a partial change in the prevailing view concerning the role of the literary artist. And I am confident that this time is near, for the creation of the material base will inevitably be followed by the need to build the superstructure – an art and a literature truly worthy of the revolution.

I know that life abroad will be extremely difficult for me, as I cannot become a part of the reactionary camp there; this is sufficiently attested by my past (membership in the Russian Social Democratic Party [Bolshevik] in Tsarist days, imprisonment, two deportations, trial in wartime for an anti-militarist novella). I know that while I have been proclaimed a Rightwinger here because of my habit of writing according to my conscience rather than according to command, I shall sooner or later probably be declared a Bolshevik for the same reason abroad. But even under the most difficult conditions there, I shall not be condemned to silence; I shall be able to write and to publish, even, if need be, in a language other than Russian. If circumstances should make it impossible (temporarily, I hope) for me to be a Russian writer, perhaps I shall be able, like the Pole Joseph Conrad, to become for a time an English writer, especially since I have already written about England in Russian (the satirical story 'The Islanders' and others), and since it is not much more difficult for me to write in English than it is in Russian. Ilya Ehrenburg, while remaining a Soviet writer, has long been working chiefly for European literature – for translation into foreign languages. Why, then, should I not be permitted to do what Ehrenburg has been permitted to do? And here I may mention yet another name – that of Boris Pilnyak. He has shared the role of devil with me in full measure; he has been the major target of the critics; yet he has been allowed to go abroad to take a rest from this persecution. Why should I not be granted what has been granted to Pilnyak?

I might have tried to motivate my request for permission to go abroad by other reasons as well – more usual, though equally valid. To free myself of an old chronic illness (colitis), I have to go abroad for a cure; my personal presence is needed abroad to help stage two of my plays, translated into English and Italian (*The Flea* and *The Society of Honorary Bell-Ringers,* already produced in Soviet theatres); moreover, the planned production of these plays will make it possible for me not to burden the People's Commissariat of Finances with the request for foreign exchange. All these motives exist. But I do not wish to conceal that the basic reason for my request for permission to go abroad with my wife is my hopeless position here as a writer, the death sentence that has been pronounced upon me as a writer here at home.

The extraordinary consideration which you have given other writers who appealed to you leads me to hope that my request will also be granted.

June 1931

A PROVINCIAL TALE

1 THE SQUARE ONE

His father nagged: 'Study and study, or you'll be like me, patching boots all your life.' But how could he get anywhere at school when he was first on the list alphabetically and therefore always the first to be called?

'Baryba, Anfim. Come forward.'

And Anfim Baryba stood before the class, perspiring, pulling his low forehead still lower over his eyes.

'Not a thing again? A-ah, and look at you – old enough to get married. Sit down, brother.'

Baryba sat down. And he sat thoroughly – two years in every grade. Thus, slowly, unhurriedly, he managed to reach the last.

He was at that time about fifteen, if not more. A moustache had already sprung up on his lip, like a good winter crop, and he ran with the other fellows to watch the women bathe. And afterwards, at night, he might as well not go to bed at all – he'd be beset by such hot dreams, they'd start him on such a merry-go-round, that . . .

In the morning Baryba would get up grumpy and mope around all day, or else he'd run off to the monastery woods till evening. School? To hell with school!

In the evening his father would take the belt to him: 'Sneaked off again? You stubborn tramp, you loafer!'

Deaf and dumb. Might as well talk to the lamp-post. Anfim would clench his teeth and nobody could get a peep out of him. Only the angles of his queer face would become still sharper, pricklier.

And true – it was all angles. No wonder the kids had nicknamed him 'Flat-iron'. Heavy iron jaws, a wide square mouth, and a narrow forehead: a regular flat-iron, with its point up.

And all of Baryba was broad, hulking, lumbering, made up of nothing but hard straight lines and angles. Yet every part was so well fitted to the other that all the clumsy pieces seemed to add up to a whole – a kind of wild, weird whole, but a whole all the same.

The other schoolboys were a bit afraid of Baryba: a brute, he could knock you right onto the ground when he got mad. They teased him from around the corner, from a mile off. But when Baryba was hungry, they fed him buns, and then they had their fun.

'Hey, Baryba, crack this one for half a bun.' And they handed him pebbles, the hardest they could find.

'Not enough. A whole bun,' Baryba would growl sullenly.

'The devil, what a glutton!' But they would dig up a whole bun. And Baryba would start to crack the pebbles with his teeth for the boys' delectation, grinding them up with his iron crushers – as many as you please! A marvel!

Still, fun or no fun, when exams came round, the wags, too, had to get down to their books, even though green Maytime beckoned outside.

The first of the matriculation exams was set by law on the eighteenth, the name day of the Empress Alexandra. And so, one evening, Baryba's father put aside his wax end and the boot he was stitching, removed his glasses, and said: 'Remember now, Anfimka, mind what I say. If you fail this time too, I'll kick you out.'

Well, then, he had three days to bone up. But as if in spite, the kids had got a game of pitch and toss going – and who could resist that? For two days Anfimka was out of luck; he lost his entire capital: seven ten-kopek pieces and his new belt, with a buckle. He could have jumped into the lake. But on the third day – thank God! – he won back everything, and even made more than half a rouble on top of that.

On the eighteenth, Baryba was naturally called first. There wasn't a sound in the room; his classmates waited to see the poor devil flunk.

Baryba stretched himself to his full height and stared at the white slip he had drawn. The whiteness of the paper and his terror made him queasy. All the words had dropped clean out of his head – not a one left.

From the first row, prompters began to whisper: 'Tigris and Euphrates . . . The garden where they lived ; . . Mesopotamia. Me-so-po-ta . . . Deaf idiot!'

Baryba spoke up – splitting off word after word, like rocks – slow, heavy.

'Adam and Eve. Between the Tigris and . . . that . . . oh . . . Euphrates. Paradise was a huge garden. In which there lived mesopotamuses. And other animals . . .'

The priest nodded, seemingly friendly. Baryba took courage.

'And who were those mesopotamuses? Eh, Anfim? Explain it to us, my friend.'

'The mesopotamuses . . . they were a kind of ancient beast. Very fierce. And they lived in paradise. Next to . . .'

The priest grunted like a pig with laughter, covering his face with his beard. The boys were flat on their desks.

Baryba didn't bother to go home. He knew: his father was a man of his word – he never spoke in vain. Whatever he said, he did. All that Baryba could expect at home was a good strapping on top of everything.

2 WITH THE DOGS

There had once been a family in town, the Balkashins, respected merchants who owned a brewery. One year the cholera killed them off, to the last one. It was said that they had heirs in some big city far away, but the heirs never came. And the abandoned house stood empty and neglected. Its wooden tower leaned askew, the windows were boarded over criss-cross, the yard was overgrown with tall weeds. The townspeople threw blind pups and kittens over the fence to die; stray dogs crept in under the fence to hunt.

And it was there that Baryba moved in. He picked for himself an old cowshed; the doors were unlocked, and there was a big wooden manger inside – it made a fine bed. Baryba had himself a time: there was no need to study, he could do whatever came into his head. He could swim until his teeth began to chatter, or tag along after the hurdy-gurdy man all day, or take off to the monastery garden, days and nights on end – anything he pleased.

It would have been fine, but soon he ran out of food. How long could a rouble last?

Baryba took to hanging around the market. With clumsy animal deftness, long-armed, hiding within himself and staring out sharply from under his brow, he dodged in and out among the raised white shafts of peasant carts, among the horses munching oats, among the gabbling village women; the moment one of the women looked away, he had his dinner.

If the pickings were lean in the market-place, Baryba would run off to the Streletsk district. Now walking, now crawling on all fours, he scoured the backyards, barns, orchards. The rank odour of wormwood tickled his nostrils, but God forbid if he should sneeze: the mistress was right there, weeding her garden patch, her red kerchief diving in and out of the greenery. Baryba would gather an armful of potatoes, carrots, whatnot, then he would bake them at home, in the Balkashin yard, and gulp them down, without salt, burning himself, until his belly was full. It wasn't fancy, naturally; still, he kept alive.

Some days he'd have no luck at all. And then Baryba would sit, starved, and stare with wolfish, envious eyes at the dogs, cracking their bones, playing with them contentedly. Baryba stared at the dogs ...

Days passed, weeks, months. He was sick to the stomach of living in the Balkashin yard with the hungry mutts! Baryba became tough and bone-hard, hairy, black. His leaness made his jaws and cheekbones still more angular, his face still heavier, still more square.

If he could only get away from this dog's life, be with people, live for a while like a man – drink a glass of hot tea, sleep under a blanket.

There were days when Baryba would lie from dawn to dusk

in his shed, face down in the straw. There were days when Baryba paced back and forth all day in the Balkashin yard, longing for people, for something human.

In the next yard, at the Chebotarevs', there were people from early morning on: tanners in leather aprons, drivers with cart-loads of skins. They'd catch sight of an eye rolling round in a knothole in the fence and crack their whips: 'Hey, who's there?' 'Hey, master, there's a goblin loose in the Balkashin yard!'

Baryba would spring with wolflike leaps back to his shed and huddle in the straw. If he could only lay his hands on those drivers – he'd . . .

At noon he heard knives clattering in the Chebotarev kitchen and smelled roasting meat. Baryba would go into a shaking fit and stay glued to his lookout hole until they had finished eating.

When they finished, he'd ease up a bit himself. They'd finish, and the Chebotarev woman would waddle out into the yard – red, bloated with too much sitting and too much grub, barely able to walk.

'U-uh . . .' Baryba would grit his teeth, iron against iron.

On holidays the pealing of the bells in the Church of the Holy Virgin would spread over the Balkashin yard from up the alley – and the bells made life seem still more bitter to Baryba. They'd ring and ring, making his ears hum, setting up a ringing in his head . . .

'But that's where! To the monastery, to Yevsey!' the church-bells suddenly gave Baryba an idea.

When he was still a little boy, he'd run off to Yevsey after a whipping. And, always, Yevsey would give him tea with mon-astery-baked pretzels, and talk to him, and console him: 'Eh, you poor lad! The other day the Father Superior grabbed me by the holy hair, and I . . . Eh, you . . . And you're bawling?'

In high spirits, Baryba came running to the monastery: he was done with the Balkashin dogs.

'Father Yevsey in?'

The novice covered his mouth with his fist and roared with laughter: 'Hu-h! You couldn't find him with bloodhounds if you tried: he's been out drinking all week in Streltsy.'

There was no Yevsey. It was the end. There was no other place to go. Back to the Balkashin yard ...

3   CHICKS

After vespers or after mass the priest of the Holy Virgin Church would catch up with Chebotarikha and shake his head: 'It isn't right, Mother. You ought to walk, to take some exercise. If you don't look out, the flesh will get you altogether.'

And Chebotarikha, spread out like dough across her three-seat droshky, would reply, tight-lipped: 'Impossible, Father, I've got steady palpitation of the heart.'

And she would roll on through the dust, spilling over the sides of the droshky – of a piece with it, lumbering, heavy, rubber-tyred. No one ever saw Chebotarikha in the street on her own feet, without wheels. Even to the Chebotarev baths (her husband had left her the tannery and the public baths) right around the corner she would ride out in the droshky every Friday – that was the women's day.

And therefore Chebotarikha set great store by this droshky, and the piebald gelding, and the coachman Urvanka. Especially Urvanka – curly, powerful as the devil, black. He might have been a gypsy. He always seemed sooty, somehow, short, squat, tendony, like a strong knot out of a good rope. People were saying that he wasn't only a coachman to Chebotarikha. But they said it on the sly, they wouldn't dare to say it in the open – Urvanka could thrash a man to death ... Beating a man till he was nearly dead was Urvanka's prime pleasure; he had gotten plenty of beatings himself during his horse-thieving days.

And yet Urvanka had his loves too. He loved horses and hens. He'd scrape and scrape a horse, and comb his mane with his copper comb and talk to it in his own queer language. Maybe it was true he wasn't a Christian.

As for hens, Urvanka loved them because in the spring they had been chicks – yellow, round, soft. He'd chase after them across the yard: 'Uti, uti, uti!' He'd crawl under the water cart, or under the porch on all fours, but he would catch them in the

end, and hold them in his palm, and – the greatest of his
pleasures! – warm them with his breath. And he'd make sure
that nobody would see his face at those times. God knows what
he looked like – who could imagine without seeing it? Urvanka
and the chick! Queer.

To Baryba's misfortune, he had also gotten fond of Urvanka's chicks. They were delicious, and he took to stealing
them. Urvanka noticed one missing, another, a third. He
couldn't imagine where the chicks could have disappeared. Unless a polecat had got into the neighbourhood.

One afternoon Urvanka lay dozing in a cart by the shed. The
heat was overpowering. Even the chicks had taken refuge under
the shed; they huddled by the wall, pulled down their inner
eyelids, and nodded. And they didn't see, poor things, that the
board behind them had been ripped away, and a hand was
stretching towards them . . . Grab! and a chick set up a frantic
chittering in Baryba's fist.

Urvanka jumped up, yelling. In a moment he was over the
fence.

'Hold him, hold him, hold the thief!'

A wild animal chase. Baryba dashed to his shed, his manger,
and dug himself in under the straw, but Urvanka found him.
He pulled him out and put him on his feet.

'You wait now! I'll show you – stealing my chicks . . .'

And he dragged him off by the scruff of the neck to Chebotarikha: let her devise a punishment for the thief.

4   GOD'S MERCY

Chebotarikha had thrown out Anisya, her fat-jowled cook.
What for? So that she wouldn't make eyes at Urvanka. She
threw her out, and now she was in a hole. She couldn't find a
decent cook in the whole town. In the end she had to hire Polka,
a worthless, scrawny chit of a girl.

The churchbells rang for vespers. Polka was sweeping the
floor in the parlour, after scattering dry used-up tea-
leaves over it, as Chebotarikha had taught her. Chebotarikha

herself sat right there on the cretonne-covered sofa, dying of boredom and staring at the glass fly-catcher: the fly-catcher was filled with cider, and flies had drowned themselves in the cider from sheer boredom. Chebotarikha yawned and made the sign of the cross over her mouth. 'Oh, Lord our Father, have mercy on us . . .'

And He was merciful: there was a sudden stamping and shouting in the entrance hall – and Urvanka pushed Baryba in. Baryba was so stunned at the sight of Chebotarikha that he even stopped trying to break away; only his eyes ran from corner to corner like mice.

The moment Chebotarikha heard about the chicks, she went into a spluttering rage. 'Raised his hand against the chicks, against God's own little angels? The murderer, the scoundrel! Polyushka, bring me the whisk. Bring it over here, bring it over, I won't listen to anything!'

Urvanka bared his teeth, kicked him from behind with his knee, and in a second Baryba was on the floor. He tried to bite, he wriggled like a snake, but how could he fight against that devil Urvanka? In a moment Urvanka flattened him out, straddled him, pulled off Baryba's tattered trousers, and only waited for Chebotarikha to say the word to start the punishment.

But Chebotarikha couldn't say a word; she was shaking in a fit of laughter. At last she forced her eyes open: why were they suddenly so quiet on the floor?

She opened her eyes, and the laughter vanished. She bent down closer to Baryba's straining body, strong as an animal's.

'Get out, Urvan. Get off, I say, get off! Let me question him properly . . .' She did not look at Urvanka, her eyes were off in the corner.

Urvanka slowly got up; on the threshold he turned and slammed the door with all his strength.

Baryba jumped up and dashed for his trousers: good Lord, there was nothing left of them but strips of rag. Well, then, he must run . . .

But Chebotarikha held him fast by the hand: 'Whose boy are you?' She pouted her lips, and instead of 'boy' she said 'buy',

She tried to look important, but Baryba sensed something else as well.

'I'm the sh-shoemaker's ...' And suddenly he recalled his whole life and began to whine and whimper. 'My father kicked me out for the exam, I li-lived ... in the Bal ... in the Balka-shi-i ...'

Chebotarikha slapped her hands and broke into a pitying singsong: 'Oh, you poor little orphan, you luckless soul! Kicked out – his own son? And he calls himself a father ...'

She wailed her song and dragged Baryba somewhere by the hand. Baryba ambled after her with gloomy submission.

'... And nobody to teach you to be good. And the tempter, naturally, he's right there: steal and steal, steal a chick! Right?'

Her bedroom. A huge bed, with a mountain of feather quilts. A small lamp in the corner before the icons, their silver mountings glinting in the light.

She pushed Baryba down on a little rug. 'On your knees, get down on your knees. Pray, Anfimushka, pray. The Lord is merciful, he will forgive you. And I'll forgive ...'

She herself settled down behind him and began to pray in a furious whisper. Baryba stood petrified on his knees, bewildered. 'I must get up, I must get out of here. I must get up ...'

'Well, and what's the matter with you, eh? Didn't they teach you how to cross yourself?' Chebotarikha seized Baryba's hand. 'There, that's how: the forehead, the stomach ...' She was pressed to him from behind, breathing on his neck.

Suddenly, unexpectedly to himself, Baryba turned around and, clenching his jaws, he sank his hands deep into something soft as dough.

'Oh, you! So that's what you are after? Eh? Well, then, well, I'll take a sin upon myself for your sake, for a poor orphan's sake.'

Baryba drowned in the sweet, hot dough.

At night Polka spread a blanket for him on the trunk in the foyer. Baryba shook his head: such wonders in God's world. He fell asleep with a full belly, well pleased.

27

5 WHAT A LIFE!

Oh, yes, this wasn't anything like living in the Balkashin yard.
Baryba had all he wanted, he lived in peace, he slept on soft
feather-beds, in rooms well heated by pot-bellied stoves. All day
he lounged about in sweet idleness. At dusk he'd snooze off on
the oven next to the purring Vaska. He ate his fill. What a life!

He ate from morning until night, until he'd break into a
sweat, until he couldn't breathe. That was the way of the house.

In the morning – tea with steamed milk, with all sorts of buns
and doughnuts baked with buttermilk. Chebotarikha would sit
there in her white night jacket (not so white at that), a kerchief
on her head.

'Why do you wear a kerchief all the time?' Baryba would
ask.

'Is that how they taught you? How can a woman go around
bareheaded? I'm not a girl, it's a sin. I've been properly wedded
to my lawful husband. I'm not one of them loose wenches,
going with their hair uncovered . . .'

Or else they'd strike up a conversation good for the digestion:
about dreams, about the dream book, about Martin Zadek,
about signs and spells and portents.

Before you turned around, it was going on twelve, and time
for lunch. Jellied pigs' knuckles, cabbage soup, sheatfish or
pickled carp, roast gut stuffed with buckwheat, tripe with horse-
radish, dilled watermelon and apples, and more and more.

At noon you could neither sleep nor go for a swim in the
river: the noontime goblin might get you. And, of course, you
could barely stay awake: the unholy one tempted you, made
you yawn.

Green with boredom, Baryba would wander off into the
kitchen, to Polka. She was a nitwit; still, she was a living soul.
He'd find the tomcat, Polka's favourite, and start stuffing him
into a boot. The kitchen would become a bedlam of squealing
and pleading. Polka would dash around him frantically. 'Anfim
Yegorych, Anfim Yegorych, for Christ's sake, let Vasenka
alone!'

Anfimka would bare his teeth in a wide grin and push the cat in still deeper. And Polka would now plead with Vasenka: 'Don't cry, Vasenka, just have a little patience, baby, just wait a moment! He'll let you go now, in a minute.'

The cat yowled in a desperate voice. Polka's eyes popped, her pigtail dropped over her shoulder, she tugged at Baryba's sleeve with her feeble hand, 'Scr-ram, or I'll whack you with the boot!'

Baryba would fling the boot with the tomcat across the kitchen into the corner, and roar with laughter, clattering like a cart over a rutted road.

Supper was early, at eight. Polka would bring in the food, and Chebotarikha would send her off to sleep, to get her out of the way. Then she would take out the decanter from the cabinet.

'Have some, Anfimushka, have another glass.'

They drank silently. The lamp smoked and hissed. For a long time nobody paid any attention to it.

'It's smoking. I ought to tell her,' thought Baryba. But he could not marshal his drowning thoughts, he could not utter a word.

Chebotarikha poured more and more, for him, for herself. In the expiring light her whole face melted into a great dim blur. And nothing could be seen except the greedy mouth – a wet red hole. The whole face was nothing but a mouth. And Baryba felt the smell of her sweaty, sticky body closing in upon him.

The lamp was dying in long, slow anguish. The black snow of soot floated in the room. Stench.

And in the bedroom – the holy lamp, the glimmering of the gold and silver mountings on the icons. The bed was made, and Chebotarikha knelt on the rug, bowing to the floor again and again in prayer.

And Baryba knew: the more bows, the more furious her prayers for forgiveness of her sins, the longer she would torment him at night.

If one could hide in some corner, if one could crawl away into some cockroach crack . . .

But there was no way out: the doors were bolted, the window sealed with darkness.

No, Baryba's service wasn't easy. But Chebotarikha adored him more and more with every passing day. He'd taken such a hold on her that all she thought of was how to pamper him some more. 'Anfimushka, another plate? . . .' 'It's bitter chill today! Anfimushka, let me tie your scarf, eh?' 'Anfimushka, you've got a bellyache again? Such trouble! Here, here's some vodka with salt and mustard, drink it down – it's the best remedy.'

Bottle-shaped boots, a silver watch on a chain, new rubber galoshes . . . and Baryba strutted like a rooster over the Chebotarev yard, ordering everybody about.

'Hey, you, clodhopper, where did you dump those skins? What did I tell you?'

And he would fine the culprit, and the peasant would crumple his torn cap in his hands, bowing low.

There was only one man Baryba gave a wide berth – Urvanka. Even Chebotarikha herself would not escape Baryba's anger now and then. He'd suffer her and suffer her, and then she'd give him such a night he couldn't see straight in the morning, and all he wanted was to run off to the end of the world. Then Baryba would lock himself in the parlour and pace back and forth, back and forth as in a cage.

And Chebotarikha would shrink down, subdued. She'd call Polka: 'Polyushka, go over and see how he's doing there? Or better, call him to supper.'

Polka would come back, giggling: 'He won't come. He's raving mad, he just keeps stomping around from corner to corner!'

And Chebotarikha would wait with supper an hour, two hours. And if she waited with supper, if she broke the sacred dinner hour – that meant . . .

6   AT THE CHURILOV TAVERN

Baryba grew fat and smooth in his steward's job, on the good, rich diet. The postman, Chernobylnikov, an old acquaintance, met him on Dvoryanskaya and spread his hands in wonder. 'A different man, I could hardly recognize him. A regular merchant!'

Chernobylnikov envied Baryba: the fellow had himself an easy life. There was no getting out of it – Baryba must stand his friends a drink in the tavern. What did it mean to him, with all his wealth? The postman flattered and cajoled him into it.

At seven, as agreed, Baryba came to the Churilov tavern. Lord, what a jolly place! Chatter, noise, lights. The whiteclad waiters dashed back and forth, drunken voices flickered in the air like the spokes in a wheel.

Baryba's head began to go round and round, and he couldn't for the life of him find Chernobylnikov.

And Chernobylnikov was already hailing him from the distance: 'He-ey, merchant, over here!'

The postman's buttons glittered. Next to him was another man – tiny, sharp-nosed. He looked as though he weren't sitting on a chair, but hopping up and down on a twig, like a sparrow.

Chernobylnikov nodded at the sparrow. 'Timosha, the tailor. A good man to talk to.'

Timosha smiled – lit a warm little lamp on his pointed face. 'A tailor, yes. I make over brains.'

Baryba opened his mouth, meaning to ask him something, but somebody pushed him in the shoulder from behind. A waiter, with a tray on his arm, was already setting out beers on the table. Voices babbled in confusion, and over them all a single one – belonging to a red-haired townsman, a horse trader – roared: 'Mitka, hey, Mitka, you dunderhead, will you bring it here or not?' And he broke into song again:

> *I'm walking for the last time*
> *Down this long wide street . . .*

When Timosha heard that Baryba had been a student in the district school, he was delighted. 'So the priest tripped you up? Oh, yes, I know him, I know him very well. I used to do some tailoring for him. He hates my guts!'

'Why so?'

31

'Oh, for my talk. The other day I said to him, "How will it be with our saints in the next world? Take St Timothy, my blessed patron saint, my guardian angel: he'll see me roasting to a crisp in hell and then go back to munching his paradise apples? That's infinite mercy for you! A saintly soul! And he can't get out of it, either, he can't refuse to see me or to know what's happening to me – it is his duty according to the catechism." The priest, he just clammed up – he didn't know what to say.'

'That's a good one!' Baryba neighed, rumbled.

' "You'd better," the priest says to me, "try to do some good deeds instead of wagging your tongue." And I say to him: "Why should I do good? I'd rather do evil – that's much more useful to my neighbours. After all, doesn't the Holy Book say they will be repaid a hundredfold in the next world for any evil I might do them?" He almost had a fit! . . .'

'Good for him, serves him right,' Baryba gloated. He could almost love Timosha for getting the priest's goat – he could almost love him, but Baryba wasn't made of loving clay, he was too tough, too heavy to be turned into paths of love.

On the red-headed man's table the glasses jumped and clanked. A huge fist, overgrown with yellow hair, was banging on the table. The man was roaring: 'Come on, say it again! Just say it once more! Come on, now, let's see you do it!'

The men at the neighbouring tables jumped up, crowded over, craned their necks: our people love a scandal – don't feed them honey, give them a good scandal!

A long-necked, lanky fellow dived out of the mêlée, approached their table, and greeted Chernobylnikov. He had a cap with a badge under his arm.

'Remarkable . . . And immediately they all pile up like sheep,' he said in a thin, high voice and pouted contemptuously.

He sat down, paying no attention to Timosha and Baryba, speaking only to Chernobylnikov: a postman, after all, was also an official personage of sorts.

Timosha loudly explained to Baryba: 'He's the county treasurer's son-in-law. The treasurer married off his last daughter, the old maid, to him, and got him a spot in the treasury, clerking. So he's full of airs.'

The treasurer's son-in-law pretended not to hear and said to Chernobylnikov in a still louder voice: 'And after the inspection he was presented to the provincial secretary . . .'

Chernobylnikov drawled respectfully: 'The provincial secretary! . . .'

Timosha could stand it no longer, and broke into the conversation.

'Say, postman, Chernobylnikov, do you remember how the police chief kicked him out of the club? . . . Let him have it – right in the you know what? . . .'

'I would ask you . . . I would ask you most earnestly!' the treasurer's son-in-law hissed furiously.

But Timosha continued: '. . . "I bet you won't!" "I bet I will!" Well, one word and another, and they made a wager. So he barged into the gentry's club. And the treasurer was just having a game of billiards with the police chief. Our fop here walks over to his father-in-law and whispers something in his ear – as if he'd come on business. And then he just keeps standing there. So the police chief starts aiming his cue and backing up, and backing up, until he "accidentally" pushed him right out of the door – with his cue against you know what. Good Lord, they almost died laughing!'

Baryba and Chernobylnikov were groaning with laughter.

The treasurer's son-in-law rose and stalked out without a glance.

'Oh, well, we'll make it up one day,' Timosha said. 'He wasn't a bad fellow, you know. Now, he's got a badge outside his forehead, and garbage inside.'

7 THE ORANGE TREE

Polka, that barefoot ninny, had a single window in her kitchen, and even in that window the glass had turned all colours with age. On the window Polka had a little jar.

About six months ago she had planted an orange seed in the jar, and now, before you knew it, there was a little tree: one, two, three, four leaves, tiny, glossy.

Polka would putter around in the kitchen, clatter with her pots, and then run to the window again to smell the leaves.

'A marvel! There was a seed, and now . . .'

She watched and tended it. Somebody had told her that soup was good for growth, and she began to water the little tree with soup if any was left over from supper.

One day Baryba came home late from the tavern and got up in the morning, sore as a wolf. He drank some tea and went off to the kitchen to ease his soul. Polka called him 'master' now – it flattered him.

Polka was fussing at her window, near her beloved little tree.

'Where's the tom?'

Polka went on puttering without turning back. She answered timidly: 'He's gone, master. Somewhere in the yard, I guess, where else?'

'What're you cooking, up there?'

She was silent, frightened, a saucer of soup in her hand.

'So-up? To water the weed? Is that why you get soup, you ninny? Give it here right away!'

'B-but, master, it's an urange . . .'

Polka fluttered with terror: oh-h, what would happen now? 'I'll show you, urange! Watering it with soup, you fool, eh?'

Baryba seized the jar with the orange. Polka bawled. Eh, what's the use of bothering with her? He pulled the seedling out with the root, and tossed it out of the window; then he put the jar back in its place. As simple as that.

Polka wailed loudly. The tears left dirty streaks down her cheeks, and she was keening like a peasant woman: 'My little urange! Father in Heaven, what will I do without you . . .'

Baryba gaily shoved her from behind, and she tumbled out of the door, across the yard, and into the cellar.

It was as though he had crushed a rock between his teeth in this little exchange with Polka over her orange, and he felt better right away. Baryba bared his teeth, grinning, becoming drunk again.

Through the window he saw her go down into the cellar. A

millstone turned slowly in his head, and his heart suddenly began to hammer.

He went out into the yard, looked around on all sides, and slipped into the cellar, closing the door tightly after him.

After bright sunshine – darkness. It blinded him. He felt along the damp walls, stumbling.

'Polka, where are you? Where are you holed up, you goose?'

He could hear her sniffling somewhere, whimpering, but where?

The cellar was damp and mouldy as a grave. He felt with his hands along the potatoes, along some barrels; a wooden lid came rattling down from some jug.

There she was – sitting on a pile of potatoes, rubbing her face, smearing the tears. There was a tiny crevice somewhere up above, and one sly, squinting ray slipped in and picked off a piece of Polka's pigtail with its ragged ribbon, her fingers, her grubby cheek.

'That'll do, that'll do, quit bawling, dry up!'

Baryba leaned against her lightly, and she keeled over. She moved obediently, all of her like a rag doll. But she began to whimper even more.

His mouth felt dry, his tongue could barely turn. He muttered something, just to divert her mind from what he was doing.

'Just imagine, such a big thing, an ur-range! And you go bawling over it? Wait, I will buy you a geranium 'stead of the urange ... Geranium ... you know ... with a smell ..'

Polka shook and whimpered, and this sharpened Baryba's pleasure with a special sweetness.

'All right, all right! Now you can blubber all you want,' Baryba repeated like a refrain.

He got rid of Polka, and remained a while longer in the cellar, stretched on a pile of potatoes, resting.

Suddenly Baryba grinned, pleased with himself. He said aloud to Chebotarikha: 'Well, you old feather-bed, take that! You thought you had me, eh?'

And he showed her a fig in the dark.

He came out of the cellar, squinting against the sun. He looked under the shed: Urvanka was puttering there, with his back to him.

8   TIMOSHA

They were having tea at the tavern. Timosha looked at him closely, observing him.

'You're a kind of hard, uncomfortable man, as I see. They must have beaten you a lot; maybe that's it.'

'They did, how else?' Baryba laughed. He was flattered: he sure had gotten plenty of beatings, but let anybody try it now.

'That's why you've turned out this way, love. You've got as much soul or conscience as a chicken . . .'

And he went off on his favourite topic – all about God: there was no God, and yet man had to live according to God's law; and on and on, about faith, and about books. Baryba was not accustomed to so much turning of the millstones in his head; Timosha's fancy words wearied him. But still he listened, lumbering after Timosha like a heavy cart. Who else was he to listen to if not Timosha? The man had a head on his shoulders.

And Timosha had already come to his main point: 'Sometimes you think – there is a God. And then you turn around and take another look – and again there's nothing. Just nothing: no God, no earth, no water, nothing but an abyss under the heavens. Nothing but what seems to be.'

Timosha turned his head, sparrow fashion, this way and that. Something troubled him.

'Nothing but what seems to be. Just to come to this! No, but just try and live with this nothing, face to face, alone, try and live with nothing but air. That, brother . . .'

Then he saw that Baryba was way behind him, stumbling, lost.

Timosha waved his hand. 'Eh, what's the good! It doesn't mean a thing to you, all that you live by is the belly . . . Your God is something to be eaten.'

They went out of the tavern. It was a June night, the air was pleasant, filled with the smell of linden trees; the crickets chirped away for all they were worth in the grass. And Timosha wore a quilted coat – a queer bird!

'Sure! Don't ask. Tu-ber-cu-losis, brother. That's what the male nurse at the clinic told me. You catch a cold, he says, and it's your death.'

'Eh, what a seedy fellow,' Baryba thought, suddenly aware of the weight of his own animal-strong body. He strode along, well satisfied with himself: it was a pleasure to step on the earth, to trample it, crush it – so! And so!

At Timosha's, three freckled, sharp-nosed children sat at the unpainted table in the small room with tattered wallpaper.

'Where's your mother?' Timosha shouted. 'Out again?'

'She went to the county chairman's; they came for her,' the girl said timidly, and began to pull her boots on in the corner: it was awkward to go barefoot in front of a stranger.

Timosha scowled. 'Get out the gruel, Fenka. And bring the bottle from the hallway.'

'Mama said not to touch the bottle.'

'I'll show you "Mama" in a minute. Come on, step lively now! Sit down, Baryba.'

They sat down at the table. The lamp overhead, with a tin shade covered with a multitude of dead flies, gave out a thin, high hissing sound.

Fenka began to pour off some of the gruel into a wooden bowl for the children, but Timosha shouted: 'What's that now? Getting finicky, with your own father? Your ma's been putting you up to it? Wait, I'll show her, just wait till she comes home! Gallivanting . . .'

The children began to eat from the common bowl, reluctantly, drearily. Timosha guffawed out of the side of his mouth and said to Baryba: 'I'm tempting the Lord, you see. They've said at the hospital it's catching, this consumption. Well, now I'll see: will it get the kids or not? Will the Good Lord raise his hand against innocent babes – will he now?'

There was a light, timid knock on the window.

Timosha hastily flung the window open and sang out venomously: 'A-ah, you're back?'

And then he turned to Baryba: 'Well, brother, get going. There's nothing for you to watch here any more. We're down to the real business now.'

9 ST ELIJAH'S DAY

The evening before St Elijah's Day is always special, and the ringing of the church bells is special. There is Communion at the church and at the monastery. In all the homes the housewives bake pies and pastries for the morrow, and in the heavens the Prophet Elijah gets his thunders ready. And the sky on the eve of St Elijah's Day is quiet and clean, like a house scoured spotless for the holiday. Everybody hurries to his church; God forbid that one should be late for troparion – he'll cry all year, his tears will flow like the rain decreed from time immemorial for St Elijah's Day.

Anyone else may be late, but not Chebotarikha; she's the most regular churchgoer in the Holy Virgin parish. Urvanka had harnessed the horses way ahead of time.

He harnessed them and walked across the yard, right past the cellar. The door was open. Urvanka muttered: 'The devils, left the door wide open. People go to church to pray, and they . . . Godless swine!'

And he added a saltier word or two. At first he meant to shut the door, then he thought better of it. He stood a while and grinned. He came to Chebotarikha to report that everything was ready.

'But let me ask you to come out the back way, if you please . . .' and his smile was like a knot, tight on his sooty face; try and guess what it means.

'You're up to something, Urvanka!' said Chebotarikha. Nevertheless, she sailed out, rustling her brown silk dress with its pattern of little flowers.

She climbed, puffing, down the stairs and walked past the cellar.

'You could have had sense enough to close the door. Got to tell them everything ...' Chebotarikha was a good house-keeper; how could she walk by an open door without doing something about it? Even if it needn't be closed, she'll close it.

'Do you want me to lock them in, in there?'

'Who's them?'

'Who? Why, Anfim Yegorych and Polka. After all, they ought to go to Mass on the eve of Elijah's Day too!'

'You're bluffing, you scoundrel! I won't believe it, never in my life – Anfimka and her ...'

'May St Elijah strike me with lightning tomorrow if I'm lying.'

'Go on, cross yourself.'

Urvanka crossed himself. So it was true.

Chebotarikha turned white as chalk and shook like dough that's risen to the edge of the bucket. Urvanka thought to him-self, 'She'll start howling now.' No, she evidently remembered she had a silk dress on. She pushed out her lower lip importantly and said as though nothing had happened: 'Kindly shut the door, Urvan. It's time for us to go to church.'

'Yes, ma'am.'

He clicked the bolt, untied the horses, and Chebotarikha's famous droshky raised the dust along the road.

Chebotarikha stood in her usual place, in front, near the right choir. She folded her hands on her stomach and stared at one spot, on the deacon's right boot. A scrap of paper had gotten stuck to the boot; the deacon stood on the pulpit before Che-botarikha, and the paper bothered her.

' "The sick and the suffering ..." That's for me, too, for my suffering. Oh, good Lord, that scoundrel Anfimka!'

She bowed low to the ground, and the bit of paper on the boot kept flickering before her eyes.

The deacon went away, and it became still worse: she could not get that damned Anfimka out of her head. And now she had pampered him!

Only during the 'Gloria' had she managed to divert herself a

39

little and almost forget Baryba. Wouldn't you know it? That
Olga, the deacon's daughter, with all her education, always
trying to do things in her own way, different from everybody
else. Oh, no, she'll have to give the deacon a piece of her mind
about it . . .

The watchman in his ex-soldier's uniform was putting out the
candles in the church. The deacon brought a little loaf to Chebotarikha: she was a model, God-fearing parishioner, and
she paid well.

Chebotarikha pulled him over to herself by the sleeve and
whispered for a long time about Olga, shaking her head.

Urvanka leaned to and released the bolt. Baryba jumped out as
though he were scalded.

'Come in to tea, if you please,' Urvanka said, grinning.

'Can it be he didn't tell her?' thought Baryba.

Full of dignity in her stiff silk dress, Chebotarikha sat crumbling the loaf presented to her by the deacon and swallowed the
pieces loudly, like pills: whoever chews Holy Communion
bread?

'If she would only speak out.' Baryba waited, his heart
flopping around with a dull pain.

'Shall I tell them to bring some boiled milk for the tea?'
Chebotarikha glanced at him, as though lovingly.

'Is she leading me on? Or maybe she really doesn't know?'

'But where can you find Polka now? She's starting to fool
around, that miserable brat. Perhaps you'd take her in hand,
Anfimushka?'

Chebotarikha spoke simply, in her ordinary way, as if she
meant nothing at all; she swallowed the pieces of the loaf, gathered up the holy crumbs from the table and poured them into
her mouth.

'I'll bet she doesn't know, I'll bet she doesn't,' Baryba suddenly convinced himself. He turned jolly, smiled his square
smile, neighed, told Chebotarikha how that idiot Polka had
been watering her orange plant with soup.

The sun was setting, copper-coloured, furious: the prophet
would send them a roaring storm tomorrow. The white cups

40

and plates on the table turned scarlet. Chebotarikha sat at the table, important, silent, without a smile.

Baryba gaily made his nightly bows in the bedroom next to Chebotarikha, thanking all the unknown saints: the danger had passed over, Urvanka had not said anything.

The lamp before the icons went out. The night before St Elijah's Day was heavy, sultry. In the darkness of the bedroom – a greedy, gaping, drinking mouth – and the fast breath of a beast at bay.

Baryba's heart stopped beating, green circles jumped before his eyes, his hair was matted on his forehead.

'Have you gone crazy, or what?' he gasped, trying to extricate himself from her body.

But she wrapped herself around him like a spider.

'Oh, no, my dear! No, my friend! You won't get away, no, you won't!'

And she tormented him with unknown, vicious caresses in the dark, sobbing and sobbing, getting Baryba's face wet with her tears.

And so till morning. Through his stony sleep Baryba heard the bells announcing the St Elijah Mass. Through his sleep he heard singing and tried to stir his petrified thoughts, to understand what was happening.

But he awakened only when the singing stopped. He jumped up suddenly, as though someone had stuck him. 'Oh, the priests had sung the thanksgiving service in the parlour.'

He dressed. His eyes were glued together, his head felt like a stranger's.

The priests had already gone. Chebotarikha sat alone in the parlour, on the cretonne sofa. She was again in her stiff silk dress, with a lace kerchief for the holiday.

'So you slept through St Elijah's service? Eh, Anfim Yegorych?'

Baryba felt constrained and anxious – perhaps because he had indeed overslept and it was already close to noon, or perhaps because the parlour smelled of incense.

41

'Sit down, Anfim Yegorych, sit down, let us have a chat.'

She was silent awhile. Then she closed her eyes and made a pious face – not a face, but a sweet, fat pudding. She leaned her head to one side and began in a honeyed voice: 'Well, well, our heavy sins. And no amount of prayer can redeem them. And in the next world – our Father will remember everything; he'll smoke out all the nastiness, my friend, in sulphurous Gehenna.'

Baryba was silent. What was she leading up to?

Suddenly Chebotarikha opened her eyes wide and shouted, sputtering: 'You scoundrel you, why do you sit there without a word, as though you've got a mouth full of water? You think I don't know all about your filthy carryings-on with Polka? Corrupting the girl, you lecherous scum? That doesn't mean a thing to you?'

Baryba, stunned, ground his teeth silently, thinking: 'They killed a suckling pig last night – I'll bet they'll serve it at dinner today.'

Chebotarikha went into a frenzy over Baryba's silence. She began to stamp her feet, still sitting on the sofa.

'Out, out of my house! You snake! I warmed him in my own bosom, the swine, and he – that's what he does to me! Exchanging me! Me! – for Polka, eh?'

Without understanding anything, unable to stir his leaden thoughts, Baryba sat before her in a daze. He stared at Chebotarikha. 'Look at her spluttering all over, just look at her spluttering, eh?'

He came to when Urvanka walked into the parlour and said to him with a merry smile: 'Well, brother, there's nothing for you here. Get scarce. There's nothing here of yours.'

Before the storm of St Elijah's Day the sun baked mercilessly. Everything waited – the sparrows, the trees, the stones. Everything was dry, languishing.

Baryba roamed the streets like a man unhinged, sitting down to rest on every bench along Dvoryanskaya.

'Where now, eh? Where to?'

He shook his head but couldn't shake off the vision of the Balkashin yard, the manger, the hungry dogs fighting over a bone ...

Then he wandered along back streets, over green grass. A water carrier went by in his cart; one of the tyres had slipped off and the wheel clanked. Baryba suddenly felt that he was thirsty. He asked for some water and drank.

And from the north, from the direction of the monastery, a heavy cloud had already loomed up, dividing the sky into two halves: one blue and grey, the other leaden, menacing. The leaden part grew, swelled steadily.

Without remembering how he got there, Baryba found himself under the awning at the entrance to the Churilov tavern. Rain was coming down heavily; a group of peasant women gathered under the awning, their skirts pulled over their heads. Elijah thundered. Eh, nothing mattered, let him clatter, thunder, let him pour the rain in buckets!

It somehow turned out of itself that Baryba went to sleep at Timosha's. And Timosha wasn't even surprised in the slightest, as though Baryba had been coming every night to sleep at his place.

10 TWILIGHT IN THE MONASTERY CELL

Four o'clock in summertime is the deadest hour in our parts. No good man will stick his nose out into the street. The heat is murderous. All the shutters are closed, and sleep is sweet after lunch, on a full stomach. And only the grey sparrows skip around in the empty streets like midday imps.

Homeless, drifting, Baryba shuffled at this hour along the streets, as if he didn't know himself where his feet were carrying him. And they were carrying him to the monastery. Where else? From Timosha – to Yevsey in the monastery; from Yevsey to Timosha.

A serrated wall, moss-grown. A small hut, like a dog-kennel, at the ironbound gates. From the hut the holy fool Arsentyushka comes out, jerking and making faces – he has St Vitus's dance;

43

he is the gatekeeper, he collects contributions, he won't let you alone until you give him something.

'Can't shake him loose, the pest!'

Baryba dropped him a coin and went in along the white, burning-hot flagstones, past the graves of prominent citizens behind gilded railings. The prominent citizens loved to be buried in the monastery, where the saintly monks could pray for them day and night.

Baryba knocked at Yevsey's cell. Nobody answered. He opened.

Two monks sat at the table without their cassocks, in white underpants and shirts: Yevsey and Innokenty.

Yevsey hissed furiously at Baryba – 'Sh-sh-sh!' – and turned his eyes again, bulging, unblinking, glassy, to his tea glass. And Innokenty, with flabby lips, an old woman with a moustache, stared motionless at his.

Baryba stopped at the door-post, gaping at them: had they gone batty or what?

At the other side of the door stood Savka the novice: oily hair straight as sticks, huge red hands like lobsters.

Savka respectfully whispered sideways: 'Wh-ee! Just watch, the fly will get into Father Yevsey's glass in a moment. Don't you see?'

Baryba's eyes goggled without understanding.

'Sure thing! It's their most favourite game today. They'll wager a five, a ten – and then they wait and wait. Whichever father gets a fly in his glass first, he's the winner.'

Savka was glad of a chance to talk to an outside man. He spoke, covering his mouth with his huge red paw out of respect.

'Lookit, look now, it's Father Yevsey . . .'

Yevsey, bluish-grey, sodden with alcohol, bent over the glass, his mouth grinning wider and wider – and suddenly he clapped his hand violently over his knee.

'Th-ere! There she is, the honey! My fiver!' and he fished the fly out of the glass with his finger. 'Well, my good fellow, you'd almost done me in – you'd scared the fly off for a moment!'

He approached Baryba and stared at him with his glassy eyes, booming away: 'Well, and we never hoped to see you again, my boy. People were saying you got to be a regular rakehell. We thought the woman would ride you to death. That Chebota-rikha, she's a glutton, she could gobble a man, bones and all.'

He poured Baryba some tea, while he himself finished the glass from which he had fished out the fly. But what was the good of meeting old friends without a proper drink? Yevsey got out a fifth of vodka too.

Savka brought in a second samovar. The table was littered with copper coins, a Psalter, wineglasses with chipped stems.

Innokenty seemed to have fallen into a melancholy after the vodka. His little eyes were closing, and he kept putting his head down on the table, resting it on his tiny fist. Suddenly he began to intone 'O Quiet Light' in a small lugubrious voice. Yevsey and Savka joined in. Savka sang in a deep bass, turning his head sideways to clear his throat and covering his mouth with his huge red paw. Baryba thought: 'Hell, what's the difference!' And he also started howling along sorrowfully.

All at once Yevsey broke off and roared: 'Sto-op! Stop, I tell you!'

Savka still drawled the melody. Yevsey lunged at him, seized him by the throat and pinned him to the back of the chair – a crazed idiot savage. He might choke the man.

Innokenty got up and, with his back humped, pattered over to Yevsey, with an old woman's tiny steps, and tickled him in the armpits from behind.

Yevsey burst into a fit of gurgling laughter. Waving his arms like a drunken windmill, he released Savka. Then he sat down on the floor and began to sing:

> On the hill there sits a cripple,
> He just killed a man.

Everybody echoed him diligently, as before, with 'O Quiet Light'.

Dusk thickened; everything blurred and rocked in the drunken cell. Nobody lit the lamp. Innokenty whined and pestered everyone, lisping toothlessly – an old crone with a moustache and a grey beard. It seemed to him that he had choked on something. Something had gotten stuck in his throat, and he wouldn't stop complaining. He dug and dug with his finger – it didn't help.

'You try, Savushka, try, darling, with your finger. Maybe you'll find it.'

Savushka poked about in his throat, wiping his finger afterwards on the skirt of his cassock.

'Nothing, Your Reverence, there's nothing there. It's only the drunken devil teasing.'

Yevsey huddled up on his cot and lay there for a long time without movement or sound. Then he jumped up suddenly and shook his tangled mane.

'I say, fellows, how about running over to Streltsy? Just the occasion – to celebrate the reunion. Baryba, boy, what do you say? The only trouble is where to get some money. Shall we try the pantry-keeper, eh? What do you say, Savka?'

Invisible at the door, Savka neighed. Baryba thought to himself: 'Why not? It may ease me up a bit. Help me forget things.'

'If you'll return it tomorrow . . . I have a bit of change, my last,' he said to Yevsey.

Yevsey immediately cheered up, shook his head like a playful dog, goggling his glassy eyes.

'Before the Living God, I swear I'll give it back tomorrow. I have it, you know, but it's hidden too far away.'

The four companions walked past the graves. The half-dead moon blinked at them from behind a cloud. Innokenty's cassock got caught in a grave railing. He began to cross himself, frightened, and turned back. The other three climbed over the wall, where the bricks had been removed to provide an exit.

11   THE POMADE JAR

And now again it was a heavy, drowsy, hot, deserted afternoon. White flagstones on the monastery path. The avenue of ancient lindens, the steady buzzing of bees.

Yevsey walked ahead, in his black cowl, with tangled wisps of hair plastered down on his forehead; it was his turn at vespers that day. Behind him strode Baryba, every now and then breaking into a square grin, as though opening a wide square gate.

How queer Yevsey looked in his cowl – altogether out of place! He should be wearing a peasant jerkin or a tall sheepskin hat – that would be closer to his style.

'Oh, well, boy, I had meant to go to the cadet school, but got to drinking instead. So I've ended up in the monastery.'

Eh, Yevsey! What a fine, red-faced, blue-nosed Cossack captain he would have made. Or else a village clerk, a drunken crony to all the peasants. And there he was now, by the grace of God . . .

'You sure gave them a show in Streltsy last night, Yevsey, eh? Some dance! . . .

The jolly monks
Bought samovars . . .

Yevsey grinned and jiggled his shoulders. Nah, not in this woman's dress, it wouldn't work. But yesterday – that was fun: he had belted his shirt with a rope, village fashion, right under the armpits; white underpants with a blue stripe; a wide red beard like a shovel; eyes fairly jumping out of his face – a real village goblin, and what a dancer! The Streltsy girls laughed till they were rolling on the floor.

They came to the monastery. Baryba stood a moment by the ancient church door. Yevsey came out and beckoned him in. 'Come in, boy, come in. There's no one here. Even the gate-keeper is off somewhere.'

A squat, old, wise church, named after the old prophet, Elijah. It has seen a thing or two in its lifetime: it stood its ground against the Tartars; the boyar Fyodor Romanov, of the royal house, known as Filaret in his monastic days, was said to have held services in it. Old lindens shade its latticed windows.

But even here Yevsey was not subdued, booming and clattering – a Cossack captain in a cowl. The ancient, emaciated, huge-eyed saints seemed to shrink deeper into the walls, away from the bearded, shouting, arm-waving Yevsey.

Yevsey got down on his knees and felt for something under the pulpit.

'Here,' he said and brought a dusty old Brockard pomade jar to the light. He opened the lid, and counted the twenty-five-rouble notes, spitting on his thumb.

Baryba's flat-iron stirred restlessly. 'The devil! There must be ten or even more. And what the hell does he need them for?'

Yevsey put aside one note. 'The rest I'll leave behind, to pay for Masses for my soul; or maybe I will take some out one day and throw 'em all to the Streltsy wenches, for a roaring binge.'

White flagstones along the monastery path. The bees hum in the ancient lindens. The heavy heat makes the drink-fuddled head turn round and round.

'What the hell does he need them for?' Baryba thought again.

12   THE OLD MONK

An old, old little monk sat on the sun-warmed stone bench near the St Elijah Church. His cassock was faded green, his grey beard had turned greenish, his hands and face looked over-grown with greenish moss. It was as if he had been lying some-where, like buried treasure, under an old oak and then dug up and put out in the sun to warm up.

'How old are you, Grandpa?' Baryba asked him.

'Ee-eh, my dear, I've lost count of the years. But I remember your Tikhon Zadonsky. He was a good priest, his holy services were something to hear.'

Baryba always hung around the little green old monk now, always sidling up to him. There was surely something behind it!

'Come on, Grandpa, come into the church, I'll help you sweep up.'

And they walked under the cool dim vaults. The monk lovingly tidied up the old church, whispered to the saints. He'd light a candle and stop before it, admiring, glowing over it.

'Just blow, and they'll both go out – the candle and the monk,' Baryba thought to himself.

He followed on the little monk's heels, bringing him this, holding that for him. The little monk became fond of Baryba. People nowadays had no respect, they had forgotten the old man, he had nobody to say a word to. And this one . . .

'Say, Grandpa, aren't you scared to be alone in church at night?'

'Ee-eh, Christ be with you, how can it be scary in church?'

'Let me sleep here with you, Grandpa, eh?'

But the little old monk spoke sternly out of his deep hollow in the ancient oak: 'For forty years I've spent my nights alone with her. And nobody's to sleep here but myself. Who knows what can happen in a church at night? . . .'

Yes, watch the church, watch it zealously. Truly, who knows what can happen in the old church at night?

'Oh, well, I'll wait a while,' Baryba thought and followed closely on the old man's heels.

At the midnight Mass before St Tikhon Zadonsky's Day the little monk had worn himself out. There was no counting the crowd. And afterwards he and Baryba had no end of cleaning up to do – it looked as though they'd never get done.

The little old monk examined all the doors, checked all the rusty bolts, and sat down for a mite to rest. He sat down, and went out like a candle, fell fast asleep. Baryba waited a while, coughed. Then he came over, touched the old man's sleeve; he went on sleeping. Baryba hurried over to the altar and started feeling under the pulpit. He moved his hand around and around, and at last he found it.

The little old monk was fast asleep – getting himself accustomed, no doubt, to sleep in eternity. The old monk heard nothing.

13 APROSYA'S HUT

Dvoryanskaya petered out with a few shabby stores and the last street lights. Beyond it was the Streletsk pond, with sickly old willow trees huddled around it. On the moss-grown, slippery raft, the women bent over their wash, battering the dirt out of it, while ducklings dove in and out of the water around them.

Aprosya's hut was right next to the pond, on the side of the Streltsy suburb; it was good enough, warm and dry. Its straw-covered roof was neatly sheared around the edges, like a peasant's hair; its windows were set with faded, blooming bits of glass. Aprosya and her small son needed little. She had rented out her small allotment of land; in addition, a holiday would come around now and then, and she would get a present from her husband – three roubles, or five. And a letter: 'And also with my love a low bow to my dearest spouse Aprosinya Petrovna ... And also to inform you that we have got a raise, three roubles a year. And so, together with Ilyusha, we have decided to remain in the army again ...'

At first Aprosya was lonely; naturally – she was young. But then her husband's face grew dim, forgotten as he stayed on and on in military service beyond his term. She thought of him now as something remote, like a stamp on a letter, or some sort of seal: his stamp, his seal. And nothing more. And so she lived on, weatherbeaten, puttering in her vegetable patch, sewing clothes for the boy, doing laundry for others.

Baryba rented a room in Aprosya's hut. He liked it at once: it was cosy and clean. They agreed on four and a half roubles.

Aprosya was pleased. Her boarder was a steady man, not some drifter, and apparently with money too. He wasn't high and mighty either – he'd say a word to her now and then. Now she had two to care for: her boy and Baryba. All day long she was on her feet, windburned, stately, brown as rye, firm-breasted – a joy to look at.

Everything was quiet, bright, clean. Baryba rested from his old troubles. He slept dreamlessly, he had money; what else did he need? He ate unhurriedly, solid, big meals.

'I guess I please him,' Aprosya thought to herself.

Baryba bought himself a lot of books. Cheap small ones, but exciting reading: *Tyapka, the Brigand of Lebedyan*; *The Criminal Monk and His Treasures*; *The Coachman of the Queen of Spain*. Baryba lolled around, cracked sunflower seeds, and read. He had no desire to go anywhere. It was awkward to face the postman Chernobylnikov and the treasurer's son-in-law; they must know everything by now. As for women, he didn't even want to look at them: he'd had enough of Chebotarikha, the nausea hadn't settled down inside him yet.

He went walking in the field. It was mowing time. The evening sky was like brocade; the golden corn lay down obediently; red, sweaty shirts; clanking scythes. After a while the men would halt and pick up mugs of kvass, drinking, drops of it glistening on their beards. Eh, they had worked their sweet fill!

Baryba was tempted to join them. His strong hands itched, his chewing muscles contracted . . . But what about the treasurer's son-in-law? What if he saw him?

'Hu-h, some idea! – to turn into a peasant. The next thing I'd be carting skins to Chebotarikha's tannery! A fine notion . . .' Baryba muttered angrily to himself.

Still, he must think of something; he couldn't last on Yevsey's money much longer without work – it wasn't thousands.

Baryba turned the thing over in his mind, and wrote out an application to the treasury department; maybe they'd take him as a clerk, as assistant to the treasurer's son-in-law. He'd get a cap with a badge – something to strut around in!

Towards evening the heat became suffocating. Nevertheless, Baryba buttoned on his velvet vest (a remnant of his prosperous days at Chebotarikha's), put on his glossy paper collar, his trousers – over the boots – and went to Dvoryanskaya: where else was he to find the treasurer's son-in-law?

Naturally, there he was. Lanky, long-legged, like a clothes-pole, looking down at everybody sourly, waving his cane. As though he was saying: 'Who are you? *I'm* an official – in a cap with a badge.'

He gave Baryba a sour grin. 'O-h, it's you! An application? Hm, hm.'

He became animated, pulled up his trousers, straightened his collar. An amiable man in authority.

'Well, very well, I shall submit it. I'll do what I can. Certainly, for an old acquaintance.'

Baryba walked home and thought: 'Eh, wouldn't I love to bash in his sour puss! Still, you can't hold it against him – he talks educated. And his collar? Real linen. And looks like a new one every time.'

14   THE MERRY WINE RUNS OUT

The pantry-keeper Mitrofan found out everything about Yevsey's excursion to Streltsy, sniffed it out like a good hunting-dog. Of course, Yevsey himself may have babbled, boasted about it all over the place. But Mitrofan knew all about it, to the last detail: how Yevsey had danced in nothing but his shirt, belted under the armpits, and his indecent song about the monks, and the wild, merry driving all over Streltsy. Naturally, the pantry-keeper reported it to the prior. The prior summoned Yevsey and gave him such a roasting that Yevsey shot out of his cell as scarlet as though he'd just come down from the top shelf in the baths.

Yevsey was sent to help out the baker as a penance. He did not attend services. The baker's cellar was as hot as hell. The chief devil, Silanty, shaggy, red, yelled at the kneaders while he himself swung forty-pound loaves into the oven with his shovel. The kneaders, in nothing but white shirts, their tumbling hair tied up with string, turned and kneaded the dough, groaning and sweating.

But now Yevsey slept as he had not slept in years. Even his glassy eyes seemed to have cleared a bit. There was no time to think of tippling.

Everything would have been fine, but his penance came to an end. The old business started all over. Yevsey began to officiate at services, to bellow prayers. Savka the novice began to hang around him again with his lobster paws; and again there was Innokenty with his songs – an old woman with a moustache.

Savka told Yevsey about Innokenty: 'The other day Father Innokenty went to the baths. There was a little deacon there, a jolly fellow, exiled to these parts. As soon as he saw Father Innokenty in his natural state, he raised a hue and cry: "Look at him, holy fathers, look, he's a woman – his tits hang down to his belly, he's given birth too!" '

Innokenty pulled his cassock closer around him. 'A shameless scamp, that deacon of yours. That's why he thinks such thoughts.'

It was this very deacon who proved to be Yevsey's undoing. He had come from the world outside; naturally, he was bored, and so he wandered from cell to cell. One day he dropped in on Yevsey. Yevsey and Innokenty sat over their glasses, at their game of 'flies' again, waiting to see who'd get the first fly in his glass. The deacon took one look and nearly died of laughter; he tumbled down on Yevsey's bed, kicking his legs – oi-oi-oi! (and his legs were short, tiny; his eyes, like bird cherries).

The little deacon got into a jolly mood and started going – on and on. He told them all the anecdotes of his seminary days – he was a master storyteller. At first the modest ones. And then – all out! About the priest who'd send the confessing sinners to sin some more: he had set a penance of fifteen bows for two transgressions, you see, and he could never figure it out without fractions; about the nun caught up in the woods by tramps, five of them, and how she would tell about it afterwards: 'It was real good, and all you'd want, and without sin, either.'

In short, he had them all rolling. Yevsey choked with laughter and banged his fist on the table.

'What a deacon! Have you ever? ... We'll have to treat you to a drink for that. Wait, Fathers. I won't be a minute.'

'Where's the storm wind carrying you?' the deacon asked.

'For money. I've got it stowed away, imperishable. Right near by. Before you blink an eye ...'

And, indeed, the deacon had not finished his next tale when Yevsey was back. He came in and leaned against the doorpost.

'Come on, you pot of gold, come over, let us see,' the deacon shouted gaily and approached Yevsey. He took one look and stopped cold: it was Yevsey all right, and yet it wasn't Yevsey. He seemed to sag, to droop, as though someone had punched a hole in his side, and all the merry wine had run out, leaving an empty skin.

'What's wrong, why don't you speak? What happened?'

'Stolen,' said Yevsey in a quiet, alien voice and threw two last notes on the table; the thief had left them just to mock him . . .

True, Yevsey had never been too bright, but now he lost what wits he had. He drank away his last few roubles. Then he wandered all over town, drunk, begging kopeks for a bracer. The corner policeman took him off to the precinct house for drunken conduct in the street; he bashed in the policeman's nose and escaped back to the monastery.

In the morning he had a visit from his cronies – Savka the novice and Father Innokenty, along with the little deacon. They began to preach at him: get hold of yourself; do you want the prior to kick you out of the monastery? What will you do then, go begging?

Yevsey lay flat on his back and would not say a word. Then he suddenly began to sniffle, drooling all over his beard: 'But don't you see, brothers? It's not the money, who cares for the money? But before, I was a man, I could get out of the monastery any day. And now it doesn't make a bit of difference what I want . . . I was a free man . . .'

'But who could have cleaned you out like that?' the deacon bent over Yevsey.

'I didn't know, but now I do. It wasn't one of ours – an outsider. I thought he was a decent fellow, and now . . . It's he, nobody else could have done it. Nobody but him knew where the money was hid.'

Savka neighed: 'Hah, I know.'

All evening, by candlelight, over the empty table – they didn't even feel like heating the samovar – they talked it over, looking for a way, but could not come to any conclusion; there was nothing to be done.

15 AT IVANIKHA'S

After morning Mass, Innokenty came in, bringing Yevsey a piece of consecrated bread. He whispered: 'I know what to do now, Father Yevsey. It came to me. Let's go to Ivanikha, but quick. Everybody knows her – she'll cast a spell – o-oh! – the thief will turn up at once.'

The morning was rosy, dewy; the day would be a hot one. The sparrows celebrated merrily.

'Eh, woke me up at such an early hour,' Yevsey grumbled.

Innokenty pattered with tiny, woman's steps, holding up his cassock on his belly.

'Can't do it any other way, Father Yevsey. Don't you know? A spell works only on an empty stomach.'

'I'll bet you're lying, Innokenty. It's just a waste. And a shame too – men of the church!'

Ivanikha was a dry old crone, tall, bony, with shaggy eyebrows like an owl. She met the monks without much courtesy.

'What d'you want? What kind of spell are you after? Or do you mean to pray at me? I don't need your prayers.'

And she went on puttering, clanking with her pots on the stove.

'No, we're here about ... Well, Father Yevsey here has been robbed. Could you cast a spell on the thief, eh? We've heard ...'

Father Innokenty was afraid of Ivanikha. He wanted to cross himself, but maybe she wouldn't stand for it: the devil knows, she might get sore and then you would get nothing out of her. Innokenty pulled his cassock closer over his chest with the gesture of a woman wrapping herself tighter in her coat.

Ivanikha threw him a glance from above with her owlish eyes – like the stroke of a whip.

'And what's it got to do with you? If he was robbed, he's got to stay here with me, eye to eye.'

'But I ... Sure, my dear woman, sure, I'll ...'

55

He tucked up the skirts of his cassock and hurried off with his tiny, woman's steps.

'Name?' Ivanikha asked Yevsey.

'Yevsey.'

'I know you're Yevsey. Not yours; the man you're thinking of – what's his name?'

'Anfimka, Anfim.'

'What d'you want me to conjure on? The wind? An apron's good too, if you spread it over birch twigs. Or maybe water? Then you can get him to come in, the dove, and make him drink some tea made out of that water.'

'Yes, that's just right, some tea, eh? That's a good one, eh?'

Yevsey cheered up and boomed away, full of confidence in the spell: Ivanikha was such a solid, stern old woman.

Ivanikha dipped up some water with a hollowed wooden pitcher, opened the door to the entrance hall and ordered Yevsey to stand outside the threshold; then she took up a position on the threshold and put the pitcher into Yevsey's hands.

'Hold it, and listen. But mind you, not a word to anybody, or everything will turn around against your own self.'

She intoned slowly, with emphasis, piercing the water in the pitcher with her owl's eyes.

'In the sea, in the ocean, on the island of Buyan, stands a huge iron trunk. In the trunk there is a great steel sword. Run, sword, to Anfimka the thief, stick him right in the heart, make the thief return what he stole from God's good slave Avsey, without holding back a single mite or crumb. If he holds any of it back, may he be cursed to the land of hell, to the Ararat mountains, to boiling pitch, to burning ash, to bog and mire, to a homeless home, to a bathhouse bucket. If he holds it back, may he be pinned to a door-post with an aspen stake, may be dried out drier than grass, frozen colder than ice, and may he die away from his bed.

'That will do,' said Ivanikha. 'Make him drink some of that water, our dove.'

Yevsey carefully poured the water into a bottle, gave Ivanikha a rouble and went away, well pleased.

'I'll treat you to some tea, my love. I'll untie your tongue!'

16 FOOLPROOF

All of a sudden, in the middle of the night, Baryba started shaking with an ague. He shook and he doubled up with cramps, and all sorts of unnatural dreams tormented him.

In the morning he sat at the table as in a fog, resting his lead-filled head on his hands.

There was a knock at the door.

'Aprosya?'

He could not turn his head, it was so heavy. Somebody coughed at the door in a thick baritone.

'Savka, you?'

It was Savka all right: straight hair like twigs, red lobster paws.

'You are invited, without fail. Father Yevsey's been missing you, he says.'

He came up nearer and neighed: 'He wants to treat you to some charmed tea. Heaven preserve, don't touch it.'

'Charmed? What sort of charm?'

'What sort! But naturally, against a thief.'

'Aha!' Baryba understood. This was hugely funny. That fool Yevsey! Something moved mistily, something hammered in his head, something merry grimaced and jumped around.

In Yevsey's cell the air was blue with smoke; the jolly deacon had been smoking.

'Ah, welcome now, dear guests!'

And, wiggling his behind, the deacon offered his arm to Baryba.

There was no vodka on the table. They had decided not to drink, to keep their heads clear – so they might easier catch Baryba.

'You've gotten thinner, Yevsey! What's wrong, has anybody put a spell on you?' Baryba grinned.

'I've plenty of trouble. Haven't you heard?'

'They've swiped your money, eh? Sure, I heard it.'

The little deacon sidled up to him, jolly, taunting: 'And where did you hear it, Anfim Barabych?'

'Why, Savka here just told me. That's how I heard it.'

'You're a dope, Savka,' Yevsey turned around glumly.

They sat down to tea. One glass, half filled, stood separately on the tray. Innokenty busily poured more hot water into the glass and gave it to Baryba.

Everybody stared and waited: now . . .

Baryba stirred the tea and sipped it unhurriedly. They were silent, watching him. Baryba could not stand it any longer and broke into loud laughter, like iron wheels clattering over cobblestones. Savka neighed after him, and the little deacon joined in with a small high-pitched giggle.

'What's all this about?' Yevsey asked, staring with the eyes of a boiled fish.

Baryba clattered, rolling down and down, no longer able to stop; his head was throbbing, whirling in green fog. The imp of laughter tugged at him, prompted him to say: 'It was me all right. I stole it.'

Baryba drank down the tea, but still kept silent, smiling his square, brutal smile.

Yevsey fidgeted.

'Well, tell us, Baryba. Go on, don't hold it back.'

'Tell you what?'

'You know what yourself.'

'So that's what you're driving at? The money, eh? Well, I told you – Savka told me all about it. That's all I know.'

He spoke in a deliberately false tone, as though taunting: sure I'm lying, but try and catch me.

The little deacon jumped up to Baryba and slapped him on the shoulder. 'No, brother, you're foolproof, no witch's brew could get you! Tough as a rock.'

Yevsey began to shake his tangled mane. 'To hell with everything! Run for some wine, Savka.'

They drank. Baryba's head throbbed, whirled in a fog. Cigarette smoke floated in the room, the air was green. The deacon stomped around in a sailor dance.

Baryba came home at dusk. At the very gate he suddenly felt his knees buckle; his eyes went dim. He leaned against the door-post, frightened. He had never felt like that before.

Aprosya opened the door and looked up at her roomer. 'You're white as a ghost! You aren't sick?'

As in a dream, he found himself in bed. A small lamp burned on the table. Aprosya sat at his bedside. On his forehead was a cloth dipped in vinegar.

'You poor ailing soul,' Aprosya drawled pityingly, comfortably.

She had run over to her neighbour's and gotten him some healing powders. All through the night he kept dropping off into a mist and then his head would clear again and he would see Aprosya by the bed, dozing in her chair.

By the third morning he felt better. Baryba lay under a white sheet, with grey, autumnal shadows on his face. He looked somehow more transparent, more human. 'But sure, I am a stranger to her, yet she sat up all night without sleep . . .'

'Thank you, Aprosya.'

'Why, it's nothing, poor soul. You were sick.'

And she bent over him. She wore nothing but a varicoloured homespun skirt and a cotton shirt, and two sharp stinging points flashed suddenly before Baryba's eyes under the thin cotton.

Baryba closed his eyes, and opened them again. The hot summer day looked into the window. Somewhere outside, the Streletsk pond glittered, women were bathing, white bodies gleamed . . .

His head throbbed still more furiously. Baryba restlessly moved his heavy jaws and pulled Aprosya towards him.

'Oh, so?' she was surprised. 'But maybe it's not good for you. Now, now, wait, it's time to change the compress.'

She calmly changed the cloth and calmly, comfortingly, lay down in Baryba's bed.

And so it went. All day she busied herself with her housework, clattered with her pots – Aprosya, the soldier's wife. She had her own boy, and now Baryba to care for. True, he recovered soon enough; still, it was not easy to look after everything all by herself.

In the evenings, Anfim Yegorych would come home from

somewhere and look in on Aprosya: 'Drop in later, in the evening.'

'Drop in, you say? All right. You've gotten me all addled now. Something I had to do – now it slipped my mind. Oh, yes, get out the eggs from under the hens, or else that damned polecat will get them all again.'

She ran to the coop. Afterwards she made the samovar. Baryba drank tea by himself in his room, turning the pages of a book. 'Keeps reading and reading all the time; he'll spoil his eyes before he knows it.' She'd put her boy to bed. Then she would sit down on the bench and spin grey thread for winter socks, the spindle whirring, humming in her hands. A fat black cockroach would drop loudly from the ceiling onto the floor. 'I guess it's late, time now.' She scratched her head with the blunt end of the spindle, yawned, made the sign of the cross over her mouth. Carefully, thoroughly, spitting on the brush, she polished Anfim Yegorych's boots, undressed, neatly folded everything in the corner on the bench, and took the boots to Baryba.

Baryba waited for her. Aprosya put the boots by the bed and lay down.

Half an hour later she would leave, yawning lightly. Then she would make her ten bows before the icon, recite Our Father, and fall fast asleep: she had done a full day's work, without a minute's rest.

17   SEMYON SEMYONYCH BLINKIN

One day Baryba said to Timosha: 'What sort of a tailor are you, anyway? I see no work around your house.'

The answer was simple enough. There was no work because Timosha – he might be all right for a while, but then he'd go on a bender, and good-bye to the customer's pants – he was sure to drink them anyway. People knew his habit and were afraid to give him work at home. And so he did his tailoring in other people's homes. He made the clothes of many a merchant, and even of some gentry – he was a master tailor, the scamp. One of his customers was the lawyer Semyon Semyonych Blinkin; in fact, he was almost like a member of the Blinkin household. Semyon Semyonych called him 'my court tailor'.

Timosha seldom wore boots; most of the time they were in pawn. And he would come to Blinkin's house in old rubber galoshes, carrying white canvas slippers wrapped in paper under his arm. In the foyer, he would take off the galoshes, put on the white slippers, and he was dressed. And they would go off into marvellous conversations, Timosha and Blinkin: about God, about saints, about everything in the world being nothing but appearance, illusion, and about how a man should live. Timosha respected Blinkin as a man of intelligence. And that, indeed, he was – Semyon Semyonych Blinkin.

Blinkin, by the way, was not his real name; it was more of a nickname – the boys in the street would tease him, calling it after him. And it needed one look at him to see – he was Blinkin all right.

Semyon Semyonych had a gaunt, dark face, like an old icon. Huge, black eyes. And you could not tell – were they wide open with astonishment, or were they the eyes of a scoundrel? But they were huge; there was nothing to the face but eyes. And they kept blinking constantly: blink, blink – as though he were somehow ashamed of them.

But it wasn't only the eyes. All of him seemed to blink. Semyon Semyonych! He'd walk along the street and limp on his left foot – his whole body, his whole being, blinking.

And how the merchants loved him for his cunning!

'Semyon Semyonych? Blinkin? O-ho, there's a fox for you, a slick one – slippery as an eel. Just look at him, just look at him blinking away – eh?'

And so it went: he handled all of the merchants' shady deals: fake notes, bouncing cheques, contracts without anything to back them. In one way or another, he'd get them cleared in court. And they paid him well.

Timosha took Baryba to visit Blinkin. It was high time too.

The autumn was a crazy one: snow fell, and melted. And with the snow Baryba's money – Yevsey's money – kept melting

61

away. The treasury rejected his application; the devils, who knows them – what else did they want? And so, he had to find something to do; the stomach, after all, had to be filled.

Semyon Semyonych took Timosha aside and questioned him about Baryba: 'Who's that?'

'That's an assistant of mine, in a manner of speaking. I work and I talk, and he listens. After all, you cannot talk without an assistant – you can't talk to your own self.'

Semyon Semyonych broke into a quavering laugh.

'He's in a good mood – it'll work,' Timosha thought to himself.

'And what did you do before?' Blinkin asked Baryba. Baryba hemmed and hawed.

'Oh, he was with a respectable widow – for her solace and amusement, kind of,' Timosha helped out, his needle darting in and out of the cloth.

Blinkin quavered again: some occupation!

And Timosha went on imperturbably: 'Nothing to sniff at. A business. Everything's a business nowadays, that's how we live, buying and selling. A tradesman sells herring, a whore sells her flesh. Everyone to his own trade. Why's the flesh worse than herring, or herring worse than conscience? Everything is a commodity for sale.'

Blinkin was now in the merriest of moods; he winked, quavered, slapped Timosha on the shoulder. Then he suddenly turned serious, stern, as though he had just come out of an icon, as though he'd swallow you up with his enormous eyes.

'So, you'd like to earn a bit of money?' he asked Baryba. 'I'll find some work for you. I need witnesses. You look imposing enough; I think you'll do.'

18   THE WITNESS

And so Baryba went to work for Blinkin as a witness. In the evening Blinkin would instruct Baryba, fill him to the gills with information: now, mind you, don't forget this and remember that; Vasily Kuryakov, the merchant's son – he's the fat one –

he only raised his hand. But the first blow was struck by the workman, the redhead – yes, the redhead. And you were at the garden fence, you saw it all with your own eyes.

In the morning Baryba would stand before the judge, neatly combed, a steady man. At times he'd grin to himself – it was a funny kind of business. He would tell his story carefully, as Blinkin had taught him. The merchant's son Vasily Kuryakov would triumph; the workman would be sent to the clink; and Baryba would receive a three-rouble or a five-rouble note.

Semyon Semyonych had nothing but praise for Baryba: 'You're a solid, respectable-looking fellow and stubborn, too. They never shake you. Before long I'll be starting you in criminal cases.'

And he began to take Baryba with him to the neighbouring town, where the criminal court was held. He got Baryba a long-skirted coat, like a merchant's. In this coat Baryba hung around for hours in the corridors of the courthouse, yawning and lazily awaiting his turn. He testified calmly, in a businesslike manner – and was never confused. Sometimes the prosecutor or the defence attorney would try to rattle him, but they couldn't get anywhere with him: he'd stick to his story and wouldn't be budged.

Baryba earned a good bit of money on a certain will. The merchant Igumnov had died. He was a well-respected man, a family man, with a wife and a daughter. He ran a fish store, and everybody knew him, because fasts are strictly kept in our parts. This Igumnov's hands were covered with warts all over. People said it was from the fish – he had gotten stuck with fishbones.

Igumnov lived, thank God, like everybody else. But in his old age he got into trouble – the devil poked him in the rib. His daughter's teacher – her governess – just turned him around her little finger. He threw out his wife and daughter, and started living like a lord: horses, wine, guests, banquets – the sky was the limit.

It was only on his deathbed that the old man came back to his senses. He called in his wife and daughter, begged their forgiveness, and wrote a will leaving everything to them. But his first will remained in the hands of his mistress, the governess, and that will had left everything to her. This led to litigation. And, naturally, Semyon Semyonych was brought in.

'Semyon Semyonych, darling. We must prove that he was not in his right mind when he wrote the second will. With witnesses. I'll pay whatever you say.'

Semyon Semyonych and Baryba talked it over, inside and out. Baryba thought and thought, and suddenly remembered: one day he had seen Igumnov run out of the baths in winter-time and roll in the snow. It's nothing out of the ordinary in our town, people do it all the time. But the lawyer presented it as though the old man had run about the streets in wintertime in his natural state. He found other witnesses: why not? they had seen it too.

And when Baryba testified to it in court, he spoke so reason-ably and weightily – as though laying a stone foundation – that he even began to believe it himself. And he didn't blink an eye when Igumnov's widow, like a nun in her black kerchief, stared hard, straight in his face. And the lady-love made eyes at him after the trial: 'You are truly my benefactor!'

She gave him her hand to kiss and said: 'Drop in sometimes.' Baryba beamed with pleasure.

19   THE TIMES WE LIVE IN

'N-no-o, all that excitement, it wouldn't reach us,' Timosha spoke gloomily. 'We're like the sunken city of Kitezh, living at the bottom of the lake. We do not hear a thing, and the water over us is muddy and sleepy. And on the surface, way above – why, everything's in flames, and the alarms are ringing.'

Well, let them ring. People around our parts used to say: 'Let them go crazy out there, in their Babylons. All we want is to live out our days in peace and quiet.'

And true enough: look at the newspapers – the people out there have lost all sense. For centuries we've lived in fear of God and veneration of the Tsar. And now – they're like a pack of dogs that broke loose from their chains, may the Lord forgive us. And where did all these troublemakers come from in this land of the fat and the slippery?

Oh, well, in our parts we've got no time for such tomfoolery: our main worry is to keep the young ones fed – there is no house that isn't overrun with kids. Maybe it is from boredom, or whatever, but folks around here breed like flies. And that's why everybody is so God-fearing and steady – good family men all. The gates have iron bolts; in every yard a mongrel runs around on a chain. Before they'll let a stranger into the house, they'll ask him three times over who he is and what's his business here. All windows are filled up with geraniums and rubber plants. It's safer – nobody can look in from the street. And everybody loves warmth; the stoves breathe fire; all winter the townsfolk wear quilted vests and skirts and trousers – you will not find the like of it in any other place. And so they live in peace, sweating like manure in the heat. And a fine way of life it is, too: look at the chubby, blooming kids they raise.

Timosha and Baryba came to visit Blinkin. Blinkin sat in his chair with a newspaper.

'So they've popped off the minister now, have you heard?'

Timosha smiled – lit a merry lantern.

'Naturally, we heard about it. We were walking across the market, and I hear them talking: "What a shame! I'll bet he was getting all of twenty thousand a year, the poor soul. A great pity." '

Blinkin shook in a fit of laughter. 'That's our people for you, in a nutshell: twenty thousand ... A pity ... A scream!'

They were silent for a while, rustling the newspapers.

'There were some from our town in it too,' Baryba remembered. 'Anyutka, the archdeacon's girl – they arrested her in Petersburg. That's what comes from all that studying.'

Blinkin took up the topic at once and began to egg Timosha on. He knew Timosha's views: tangling with skirts in serious business was like mixing jam with beet soup.

'Letting a woman visit you is one thing. But let her into your soul? Oh, no!' Timosha wagged his dry little finger in warning. 'Once you let her in, you're done for. A woman, brother – she sends down roots like a weed. Before you know it, you'll be overgrown with weeds all over.'

'Weeds,' Baryba boomed, laughing.

And Blinkin banged his fist on the table, yelling in an unnatural voice: 'Atta boy, Timosha! Right you are! Come on, exhort some more, King of Judea!'

'What's he clowning for, why does he yell so much?' Baryba thought to himself.

And it was true, Semyon Semyonych liked to clown. An unreal man, somehow, a faker; kept winking, spying on you, with a rock in his bosom. And his eyes – either shameless or saintly, you couldn't tell.

'Beer now, bring in some beer!' shouted Semyon Semyonych.

The beer was brought in by Dushatka, clear-eyed, fresh as grass after rain.

'A new one?' Timosha asked without looking at Blinkin.

Semyon Semyonych changed them almost every month. Fair, swarthy, plump, lean. And with all of them he was equally genial. 'Why not, they're all the same. As for a real one, you can't find one anyway.'

Over the beer Timosha took up his favourite subject – God – and began to press Blinkin with sly questions: If God can do everything and does not want to change our lives, where's his love? And how can the righteous remain in paradise? And what will God do with the minister's assassins?

Blinkin did not like to talk about God. A mocker, full of malice, but the moment you talked of God he'd darken like a devil at the smell of incense.

'Don't you dare to talk to me about God, don't you dare!'

He'd say it almost in a whisper, but it scared you to hear him. And Timosha was pleased and laughed.

20   JOLLY VESPERS

During Lent tempers are frayed, people snap at each other – it all comes from the skimpy diet: carp and cider, cider and potatoes. But as soon as Easter comes around, everybody is suddenly in high good humour – from the savoury fat meats, the brandies and liquor, the merry church bells. People become kinder: instead of one kopek, they'll give a beggar two; the gentry will send a slice of Easter cake to the cook in the kitchen; and if Mishutka spills some brandy on the fresh tablecloth, he won't be whipped, for the holiday's sake.

Naturally, the postman Chernobylnikov got his tips as he made the rounds, delivering picture postcards and wishing everybody a happy Easter. Here he would get a quarter, there a half rouble. He collected a good round sum, and took his cronies to the Churilov tavern: Timosha, Baryba, and the treasurer's son-in-law.

Timosha seemed to have lost his bounce by spring; he went around like a moulting sparrow, shaken by every wind, yet puffing himself out, putting on a brave face.

'You ought to see a doctor, Timosha, by God you ought to,' Chernobylnikov worried. 'Look at you now.'

'What's there to medicine? I'll die all the same. And then, it's sort of interesting too – to die. Sure. All my life I've been stuck in this town, and suddenly there's this chance to travel to lands unknown – on a free ticket. It's a real treat.'

Timosha mocked at everything.

'At least, if you didn't drink so much, it's bad for you.'

Not a chance. He drank as much as the next man, mixing, as his custom was, beer with vodka. And all the time he coughed into his red cotton handkerchief; he had gotten himself a handkerchief, big as a sheet. 'So that I wouldn't spit on the floor of a respectable establishment,' he explained.

The church bells rang for vespers. Old man Churilov changed the silver from his right hand to his left, and crossed himself piously, with slow dignity.

'Hey, Mitka, get your money!' Chernobylnikov shouted to the waiter.

The four friends went out together. The spring sun was merry, the bells danced liltingly. Nobody wanted to go home, to break up the company.

'Eh, I love the Easter vespers,' Timosha screwed up his eyes. 'A regular dance; let's go to church, the whole party, eh?'

Baryba suggested the monastery – it was near by.

'And after vespers I'll take you to a monk I know, for some tea. A queer duck.'

The treasurer's son-in-law took out his watch. 'Can't make it, I promised to come to dinner; the treasurer won't stand for lateness.'

'Won't stand!' Timosha mocked and began to cough. He wanted to get his handkerchief, but it wasn't in his pocket. 'Wait, fellows, I dropped the handkerchief upstairs. I'll get it in a moment.' He flapped his hands and took off like a sparrow.

The merry bells were jingling; well-dressed people walked to the joyous Easter service.

'Wait, they're shouting upstairs ... I wonder what it is,' Baryba pricked up his huge bat ears.

The treasurer's son-in-law pulled a face. 'Another fight, I guess. People don't know how to behave in public places.'

Dz-zing! A windowpane crashed upstairs, and glass splinters showered down, ringing on the pavement. Then there was silence.

'O-ho,' Chernobylnikov listened. 'No, there's something ...'

And suddenly Timosha bounced out like a ball, red, dishevelled, gasping.

'There ... upstairs ... they ordered. And everybody raised their hands and stood like ...'

Cr-rack, cr-rack! there was a clattering upstairs.

The treasurer's son-in-law stretched out his long neck and stood for a second, cocking one eye upward like a turkey looking at a hawk. Then he let out a thin, frightened squeal: 'They're shooting!' And he took off at a run.

On the stairs in the meantime there was a thumping of boots, a bellowing; everybody came rushing down. 'E-e-eh! Hold him, hold . . .'

And again: *cr-rack, cr-rack.*

For an instant, an eyeless red face burst out of the door ahead of everyone.

'He must have closed his eyes with fright,' the thought flashed in the minds of the watchers.

And the eyeless one was already in the alleyway across, and vanished from sight. The mob rushed in his tracks, tumbling down from upstairs; everybody seemed drunk – a pack of wild, unleashed hounds. 'Hold him!' 'Don't let him go!' 'There, there he is!'

Somebody was grabbed downstairs at the entrance, and everyone piled up on him, crushed him and battered him – still yelling, 'Hold!' As though the word just had to burst out of the throat.

With his head thrust forward like a ram, Baryba pushed his way through to the front. For some reason this was necessary, he felt with all his guts that it was necessary. He clenched his iron jaws. Something bestial stirred in him, something he hungered for, some murderous instinct. To be with everybody, to howl like everybody, to hit the one that everybody else was hitting.

Within the circle a young boy lay on the ground – swarthy, with closed eyes. His collar was torn at the side, exposing a small black birthmark on his neck.

Old man Churilov stood in the centre of the circle and kicked the boy in the ribs with his foot. Always so neat and stately – now his beard was rumpled, his mouth twisted; where had all his piety gone to?

'Carried it off! The devils! The other one ran off with a hundred roubles! The devils!'

And he kicked the boy again and again. Sweaty fists stretched toward the prone figure from behind his back, but now they did not dare to strike. Churilov had been robbed, hence he was master here: it was for him to mete out punishment.

Suddenly, from somewhere in the crowd, Timosha dived up right under the old man's nose, jumped at him, red-faced, furious, and pecked away at him, waving his arms and chattering: 'You old bastard, you antichrist, what are you doing? Trying to kill the boy for a lousy hundred roubles? Maybe you've killed him already? Look at him, he isn't breathing. Devils, beasts, is a man's life worth less than a hundred roubles?'

Old Churilov was stunned for a moment, then he snarled back: 'What's this, are you in with them? A new defender! Look out, brother. With all your fancy talk in the tavern! Plenty of people heard you. Hold him, Christians!'

Some of the men moved closer, but hesitated: after all, Timosha was one of them, and those others were outsiders. The old man might just be talking . . .

A red-faced, red-haired townsman, a horse trader, had put on glossy paper cuffs in honour of the holiday. In the mêlée, his cuffs crept down; red hair stood up between the sleeves and the white of the cuffs, and this made his huge hands look still more formidable.

The red hands stretched towards Timosha and pushed him out of the circle. The man said: 'Clear out, clear out while you're still alive, defender. We'll manage here without you.'

And he began in a businesslike manner to frisk the swarthy boy, turning him over like a carcass.

No one wanted to go to the monastery any more. Baryba stayed all evening at Timosha's. Chernobylnikov joined them later.

'I walk along Dvoryanskaya,' he told them, 'and see some people on a bench in a gateway, talking: "Our own Timoshka, the tailor," one of the men says, "was in with them, the lost soul." '

'Damn fools,' Timosha said. 'Nothing better to do but gossip. And Churilov, that beast, it serves him right, the old devil. What's a hundred roubles to him? And those fellows – maybe they hadn't eaten for two days?'

He was silent a while and added: 'So maybe things will start here too. If they did – by God, I'd dive right off the deepest end, into the thick of it. What if they knocked me off? It's all the same – I've half an inch of life left anyway.'

21   THE CHIEF OF POLICE HAS HIS TROUBLES

Well, things were too quiet, so the devil got busy! Hands up! In our town too! And now the chief of police, Captain Ivan Arefych, had his hands full.

A court-martial arrived from the provincial capital – and all because of some snotty boy. The judge, a colonel, a lean man with closely cropped grey hair, suffered from poor digestion. Ivan Arefych went frantic trying to please him. He couldn't eat this, he couldn't eat that – a plague!

When the uninvited guests had first arrived, Ivan Arefych set up a feast of a breakfast: bottles on the table, biscuits, hams, pies. And the colonel turned green with bile. He'd poke his fork into one piece, into another, sniff at it and mumble, 'All that fat.' And sat there sourly, without eating.

The chief's wife, Marya Petrovna, was at the end of her wits: 'In heaven's name, Colonel, why don't you eat?' And she thought to herself: 'He'll have it in for my Ivan Arefych now.'

The prosecutor, though, did their hearts good. A roly-poly, bald, pink as a suckling pig, he looked as though he visited the baths at least twice every week. He shook with laughter at every word and kept taking double portions of everything.

'Another piece of pie, my dear woman. You know, it's only in such musty places as your town that the art of baking in the good old way is still preserved in Russia . . .'

And in the evening, candles were lit in the police chief's study (this had never happened before) and the papers were spread out on the desk. Ivan Arefych puffed at his cigarette, waving away the smoke; heaven forbid that it should blow in the colonel's direction.

The colonel read the papers and made a sour face. 'Are we to bother just with this boy? What's the good of it if you can't get a word out of him? A nuisance. After all, you are the chief of police here, it's your job to find the criminals.'

Sitting on his bed at night, Ivan Arefych pulled off his boots and complained to his wife: 'I'm losing my wits, Masha. Go and give them more – one thief isn't enough. Where am I to get him if he ran away? And don't forget now: at noon the colonel must have oats with milk, well boiled, and a bottle of mineral water. I'm afraid of the man, he can make trouble – a sorehead!'

Marya Petrovna wrote down: 'Oats ... Mineral water ... You ought to talk it over with Blinkin, Ivan Arefych. He's a fox, he'll get you anything you wish – really, you ought to try him.'

It was a good idea, and Ivan Arefych went to sleep with an easier mind.

In the square before the police building, with its yellow peeling walls, the market day was in full swing. Wagon shafts, raised to the sky and tied together; horses with sacks of oats over their muzzles; squealing pigs; barrels with pickled cabbage; wagon-loads of hay. People slapped hands, striking up bargains, called out loudly for customers; peasant carts creaked; the county chairman's coachman tried out a new accordion.

And in the police chief's office an interrogation was in progress. The colonel listened anxiously to the sounds within himself: his stomach rumbled heavily. Good Lord, for a whole week he had been all right, and now it seemed to be starting again ...

The old man Churilov entered, slow and dignified, in a long-skirted coat, grey-bearded. He crossed himself.

'How it happened? Well, to tell you everything in order ...'

He told his story and mopped his face with a calico kerchief. Then he stood a while and thought to himself: 'Might be a good idea to complain about that impudent scoundrel Timoshka; the gentry seem to be kindly disposed.'

'And then, again, your honours, we've got a tailor here, Timoshka, a worthless character, a brazen scamp. He started to protect the young fellow – the one who had been shooting. And I said to him: "Are you in with them too?" And he turned on me in front of everybody ...'

The old man was dismissed. The prosecutor rubbed his soft

small hands, undid the lower button of his uniform jacket, and said to the colonel quietly: 'Hm. This Timosha . . . What do you think?'

Behind the window there was bargaining, shouting, creaking. The colonel lost his temper. 'Ivan Arefych, won't you close the window! My head is splitting. What customs – a market right in front of the police office!'

Ivan Arefych tiptoed to the window, closed it, and called out: 'Next.'

The treasurer's son-in-law told his story languidly, with genteel airs.

The prosecutor asked: 'So you say he returned to the tavern, and then ran out again? I see. And the handkerchief? I think you mentioned something about a handkerchief? Did he go back for the handkerchief?'

The treasurer's son-in-law recalled Timoshka's red phlegm-spattered handkerchief, made a sour face, and drawled out nasally, in an offended tone :'What handkerchief? I don't recall any handkerchief.'

It was beneath his dignity even to remember that handkerchief.

Baryba followed the prosecutor's questions with his well-practised scent. And when the handkerchief was mentioned, he said confidently: 'No, there was no handkerchief. He simply said he had some business upstairs.'

After Baryba was dismissed, the prosecutor swallowed some cold tea and said to the colonel: 'Would you please instruct the clerk to write an order for the detention of this Timosha? It seems to me that all this testimony . . . I know, you are sometimes excessively careful, but this . . .'

The colonel had griping spasms in his intestines, something seemed to rise to his gullet, and he was thinking: 'The devil knows them! That bloated idiot, the captain's wife! Their stupid provincial manner of making everything fat . . .'

'I was saying, Colonel . . .'

'Oh, leave me alone, for Christ's sake! Write anything you please. I have a frightful stomach ache.'

22 SIX TWENTY-FIVE-ROUBLE NOTES

Nobody was surprised when Timosha was picked up.

'He's been asking for it for a long time.'

'All that he knew was to wag his tongue. No respect for anything! Talked about God the same as he would talk about the grocer Averyan.'

'And stuck his nose in everywhere, judged everybody. Just think of it, a new saint, a protector!'

And Blinkin said: 'Such heads don't last long on their shoulders hereabouts. Take me and Baryba; we'll live.'

He slapped Baryba on the back and looked at him with his huge eyes, straight out of an icon, but it was hard to tell whether his look was friendly or contemptuous – the faker.

That same evening, Semyon Semyonych was invited to visit Ivan Arefych, for a cup of tea. The police chief implored Blinkin, in the name of Christ the Lord: 'Instruct your ... what's his name, to do the right thing. Oh, that Baryba of yours. So he will give some definite testimony at the trial. I know he's a specialist in these things – oh, never mind, we are among our own here. By God, my head is going round and round with those guests of ours from the capital. If we could only get rid of them, and have the whole mess done with. That colonel with his choosy ways – give him this, don't give him that ...'

After a bit of bargaining, they agreed on six twenty-five-rouble notes.

'What's a little more, a little less. And that fellow ... what's his name ... that Baryba can be fixed up with a post somewhere. What could be better? Say, a clerk, or a police sergeant ...'

On the following day, over a mug of beer, Blinkin used every possible wile to persuade Baryba, now tempting, now flattering. Baryba demurred.

'But we've been pals, it's queer somehow, it's too awkward.'

'Eh, my dear, is it for us to stop at anything, to worry about such things? We'll sink into the mire, we'll lose our heads. It's like the fairy-tale: if you look back, you'll die of fear. So it's better to rush in without a glance. And then, there's plenty of time before the trial. If it bothers you, you can always get out of it.'

'Right, too,' Baryba thought to himself. 'And the devil with him, he's got consumption anyway ... And I'd get a position ... Am I to spend my days on bread and cider?' And Baryba said: 'Well, it's only for your sake, Semyon Semyonych. If it weren't for you, I'd never think of it.'

'If it were not for me ... Why, my dove, I know you never would have turned into such a treasure without me. You'd still be neither here nor there. And now ...'

He was silent, then suddenly he bent down to Baryba's ear and whispered: 'But don't you dream about devils? I see them every night, every night – do you understand?'

23 THE TROUBLESOME ANT

Baryba agreed. He went to the police chief, and the chief gave him a pile of money and promised the world ... Baryba should have been happy. And yet something nagged at him, something bothered him – like a gnat, or an ant that had gotten into his guts and crawled around and around, and there was no way of catching it or squashing it.

Baryba went to bed, thinking: 'Tomorrow evening. There's still a whole day to the trial. I'll take it in my head, and go and back out. I'm my own master.'

He slept, and he didn't sleep. And kept trying to complete an unfinished thought in his sleep: 'But he hasn't more than half an inch of life left anyway.'

And again he dreamt of the district school, the examinations, the priest chewing at his beard.

'I'll flunk again, a second time,' thought Baryba.

And thought again: 'He was a brainy one, Timosha; you have to give him credit,' But why 'was'? How come he 'was'?

His eyes were gaping wide in the darkness, and he could no

longer fall asleep. The persistent ant crawled around inside him, didn't let him rest.

'Why "was"?'

24   GOOD-BYE

Baryba woke late, at noon, in his small room in Streltsy. Everything around was bright, clear, and what he had to do in court was suddenly plain and easy. As though none of what had bothered him at night existed – there had been nothing at all.

Aprosya brought a samovar and a fresh rye bread, and stood on the threshold. Her sleeves were rolled up, her right elbow rested on the palm of the left hand, and her simple head was propped by the right hand. And all she wanted was to listen to Anfim Yegorych, to stand there, listening, sighing pityingly, shaking her head with horror and commiseration.

Baryba finished his tea. Aprosya brought Anfim Yegorych his coat and said: 'You are in a jolly mood today, Anfim Yegorych. Are you about to come into some money?'

'I am,' Baryba answered.

At the trial, Timosha was all right, tried to keep up his courage, turned his little head this way and that, and his neck was long and thin – it gave you a turn to see it.

And the swarthy young fellow had gone altogether queer: he seemed to sag, as if his bones had suddenly gone soft, melted away. He kept toppling over sideways. The guard was always straightening him up and leaning him against the wall.

Baryba spoke confidently and convincingly, but he hurried: if he could only get away from there, quick, and go off somewhere. When he had finished, the prosecutor asked: 'But why didn't you speak up before? So much valuable material.'

The trial was about to dismiss, when Timosha jumped up suddenly and cried out: 'Yes! Well, then, good-bye to you all!'

Nobody answered.

25   THE MORNING OF A MARKET DAY

It was the morning of a merry, lively market day. The air before the jail, before the courthouse and the police, was thick with the squealing of suckling pigs, with dust and sunshine, with the smell of horses and of apples piled in carts. There was a tangled pealing of bells, overlaid with market noises: a church procession somewhere was praying for rain.

The chief of police, Ivan Arefych, in a faded uniform, with a cigarette, well pleased with himself, came out on the steps and said, looking sternly at the crowd: 'The criminals have suffered lawful execution. I warn you . . .'

The crowd, quiet for a moment, suddenly rustled, swayed like a forest under a gust of wind.

Somebody took off his hat and crossed himself. And in the back rows, further away from the police chief, a voice said: 'Hangmen, devils!'

'Who're you talking about, eh?'

Ivan Arefych turned sharply and went in. And all at once, the crowd seemed to come awake before the porch. Everybody shouted at once, hands were raised, everybody wanted to be heard. The red-headed townsman waved his long arms.

'They're lying, they didn't hang them,' he spoke with conviction. 'It's an unthinkable business: how can you hang a living man? Would he ever let himself, a living man? He'll fight with tooth and nail . . . For a man alive to let them put a noose around his neck – it makes no sense!'

'That's education for you, that's where books will get you,' said an old shopkeeper. 'That Timoshka, he was too smart, he forgot God, and there you are . . .'

The red-haired man looked angrily at the old man from above and saw the long grey hairs sprouting from his ears.

'You'd do better to keep quiet,' the red man said, 'with one foot in the grave yourself. Look at you, growing hair from your ears already.'

The old man turned indignantly and muttered, making his way out of the crowd: 'All sorts of characters hanging around nowadays ... The good old days are over in our town; they've churned up everything, they have.'

26   SHINY BUTTONS

A white, still unlaundered tunic, buttons like silvery suns, gold braid on the shoulders.

'Holy Mother of God! Can it be true? The Balkashin yard, and all the rest of it – and now here I am – Baryba, with shoulder-straps.'

He felt them: yes, there they were. It must be true, then.

The postman Chernobylnikov came out of the notary's house and stopped with his mailbag under the gateway with the sign. He looked closely and saluted, clowning: 'My greetings to the sergeant, sir.'

Baryba almost choked with pride. With a negligent air he raised his hand to his visor.

'How long since they promoted you?'

'Umm, about three days. The uniform was just finished. All the trouble now – getting it made.'

'Gr-reat! So you're one of the higher-ups now? Well, my very best.'

They parted. Baryba walked on: he had to report to the chief today. He walked, beaming, pleased with himself, with the May sun, with his shoulder-straps. And he smiled his rectangular smile.

At the jail Baryba stopped and asked the corner policeman: 'Ivan Arefych in?'

'No, sir, he's gone to a murder.'

And the corner policeman, from whom Baryba had had to duck during his market-pilfering days, saluted him politely.

Come to think of it, Baryba was glad that the chief had gone to the murder: it was fine to walk about in his new tunic, with everybody saluting him. 'It's good to be alive in the world! What an ass – I'd almost backed out.' The iron jaws clenched tightly. If he could get the strongest, hardest pebble in his teeth now, he'd grind it into dust just as he used to in the old days, at the district school!

Ah, that's it! This was the time to visit his father. The old fool – he kicked him out, let him take a look now.

He walked past the Churilov tavern, past the empty market stalls, along the sidewalk of decaying boards, and then over the grass-grown alley, with no sidewalks at all.

At the door covered with tattered oilcloth – the old familiar door! – he halted for a moment. He almost loved his father now. Eh, he was ready to kiss the whole town at that moment: sure enough – his first day in the tunic with the shoulder-straps and shiny buttons!

Baryba knocked. His father came out. Oh, brother, he had aged! Grey bristle on his cheeks, his glasses pushed down on his nose, the old man stared at him for a long time. You couldn't tell whether he recognized his son or not. He didn't say a word.

'What d'you want?' he grunted after a while.

Uh, what a sorehead. Well, clearly he hadn't recognized him.

'Well, don't you know me, old man? Remember how you threw me out? And now – see? I got the appointment, three days ago.'

The old man blew his nose, wiped his fingers on his apron, and said calmly: 'I heard about you. I sure did. Good folks are talking . . .'

He looked at him again over his glasses, calmly. 'They talk about Yevsey, the monk. And about the tailor.'

The grey bristles suddenly quivered on his chin. 'And about the tailor, they do, they do.'

And the old man suddenly began to shake and scream, sputtering saliva. 'Out! O-ut of my house, you scum! I t-told you never to come to my doorstep. Get out, get out!'

Stunned, Baryba goggled at him and stood there for a long time, unable to understand. When he finally digested it, he turned silently and went away.

A muddy twilight had fallen in the street. A dismal breeze blew from the window.

Baryba, already well loaded, sat at a table in Churilov's tavern, his feet spread wide apart, his hands in his pockets. He muttered under his nose: 'I spit on him. The old man's off his rocker. To hell with him . . .'

But something had already settled at the bottom, something muddied the waters. The jolly May day was gone.

In the opposite corner three shopkeepers' assistants from Market Row sat at a table. One of them leaned forward and was talking, the other two listened. And suddenly all three burst into laughter. He must have told them something very funny.

'A-ah, I see! So? Well, I . . . I'll sh-show them,' Baryba muttered under his breath.

His eyes narrowed, the square mouth opened, baring his teeth, the iron jowls worked tensely.

The shop assistants broke into a new fit of merriment.

Baryba suddenly took his hand out of his pocket and banged his knife on his plate, with drunken, stumbling blows.

The waiter Mitka ran over and bent down to him, grinning with the cheek turned to the shop assistants, and expressing due respect with the cheek turned to his honour the sergeant. The assistants pulled long faces and listened.

'Sl-listen to me. T-tell 'em that I f-forbid them to laugh. I'll з . . I'll . . . From now on laughter is strict-ly forbidden hereabouts . . . N-no, wait, I'll tell 'em m'self!'

Swaying from side to side, huge, square, crushing, he rose and started, clattering, towards the shop assistants. And it was not as if a man were walking, but an idol from an ancient burial mound suddenly come to life, a crude, uncouth, preposterous stone idol out of prehistoric Russia.

[*1912, published 1913*]

THE DRAGON

Gripped with bitter cold, ice-locked, Petersburg burned in delirium. One knew: out there, invisible behind the curtain of fog, the red and yellow columns, spires, and hoary gates and fences crept on tiptoe, creaking and shuffling. A fevered, impossible, icy sun hung in the fog – to the left, to the right, above, below – a dove over a house on fire. From the delirium-born, misty world, dragon men dived up into the earthly world, belched fog – heard in the misty world as words, but here becoming nothing – round white puffs of smoke. The dragon men dived up and disappeared again into the fog. And trolleys rushed screeching out of the earthly world into the unknown.

On the trolley platform a dragon with a gun existed briefly, rushing into the unknown. His cap was down over his nose and would have swallowed the dragon's head but for his ears; on the protruding ears the cap had come to rest. His army greatcoat dangled to the floor; the sleeves flapped loosely; the tips of the boots were turned up, empty. And in the dimness of the fog – a hole: the mouth.

This was now in the leaping, rushing world; and here the bitter fog belched out by the dragon was visible and audible: 'So I was taking him along, the bastard: an intellectual mug – it turned your stomach just to look at him. And it talks, the scum! Wouldn't you know? It talks!'

'And did you bring him in?'

'I sure did – non-stop to the heavenly kingdom. With the bayonet.'

The hole in the fog closed up. There was nothing now but the empty cap, empty boots, an empty army coat. The trolley sped, gnashing, out of the world.

And suddenly – from the empty sleeves – from out of their

depths, a pair of raw, red dragon paws emerged. The empty coat squatted down on the floor, and in the paws there was a tiny, grey, cold lump that had materialized out of the bitterly cold fog.

'Mother in heaven! A baby starling – frozen stiff! Just look at it!'

The dragon pushed back his cap – and in the fog two eyes appeared, two small chinks from the nightmare world into the human.

The dragon blew with all his might into the red paws, and there were clearly words, spoken to the starling – but in the nightmare world they were unheard. The trolley screeched.

'The little bastard: he gave a flutter, didn't he? Not yet? He'll come around, by Go . . . Just think!'

He blew with all his strength. The gun dropped to the floor. And at the moment ordained by destiny, at a point ordained in space, the starling gave a jerk, another – and fluttered off the dragon's paws into the unknown.

The dragon's fog-belching maw gaped open to his ears. Then slowly the cap slid down over the chinks into the human world and settled back on the protruding ears. The guide to the heavenly kingdom picked up his gun.

The trolley gnashed and screeched and rushed into the unknown, out of the human world.

[*1918*]

THE PROTECTRESS OF SINNERS

Black, shaggy depth: the bottom of a wooded ravine. Through
the blackness, high overhead – the white serrated walls of the
convent, and over their jagged line, the stars. And you can hear
the watchman by the wall, tapping on his board.

The watchman has the key to the convent gate. Sikidin knows
all about it; he got his information from Dushatka, who bakes
Communion bread for the nuns. Now he must only get hold of
the key somehow – then they can do the job at night, quiet and
gentle-like. Because if you tried it in the daytime, there'd be no
end of fuss and squealing all over the place.

And Sikidin speaks sternly into the darkness behind him:
'Mind you, no physical beating without no need. And no shov-
ing like fools. Everything must go strictly according to the resolution . . .' From the way he whispers, you can tell Sikidin is
scowling, but he himself cannot be seen – only his teeth flash in
the dark.

While they had been talking it over in the village and writing
out the verdict, the soldier Sikidin took a back seat. The big
shot, naturally, was Zinovey Lukich, with his fancy gab. But
now, when it came down to business, it somehow happened of
itself that Sikidin took command, and Zinovey Lukich shrivelled
up before him. As for old Onisim, it goes without saying: at
every word Sikidin says, his mouth puckers up into a round
little O: 'Oh? So-oh!'

They climbed up to the top, to the serrated wall. Close by the
wall a small red fire was burning; by the fire, a red dog. The fire
went up and down, flared and dimmed, and the red peasant near
the fire sat with his arms around his knees, a gun between his
knees.

'Lord Jesus Christ, the Son of God . . .' Zinovey Lukich's

little head leaned to the side, and he looked humped and sickly. 'We want to see the Mother Superior – about some wood, you know . . . I guess we're a bit late, we got held up . . . N-no-no-no, doggie! The Lord be with you, doggie, hush, doggie, hush . . .'

'Down, Belka, quiet!'

The watchman's red hand grasped the collar. The hand had six fingers: the sixth struck out, stubborn and hard like a rooster's spur. And Zinovey Lukich started weaving his little hands in the red light, around the watchman, around Belka, flickering, hurrying, spinning a spiderweb so fine you could not see it with your eye.

He talked about some general's dog, about St Seraphim Sarovskoy. The dog, it seems, relieved himself on the church steps, and the sainted father pinned him down with his holy staff right there on the steps. And in the Nil-Stolbensky Hermitage, a dog had swallowed the Communion bread, and at that moment the dog's head suddenly became a human head, and he says . . .

And now the web is spun all round and round the fire. The rooster's finger stands up, motionless. Belka put down her head on her front paws and closed her eyes . . .

'I guess we need more firewood . . .' Sikidin stretched himself and got up lazily. Belka followed his movements with a sidelong yellow glance. Zinovey Lukich watched out of the corner of his eye.

'And the dog says: Faithful Chris . . . Christians . . .'

Zinovey Lukich caught his breath: 'Mother of God . . . Protectress of sinners, help us!' Behind the watchman he suddenly saw Sikidin's teeth.

Wham! The teeth flashed, the watchman grunted like an ox and was down on the ground with Sikidin's worsted muffler in his mouth.

Belka leaped up, yelping, sank her teeth into Sikidin's hand. Sikidin poked his knife into her, wiped it on the grass, and Belka was quiet.

The moon climbed out of the ravine, blue, skinny, as if it had been fed on nothing but skimmed milk. It climbed out, and quickly slithered up and up along the finest thread – away from trouble, and on the very top it huddled, crouching on thin legs.

To keep the nuns from wondering if something was amiss, to keep them sleeping quietly, they left old man Onisim up above with the rattle, and he went on tapping at it lightly. Meanwhile, they busied themselves with the watchman down in the ravine.

They knocked themselves out with him, the stubborn bastard! He kept harping on one thing: 'Sure I had it,' he says, 'I had it on my belt. It's your own fault, you made me lose it, dragging me down here from above.'

They showed him the paper.

'Lookit. Here . . . "And all the monetary finances of the convent, in the name of the Holy Mother of God, the Protectress of Sinners, unanimously for the benefit of the peasants of the village of Manayenki . . ." According to the paper! Understand? Hand over the key!'

But he kept silent. Then Sikidin went to work on him: physically, on the jaw, he let him have it. Not a sound. The son of a bitch!

'The devil knows him, maybe he isn't bluffing?' And Sikidin crawled off on all fours to look for the key. Try and find a needle in a haystack!

Sikidin came back sore as hell – a holy terror. He pulled out his knife, slashed off a piece of bread, and sits there chewing, glaring at the watchman: six-fingered devil! On account of him, they'll have to do it in the daytime now . . .

Silence. As if nothing at all has happened. Old man Onisim knocks on his board by the convent gates, and only Belka isn't barking, and Sikidin's hand is wrapped in a piece of rag – the mark of Belka's teeth.

Suddenly Sikidin grins – teeth just like Belka's – and turns to the watchman: 'Hey, you – give out, in place of your old Belka! Bark, I say!'

He holds the knife to the rooster neck. The watchman's face cannot be seen behind Sikidin – only his hands, tied up over his belly, with the sixth finger jumping around, faster and faster.

'Come on, now! Bark, I tell you!'

Sikidin presses the knife harder. The watchman hiccups,

gulps, and begins to bark. 'More!' – the barking rings out louder and clearer.

Laughter comes bubbling out of Zinovey Lukich's nose – silently, like air out of a pricked balloon. Onisim came running down from the hill – his eyes clear as a baby's, his mouth a puckered *O*.

'O-oh? So-o! You jokers! And I thought there's somebody here really with a dog . . .' And he crows with laughter, gaily as a child, his eyes pure as an infant's. 'Come on, come on, let's have some more!'

But Sikidin has already thrown away his knife and the watchman lies silent. The sixth finger, like a rooster's spur, is stirring faintly.

The moon is hurrying, climbing higher and higher: it can hardly be seen now. The black leaves turn green. The dawn burns with an even flame, like haystacks in a drought. The day will be pleasant, calm.

But what will happen on this calm and pleasant day?

Mother Naphanaila, the Mother Superior, once had a small-holding of her own, right here in the district. She had borne nine children in the world, all of them daughters, and all the image of their mother: tiny, blue-eyed, waddling like ducklings. Widowed, she raised the nine all on her own, and before you knew it, it was time to marry off the older ones. Soon there would be a flock of grandchildren, fresh and firm as mushrooms: all the noise, all the fun she'd have around her!

The girls would need their strength, and she fed them well. She was a great cook: what buckwheat puddings she baked, what liquorice tarts!

'Eat, girls, eat, build up your juices. Ours is a woman's job, a hard job.'

One day they had jelied sheatfish on ice. It was a cholera year, and all nine were laid up. Inside a week the house was empty, swept clean. She was left alone.

She went into the convent, and now Naphanaila has ninety daughters. She is all shrivelled today, black, tiny as a beetle, but she still walks with the old waddle; her lips are sunken like a little trough, but the eyes are the same: wide open, blue, and clear. It sometimes happens that a tree dries out and stands blackened, gnarled, yet in the spring a single green branch will shoot out, and the eye rejoices in the whole tree.

Mother Naphanaila loves the spring, the thaw, the patches of black earth appearing through the snow. And when the first smooth stalks push up, and the red bugs come climbing out from under rocks, their wings still glued together, and silly faces painted on their backs, and Easter bells begin to ring . . .

'Out into the woods, girls, you lazy good-for-nothings – out into the woods this very minute to pick flowers! It's your season – springtime. Get out now!' and she pretends to stamp her feet.

Many a nun has gotten married out of the Manayenki convent. And many a child has been born there. The old woman's sunken lips would chide, but the clear eyes laughed.

And all her ninety daughters doted on Mother Naphanaila. They shielded her from every harm, and now . . .

'Goodness, mercy, how can we tell her now? The watchman gone, and nobody knows where, and Belka. It'll get her all upset, and on such a day . . .'

On such a day: Mother Naphanaila's birthday.

They went to the Mother Treasurer for advice. Katerina the treasurer is hefty as a man: sinewy, beetle-browed. And if she gives you a word of advice, it's like a key turned in a lock, turned and sealed.

'There's time enough tomorrow. Not a peep about the watchman today,' decided Katerina.

And the day went at its own pace. A smell of good things came from the cellar under the refectory. Dumplings in cream, pies with cabbage soaked in milk, millet pancakes. The Mother Superior was feasting her girls. For late Mass the big bell was rung, as on holidays. The nuns came in new habits, most of them pink-cheeked – squeeze and the juices will come spurting out; under the black cloth the breasts push out stubbornly, no matter how they try to hide them.

'The darlings!' Sikidin hankered after the nuns, his teeth flashing, lips widening.

There were few outsiders in the church for prayer – only four or five pilgrims and the three men from Manayenki: Sikidin, Zinovey Lukich, and old Onisim.

But a mob of people came to worship before the Miraculous Icon – the Protectress of Sinners. And everything was turned to her – heads and hands – and she looked down lovingly on everybody with her clear blue eyes.

'Protectress . . . Virgin Most Powerful . . . save us, help us . . .' Zinovey Lukich stood before the Virgin, his little head bent to the side, all of him humped, infirm . . .

Dushatka, the baker, brought out the birthday Communion bread, a three-pound loaf. As soon as she was free, she slipped out of the door. And glancing back over her shoulder, she ran down the flagstone path to the left, toward the cemetery. After a while Sikidin also came out of the church.

The linden trees stand breathless in the heat. The bees are fairly clinging to their honey fragrance. On a warm gravestone Sikidin sits with Dushatka. And Dushatka is all limp, her arms hang down, and there is only one thing in the world: Sikidin's paw on her right breast.

'Now look, Dushatka, no fooling now. Soon as they go to sleep after the meal, you'll take us through the corridor across the building to her chamber. Then scat. And later on, at night, I'll wait for you in the clearing, categorically.'

'Vanyushka, but promise, for Christ's sake, there shouldn't be no trouble for her!'

'Stupid! We mean to go about it delicately, according to the resolution.'

And now there is only one thing in the world: Sikidin's paw on her right breast.

After Mass, Mother Naphanaila's chambers buzzed with guests: the clergy from Manayenki, Krutoye, Yablonov. Like a little waddling duck, tiny, dried up, dark, the hostess fussed over her guests. And her clear blue eyes were like a fresh spring shoot . . .

The deacon from Krutoye had just married off his daughter Nonochka, and Naphanaila rejoiced and questioned him about everything: 'And what kind of a wedding dress?'

'White muslin, with an inset over here, and ruffles all around.'

'Thank God, thank God! And was there music?'

'Oh, well, what kind of music do we have? Two Jews in three rows.'

'Thank God, thank God! More pancakes?'

It was a pleasure, yet Naphanaila had worn herself out with her guests. As soon as they had gone, she sent Katerina away, pulled the shades, and lay down on the sofa. The shades were yellow, and everything in the room was golden, gay: the stack of dishes looked gilded, and the three-pound loaf, and on the windows the honey-fragrant linden twigs and the buttercups and daisies.

And then, as soon as she had closed her eyes, all her nine daughters were there – come to her birthday, laughing, merry.

'And do you have music there, my dears?'

'How else? But naturally . . .' and they went into a dance, tapping their feet, louder and louder. They must be wearing heavy boots out there – who would have thought?

Naphanaila opened her eyes. Three peasants were shifting from foot to foot in the doorway.

'Oh dear, how come I fell so fast asleep? And Katerina must have knocked and knocked, and I didn't hear a thing . . .'

She jumped up, straightened out her habit, and waddled over to the peasants.

'You look to be from Manayenki, no?'

'Sure enough, we're from Manayenki. And we've come to you according to the resolution.'

'My good souls, such a happy day! Thank you, thank you kindly! So you remembered the old woman too, and came to do her honour. Wait, I still have some birthday cake, and everything. One moment, just a moment . . .'

And like a little duck she waddled off into the next room and started tinkling with the dishes.

Old man Onisim's mouth puckered up into an *O*.

'Well, now! Isn't that a fix!'

They could hear the knife going through something soft, clicking lightly against the plate, cutting the cake into slices.

Sikidin's teeth flashed; his eyes were hidden in his cap–the cap was in his hands: 'Oh, well, we haven't eaten since morning. Only, no privileges after that – categorically.'

The Mother Superior brought in a heavy tray: cake, a decanter of Visant wine, a piece of roast carp.

'Well, my dears, such a pleasure ... So you remembered my birthday? Here you are, please, please. And you, old man, sit down here, in the armchair. Your health! I'll join you.'

The Manayenki men had struggled with the damned watchman all night. And the birthday Visant was good and strong: it spread through all the bones and hit one in the back of the head. Sikidin tore at the cake more and more furiously with his wolf's teeth. Zinovey Lukich's head bent further and further to the side.

Another glass, and Zinovey Lukich began to beat his breast.

'I'm a sinner, Mother, I confess it in front of everybody ... Between last Christmas and Shrovetide, I married for a third time, a young girl ... And again, my heifer, it had hoof and mouth disease ... But the Mother of God, she's the Protectress of Sinners – she must deliver us out of this hardship. It's true, I sinned, and the heifer ... but as we're out for society, so to speak, not for our own selves ... Am I right, Sikidin? Eh?'

There was a knock on the door: the Mother Treasurer. Heavy steps, like a man's. She raised her eyebrows at the sight of the Manayenki men.

'Got wind of the cake and barged in. Might have given her an hour's rest!'

'Katerinushka, bring us some more Visant, dear – on such a day! Do me a favour, the keys to the cellar are over there, in the cabinet.'

Well, then, it's either now, while she is in the cellar, or everything is lost ...

Sikidin got up, thrust out his forehead, like a butting ox, and leaned his hands on the table, the right hand wrapped in a piece of rag.

'Heavenly Father, what's that on your hand? Come, let me wrap it in a clean cloth, or you can get ...'

Sikidin held up his hand. He looked at the Mother Superior, at his hand, and the words stuck in his throat ...

At this moment, Onisim finished eating too. He was red from the wine, and his baby-soft old man's hair seemed whiter than ever.

He grunted, wiped his lips, and bowed low, to the waist: 'Well, Mother, thanks for the fine treat. Full – up to here! And such a cake – o-oh . . .'

The Mother Superior glowed like a lighted candle. Lord, such a happy day! And Sikidin stood – stiff as a post, a lead weight on his tongue. Then suddenly he scrunched his teeth, and shot out of the door like a bullet.

'Oh, but why . . . But wait a moment! There she is, there's Katerina, I can hear the keys . . .'

But who could wait? They clattered down the stairs, across the warm flagstones under the lindens . . .

And down in the ravine, by the cart, they turned on old Onisim.

'You dunce! You empty-headed nitwit! "Tha-anks, Mother!" What did we agree on, eh? If you had kept your mouth shut, everything would've . . . "Tha-anks, Mother!" '

'Well, if you're so much brainier than I, why didn't you talk business to her right off? And what did you do? Sure enough! Well, don't you rail at me!'

And in the cart, on the way home, Sikidin worried: 'What can we say to them in the village now? Naturally, there were facts against our expectation. Still, it's a disgrace, it is. We've got to think of something tellable. How can you get that off your tongue? – "Tha-anks, Mother!" '

And he lashed out and lashed out at the horse, as if it weren't a horse at all, but old Grandpa Onisim himself.

Oh, well, they still have seven versts to go. Maybe they'll think of something tellable.

[*1918, published 1922*]

TWO TALES FOR GROWN-UP CHILDREN

THE CHURCH OF GOD

Ivan decided to build a church for the glory of God. But a church – to make the heavens sizzle and the devils wilt! So the fame of Ivan's church would spread to the ends of the world.

Well, naturally, building a church isn't like putting up a hut – it takes plenty of money. So he went out to dig up some money for the church of God.

It was already going on evening. Ivan hid out in the hollow under the bridge. An hour, two hours. And then there was a clattering of hooves – a three-horse carriage rolling across the bridge: a travelling merchant.

Ivan gave a rush and a hoot and a whistle – a regular Dragon Gorynich out of the fairy-tale. The horses reared, the driver tumbled out onto the ground, and the merchant in the carriage shook with fright like an aspen leaf.

Ivan sent the coachman to his maker, and turned to the merchant: 'Hand over the money.'

The merchant began to swear by all that's holy and to plead: 'What money?'

'It's for a church, you fool! It is a church I want to build. Hand over!'

The merchant swears and pleads: 'I'll build it myself.'

'A-ah, yourself? Come on, now!'

Ivan lit a fire under a shrub, crossed himself, and started roasting the merchant's heels with a burning splinter. The merchant couldn't take it and revealed the money: a hundred thousand in the right boot; another hundred in the left.

Ivan bowed low to the ground: 'Praised be the Lord! There will be a church now.'

And he put out the fire with handfuls of earth. And the merchant groaned, doubled up, and gave up the ghost. What can you do – it's for the Lord's sake, after all.

Ivan buried the two, prayed for their souls, and off to town: to hire masons, carpenters, icon painters, guilders. And on the very spot where he had buried the merchant and his driver he raised up a church – taller than Ivan the Great. The crosses – way up in the clouds, blue cupolas with stars, and crimson bells: a church to put all churches to shame.

And Ivan sent out word: God's church is ready, welcome, one and all. A mob collected, you couldn't see from end to end. The bishop himself came, riding in a golden coach, and forty priests, and forty times forty deacons. But just as they began the service, the bishop beckoned to Ivan with his finger, this way: 'Why is it,' he says, 'you've such a rotten smell around here? Go tell the old women they aren't back home, stretched out on their ovens. After all, this is a church of God.'

Ivan went over and told the old women, and the old women shuffled out. But no, the smell was still there! The bishop made a sign to the priests, and all the forty priests began to swing their censers. What the . . .? It didn't help! The bishop nodded to the deacons; the deacons swung their censers, forty times forty of them: the smell got even worse. You couldn't catch your breath, and it was clear now – it wasn't the old women at all, it was the smell of human corpses. Impossible to stand it. And all the folks began to leave the church; the deacons slunk off quietly, the priests backed out one by one. Only the bishop was still in his pulpit in the middle of the church, and Ivan before him, white as a ghost.

And then the bishop looked at Ivan – right through him, to the very bottom – and walked out without a word.

And so Ivan was left all by himself in the church. Everybody else cleared out – they couldn't take the stink of death.

[*1922*]

THE IVANS

And then there was this village, Ivanikha, with all the peasants in it called Ivan. Only their nicknames were different: Ivan Self-Eater (chewed his ear off in his sleep), Ivan the Bald, Ivan Nose-Poker, Ivan Salt-Ears, Ivan Berserk, Ivan Spit-Furthest – no end of them! But Ivan Spit-Furthest was the chief of the lot. Others plough and plant, but the Ivans, they don't do nothing but lie stretched out with their bellies up and spit into the sky: to see who'll spit the furthest.

'Eh, you, Ivans! You should be planting wheat!'

But all you get from the Ivans is 'Ts-s-rk!' through their teeth.

'Now on the new lands, folks say, there's real wheat: first class, every grain big as a cucumber. That's wheat for you, yes, sir.'

And back to their spitting: who'll outspit whom.

They lay around like that, and then all of a sudden luck dropped their way – who knows from where. A stamping of hooves on the road, clouds of dust, and a horseman gallops into Ivanikha, bringing word: whichever Ivans wish to move to the new lands – they can come, and a welcome to them.

The Ivans crossed themselves, grabbed hold of the horse's tail, and off they went like the wind, with everything aflicker before their eyes: a church, a field, a field, a church.

The horseman let them off. No houses, nothing. Bare flat-land for a hundred versts around, and only a stand of nettles in the middle of it. But what nettles: stems thick as a bottle, and if you look up at the top, your hat will drop off. And if it stings you, the blisters are the size of a half rouble. The Ivans poked the soil: black as cobbler's pitch, fat as butter.

'Well, brothers, unsling your bags: that's it – first class.'

They sat down in a circle, chewed some crust with salt. Now for a drink, and to work. They looked here, there – no water. Nothing to be done, they must dig a well.

They went to it. The earth was light, crumbly, lumps flew in all directions. And Spit-Furthest stopped every now and then, screwed up his eyes.

'Oh, brothers, what water they must have here – the sweetest you can find, nothing like ours . . .'

And then the iron struck a stone – *twing!* A huge stone. They turned it over, and a spring shot up. They dipped their pitchers, tasted it: cold, pure, but water like every other.

Spit-Furthest only spat through his teeth – Ts-s-rk: 'This kind of water you get in Ivanikha – all you want. Try deeper: the water round here must be first class, not like . . .'

They dug and dug till late into the night, but the water was still the same. They spent the night turning and twisting under the nettles. In the morning, back to their digging. Now they were way down; it was getting scary, full of worms – nasty, naked, pink, with ugly snouts. They dug and dug, then they would halt a while, the Ivans, and get to thinking. And Spit-Furthest from up above – they could hardly hear him now: 'Deeper, brothers, try deeper! Just a little more, go to it!'

And then they came to some sort of hard crust, the spade couldn't take it, and the water was in the way – plenty of water, but all of it the same as in Ivanikha. They took a crowbar, banged it, and a booming came at them as from a barrel, as if there was a cave below. A harder knock – and everything came rumbling, crashing down – the water, the rocks, the clumps of earth, and all the tools. Deafened by all that noise, their eyes full of dust, the Ivans just barely managed to hang on to a ledge.

After a while they rubbed their eyes, looked down under their feet . . . Merciful heavens! A hole – and in the hole, blue sky. They looked up: far, far above the blue sky glimmered. Merciful heavens! They'd dug right through the earth!

They lost their nerve, grabbed hold of their hats, and started climbing: Self-Eater up on the Bald one's shoulders, the Bald one up on Nose-Poker, Nose-Poker on Salt-Ears, Salt-Ears on Berserk, and so at last they made it to the top.

They got out, and first thing they did was give Spit-Furthest a good thrashing. Then they threw their few belongings into their sacks, and back to Ivanikha: what could they do now – without water, without tools? Their only comfort was to bring a handful of earth each from the new lands back home.

They show it to their neighbours, and the neighbours don't believe it.

'Bluff some more! If there was that kind of earth out there, would you have come back?'

And, naturally, they couldn't say a thing about how they'd dug down through the earth – they'd be laughed off the face of the land. And so the Ivans got to be known as a bunch of liars and braggarts, and nobody believes to this day that they had been to the new lands. And yet they really had.

[*1922*]

THE NORTH

This is how it happens: the sun flies slower and slower, until it hangs suspended, motionless. And everything is locked, embedded for eternity in greenish glass. On a black stone near the shore a seagull has spread its wings and poised for flight – and it will sit forever on the black stone. Over the chimney of the fat-rendering works a puff of smoke hangs, petrified. The quick, tow-headed urchin in the boat leans over the side to splash his hand in the water, and is caught, immobile, still.

For a long moment everything is made of glass. This moment is night. But then the sun stirs faintly, strains, a little more – now! It starts, and everything is shattered: a spray of vari-coloured sparks fans out over the sea; the gull breaks from the stone, and all at once there are hundreds of them, piercing, pink; the orange puff of smoke flies upward; the tow-headed urchin slips, frightened, out of his uncle's huge boots and hurries to his work.

The day is in full swing. And Kortoma, the storekeeper, comes down from upstairs, from his own private office, into the store, well pleased, blowing smoke out of his stubby pipe, his cheekbones as shiny as copper.

The women of the nearby village have come to buy flour and salt from Kortoma. He writes down what they owe him with his own hand in his little green book: everything is there, in that green book. And Kortoma reigns over the women benignly, and banters with them graciously.

'Hey, Holmogorian, what have you got there, stuffed in your bosom? A man just has to turn away, and they . . . Nothing, you say? Come over, let's see . . .'

The Holmogorian woman's breast is hot and fluttery. And

Kortoma cannot remember for the life of him: had she ever come upstairs, to his office? Just to make sure, Kortoma marks the place in his notebook with the letter *N*.

The woman, red as calico, buttons her calico blouse in the corner. Grandma Matrena-Pleseya, broad and warm like a Russian oven, helps the Holmogorian, coaxing her like a child: 'Hush, hush now, sh-sh ... Everything's left in place, ain't it? Well? Stop whining like a fly!'

Grandma Matrena gets all she needs at the store, and it is never entered in the book: with Grandma Matrena, Kortoma had his own special accounts ...

On the table in the office there is a samovar: high-cheeked, arms akimbo, rubbed to high polish with a brick. The shiny belly of the samovar reflects the whole world – in its own way: stretched, flattened, upside down. In its own samovar language, the samovar undoubtedly thinks: 'The world is mine. The world is in me. And what would the world do without me?'

The samovar grins benignly at the world ...

Kortoma sits at the table before the samovar. Kortoma is reflected in the samovar as in a mirror: flattened, with wide cheekbones, shining with coppery good humour. And the samovar is reflected in Kortoma as in a mirror: broad-jowled, merry, boiling and bubbling like a spring the whole day long, sending out puffs of white smoke.

The samovar confers the benefits of tea on Kortoma. Kortoma is entering debits in his ledgers. Kortoma's bookkeeping is shipshape: he does not keep his books just any old way, but by the triple-entry system.

'It's time for us to live according to the Western European nations!' This is his favourite saying.

Kortoma feels hot in his blue knitted shirt, and sweat pours down his face. He puts his hand into his pants pocket, takes out a batiste handkerchief, wrapped in a piece of newspaper (the pocket is dirty), and mops his copper cheekbones. Then he blows his nose with two fingers, dabs it with the batiste handkerchief, and wraps the handkerchief neatly again into the piece of newspaper.

Against one of the names in the debit column Kortoma writes the letter *N*. After a moment's thought he deducts one rouble from the total, and grins benignly at the world.

Behind him, waiting respectfully, is his shop assistant, Ivan the Monk, a runaway from a monastery. Ivan's head does not sit upon his shoulders like everybody else's; it is buried in his shoulders, peeping out like a mouse from its hole.

'Stepka fell asleep in the vat ... A scream! Come take a look ...'

'Hm? All right, let them wait. I'll be over soon.'

Stepka, the bait setter, had baited tackle all night long till he was ready to drop. Then he slipped off and climbed into the cracked fat-melting vat on the shore, crouched down on his heels, and snored away. All you could see of him were his tow head and his uncle's boots. The men from up and down the shore collected around the vat. They called and called to him, but Stepka didn't hear. They neighed like horses – Stepka didn't hear and went on snoring in the vat, doubled up on his heels.

The shop assistant Ivan the Monk covered the vat with boards and weighed them down with forty-pound weights. Then he clambered up on top, and the fun began.

'Let's have it now, fellows!'

And they started bringing water, pail after pail, from hand to hand in a living chain, as at a fire, and down into the vat where Stepka was sleeping. Stepka jumped up and bumped into the boards. He's trapped, and water keeps gushing in, and he cannot make head or tail of anything in his sleep-dazed state.

He started banging on the walls, howling: 'Oh, my God, where am I? Uncle, Uncle! Let me out!'

His Uncle Marey is right there, in the back. He is as tow-haired as Stepka, and heaven knows how much older he is than Stepka. A giant, broad-shouldered, but his eyes are blue and childlike, gaping at the seagulls as though he were seeing them for the first time in his life.

Stepka had already stopped yelling and was merely whimpering faintly like a puppy through his nose. And it was only now that Marey finally heard him. He flushed a fiery red – his ears, his neck. With his shoulders and elbows he ploughed through the crowd, seized the pail from Ivan and brushed off the weights.

The shop assistant bristled at him: 'What's the matter? A new fine gentleman around here! What's it to you? Can't you see the boss is here? Might know enough to keep your place . . .'

And he flung another pailful of water into the vat, directly on Stepka and on Marey's head, bent over the vat.

With one hand Marey pulled Stepka out, wet, shivering like a pup, and with the other he grabbed Ivan the Monk by the feet and plopped him down into the vat.

The big toothy mouths belch with laughter. Kortoma beams with coppery good nature. In the vat there is a squealing and a snorting.

The shop assistant Ivan the Monk crawled out, streaming rivers, everything clinging to his puny body, and bared his toothless gums at Marey from below. A moment, and he'll rush at him . . .

'Crack him one, Vanka! Come on!'

Ivan raised his fist, measured Marey's yard-wide shoulders, and the fist dropped.

'You just wait! I'll get you, wait and see!' and he dived back into his hole, between his shoulders, and slunk away between the feet of the crowd.

The show is over. Reluctantly, the men return to their places: to split cod, to fill baskets with cod livers and carry them on their backs to Kortoma's fat-rendering works.

Before leaving, Kortoma slipped the wet, whimpering Stepka a twenty-kopek piece, thinking in his samovar language: 'I'll bet the kid is tickled; it isn't every day he gets a twenty-kopek piece . . .'

Nobody knows when it happened, but one day a whale had swallowed the Prophet Jonah. And then a voice came from heaven: 'Don't you dare to sup on the prophet! Spit him out!'

The whale hated to start looking for another catch, and yet he was afraid to disobey. He waited for three days, and on the fourth he spat him out. And in reward for his obedience, it was decreed that the whale should have life everlasting.

And he is still alive. He's gotten huge and fearsome, his whole back overgrown with moss and bushes from old age. And nobody has touched him: everybody knows it's Jonah's whale, the one that was decreed to have eternal life.

Then came a hell-bent Russian whaler and drove a harpoon into his back. The whale just turned around – gulp! – and swallowed the schooner with the whole crew. And the crew lives in the belly of the whale to this day, praying for forgiveness of its sin. And when a man's forgiven, the whale spits him out, and he goes off into the woods and lives a hermit's life – wise, from out of the belly of the whale. He prays and rejoices in the never-setting summer sun, the never-setting winter night, in sinners and in righteous men, and in death – when death comes . . .

Behind the village, where the road divides to the right and the left, at the very fork, there is a tumbledown chapel. Near the chapel there is an earthen hut, and in the hut – the ancient hermit Ivan Romanych; he may be a hundred years old, or two hundred.

He creeps out of his earthen hut and stands there, his hand over his eyes, as tiny as a raindrop, green, with a round skullcap in his hand and white down on his head. Just blow, and it will fly away like dandelion fluff.

Dawn. Dewdrops on the tips of the green pine needles; in the dewdrops, pink and green sparks. Thank God: the dawn! The sun rises higher and higher, the sky is blue. In the blue, two yellow butterflies wheel round and round one another, glue themselves together, and fly off – just one.

The hermit Ivan Romanych looks out from under his hand and smiles: thank God . . .

When he was a boy, Marey was just like Stepka; they called him Maryushka. Then something happened to him.

Maryushka was sitting over the Tunezhma, fishing with a line and hook. The river rushed, singing, over sharp stones, lulling to sleep, telling old tales. And perhaps the boy had looked or listened too closely, but he toppled over straight into the water. When his mother came to call him to supper, all that was left of Maryushka was the line over the water, stuck among some rocks.

'Merciful Father, my Maryushka is drowned, dragged off into the whirlpool!'

People came running and pulled him out, all blue. Well, they brought him around somehow; he came to. But he turned kind of queer, always keeping to himself. And you couldn't tell if he was looking at you or not looking at you. His eyes were always staring somewhere past you, and who knows what they saw.

His late mother took Marey to the hermit Ivan Romanych.

'Father Ivan Romanych, what shall I do with him? Tell me, give me some advice. The boy is growing up all addled . . .'

'Well, and thank God . . .'

And he stood there, tiny as a raindrop, his little skull-cap in his hand, his hand over his eyes.

'Your child, Mother, was in the other world, and then they brought him round. He forgot it all, and tries to remember – but cannot. It's all right, one day he will remember! Go Mother, go in peace . . .'

And to this day Marey's favoured spot is where he had almost drowned as a boy: under the rock, over the boiling white Tunezhma.

The fish must have been biting for a long time, the rod curved over like a bow, but Marey saw nothing, thinking some thoughts of his own. And for a long time somebody's red head looked at him from the other bank, thrust out among the dense green juniper shrubs, deliberately rustling the leaves. The tow-haired infant giant continued to gaze past, hearing nothing, thinking his own thoughts. She seized a stone and threw it; the stone splashed into the water at Marey's feet.

Marey started, dropped the rod. The water caught it, whirled it away, and now it was no more than a twig in the foam, far, far away. And far among the pines on the other shore a rusty spot flickered, like the sun on the pink trunks.

Gone. The Tunezhma boils and whispers. It carried off the fishing rod; the rod will never return.

A glove on the hand. And now the glove is off, and it lies on the counter, seemingly the same, yet different: unalive, the flesh and substance taken out of it. And so with Kortomikha behind the counter: the innards have been taken out of her, and her cheeks are sunken forever, and the chest is hollow. But her hat is pink, with flowers, and the pink hat makes it still more painful to look at her. Between the wrinkles at the corners of her lips there is a smile, and the smile is even more painful than the hat.

Kortomikha always comes into the store dressed up, in the pink hat, in gloves, in a smile. This is her husband's order: 'Let everybody see you're not just anybody.'

But Kortomikha rarely comes out. She is mostly upstairs, sitting on her little trunk by the door of the office. Unless there is something special.

On this day there was something special. The Lapps had come. They hadn't been there for nearly two years, but now they came. And the first thing they did was to go to Kortoma's store, to barter furs for salt and calico.

A crowd gathered from the whole village. People were in the store, and outside in front of the store. It was a regular fair – talk, buying, selling. The local girls peeked from around the corner, heavy, slow. One would rise on tiptoe, show her fair head – like a seal rising out of the sea. And the Lapp girls were dark, quick, darting around like fry in sunlit shallow water. And only one red head flashed like a hare among the black.

'Hey, you, red beauty! Come closer! Don't fear, I will not eat you,' Kortoma's cheekbones shine like copper, spreading wide.

'Look out you don't choke!'

She stands before the counter, her red head high, straight as a green shoot springing from the earth, and it is not a rough plank floor under her feet – it is the earth itself, and moss, and her feet are like white roots, firmly grasping the earth.

Kortoma has a piece of grass-green calico in his hands. With a practised hand he gathers it into pleats and ruffles and brings it up against the red-haired girl, just below her throat: red and green, o-ho!

Smoothing out the folds on her breast, stroking it through the cloth, he feels it: like a young fir cone, like a still unripe, still faintly rosy cloudberry.

An iron yardstick lies on the counter. The red head flashes, and the yardstick comes whistling down on the hand, right on the knuckle.

Kortomikha, whose eyes have never left them for a second,

flicks toward them with her pink hat, and she is right there, shielding him with her dried-out, empty hands, and with her body, and her hat. She caught her husband's wrist.

'My darling, how's that . . . the bitch! Does it hurt? Tell me!'

Just to think of it: her Kortoma, the best man in the world! She stroked his hand.

The people in the store giggled. Kortoma shook her off, and she fell against the counter, like a flabby, empty glove.

Midsummer Night was roasting hot. The shore, of red granite, glowed with the heat; the dark blood of the earth seemed to be rising from below. There was a sharp, unbearable smell of birds, of cod, of green decaying seaweed. Through the mist the huge ruddy sun loomed nearer and nearer. And in the sea, dark blood welled up to meet it – in bloated, rearing, huge white waves.

Night. The mouth of the bay between two cliffs was like a window. A window shutting out curious eyes with a white shade – white woolly fog. And all that you could see was that behind it something red was happening.

The village was deserted. Black gaps in the fog – the open windows of empty huts. Everybody was on the other bank, across the Tunezhma. There, in the clearing with the trampled white moss, columns of smoke, still whiter and more pearly than the fog, rose from the fires. The three-stringed lute strummed quietly; figures circled in the fog, came out of it and disappeared again. Lapp fellows with slow, tow-haired local girls. Local fellows with dark Lapp girls. And among the dark ones, a quick, red, flashing spot, like the sun on a pine trunk.

And Kortoma is also here, his arms akimbo, puff, puff, the grey smoke rising from his pipe. Eh, if he could only throw his arms around a hot young body and whirl and whirl around till he was dazed and breathless. But that's impossible: Kortoma is not just anybody. And so he puffs with dignity, and slowly pulls out the handkerchief wrapped in paper, and slowly measures out his words.

'Well, everything depends on the man himself. When I first set my foot here – what did I amount to? A nobody – a mangy sandpiper, like Stepka. And now? Oh, yes! ... We have to live according to the Western European nations, we must see educated cities. Take, let's say, Petersburg...'

Yes, Kortoma is somebody; he has seen everything. And the others listen silently, with eyes and mouths wide open. The urchin Stepka – a small head poking out of his uncle's bottomless boots. And Marey: blue, baby eyes, white hair, lips plump like Stepka's, and terrifying shoulders, a yard across – an infant giant.

'And how many streets are there in Petersburg?' Marey asks, staring greedily into Kortoma's mouth.

'Oh, well, around forty, or maybe even fifty ...' Kortoma puffs out his cheeks – puff, puff!

God knows whether there is really such a city – with fifty streets, and houses all over, and people. How come they don't get lost in all those streets? After all, it isn't like a forest, with all kinds of trees, and moss on the bark, and junipers, and rocks – and everything different; all you have to do is keep your eyes open. But there, in the city?

The childlike eyes grow wider and wider with astonishment. Marey is far away, in Petersburg. And he does not see the redhaired Lapp girl pass by – once, and twice, with a juniper wreath on her head, for this is Midsummer Night. A gang of fellows tags after her at every step. Perhaps she smells of something special – green pine needles, sea birds – and they are drawn by the scent and follow in her tracks.

'Eh, I'm sick of all of you, get going!' The redhead sits down on a stone near by. Perhaps she wants to listen to Kortoma. Kortoma beams slowly with his cheekbones, puffs at his pipe, as though the redhead weren't there at all – and keeps a dignified silence. Kortoma knows his own worth ...

The three-stringer hurries, the couples whirl more rapidly on the white meadow, their breath comes faster. The white smoke columns sway. Silently, pair after pair disappears into the fog, or maybe into the downy white forest out there, beyond the fog, and the white curtain shuts them out.

Kortoma puffs at his pipe.

'Then also, there's the light at night – a huge lantern, in the very middle, over the whole city ... Good God! You'd think it's daytime ... Even brighter than daytime! All night long, summer and winter, you can see every pebble, every blade of grass ...'

The three-stringer hurries, breath comes faster.

'You hear? I say, come with me into the circle!' The green wreath on the russet hair is right under Marey's eyes; she must have been tugging at his sleeve for a long while.

'Oh-h, wait ... Let me listen ...' Marey is far away, in Petersburg.

Somebody in the band of fellows giggled. The redhead flushed, let go of Marey's sleeve, and slipped off into the fog.

But she came back at once: she had forgotten the most important thing. She went to Kortoma and took his hand.

'I didn't hurt you too much with the yardstick, did I? Let's see.' She looked and stroked the welt, smiling: a squirrel's teeth, sharp, sweet, dangerous. Lightly she twitched her shoulders, swayed in time to the music.

'Eh, shall we have a go at it?' Kortoma could not resist and threw his arms around her. But try and catch her. She slipped out of his arms like a lizard, and stands two steps away, swaying, teasing. And then, as though to spite him, she stretched her hand out to some fellow right under Kortoma's nose, and all that you could see of her was the vivid red spot, like the sun on a trunk, growing faint through the dense curtain of fog.

She did not return. Perhaps she whirled herself to dizziness and went home, or perhaps she had gone into the downy white forest, beyond the fog – who knows?

Marey met her again in the morning, when he went out hunting with his father's heavy musket. He glanced up towards the Tunezhma, and there she was, driving a young bay deer.

'Hello, there!' Marey shouted from the distance.

The deer turned his brown muzzle, the skin drawn tightly over it, but the red-haired girl did not hear: she never looked back. Or maybe she was in a hurry to get home: she slapped the deer and ran after him still faster.

For many days the wind blew from the summer shore, driving

all bait into the ocean, and there was no catch. Then the wind shifted, the northeaster boomed, the swollen waves plashed on the shore – and again Stepka sat bent over for hours, baiting the lines.

His uncle's bottomless boots; over the boots, a small tow head; and on the right ear, on the lobe, a drop of congealed blood. Every now and then he would remember and put a finger up to his ear.

The men behind him neighed: 'Hey, Stepka, watch out! You'll pull it off altogether – it hangs on a hair.'

What if it was true? How would it be, living lop-eared? And silent drops crept down the grubby face as down a sweaty windowpane in autumn.

Marey scowls: it's all the fault of Vanka the Monk – he almost tore away the boy's ear. Because of what had happened yesterday; to spite Marey. Just wait – the time will come . . .

White-crested waves crash on the shore. The masts sway violently, every which way. In the grey sky the gulls are circling like white flakes. Rain squalls blow past like grey slanting sails, and blue gaps open in the sky. The air brightens.

A cold silvery evening. The moon is overhead, and down below, in the water; and all around it – a wide frame of old, hammered, scaly silver. Etched on the silver – silent black fishing boats, tiny black needles of masts, little black men casting invisible lines into the silver. And the only sounds are the occasional plashing of an oar, the creaking of an oar-lock, the springlike leap and flip-flop of a fish.

Marey has his own lines, inherited from his father. He did not sail far, but set them out right by the shore. His practised hand worked quietly, on its own, dropping the lines neatly overboard. And his head was also on its own over the silvery mirror, seeing streets in the mirror, perhaps forty, perhaps fifty, and over them all a lantern like the sun . . .

The lines were to be out all night. Those who had sailed far out slept in their boats; the others returned ashore. And just as the sun leaped up and gulls began to scream and the black shore turned pink, they all swarmed back into the water, to pull in their lines.

Marey began to pull the rope, and it came easily – quite empty. He glanced at Stepka in anger.

'All he thought of was his ear, the rotten brat! A fine job of baiting! Wait till we get ashore . . .'

'But . . . b-but . . . I didn't . . . Really, Uncle, cross my heart, I didn't . . .' Stepka was beaming this morning: his ear grew back; tug all you want, and nothing happens.

Marey pulled up more line: still just as light. More. And he was petrified: all the hooks on the line had been cut, to the last one.

The others had had a good catch. Red watersoaked hands shovelled out the fish, and silver piles grew on the beach. Marey alone returned empty-handed.

The men piled into Marey's boat, stared at his lines, felt them with their hands, turned them this way and that. Swore strong, salty oaths.

'What the hell! Today it's Marey, tomorrow it will be somebody else? We must find the man. Tie a stone around his neck, and down into the water.'

Marey scowled, glancing at Stepka. Every now and then the boy tugged at his ear: it had grown back, thank God! The ear, the hooks . . . oh, well! But for a while Marey kept silent, he didn't want to blame a man for nothing.

'Say what you will, Marey, but you must find the thief. We can't go around squinting at every other man.'

'Don't you worry. He won't get away from me . . .'

One silver night. Another. A third. For three nights Marey watched for the thief without shutting an eye. But no one came. Little by little his anger settled and he began to feel sorry for the man. All right, so Stepka was hurt. All right, so the hooks were cut. That's true. But if he's caught – if they don't drown him, they'll batter him to death with their fists anyway. Poor fellow. But then, he couldn't shield him either . . . Such a fix . . .

From behind the big stone on the shore Marey could see everything as clearly as the palm of his hand: the silvery path on the water, and all along the silver, black dots bobbing up and down – the floats. For a moment the moon would slip behind a cloud, then everything was lost and nothing could be seen. And then again the black dots – up, down, up, down – flickering before the eyes, and the eyes would start closing by themselves.

Then, with his eyes half closed, Marey just barely could see a bay deer coming out of the woods. The deer came over to Marey and spoke with the voice of Ivan the Monk: 'Don't ruin me, Marey, I am from Petersburg.'

Marey jumped up and stared around: no deer, only a distant plashing of oars in the water, and far off on the left, scarcely visible, the small black shape of a canoe nosing in among the rocks.

Hell, he slept through it! Damn! And he forgot his pity, and forgot that they would kill the man. He forgot everything, and now, like a hunter after quarry, he crawled on all fours, as quickly as he could, to cut him off . . .

A long rocky clearing in the woods. Trees behind him, and trees in front, and in the middle – a bare spot under the moon.

Marey crouched in the shadow of a bush. His eyes and ears razor-sharp, his heart hammering away. From the other side of the bare spot, always nearer and more audible, came a light, cautious snapping among the trees. He's coming.

Somewhere right there, no more than twenty paces away, across the clearing. Now you could hear: he stopped and turned left. And Marey crept on his belly to the left. His gun caught at some fallen branches; he tugged at it, they snapped, and he lay still. The other, across the clearing, was also still. Both waited: who would be the first to come out into the white clearing, exposing himself to shots?

'Hey, Vanka!' yelled Marey. 'Come out, you hear? You won't get away in any case.'

The other side was silent. The moon slid into a dark burrow, the white patch was extinguished.

Marey got up. He gathered up all of himself, like a bullet, and vaulted in a single leap across the patch, to the other side. And there, the wood was full of crashing, the breaking of twigs – away, into the heart of the forest!

'Stop, stop, Vanka! Stop, you won't get away!'

Marey plunged into the thick, into the dark, leaped on the other, threw him over, and sat astride him. He bent down to tie him up, and suddenly his hands went limp and he was dazed: the girl, the redhead . . . Some Vanka! . . .

'But . . . but why . . . but why the hooks?' Marey stood over her, his legs wide apart, his gun on the ground.

And the redhead threw her face into the moss and broke into a wail, like a baby, harder and harder. What could you do with her?

'Oh, God! Stop howling, stop now – what's the matter?' and he lightly stroked her head as though she were a child. And his heart went – *bump!* – and quietly turned in its nest and started sinking down.

The redhead got up from the ground. On her knees, she stretched her arms to Marey, closed her eyes, with trembling lips, without a word.

'She doesn't want me to tell . . .' Marey gently pushed away her arms.

'Don't be afraid, I won't tell anyone, I swear I won't. Truly, I'll cross myself – there!'

She jumped up to her full height, screaming: 'Tell everybody! If you don't, I'll tell them all myself. I don't want anything from you – I cannot bear to look at you – go away, this very minute – go a-way!'

She flashed across the clearing, and nothing was left of her but a light snapping of twigs far in the forest, and her hat on the moss.

Marey stood for a long time, turning the hat in his hands. The moon was diving from burrow to burrow: silver – black – silver again, and everything was confused, and you couldn't make head or tail of anything. Marey slung his gun over his shoulder and slowly ambled home, stepping heavily-lightly on his heels, bear-fashion.

In the morning everybody was giving him hell.

'You blockhead! You nitwit! Again they've cut the hooks, eh? How was it you snored through it all?'

'It happened. I hadn't slept three nights, it knocked me out, heaven knows how. And then I had a dream about a deer ...'

'You, deer dope! And you didn't see a soul?'

'No, nobody.'

They left Marey alone and set up watch themselves, taking turns by lot: the vermin had to be exterminated; you couldn't let such things go on.

But nobody touched the lines again. The thief had disappeared by himself.

The nights were long, like the braids of a pretty girl, and the days were short, like a girl's sense. The tom-tits started singing, tinkling like crystal. Swans and geese were flying in flock formation, exercising their wings, preparing for the distant journey. The Lapps were gradually packing up. Today or the next day they would start moving south, to their ancestral burial grounds.

Marey spent whole days wandering in the woods with his father's long-barrelled musket. On quiet days he could hear from far off, from the Lapp clearing, human voices and the sound of axes. On windy days the golden leaves sang out their farewell song, dropping away from the trees, whirling slowly down and catching at every twig – if only for a moment longer ...

Marey's sharp-muzzled white husky roused the geese. Heavy, they flew low overhead, whistling, cutting the blue with their wings. Marey did not even raise his gun. On the pale-blue moss the husky found bear tracks: all the moss was churned up – there must have been a bear wedding. The dog barked shrilly, running from Marey to the track, from the track to Marey. 'Why, right here, why, right this way – have you gone blind or what?'

Marey angrily thrust the husky aside. She hung her head and ambled behind him with an injured air: those humans! What can you make of them?

For days Marey wandered about, looking for something among the birches, among the rusty pine trunks. Nothing was there, only the blue autumn.

*

All the outsiders, all the summer people had gone. The shore was empty. The fat-rendering works stood cold and silent. And only Kortoma still ran around, seething busily: 'Get going, build, chop down! Lively, a hundred versts an hour!'

In the vacant lot behind the fat-rendering works there was an abandoned whaling plant; nothing was left of it but crumbling roofless walls. It must be torn down, and a new building erected by summer: a canning factory. People must live like Europeans ...

Kortoma was on the vacant lot from morning till night with his pipe, speeding the work, bantering, goading the men on.

They'd set the lever to a row of logs – it wouldn't budge. And Kortoma would strike up a bawdy song about Kortoma:

> *Mikhailo Kortoma,*
> *A hell of a fellow ...*

'Once more now! Heave, go!' and he would grasp the crowbar himself. Flattened, copper-red, chunky, he'd bear down – and the logs would start, dust flying thick and fast.

They finished and removed the rubble. And now the office window looked out on the empty shore. And the northeaster boomed along the empty shore, the whitecapped rollers hammered at it.

Kortoma had leafed through all his ledgers: everything was tallied and totalled according to the triple-entry system of bookkeeping. He shut the ledgers. The samovar on the table had cooled off and was not singing any more.

'Hey! How about a samovar?'

Behind the office door Kortomikha sat on her little trunk, all ears. She started, and a flush spread on her sunken cheeks, and a smile squeezed through the wrinkles at the corners of her lips.

'Have you slept badly? My precious one ... You ought to take a little piece of sealing wax into your hand for the night: it helps. My handsome one ...'

'All right, I've heard it all ... Some rum!'

The rum is in the trunk. An antique, lop-eared lock. The antique spiral key hung on a nail all summer; now the nail is empty.

Kortomikha is all ears behind the door. The clock strikes, ticks, strikes. Evening. Far off, on the edge, between the water and the sky, a strip of pink is tightly held, and the pink makes the black watery endless waste still emptier, still more naked.

'More rum, hey, there! And get Matrena – lively!'

Matrena-Pleseya is broad and warm and comforting, like a Russian oven.

Once upon a time, nobody was turned away: come, snuggle down, she'll warm every comer. If a man's wife was a shrew, she'd ease him. If a boy had come of age, she'd teach the lad how – properly, patiently. But now she has become Grandma Matrena, with a black old-woman's shawl on her head. She hardly ever does anything herself now; nowadays she only provides others.

Before an hour went by Matrena was there with a nimble, swarthy Lapp. With empty, sucking eyes Kortomikha examined the swarthy girl from head to toe and turned up her nose: 'Who do you think you've come to? No, tell me, who do you think, eh? Look at her, muddy as a pig! All right, all right, come over here, get everything off, I'll give you clean things.'

The clock strikes, ticks, strikes. On the trunk by the door Kortomikha sits, all ears.

On the third day – his pipe in his teeth, his arms akimbo – Kortoma was back behind the counter, solidly, weightily as ever, and only the copper was screwed down harder on his cheeks, drawn still more tightly over the cheekbones.

The store was full of talk and laughter, crowded with Lapp women: tomorrow the Lapps were leaving, it was the end, and they must get a bit of this and that before they go.

'Hey, you, swarthy one . . . No, no, not you – the one with the birthmark on her back. Come on, you with the birthmark! Here's a belt, try it on . . .'

The store was full of gaiety; the master was generous. The money was counted by the mistress in her pink hat and gloves, a gay smile held tightly between two wrinkles.

A rich man who feels the coming of the end goes out to the people, tears open his collar, and throws gold in handfuls right and left: 'Here, take it, good Christians, take everything, I need nothing any more!' So, just before the end, the sun poured gold in pailfuls on the forest: golden trees, a golden sky, golden moss.

It was there, towards all that gold, that Marey walked, hurrying, making his way among the tangled branches. Another hour, another half hour, and everything would fade, go out.

And at the last hour she came out to meet him from the gold. Her head – a rusty patch, her lips – blood, a rifle in her hand. And not a word, nothing: she caught sight of him, and rushed straight at him. A wave is driven toward the rock: it strikes and shatters to bits. Yet there's no tripping it, no holding it, no crying out to stop. The wave must rush to shore.

'Hey, your gun . . .' Marey wanted to shout . . . But the redhead had already raised it, aimed – *boom!*

Is he all right? No? Later . . . He leaped, before she loaded again – toppled her over, twisted her on the ground, bore down with his whole body.

'A-ah, with the knife, eh?' Her hands, if he could catch her hands!

And then his breath was stopped. The hot hands locked themselves around his neck, her lips found his, harder and harder. The taste of salt upon his lips – blood.

It was as though someone had struck a blow at his head, and everything went round. He seized her with both arms, with all his strength, till something cracked. The girl moaned, closed her eyes, and was like wax.

'Oh, no, you won't . . . Where is the knife? There – it is mine now. And the lips, and the arms, and all of you . . . Ah, it hurts?'

'It doesn't hurt . . . oh! Make it hurt more, more – oh, do!'

'You! You wild cub! Don't you touch the knife! My beauty, my golden deer, my hair . . . Why did you turn the gun on me?'

'Because I love you, and you . . . Because you . . .'

'My forest deer . . . No, what's your name – what shall I call you?'

'Call me Pelka . . . No, call me what you wish, whistle for me as if I were a dog, I'll run after you . . . you can beat me . . . You're the only one – you, you!'

They do not need the sun. Who needs the sun when the eyes glow? Darkness. A woollen fog has wrapped the earth, has dropped a heavy curtain. From far away, from beyond the curtain, comes the sound of drops falling on stone. Far, far away – the autumn, people, tomorrow.

'Tomorrow we go. Everything is packed, the tents are folded.'

'You won't go anywhere. Just try to go! Come, try and move!'

'Oh! No, no, hold me tighter, don't let me, tighter still . . . So!'

'Look, Pelka: it will be night, snow, and we'll have a skin over the window, and a fire in the stove. And there will not be anybody in the whole wide world – only the two of us in the whole world.'

'Yes . . . tell me. Tell more. Give me your hand, this way. But let my deer come with us. He was little, red . . . And I was little . . .'

'But you're sleeping. Sleep, cub. Sleep, my golden deer.'

Night. Snow is falling, rustling gently, quietly, lulling. And when the people fell asleep, it started in earnest, blowing without a stop, droning in the chimneys, confusing everything, enfolding everything in white mist, covering all.

White smoky drifts up to the roofs. Everything is dark-white, silent, soft. Who knows when it's day and when it's night. Everybody is asleep, and the slow, clinging dream goes on and on, always the same. Again, it seems as though somebody has come out into the street – again the cold stars glimmer – the same repeating dream of a red deer dozing, tethered near someone's hut. The window is covered with a skin, a warm flame dances behind the curtain; red strips slant on the snow.

The tiny man in the skullcap walks past and understands everything as in a dream – without thinking, without naming, without a word. And he understands: they forgot to feed the deer. The good man brings an armful of dried white moss from the yard and throws it to the deer – and falls asleep again, to see the same old dream. And night goes on without end. Or maybe only for a second – from one sigh to the next . . .

A naked man pulled aside the skin over the window. Behind the window, in the sky – a pink, bright slit, pink snow, pink smoke over the roofs.

'But no! The night is over? No, it's just a . . .'

And the skin was dropped once more. But daily the slit grows wider, brighter. And now there are red strips outside, on the snow – and red strips inside, in the hut, on the white curve of a leg with its pale-blue network of tiny veins, on the closed lids, the rusty head. The lids are held together with sweet glue. If only one need never open them . . .

The wind blows, the ice is piling up from the sea, booming and crashing. The ice floes glitter in the sun, climb one upon the other, like beasts in springtime, love-maddened. Playfully, they scratch, rear up, gnaw at each other, topple and crash – shivering to white dust. Let the end be dust – it doesn't matter. The new ones climb, hurrying to smash themselves – with ever greater glee.

On the hillock behind the village, a man stands near the chapel, tiny as a raindrop, wrinkling up his eyes, his hand held like a visor over them. From the hillock he can see two figures flying on skis along the shore, and then straight down, into the sea, over the blue, warm ice, across the gaps and cracks, without care or caution, on and on. Where? Anywhere. Simply to fly at full speed, laughing and shouting: Ho-o!

On a distant icy-sunny field they dropped, rolling and clutching one another like beasts in springtime. The sound faintly reaches the chapel: 'Ho-o!'

Under the visor, the eyes wrinkle up, smiling. God be with them!

From below, from the village, Grandma Matrena crawls towards the chapel – broad, heavy, bulging out in every direction like an oven. Her face is red, she staggers; the neck of a bottle peeks out from her bosom. Her lips are smiling but tears roll down her cheeks.

'What's wrong, Grandma?'

'What do you think, my dear: it's spring. Once upon a time, in spring . . . Eh! And now – nobody comes to me at night but the house goblin. I even have to drink alone.'

'Oh well, I'll join you.'

'Thank you, good heart! Holy soul!'

They warm themselves on the hillock, drink from the same bottle. Below, on the ice floe – two black dots.

A long slow cracking sound: the ice field has split off and silently begins to move out to the sea. The two on the floe do not rise, do not stir, perhaps they never noticed. Slowly the two black dots are floating outwards.

And on the shore, there is panic, running, shouting. 'They'll be pulled out to sea . . . If it were high tide, but it's ebbing . . .'

'And where's the wind from, stupid greybeard? Hey!'

'Where are the boathooks? Hey, you, quit wagging your tongues, get moving – get the hooks!'

'Quick, quick! There are people on the ice . . . Quick!'

Kortoma has harnessed a deer to a light sled; the sled is piled with hooks, a folding canvas boat. He'll race across to Mysh-Navolok, the floe may ground on a shallows. Things might turn out all right without Kortoma, but he must do it all himself. Perhaps it is the spring, perhaps it is the sun that makes him feel as though he is bursting out of his skin, and he must simply race at breakneck speed, act, shout, command. Or maybe Kortoma is moved by some sort of his own triple-entry bookkeeping.

And those two? There they go, jumping from floe to floe, across the gaps and cracks.

Tired, drunk with sun, with leaping over glittering blue ice, the two returned home. Near the hut, the red deer stood quietly, on his tether. Pelka embraced him, pressed her face to the warm muzzle.

'Happy, darling? Eh? Tired of standing still?'

She untied him, and the deer darted off like an arrow, made a wide circle, leaped on a knoll, and stood, thin-legged, thinking: should he run out there, to the low northern woods blue in the distance, or come back to the hut for moss?

Now the mosquitoes have begun to sing. The green velvet moss is speckled with the pink, cool corals of the cloudberry, with grey-blue blueberries. Somewhere far off there is a forest fire, and the sun floats in a mist.

The three of them – Pelka, Marey, and Marey's foam-white husky. Pelka's red hair is tangled, a green wreath on the red. She is like a firm young shoot in spring, just risen from the earth, still carrying on its tip moist soil and a bit of green moss.

Pi-i-u! Pi-i-u! The hazel grouse sings as through a slender reed. Then he falls silent and listens: will his mate reply among the green rustling treetops?

'Pi-i-u!' Pelka replies in grouse language.

And the grouse comes nearer and nearer. Now he is on a branch just overhead, trembling, spreading his wings, opening his love-stricken heart.

The grouse does not hear the shot. Nothing but a flash of fire in his eyes, and he drops into the fire. With gay forest cruelty Pelka tears off his head and goes on.

She talks with all the forest creatures. Her green-red sister-pines run after her in an obedient herd. It grows warmer: dew-drops on the forehead, transparent drops on rusty trunks. Somewhere ahead the husky breaks into frenzied barking.

'Load it with larger shot, Marey: geese ...' Pelka hears the husky shout: geese.

The trees spread out like a curtain. A long still lake, with banks of smooth red stone. The geese are gabbling, rising from the lake in slow flight. Two rifle shots break the quiet mirror of the lake: Marey's, then Pelka's. Two grey lumps somersault awkwardly and plop into the water.

The husky sneezes and squeals in the water. The goose is too heavy for her; Marey must climb in after it himself. It may be deep.

Marey strains, bending his tow head to his shoulder, slowly pulling off his boots: they're wet and will not budge.

'You, slowpoke!' Pelka lost patience, quickly threw off her

light sandals, and, pink-bodied, wades through the cold water. Only her head shows – now she must swim.

She comes back, shakes herself, laughs, smelling of fresh water and seaweed. Near her the husky shakes herself, jumps, licks Pelka's knees. On Pelka's red hair – a green wreath; the drops slide off her breasts, slide off the tender, cloudberry-pink tips – they must be cold. In her hands she carries the geese; blood drips from them, trickles down the smooth, carved legs.

Marey can't bear it any longer. On the warm red stones he warms with his lips the cold pale-pink cloudberries.

'No, they are not warm yet; you see, they are still cold.'

Somewhere the forest burns. On the red stone by the quiet lake a fire of fragrant needles sends up smoke. Pelka is roasting a fat goose over the fire: the flames are playing on the green, the red; her lips and hands are bloodstained. Faintly she smiles with her eyes to Marey; there is no need to speak.

From afar, a snapping of branches: a bear is plunging through the thickets. Then all is quiet, and only the white husky still grumbles angrily in sleep.

The fire goes out. The sister-pines come nearer from out the dusk. The world grows ever darker, ever narrower – and now there are only two in the whole world.

Who needs people? Marey had left the fishing team, hired out his lines and his hut to visiting summer fishermen; they paid him with a share of fish from their catch – there would be enough to last the winter. He lived with Pelka in the woods, in a Lapp tent: a frame of slender poles interlaced with twigs and covered with moss; and within, green moss, like a carpet of down.

Every morning Pelka changed the trampled moss. Every morning, singing, weaving charms, she plaited a fresh juniper wreath and hung yesterday's wreath on the wall. Maybe the green wreaths were a sacrifice to God. Or maybe the green wreaths were a record of days and nights. With eyes shut tightly, the days and nights rushed through the forest thickets, beneath the white unsleeping sun, past silent forest lakes. And as you flew with them, you might catch hold for a moment of a rushing tree, and, holding fast to your hat, turn back your head to face the wind: no, it is not a dream; there is one wreath, and another, and the trampled, drying moss. And then you closed your eyes again – let the wind carry you . . .

Marey had gone to the village, to people, to Kortoma's store for gunpowder and salt.

Alone, she languished, waiting, asking the dog: 'Isn't he coming yet? Will he come soon? – Tell me!' And as soon as the husky jumped up and pricked up her grey ears, she'd drop everything and dash with the dog to meet him until he came into sight – just faintly stooping, a tow-haired, slow, infant giant.

'You-you-you!' a single word, just like the eider crying out the same word endlessly at dawn in her stone nest . . .

There were cloudy days. Gradually the shell of cloud grew thinner, rosier, split – and there was the sun, among green tree-tops, in a blue gap. Marey heard nothing; his blue eyes stared into the blue, far off.

To brush against him, to sting him as though accidentally with her breast? No. To knit her brows so that they met, to cry: 'What are you thinking of? I do not want you to! Don't dare!' And in reply to the astonished childlike eyes, to burn to ash, to curl up into a ball at his feet, together with the white husky, and, like the husky, to close her eyes, grow still under his stroking hand . . .

At night it rained: a quiet silken music in the tent. And all she needed was to awaken, stretch her hand, to touch him lightly in the dark, and laugh with the intolerable happiness. Rain.

And then to fly again – from dream to dream . . .

One night she stroked the moss in her sleep: empty. Incredulous, she threw off sleep, opened her eyes in the dark, and touched the empty flattened moss. Marey was not there.

She ran out, crying in a ringing voice: 'Ma-rey!'

No one. The moon hangs alien, heavy, like a lock on a door; the door is tightly shut. Everything is quiet; and only far away, the sleepless Tunezhma rushes and sings.

Below, there is a shadow on the water. From above, she can

see against the dark mirror of the backwater Marey's white head. And he never sensed her bending over from above, calling him, calling with her eyes.

She came back to the tent, lay down. And only when the stars cooled, paled and trembled with the morning chill, he tiptoed quietly into the tent and quietly lay down in his place.

Autumn was coming swiftly on grey owl wings. At dusk small flocks of swans flew south, blowing their melancholy trumpets. In the mornings the moss was covered with hoary silver.

'There's nothing to be done, Pelka: we must take up the tent and move to winter quarters.'

'No!'

'But you tremble at night, dear girl. It is cold.'

'I am not cold – that isn't why ... I do not tremble! Let's not go from here!'

But you can't plead with autumn. No. The midnight wind stalked through the woods, hooted to frighten you, swept everything away for the approaching winter, whirled the leaves.

On a feverishly ruddy, windy evening they returned to the village. The hut smelled empty, sooty, cold. But the wide bench in the corner was the same, and all you needed was to hang the skin over the window and to light the stove ...

'Start up the stove, Pelka, and I'll be back in a moment – I'll just run over to Kortoma's; there's nothing in the lamp.'

The fire sang in the stove and Pelka hummed. She scattered juniper and made a soft bed on the bench: everything just as that first winter.

The bundle of twigs burnt out. Pelka threw in another; the fire danced, crackled. And again the tongues sank lower, moved lazily. Here and there – the last slow blue ones; then they went out, and it was dark.

She came out into the street. The night wind boomed, the waves crashed on the shore, the stars trembled, lights flickered in the huts.

Through the uncurtained window of Kortoma's store she could see: Kortoma astride a barrel, with his pipe, his forefinger raised instructively. Leather jackets, fur hats with ear-flaps, a fair head with childlike, astonished eyes . . .

In Marey's hut it is dark. The mouth of the stove still glows faintly red from the last embers. On the bench Pelka glimmers faintly white, her feet swing down, her hands held tightly between her knees.

'Where are you, Pelka? You said you'd make a fire in the stove, like last winter.'

'I made it.'

'It went out. Eh . . . Let's start it again, eh?'

'No, there's no more brushwood.'

In the stove, the coals crackle quietly, stir, rustle under the ash.

The snow had covered everything. A bitterly cold silence in the village.

In the dark people got up reluctantly, went out into the yard to chop some snow, to boil some water. Reluctantly, they ate, glancing up at the window: the panes were black.

Should a man run down to Grandma Matrena's? What time is it?

In Grandma Matrena's hut there was a clock on the wall, ticking endlessly, groaning, coughing, running without a rest – seeing in the dark night.

'Going on one already! . . . Have you a bottle by any chance, Grandma?'

Of course, she had. And then it seemed a little easier, as though the darkness outside the window had blanched a little, as though there were just a small faint glimmering of light.

Tipsy, they tumbled early into bed – to get as much sleep as they could. So they would feel less hunger. The summer catch had been poor; there wasn't much food. They ate with care and looked sideways at the old: the old were gluttons, everybody knew it, and what was the good of feeding them? It wouldn't harm them to starve a little.

The hungry dogs howled. The women rinsed the children's bellies with hot water three times a day, so they wouldn't cry so much for food. The old starved silently.

And, gradually, it started with the old: their feet and gums swelled up, they groaned and lay all day long on the ovens, babbling heaven knew what. The sickness went from hut to hut. Ivan Romanych went from hut to hut, curing the sick with bows: a hundred, two hundred low bows, to the very ground, before the icons, till sweat poured off the ailing man – and then, before you knew it, he felt better.

And Matrena-Pleseya laughed at Ivan Romanych from her place up on the stove: 'Eh-he, dear man! While your feet can carry you, it's best to dance. Much better for getting you into a sweat than all your bows . . .'

And she would not come down off her stove. She sipped from the bottle, and played songs, the house goblin following her tunes on a comb.

'You hear, Stepka? Hear him playing? And now he's got the glasses jumping on the chest. Just hear him go!'

Stepka had been installed in Grandma's hut to watch her. He huddled in the corner, round-eyed. Good God, if it would only brighten up a bit! It was scary: Grandma was babbling heaven knows what, she'd lost all sense.

The darkness paled a little in the window. Stepka rushed headlong to Ivan Romanych: Grandma Matrena was dying, someone should say a prayer.

Ivan Romanych came, climbed up the stove to Grandma, a carved wooden cross in his hands. And Grandma Matrena opened her eyes and pulled out a deck of cards from under her: 'Thanks for coming. Stepka's a fool, he doesn't know how to play. Let's have a game of trumps, eh?'

Ivan Romanych smiled and sat down. His black cassock green with age, tiny as a drop, dark-faced – as though he had just stepped out of an ancient icon.

They began to play. Grandma was lucky – she had never had such luck in all her life. Now all she needed was the Queen of Hearts – and there would be no need to go on playing.

The Queen of Hearts turned up. Grandma laughed, and gave her soul up to the Lord without finishing her trumps.

Stepka had fallen asleep on the bench in the corner. On the oven Matrena lay, the cards clutched tightly in her hand. Ivan

Romanych placed the wooden cross over the cards, made the sign of the cross over the woman and the boy, and went out.

Under the black ceilings, on the ovens, the old shivered and babbled gibberish – lower and lower, till they grew silent, and rested silently in blue caves chopped out in the ice. In spring the earth would thaw; God willing, they would then lie properly in the earth, in the graveyard.

Blue northern lights rose in the sky, and the silence became still deeper, more bitterly cold. As though everything had sunk to the very bottom, pressed down by thick, impenetrable blue ice, and frozen sunlight filtered wanly down to the bottom through the thousand-verst-thick ice.

In a blue cave, down at the bottom, the slender-legged deer stands quietly, tethered. A hot hand strokes its neck; warm drops fall on the tightly drawn skin of the brown muzzle. A thousand versts of ice above. But surely it must thaw at last, the spring will surely come, with green moss, and cool pink cloudberries, and the warm rustle of rain?

The deer is silent.

Marey had had an inspiration.

A light! He'd build a lantern, like those in Petersburg. It would be raised over the village, and there would be no night: life would be new and different.

And it seemed to him that this was what he had lived for all his life; this was what the Tunezhma had sung about, though it was only now that he had finally understood the word itself: a light.

Well, Kortoma had promised he would not stint on materials. 'We're not just anybody, we'll have enough and to spare!'

'But I was telling you: over there the lamps are small, with wire netting over them. And you are trying to change it over your way – you want a giant lantern – this big!'

No, what's the good of tiny lamps! You need something to kill the darkness once for all, for good. Besides, Kortoma used to tell of a big light. Now he's trying to back down. Little lamps! Hu-h . . .

Who knows what lay beyond the window: dark day or dark

night. But now it did not matter. The hanging tin lamp in the hut cast a circle of brightness. Marey lived inside the bright circle, building his lantern. He bound up boards into a round frame, soldered tin pipes, wove a wire netting.

Far away, outside the bright circle, was the red-haired Lapp girl. The one who had once – a long, long time ago – snipped off his hooks, the one who had once come out of the golden wall of trees with a gun, aimed straight at the tow head. Why had she missed?

'I've left some cod with cider for you, over there. On the bench . . .'

Marey heard her from afar, from the bright circle. He recognized her voice and smiled.

'Thanks, Pelka, thanks, darling. And I've forgotten all about it, at work. And you? You don't want any? Now, now . . .'

A pity – Marey was interrupted all the time. Today, it's Kortoma, tomorrow, Kortoma. He keeps coming every day. Well after all, it's his material, nobody else's.

'You're a smart one, Marey! Look at that contraption he thought up, eh?'

Kortoma bubbles with laughter, his copper cheekbones spreading even wider. In the shiny copper, Marey's reflection is flattened as in a samovar – a simpleton! Never mind, so long as he gets all the materials he needs.

Somewhere far away Kortoma banters with the proud Lapp girl.

'Well, Pelka, I'll be off to Norway soon for goods. Come with me, eh?'

'I do not travel your way. Let go of my hands! Let go, you hear?'

Kortoma releases her hands. But then the redhead leaves her hands in his anyway. Kortoma paws at her, crushes her, pants and puffs. The redhead glances back over her shoulder – at Marey. She must be frightened he may see.

No, it does no good: Marey is far off, tapping away with his mallet . . .

'Now, listen: if you want, I'll bring you a dress? Something to match your hair! Just tell me, eh?'

The redhead glances back again over her shoulder at Marey.
Those wives!

Kortoma winks slyly: 'Forget him, never mind; he doesn't
hear, don't be afraid.'

Well, if he doesn't hear . . .

'Bring your green dress . . . bring two dresses, bring more, I'll
take them all!'

'Oh, no-o! You think, for nothing? You've got to love me,
woman. Well? Agreed?'

'Let go! . . . But . . . well – here, take, here, here, here!'

Oh, yes, Kortoma knows how to deal with her kind. You
can't put anything over on Kortoma.

'Well, good-bye, my little beauty. But remember: a promise
is worth more than money . . . Oh, yes, about materials: You,
there, Marey, come over tomorrow first thing in the morning,
take some more. I won't stint. We aren't just anybody.'

'Ah, thanks for that!'

That's when Marey stopped hammering and turned
around . . .

In the morning – and how did it happen? – Marey and
Kortoma had missed each other on the way. Marey came to the
store and nobody was there but the assistant, Ivan the Monk.

'And where's the master?'

'He went out with a pitcher for some beer . . .' guffawed the
Monk – and dived back into his hole.

'What beer?'

'A-ah, I was just . . . He'll be back soon. Meantime, pick out
what you need . . .'

The tow-headed infant giant squatted on his heels over the
rolls of wire, the gleaming tin, his blue eyes all on fire . . .

Kortoma came to Marey's hut – and how did it happen? –
Marey was out. Only the redhead was home.

'Hello! Alone, hm . . .'

'Hello.'

'I mean, the things we talked about last night. The dress . . .
You haven't forgotten?'

Kortoma has shaved his face until it shines like copper to the
world: 'The world is mine! Hurrah!'

He turned to the door, slipped on the hook. Spread out his arms, his cheeks stretched wide: soon they will swallow up the little red-green world . . .

Pelka is in the corner. Behind her, on the wall, is a harpoon. She seized the harpoon and flashed it!

'Out, this minute! Go!'

Kortoma wanted to laugh. The harpoon flew up. The crazy one: she'll bash him, she will . . .

Slowly, he backed up to the door, slipped off the hook and edged out.

In the street, he stood a long time at the door. His samovar world was shattered, the samovar could not contain it: what sort of a wild one was that? The other day she had let him, in her husband's presence. And now? . . . How come? Why?

The blue cold northern lights sway, fold, unfold. The snow crust gleams, and on the snow – the tangled shadows of deer horns. A light sled, fully harnessed, waits before Kortoma's store: he is leaving for Norway today, to buy goods. In torn deerskin coats, with faces green under the northern lights, the villagers stand around to see him off.

'Come back soon, love, I cannot wait!'

'Bring something sour . . . Don't forget, eh?'

'Don't catch a cold, dove! Take another coat, eh? Take another, my darling, do . . .'

Kortoma angrily shakes his hand, and Kortomikha drops off. Kortoma is silent, glum.

The runners whistle, squeal along the snow, the deer takes off at a flying start – and all you can see now is a black dot climbing the white hill . . . Gone.

An hour later Kortoma's sled slowly creeps along the village street, the runners screeching, grating. He draws up at the gate – halt!

Kortoma knocks harder and harder. Kortomikha jumps out, frightened.

'My dove! What happened? What?'

'Nothing. I'm not going.'

Kortoma is upstairs, in his private office. The samovar is

boiling, spurting steam. Glass after glass of tea, as thick as home-brewed beer.

A gun hangs on the office wall. It's been there since last summer, loaded. It must be bursting with its charge; if it could only crash, just so, for no good reason, so that the panes would shiver to bits ...

Kortoma takes down the gun, aims, and – *cra-ack* – into the ceiling!

Behind the door, on her little trunk, Kortomikha starts, jumps, and hears the familiar: 'Hey! Some rum!'

Hastily, she takes the spiral key off the nail.

Perhaps it is the blue northern lights that make Kortomikha's lips so blue. In a moment the blue smile, clenched tightly between the wrinkles at the corners of her lips, will slip out and drop onto the snow.

But it still holds. And the pink hat, though awry, still clings to the head. And again – how many times now? – Kortomikha approaches Marey's hut. She cannot get her hand to knock ...

Marey sits tapping with his hammer in the bright circle. His eyes are tired. It would be good to have a bite to eat, and back to work ...

'Say, Pelka, shall we eat?'

'You've been so busy with your light – did you go out to get some food? There's nothing ...' Her brows are knit severely.

'Eh, trouble ... If I could eat and go to work again ...'

'What do you want me to do – go and kill my deer? I'd sooner kill you ... Who's there?'

Kortomikha in her pink hat: empty, hollow, with the innards taken out, with blue lips – probably from the cold.

She came up close to Pelka and took in, sucked in all of her with her empty eyes: all of her – light, slender, finely carved, glittering. If eyes could kill ...

Clenching tightly her blue smile: 'It's simply terrible ... My husband has taken ill, and I can't manage by myself – bring him this, take away that ... Matrena used to help out. Maybe you'll come, eh? He begged so much – so much ...'

Marey put down his mallet and listened. Pelka glanced at

Marey over her shoulder and suddenly flushed; her brows ceased scowling. And God knows why, her eyes shone brightly at Kortomikha.

'I have no time . . . I'd be glad to, but I have no time!'

She didn't! She won't come! Kortomikha's smile turned pink; glowing pink, she went out.

'You better watch out, Pelka! You don't know Kortoma, don't ever get it into your head to go . . . I may be good, but I can kill . . .' Marey frowned in jest.

Pelka went about the hut gaily, humming a warbling, fluid Lapp song. She took the gun from the wall, fell silent for a moment: maybe she ought not . . . maybe she ought to put the gun back in its place?

No. She went out with the gun.

'I've seen some tracks, maybe I'll shoot something . . .'

The blue northern lights sway, folding and unfolding. In the blue cave at the bottom of the ice the slender-legged red deer is barely visible. Hot arms embrace his neck, hot lips are kissing, kissing the hoary muzzle.

And God knows how it happened, the trigger must have caught in her sleeve, but the rifle inadvertently fired straight at the deer. The deer fell.

Marey jumped out to the shed: the deer had already stopped twitching. Such a mishap!

In the evening the fire danced in the stove, a piece of venison was sizzling in the frying pan.

'Let us lock ourselves in, Marey, so nobody, not a single soul . . .'

'You're right, let's lock up! They keep bothering me. And I have only just a little more to do. You know, soon . . . But wait, wait – where are you going?'

In the black sky the dawn is an ever widening crimson ribbon. At the bottom of the blue ice caves there are scarlet fires; hurried work goes on there, at the bottom – the sun is being forged. The snow turns pink, the dead blue light recedes into the depths. Perhaps, a little more, and the pink lips will smile, the lashes will rise slowly – and summer will shine forth . . .

No, there will be no sun. Pelka's lips are tightly shut, her brows are severely knit.

'Marey! Perhaps you'll come too? Or, if you want, I'll stay. Just say so, and I won't go!'

Kortoma has returned from Norway. Kortoma is celebrating, as he does every year.

'No, no, go by yourself. I'd better do some work . . .'

Pelka sits for a long time on the bench – the same bench – hands locked between her knees. For a long time she paces the hut. Once something cracked – maybe it was a piece of twig she stepped on. She takes her dress off the nail and starts to put it on.

The green silk dress. Kortoma had not forgotten – he had brought it. The other day Ivan the Monk came with a bundle tied with a green ribbon.

'For you, from the master. He says you must come to the party. As for the dress, he says it's up to you. If you want to, you'll put it on, if not, you won't – as you please . . .'

His head kept diving in and out of its hole between the shoulders, his eyes kept jumping like a pair of imps, and he stroked the bundle caressingly, as though he would fain stroke Pelka, and stroke Marey: such fun!

Pelka put on the green dress. In her red tangled hair – a dry green wreath. Her lips were dry and pressed together so hard that, just a little more, and blood would spurt out: yet the lips trembled.

'Marey!'

'What? Oh, you are dressed? You're beautiful, Pelka! There, what's wrong now?'

'No, nothing. I'm going.'

'A shame I have to work . . . If not for the work, I guess I'd come along . . . But it must be finished, there!'

'Yes, it must be finished.'

Kortoma is giving a party, as every year. The mistress is dressed up, in a pink dress, in a smile. The master is in a gala outfit: new high boots, above the knees; a blue knitted vest; and over it – a frock coat.

The master impatiently pulls his watch from the back pocket of the frock coat: his eyes turn to the watch – the door – back to the watch.

'Did you tell her everything just as I said?' he whispers angrily into the ear of his assistant, Ivan the Monk.

'Good Lord, you think I . . .'

And finally, a frosty cloud of steam in the doorway, and in the white cloud – a green dress.

The wide copper cheekbones gleam; gulp, squash the world: mine!

'Mine? The green one? What a smart girl you are! But I knew it. You're a smart one – just teasing . . . You sly thing!'

Well, let him bring her in with his arm around her, let everybody see, let them . . .

On the table there were dainties of every kind: fresh meat, tarts with millet, pancakes, turnovers, white-tipped vodka bottles, green-tipped bottles of liquors and red-tipped wines. The host pushed up the sleeves of his frock coat, to make it handier, poured out drinks, and pronounced a toast – according to the Western European peoples:

'Well, fellows, here's to you and all your spawn!'

And the jaws went to work. Smoke from the pipes, frosty steam from the cracks in the door that wasn't properly shut to. In the mist there is nothing but mouths: champing, gulping, cracking bones between the teeth. Pelka sits next to the host, on his right hand. Across the table the hostess smiles gaily, never taking her eyes off the green dress, swallowing up, sucking in all of Pelka with the huge empty eyes: her red hair, her tightly knit brows, her clenched teeth.

'No-o, but look at the material – look at the material I picked for you: pure silk!' Kortoma strokes the green silk, now here, now there.

'More wine for me, pour me some more!'

'You smart girl, I knew you're a smart girl, just teasing . . .'

Faces turn red, the dark earth blood is rising.

They wink at Pelka, wink at the host: 'He knows his goods!' The women feel the buttons constricting them – they undo one, another, a third. By twos the guests go outside to get some air.

'Well, my dear guests, are you soaked to the gills? Eh? And now – to dance! Get lively!'

The table and the chairs vanish. The middle of the room is empty. Ivan the Monk jumps out of his hole, a tambourine in his hands: 'Tim-ta-a-am! Tim-ta-a-am!'

'Eh-hey!' the redhead suddenly snatches the tambourine and sweeps off, tapping wildly in a circle. Eyes closed: a white sleepless sun – white night on the meadow – white columns of smoke swaying over fires . . .

'Eh-ah!' – to whirl herself to death, to whirl out everything, to empty herself – nothing has ever been . . .

Heavy boots are thumping on the floor, beards fly in the wind, the frock-coat tails go flying . . . hey, get going, faster, faster – a hundred versts an hour!

'And what about you?' Kortoma cries to the hostess, flying past. 'Sits there alone, like an eider on her eggs!'

The hostess rises slowly. A gay smile between the wrinkles at the corners of her lips. Her pink dress flickers in the ring, sweeps out, sways . . .

'Wait-wait-wait! She's fallen . . . but wait a moment!'

The pink dress is sinking to the floor, melting – in a moment there will be nothing but a small pink blob on the floor . . .

Kortoma caught her and led her off into the next room: 'Always something! Can never do things right! Well, what's the matter? Well?'

'My darling – it's nothing . . . I've worn myself out today – just a moment . . . Now, it's all right now.'

'You'd better go upstairs. Is everything prepared there, in the office, as I said?'

'Everything is as you said. Don't worry, dear, go back to the guests. I'll be . . . in just a moment . . .'

Everything was set to rights. The hostess came back and poured sparkling wine for the guests with a gay smile. In the excitement the host had disappeared somewhere. Through the loosely shut door a frosty steam was pouring into the room. It was a little chilly in the pink dress; one shivered now and then. But it was nothing. In a moment somebody would come in and shut the door more tightly – that's all.

And finally the host came in and shut the door. He must have stepped out for some air. The room was full of noise and smoke, like a steam bath. And Kortoma was not the only one who could not stand it. Right after him the door swung open and the redhead returned in her beautiful green dress.

Ivan the Monk fluttered out from somewhere behind the stove, like a Yuletide mummer in a devil mask.

'A merry holiday, master! A merry holiday, my beauty! How about a tip for a drink from your graces?'

Now Kortoma is off somewhere on the side, peacefully puffing at his pipe, instructively waving his forefinger. The shop assistant Ivan the Monk hovers around Pelka, bares his toothless black gums at her. He holds out his fingers like two horns, wriggles them and tickles Pelka's side, under her breast. Well, let him – what's the difference!

'And tomorrow I'll tell the husband every-thing! Tomorrow ... shoo-oo ... the husband ...' the devil mummer rustles in her ear.

And suddenly, as though this was all she wanted, Pelka's lips are suddenly alive, a flush comes to her cheeks.

'Well, then, do tell him. Scared me!'

All right! Pretending! And her heart must have dropped into her heels!

'Oh, well, I will not tell him then. Will you go walking with me?'

'With you? Hey, master! Tell this ... creature of yours to scram. Hey, master, wine!'

A whip strikes the sky with full force – and the welt glows red: the dawn. But not a sound, not a moan: there's no one to hear it anyway.

Still in the green dress, Pelka stands at the window, silently, without a sound. Marey is far away – just barely visible in the bright circle under the tin lamp. He hurries, taps his mallet – his heart is hammering, singing, rushing: tomorrow – the light, tomorrow all of life will become new and different ...

'Well, Pelka, how was it yesterday?' and instantly forgets that he has asked her anything, and nothing matters in the world: only the lantern.

The welt in the sky grows more vivid. The trembling in the shoulders, in the knees becomes more violent. She must have caught a cold running out the other night; that must be it.

'Hey, Maryukha, are you deaf? Hello, I say. Greetings and thanks from the master.'

'Ah, Ivan, hello.'

'And you, my beauty, how are you? What do you say? Still the same as last night?'

'Still the same.'

'U-hum . . . I see . . . Well, then, Marey, have you finished your lantern?'

'Just a bit to polish up here and there – and tomorrow . . . By God, there's nothing in the world I care about, if only . . .'

'Oh, yes, I see there's nothing you care about. You've even traded in your wife for that lantern! Bye-bye, wife, she's run out on you.'

'Why, there she is, by the window.'

'She's there all right – but she ain't yours.'

'Go on, joker . . . Whose is she, if not mine?'

Ivan the Monk's hands are behind his back, his fingers sticking out like horns, waggling at Pelka. But Pelka is silent.

'Whose? My master's, of course. Kortoma's. Since yesterday. Stamped and sealed . . .'

With a whip, full strength . . . Well, go on, well?

'. . . Lookit her dress – you think such dresses come for nothing? Eh, you blind mole!'

Marey stops polishing. Tow head, astonished blue eyes: Stepka!

'That true, Pelka?'

'It's true . . .'

The welt is darkening with blood – in a moment it will burst . . . In a moment he'll rush, strike, kill her. Darling, kill me, kill me!

Blue eyes, like Stepka's. The eyes turn to Ivan, to Pelka, back to Ivan. Ivan squints and bares his gums; Pelka's lips tremble: in a moment she'll smile.

'Ah, go on: found a time to joke! I know you, Ivan, you're an old wag, you devil's doll. Go away, I have no time, I have to finish for tomorrow . . .'

There's no unholy power that can cross into the bright circle. The walls of light are stronger than stone. Ivan the Monk spat in disgust and turned to the door.

At the very end of the village, where the road forks out, people laugh and whisper. Pelka is somewhere among them. In a moment the brightness will illume them all – their faces, smiles, eyes – and all of them will be renewed, and everything will change . . .

With trembling fingers Marey could barely light the match. The pulleys screeched, the lantern was raised aloft, and up above, in the very heart of darkness, a light glowed over the world. Now, to pump it up a bit, and then . . .

Faintly, in the dark, Kortoma's pipe glimmered red. In the dark, no one could see the small cold hands trembling in Kortoma's paws.

'Well, beautiful, so it's settled? You're coming straight to me from here; we'll bring your things over later.'

'I cannot tell him – how can I tell him? If you would . . .'

'Oh-o, that's easy. So it's settled, eh?'

The pump gulped, creaked. The flame in the lantern strained, leaped up and gasped – but did not grow larger. That's nothing: surely, if you look at it from a distance . . .

But it was the same from the distance: under the blinking feeble little flame, above and below – for thousands of versts – there was nothing but frozen, deadly darkness. And from the little flame it seemed still blacker, still more impenetrably dense.

Feverishly, desperately, Marey began to pump with all his strength.

Cr-rack! There was a crashing, a splitting overhead. The flame tossed upward, dazzled the eyes, a shower of splinters hailed down on Marey's head – and all was over: darkness.

Invisible in the dark, the villagers surrounded Marey, pulling and pushing at him.

'You nitwit! With a lantern against the night . . .'

'Fool! Everyone laughs at him, and he . . .'

The tow-headed bear reared up and plunged, bellowing: 'Kortoma . . . Where's Kortoma? A-a-ah, here you are! Why did you lie to me? Why did you tell me tales about the light? Eh? Why – why, eh?'

'Easy, brother, easy. You'd better yell politely. What's all this fuss about the lantern? Take five like yours – and it'll be pretty bright.'

'To hell with "pretty bright"! I don't want it "pretty bright"! I'll kill you!'

Like the flame, Marey flared up full force – and *cr-rack*! He sputtered out, and nothing was left around but the thousand-verst darkness.

From beyond the thousand versts, the voice of Kortoma: '. . . Your wife is coming to live with me, to take care of the house . . . and generally. As for money or materials – you know I'm not just anybody, you know . . .'

Pelka bent over, greedily looking into Marey's face: now . . . this moment . . . But Marey was silent.

'That's the long and short of it. Well, then, my beauty . . . But where are you, hey!'

She wasn't there. Kortoma was alone. Crazy, those women – try and understand them.

One day – it had been long ago, everything had been long ago. One day Marey walked in the woods, his gun loaded with bullets, for bears, and suddenly a goose flew out from underfoot. He fired straight at the neck, the head was cut clear off. There was no head, but the goose still flapped his wings in flight; it fluttered a few yards more, and then dropped on the ground.

Just so, as though still in mid-flight – Marey still flapped his wings, and Pelka hers.

The ice had melted. All silver, the sea was purring under the sun. Silently the sails slid over it: it was time to go fishing. And Pelka and Marey went fishing, like everybody else, but they looked differently into the blue depths.

The swans came, blowing their melancholy trumpets. Geese cackled on the quiet lakes. The three of them wandered about the woods: Pelka, Marey, and Marey's husky. But they did not build a tent as last year; they slept in the hut.

Sometimes Marey would be somewhere ahead, and Pelka behind him, alone. She would raise her gun and turn it this way and that. There'd seem to be no quarry around, yet she'd turn her gun and aim. No. She lowered it.

'I can't ...'

'What is it?' Marey would glance back.

'No, nothing. I was just talking.'

The husky broke into furious barking. Pelka heard it crying in its own, husky language: geese! They must go ...

They shot geese, smoked fish for the winter – as though there were still the winter to live through. They still fluttered their wings the last few yards by the sheer impetus of flight.

In August the bear weddings began. The bears went about in twos and threes. The villagers trekked out to hunt bears.

'We ought to go out too ...' Pelka's brows were tightly knit. 'All the money's been squandered on the lantern.'

'Oh, well, why not? We can start tomorrow.'

'I met one yesterday, quite near – just where our tent had been. My gun was loaded with shot, though.'

'Well, we have bullets.'

They rose at dawn, first thing. The moss was hoary; implacable autumn had already blown its first breath from afar – the first morning frost. The trees stood golden, red, and pink – their autumn dress. In Pelka's red hair there was a green juniper wreath.

'Well, I've loaded the guns ...'

Marey's inherited musket must be heavy – it trembled in Pelka's hands. Or had the woman worn herself out, lost her strength? Perhaps so.

Marey's foam-white husky tangled around Pelka's feet, looked up with her clever eyes: 'I know.' For a long time Pelka talked with her silently, stroked the fluffy neck.

'Well, that will do . . . Come on!'

Trampled moss, wood splinters, ash. Yes, this was where the tent had stood. Long ago.

'Marey!'

'Yes?'

'There . . . the husky, do you hear? Marey!'

The green sister-pines opened out like a curtain: a clearing. The acrid bear smell struck the nostrils. A huge bear stood on his hind legs in the clearing, throwing the husky back over and over, like a toy. The husky was in a frenzy – dashing, howling, squealing.

'Marey – you first. Then I . . . Hurry . . .'

Yes, things have changed – Pelka no longer relies on herself, her hands tremble; what will you do?

Unhurriedly, Marey rested his rifle on a branch; let the bear come to within ten paces: at ten paces, under the shoulder – a sure kill.

Boom! the smoke dispersed, the bear swayed, now he will drop . . .

But he did not drop. He let out a roar and, grasping the injured spot with his paw, he lunged straight at them.

How was that? At ten paces . . . Could the gun have been loaded with shot? Good God . . .

'Shot . . .' Pelka nodded to him. 'And mine's unloaded.'

Marey understood all. Suddenly – the sun, the red spot – only to live, to live . . .

'Drop!' cried Pelka.

Not to move. The bear will bury them and go. A bear is afraid of the dead. Only to keep from stirring, from breathing . . .

The bear sniffed at them, growling, pushed Marey with his paw: no, they're not alive. And he rapidly began to throw soft moss over them. He piled a high mound, stepped aside and looked.

Suffocating, Pelka moved closer and closer, lips to lips, as once, long ago, in the tent . . .

'Hm, the moss still moves!' The bear came back and piled more moss, then earth, then sat down on the mound himself, to lick his wound. The foam-white husky squealed in a frenzy, pawed at him, interfered.

Angrily, the bear crushed the husky with his paw, gathered her up from his belly – white and red – and threw her off into the bushes. For a long time, earnestly, he looked down on the grave.

No. The moss no longer stirs. Guess he can go now.

[*1918, published 1922*]

THE CAVE

Glaciers, mammoths, wastes. Black nocturnal cliffs, somehow resembling houses; in the cliffs, caves. And no one knows who trumpets at night on the stony path between the cliffs, who blows up white snow-dust, sniffing out the path. Perhaps it is a grey-trunked mammoth, perhaps the wind. Or is the wind itself the icy roar of the king of mammoths? One thing is clear: it is winter. And you must clench your teeth as tightly as you can, to keep them from chattering; and you must split wood with a stone axe; and every night you must carry your fire from cave to cave, deeper and deeper. And you must wrap yourself into shaggy animal hides, more and more of them.

A grey-trunked mammoth roamed at night among the cliffs, where Petersburg had stood ages ago. And cave-men, wrapped in hides, blankets, rags, retreated from cave to cave. On the Feast of the Intercession of the Holy Virgin, Martin Martinych and Masha closed up the study; a few weeks later they fled from the dining-room and huddled in the bedroom. There was no-where else to retreat; here they must last out the seige or die.

In the Petersburg bedroom-cave things were much as they had been in Noah's ark not long ago: a confusion of beasts, clean and unclean, thrown together by the flood. A mahogany desk; books, Stone Age pancakes that seemed to have been made of potter's clay; Scriabin, Opus 74; a flat-iron; five potatoes, scrubbed lovingly to gleaming whiteness; nickel bedsteads; an axe; a chiffonier; firewood. And in the centre of this universe – its god, the short-legged, rusty-red, squat, greedy cave god: the cast-iron stove.

The god hummed mightily. A great fiery miracle in the dark cave. The people – Martin Martinych and Masha – worshipfully, silently, gratefully stretched their hands to it. For a single hour it was spring in the cave; for one hour the animal hides, claws, fangs were discarded, and green shoots – thoughts – struggled up through the ice-crusted cortex of the brain.

'Mart, you've forgotten that tomorrow ... No, I see you have forgotten!'

In October, when the leaves have yellowed, withered, drooped, there are sometimes blue-eyed days; you throw back your head on such a day, so as not to see the earth, and you can almost believe that joy, that summer are still here. And so with Masha now: if you close your eyes and only listen to her voice, you can still believe she is the same, the old Masha; in a moment she will laugh, jump out of bed, throw her arms around you. And what you heard an hour ago – a knife rasping on glass – was not her voice at all, it was not she ...

'Mart, Mart! Just as always now ... You never used to forget. The twenty-ninth: St Mary's day, my name day ...'

The cast-iron god still hummed. As usual, there was no light; the light came on at ten. The shaggy, dark vaults of the cave swayed overhead. Martin Martinych, squatting on his heels, all of him drawn into a knot – tighter, tighter! – still stared, with head thrown back, at the October sky in order not to see the faded, withered lips. And Masha –

'You know, Mart – what if we lit the stove the first thing in the morning? To make the whole day – just as now! What? How much do we have? There must still be about a cord left in the study?'

It was a long, long time since Masha had been able to get herself as far as the arctic study; she did not know there was no longer any ... But pull the knot more tightly, still more tightly!

'A cord? Much more! I think there must be ...'

Suddenly, the light: exactly ten o'clock. And, breaking off, Martin Martinych shut his eyes, turned away. It was harder in the light than in the dark ... And in the light it could be clearly seen – his face was crumpled, claylike (many people had clay faces now – back to Adam). And Masha –

'And, you know, Mart, I would try – perhaps I could get up ... if you lit the stove in the morning.'

'Of course, Masha, of course ... On such a day ... Of course, the first thing in the morning.'

The cave god was running down, shrinking. It was quiet now, crackling faintly. Downstairs, at the Obertyshevs, a stone axe was chopping the knotty logs of an old barge – a stone axe was splitting Martin Martinych into pieces. One piece of Martin Martinych smiled a clayey smile at Masha and ground dried potato peelings in the coffee mill for pancakes. Another piece – like a bird that has flown into a room from out of the open – dashed itself blindly, stupidly against the ceiling, the windows, the walls: Where can I get some wood – some wood?

Martin Martinych put on his coat, buckled on a leather belt (there is a myth among the cave-dwellers that a belt will keep them warmer), and clattered with the pail in the corner near the chiffonier.

'Where are you going, Mart?'

'Only a moment, downstairs, for some water.'

On the dark staircase, ice-crusted from splashed water, Martin Martinych stood awhile, swaying, sighing. Then, the pail clanking like a prisoner's chain, he went downstairs, to the Obertyshevs: they still had running water. The door was opened by Obertyshev himself, in a coat held together with a rope, his face, long unshaven, a wasteland overgrown with rusty, dusty weeds. Through the tangle of weeds – yellow stony teeth, and between the stones, a flick of a lizard's tail – a smile.

'Ah, Martin Martinych! Some water? Come in, come in, come in!'

Impossible to turn with the pail in the narrow passageway between the outer and the inner door – the passageway is full of Obertyshev's firewood. The clay Martin Martinych painfully struck his side against the wood – a deep dent formed in the clay. Then a still deeper one, from the corner of the chest of drawers in the dark hallway.

They crossed the dining-room. In the dining-room was the Obertyshev female and three Obertyshev cubs; the female quickly hid a bowl under a napkin: a man had come from another cave – who knows, he may suddenly rush and seize it.

In the kitchen Obertyshev turned on the faucet, grinning with stony teeth.

'Well, and how's the wife? How's the wife?'

'The same, Alexey Ivanych, the same. In bad shape. And then, tomorrow is her name day, and I have no more wood.'

'Use the chairs, Martin Martinych, and the chests ... The books too: books make an excellent fire, excellent, excellent ...'

'But you know yourself – all the furniture in the apartment is the landlord's, all but the piano ...'

So, so ... Too bad, too bad!

And now, in the kitchen, the strayed bird could be heard fluttering up, rustling, darting left, right – and suddenly, desperately, it dashed its breast against the wall: 'Alexey Ivanych, I wanted ... Alexey Ivanych, could you ... only five, six pieces ...'

Yellow stony teeth through tangled weeds, yellow teeth staring out of the eyes; all of Obertyshev was sprouting teeth and they grew longer and longer.

'Martin Martinych, how can you! We haven't got enough ourselves ... You know yourself how things are, you know yourself, you know yourself ...'

Pull the knot harder! Still harder! Twisted tight, Martin Martinych lifted the pail – and back through the kitchen, the dark hallway, the dining-room. On the dining-room threshold Obertyshev thrust out a slippery, lizard-quick hand: 'Well, good-bye ... But see that you slam the door, Martin Martinych, don't forget. Both doors, both – one cannot keep the house warm enough!'

Out on the dark icy landing Martin Martinych set down the pail, turned, and shut the first door. He listened, but he heard only the dry, bony tremor inside himself, and his gasping breath – a broken line of dots and dashes. In the narrow passageway between the doors he stretched his hand and touched a log of wood, another, and another ... No! He quickly thrust himself out onto the landing and closed the door. Now he must only slam it to, so that the lock will click ...

But he could not do it. He had no strength to slam the door on Masha's tomorrow. And on the faint dotted line traced out by his breath, two Martin Martinychs locked in mortal combat: the old one, who had loved Scriabin and who knew he must not,

143

and the new one, the cave-dweller, who knew – he must. Gritting his teeth, the cave-dweller knocked down, throttled the old one, and Martin Martinych, breaking his nails in his haste, pulled open the door and plunged his hand into the woodpile ... one piece, a fourth, a fifth, under his coat, inside his belt, into the pail. He slammed the door and bounded upstairs with great, animal leaps. When he was halfway up the stairs ,he suddenly halted on an icy step and pressed himself against the wall. The door had clicked again below, and the dusty Obertyshev voice cried out, 'Who is it? Who's there? Who?'

'It is I, Alexey Ivanych. I ... I had forgotten to close the door ... I wanted ... I came back to shut it better ...'

'You? Hm ... How could you? One must be more careful. With everybody thieving nowadays, you know it yourself. How could you?'

The twenty-ninth. From early morning – a low, ragged, cotton sky, breaking ice through the gaps. But the cave-god had filled its belly in the morning, and began to hum benignly: never mind the torn sky, never mind the toothy Obertyshev counting his logs. It does not matter, it's all the same. 'Tomorrow' is a word unknown in the cave. It will take centuries before men know 'tomorrow' and 'the day after tomorrow'.

Masha got up and, swaying from an unseen wind, she combed her hair in the old way: over her ears, with a part in the middle. And this was like a last, shrivelled leaf fluttering on a naked tree. From the middle drawer of his desk, Martin Martinych pulled out papers, letters, a thermometer, a small blue phial (he hurriedly pushed it back, so Masha would not see it), and finally, from the farthest corner, a black lacquered box: on the bottom of it there was still some real – yes, yes! – real tea. Tilting his head back, Martin Martinych listened to the voice, so much like the voice of old.

'Do you remember, Mart: my blue room, and the piano with the covered top, and the little wooden horse, the ashtray, on the piano? I played, and you came up to me from behind ...'

The universe had been created that evening, and the astonishing, wise mask of the moon, and the nightingale song of the bell, trilling out in the hallway.

'Do you remember, Mart – the open window, the green sky, and below, out of another world, the hurdy-gurdy man?'

Hurdy-gurdy man, miraculous hurdy-gurdy man, where are you?

'And on the quay ... Remember? The branches still bare, the rosy water, and a last ice-floe, like a coffin, floating by. And the coffin only made us laugh, for we would never, never die. Remember?'

Downstairs they began to split wood with a stone axe. Suddenly they stopped. Someone was running, shouting. And, split in two, Martin Martinych saw with one half of him the deathless hurdy-gurdy man, the deathless wooden horse, the deathless ice-floe; and with the other half, his breath a broken, dotted line, he was with Obertyshev, counting logs of wood. Now Obertyshev had finished counting. Now he was putting on his coat, all of him overgrown with teeth, now he furiously slammed the door, and ...

'Wait, Masha, I think there's someone at the door.'

No. No one. Not yet. It was still possible to breathe, to tilt one's head and listen to the voice – so much like the old.

Twilight. The twenty-ninth of October was growing old, peering with the intent, dim eyes of an ancient crone – and everything shrivelled, hunched up, shrank under the insistent stare. The vaults of the ceiling settled lower, the armchair, the desk, Martin Martinych, the bed, everything flattened out, and on the bed – an altogether flat, a paper Masha.

Into the twilight came Selikhov, the house chairman. Once he had weighed two hundred and forty pounds; now half of him had ebbed away, and he knocked about loosely inside the shell of his coat like a nut in a rattle. But he still had his old booming laugh.

'Well, then Martin Martinych, in the first place. And in the second place, congratulations to your spouse on her name day. Of course, of course! Obertyshev told me ...'

'Some tea? ... a moment – just a moment ... We have real tea today. You know what it means – real tea! I have just ...'

'Tea? Well, I would prefer champagne. You have none? You don't say! Haw-haw-haw! The other day a friend of mine and I, we made ourselves a brew out of some Hoffman drops. It was a howl! We got stewed ... "I am Zinoviev," he says: "Down on your knees!" A howl! And then, as I was going home across the Martian Field, I met a man in nothing but his vest, I swear to God! "What's wrong?" I asked him. "Oh, nothing much," he says, "they've stripped me out there just now, I'm running home to Vasilievsky." A howl!'

Flattened, paper-thin, Masha was laughing on the bed. All of him tied into a knot, Martin Martinych laughed louder and louder – to give more fuel to Selikhov, to throw in a few more logs; if only he wouldn't stop, if only he wouldn't stop, if only he went on about something else ...

But Selikhov was running down; after a few last quiet snorts, he was silent. He dangled right, left inside his coat-shell and got up.

'Well, my dear lady, your little hand. Yos! Don't you know? Your obedient servant – Y-O-S, as they would say it nowadays. A howl!'

The floor was rocking, turning under Martin Martinych's feet. With a clay smile Martin Martinych held onto the door post. Selikhov was puffing, ramming his feet into his huge snow boots.

In his boots and fur coat, mammothlike, he straightened up and caught his breath.

Then silently he took Martin Martinych by the elbow, silently he opened the door into the arctic study and silently sat down on the sofa.

The floor in the study was icy; the ice cracked faintly, broke from the shore, and floated whirling downstream with Martin Martinych, and from the distance, from the sofa, from the shore, Selikhov's voice was scarcely audible.

'In the first place, and in the second place, my dear sir, I must tell you: I would crush this Obertyshev like a louse, I swear to God ... But you understand: if he makes an official complaint, if he says, – "Tomorrow I'll report it to the police ..." Such a louse! I can only advise you: go to him today, right now, and shove those damned logs down his throat.'

The ice-floe rushed faster and faster. Tiny, flattened, barely visible – no more than a splinter – Martin Martinych answered – speaking to himself, and not about the firewood ... What's firewood? No, about something else: 'Yes, very well. Today. Right now.'

'Excellent, excellent! Such a louse, such a louse, I tell you ...'

It was still dark in the cave. Cold, blind, made of clay, Martin Martinych stumbled dully against the things piled in confusion, out of the flood. For a moment he was startled: a voice, sounding like Masha's voice, out of the past ...

'What were you talking about with Selikhov? What? Ration cards? And I was lying here, Mart, and thinking: If it were possible to get up some energy and go away somewhere, to let the sun ... Oh, how you clatter! As if to spite me. You know, you know I can't stand it, I can't, I can't!'

Like a knife on glass. But it was all the same now. His hands and feet had become mechanical. To lift them and to lower them he needed chains, winches ... And one man could not turn the winch; you needed three. Straining at the chains, Martin Martinych put a tea-kettle and a saucepan on the fire, and threw in the last of Obertyshev's logs.

'Do you hear what I'm saying to you? Why don't you answer? You hear me!'

Of course, this was not Masha, this was not her voice. Martin Martinych moved more and more slowly, his feet sank in the shifting sand, it was harder and harder to turn the winch. Suddenly the chain slipped from the block, the arm shot down, clumsily catching at the kettle and the pan. Everything crashed to the floor. The cave-god hissed like a snake. And from the distant shore, the bed – an alien, shrill voice: 'You're doing it on purpose! Get out! Get out at once. I don't need anybody, I don't need anything – I want nothing, nothing! Get out!'

October twenty-ninth had died, and the deathless hurdy-gurdy man, and the ice-floes in the sunset-rosy water, and Masha. And that was right and necessary. There must be no impossible tomorrow, no Obertyshev, no Selikhov, no Masha, and no Martin Martinych. Everything must die.

The mechanical, faraway Martin Martinych was still going

through some motions. He may have tended to the fire in the stove, picked up the pan, put the kettle on once more to boil. Masha may have said something again. He did not hear. There was nothing but the dull ache of the dents in the clay, made by words, by the corners of the chiffonier, the chairs, the desk.

Martin Martinych slowly drew out of the desk drawer bundles of letters, the thermometer, some sealing-wax, the box of tea, more letters. And finally, from somewhere at the very bottom, the dark-blue phial.

Ten o'clock: the light went on. Electric light – barren, harsh, plain, cold, like life and death in the cave. And just as plain, beside the flat-iron, Opus 74, and the pancakes, the small blue phial.

The cast-iron god hummed benignly, devouring the paper of the letters, parchment yellow, bluish, white. The tea-kettle tapped its lid, gently calling attention to itself. Masha turned, 'Is the tea boiling? Mart dear, give me . . .'

And then she saw it. An instant, pierced through by the clear, naked, cruel electric light: Martin Martinych, crouching before the stove; the letters glowing pink like the river at sunset; and, over there, the blue phial.

'Mart! You . . . you want to . . . already . . .'

Silence. Indifferently devouring the deathless, bitter, tender, white and pale-blue words, the cast-iron god purred softly. And Masha – as simply as she had asked for tea: 'Mart, darling! Mart, give it to me!'

Martin Martinych smiled from far away. 'But you know, Masha, there is only enough for one.'

'Mart, but there is nothing left of me, anyway. This is no longer I – I'll soon be . . . anyway . . . Mart, but you understand – Mart, have pity on me . . . Mart!'

Ah, the same, the old voice . . . And if you tilt your head . . .

'I lied to you, Masha. We do not have a single piece of wood left in the study. And I went to Obertyshev, and there, between the doors . . . I stole, you understand. And Selikhov said . . . I must take it back at once – but I burnt everything, everything! I don't mean the wood – what's wood! – you understand me?'

The iron god was dozing off indifferently. Houses, cliffs, mammoths, Masha flickered, going out.

'Mart, if you still love me ... Mart, remember! Mart, darling, give it to me!'

The deathless wooden horse, the hurdy-gurdy man, the ice-floe. And that voice ... Martin Martinych slowly rose from his knees. Turning the winch slowly, with great effort, he took the blue phial from the table and gave it to Masha.

She threw off the blanket and sat up on the bed, rosy, quick, deathless – like the river at sunset long ago. She seized the phial and laughed.

'Well, now, you see: it wasn't for nothing that I lay here, dreaming of going away. Light another lamp, that one, on the table. So. Now put something else into the stove. I want the fire ...'

Without looking, Martin Martinych swept out some papers from the desk and threw them into the stove.

'Now ... Go, take a little walk. I think the moon must be out – *my* moon, remember? Don't forget to take the key, or you will shut the door and there won't be ...'

No, there was no moon outside. Low, dark, thick clouds like a vaulted ceiling, and everything – one vast, silent cave. Narrow, endless passages between the walls; and houselike, dark, icy cliffs; and in the cliffs – deep, red-lit hollows. There, in those hollows, people were squatting by the fires. A light icy draught was blowing white dust underfoot, and over the white dust, the boulders, the caves, the crouching men, unheard by anyone, went the huge, measured tread of some unknown monster mammoth.

[*1920, published 1922*]

THE HEALING OF THE
NOVICE ERASMUS

ABOUT THE BLESSED ELDER PAMVA, HIS EXCEEDING WISDOM, AND THE MIRACULOUS EVENTS THAT CAME TO PASS

The said novice Erasmus had been dedicated to God while still in his mother's womb. His parents had loved one another zealously but vainly for many years, and at last, having exhausted all the worldly, human remedies, they came to the cloister to seek help of the saintly Pamva. When she entered the Elder's cell, the wife dropped to her knees, and the woman's modesty sealed her lips. And thus, without speaking, she knelt before the Elder. But the blessed Pamva had no need of words: from the days of his youth the dust and ashes of female vestments were as glass to him, and through them he saw at once the woman's bitter, barren loins.

'Put away thy sorrow, woman,' the Elder said to her. 'Be seated here and share my repast.'

So saying, he took a baked fish, drew out the milt and, blessing it, he gave it to the woman. With tears and faith, she partook of the consecrated food, and suddenly she felt a fluttering within her, as though she had taken her husband unto her lap.

When the saintly Pamva saw her closed lids open again and red return to her cheeks which had grown pale for a short moment, he smiled to her and said: 'Henceforth thy husband shall no longer be like unto the ploughman who tills the sand, but his labours shall bear fruit. But thy firstborn, when he learns to sing the praises of Him who caused him to be born and who brings darknesses into being – thy firstborn thou shalt bring to the cloister and leave with me.'

Thereafter the sun rose many times over the cloister and sowed its golden seed in the blue snow and in the black bowels of spring; grasses sprang upward and, having accomplished their allotted task, bowed unto the earth again. And only Pamva walked upright as of old, even as the cypress, the tree of the cross, and the silver crown of his hair shone strong as ever; and many ailing men were healed by him, and those possessed of devils, and barren wives. And there were some who saw in this the workings of the blessed food that he partook of.

On Whitsuntide, after he celebrated the appointed services, Pamva came forth from the church. The zealous brethren had scattered fragrant spring grasses over the white flagstones before the church, and crowned with wreaths the crosses on the graves of monks who had departed and who were even now rejoicing together with the living. And, crowned with a green wreath, a youth with golden hair, led by the hand of a woman, appeared before the blessed Pamva.

'On this day of the earth's marriage, enter and live with us, Erasmus,' said Pamva and raised his hand to bless the youth, but at this instant two devils who had taken the shape of doves alighted on a cross and, throwing down the wreath, gave themselves over to the rage of the flesh.

'He will peck her to death! Save her, good Father!' cried the youth Erasmus to the blessed Pamva.

The Elder raised his eyes up to the devils, and they melted away as smoke in the sight of all without consummating their unseemly play. And the Elder laid his hands on Erasmus, saying: 'Happy is thy lot, Brother Erasmus, and also troublesome, for the devils are already casting their nets for thee. But they seek only precious quarry.'

And, in order to keep Erasmus from the devil's snares, the blessed Pamva brought the youth to live with him in his own cell. The novice Erasmus served the Elder; he took him water for his ablutions, he brought his frugal meals, and censers, and candles. And many a time he witnessed how the holy Elder healed the sick and read into the souls of those who came to him as though their clothes and their very bodies were of glass.

'How dost thou look, Father, to read their souls?' Erasmus inquired of Pamva.

'I look into their eyes,' answered the Elder. 'A man's body –
all of it – lives in this world, and only his eyes are wells that
reach down from the surface of this world into the world where
the soul dwells. And even as wells in the earth are of different
depths, so are they in man. And the deeper they go, the closer
they are to the heavenly mansions, but also to the gates of hell.'

'And mine?' asked the novice Erasmus.

But the wise Elder made no reply, immersing himself in
prayer. For he saw no bottom in those blue wells that were but
lightly shaded by the delicate tracery of lashes. So the experienced traveller goes warily along unknown paths, avoiding the
places that beckon with their tender green in order not to sink
into deceptive quagmires.

Soon the novice Erasmus became greatly accomplished in
reading and in letters. And when the blessed Pamva wearied of
prayer, and of talk with those who came to seek his wise coun-
sel, and of his constant wrestlings with the devils who beset
him tirelessly like flies, the novice Erasmus read to him aloud
from the Bible, or the Lives of our Holy Fathers, or other
sacred books. The young monk's voice was pure even as a
mountain stream that tumbles ringing from the heights. And as
the sun-baked rock along the path of the rushing stream is
clothed in green and speckled with a multitude of flowers, white
and crimson and blue as the firmament, so the words recited by
Erasmus seemed washed by some sweet and turbulent waters.
And hearing their beauty, made strange now, and as though no
longer divine, the Elder would stop the reading, saying: 'I shall
pray, Erasmus. Go now and read unto thyself.'

Then, seated on the sun-heated white stones outside the cell,
Erasmus would open once again the pages of the ancient book,
bespattered with waxen tears, and he would read from it. And
drunk with the wine of the words, he heard naught around him,
and neither saw nor knew what his reading did to those who
heard him.

One day at such an hour, the blessed Pamva, faint with the
heat, lifted the shutter in his cell and stood in amazement, for
beneath his window he heard deep sighs and moanings as of
some huge beast. He went forth and beheld Erasmus on the step

of his cell with a book, and around him, monks – youths and men and ancients. And their faces were red and their breath came fast, as after too much running. And many groaned, as with some raging torment, and furiously embraced with both arms the white bodies of the birches or, prone upon the ground, kissed the round stones that were like unto bellies.

'Madman, what hast thou done with them?' the Elder cried in anger.

'I am reading to them from the Holy Books,' Erasmus answered artlessly.

Thinking that the young monk, prompted by the devil, had defiled himself with falsehood, Pamva stepped nearer and, lowering his eyes to the pages of the ancient book, he saw that he had thought unjustly of Erasmus, for the youth was reading the Song of Songs of that wisest of mortals who was also a prophet before the Lord. Then the saintly Elder knew that the novice Erasmus was guiltless, but the guilt was of the brethren, and he said unto them: 'With what thoughts, ye impious ones, do ye listen to the words about divine love for our immaculate Bride – the Church?'

But the brethren were silent.

'Raise up your eyes, ye men of wicked heart, and ye shall see.'

For a brief moment, in answer to the blessed Pamva's prayer, their spiritual eyes were opened and they beheld: at a small height, at the level of the monastery roofs, a heavy cloud was rolling, infused with red as though of blood. And after a short while, they saw that it was not blood, but heavy puffs of cloud hanging down like female breasts, with the sharp nipples pointing downwards; and the cloud tossed and billowed with the shapes of navels like unto chalices, and of thighs and loins wreathed lightly in transparent veils.

Struck by the vision, the monks were silent. Then the cloud of diabolical enticements shook at the movement of the saintly Elder's hand and poured forth a malodorous rain, as thick and white as milk.

'See ye now what ye have planted with your thoughts?' the blessed Pamva asked them.

'Forgive us, Father, we see,' the shamed monks echoed.

And from that day forth, the novice Erasmus was forbidden by Pamva to read books, but was set to another task, where the devils could no longer turn to evil the sweetness of his tender voice. Under the unremitting surveillance of the Elder, Erasmus began to learn the craft of painting holy icons.

Fearing more devilish temptations, the Elder set Erasmus apart from the brethren, shutting him up in a small cell, and no one saw or heard Erasmus save the Elder. And the walls of that cell were white as the vestments of an immaculate virgin, and there was a small window covered with a lattice. After the noon hour the shadow of the lattice lay on the wall and slowly moved higher and higher till, at the hour when the river opened its lap unto the sun, the shadow halted on the ceiling and faded out, while below, on the virginal vestments of the wall, a crimson stain appeared, as though of blood. And consumed by an unknown fire, Erasmus would approach the wall and touch the crimson stain, as if seeking to dye his fingers with the tender blood. But in the morning the wall gleamed as before with the hue of innocence. And Pamva, entering the cell, rejoiced in secret, thinking that the very colour of the wall would whiten the young monk's thoughts. And he rejoiced, seeing the youth's zeal and his cunning as he applied himself to the great and sacred labour of painting holy images.

It came about at that time that the blessed Pamva healed a certain well-born woman called Mary. This woman had been in the power of a devil who drove her into ungovernable and insatiable lechery. Laying his finger three times upon her nature, which was burning up with wanton fire, the saintly Elder sated her with peace and freed her of the diabolic power. This woman had been named in honour of St Mary of Egypt, and as she was healed, she said unto the Elder: 'I pray thee, Father, if thou knowest of any who is skilled in the painting of icons, bid him to paint the life of St Mary, her passion and her torments and her excellent deeds in the desert of Egypt. And when it is done, I will shut myself up in a cell and gaze with tears upon the image of the sainted Mary's life and seek to follow in her path.'

The blessed Pamva summoned Erasmus on that very day and questioned him, saying: 'Dost thou know the passionate life of St Mary of Egypt?'

And Erasmus answered: 'Forgive me, Father, but I know it not.'

And the Elder gave him the opened book of the Lives of the Saints and instructed him to read the life of St Mary. And Erasmus read it all day, leaving his food untouched. And now it was evening, and the shadow of the lattice had faded on the vaulted ceiling of the cell. Erasmus lighted a lamp and read again how the fair-limbed maiden drew the youths and men of Alexandria to her couch by the snare of her beauty, and how she inflamed all men on the storm-tossed ship with the unsated fire of her desire, and how, withdrawing to the desert, consumed with carnal lust, she called for help to the Heavenly Bridegroom.

And it was this visage of the Saint – alone in the desert, her eyes veiled with a light mist, such as the mist that hangs over the distance scorched by furious heat, with lips apart, panting even as the earth that is dried out with rain – it was this visage of the Saint that the novice Erasmus painted in the centre of the icon. At her feet he painted yellow sand and grasses and flowers wilted by the heat that flowed from the sun or from the Saint's body, hidden under its filmy white garment.

And Erasmus did not hear when Father Pamva entered his cell and stood beside him like a guardian angel. For a long while the blessed Elder looked upon the image of the Saint, and then he said to Erasmus: 'Praiseworthy is thy zeal, and I behold upon thee the stamp of God's gift.' ('But is it God's?' the Elder asked himself.) 'Yet still there is an imperfection in thy work: there is beauty in the Saint's face, but under her tunic I see the body of a man, not of a woman. For thou art young, and must yet come to know the mysteries of her who was created by the Lord out of Adam's rib.'

With these words, the Elder departed: the evening's blood glowed on the pure white vestment of the wall, and the iron knocker was calling the brethren to church. As for Erasmus, he was dispensed from church prayer and stayed in his cell alone.

Sorrowing, Erasmus prostrated himself before the image in fervent prayer, calling out: 'Take mercy on me, saintly woman, teach me to know thy virtuous body so that I may more fitly glorify thee.'

At that instant he heard low laughter behind him. Turning around, he sought with astonishment to see who might have entered his cell, but he saw nothing save for two doves playing on the window lattice. He remembered the doves in the graveyard on the day of his coming to the cloister, and he made a sign of the cross over himself, whereupon the doves melted away into the rosy sky. Then he heard the same laughter again, but this time nearer and more distinct.

And then, near the sun-brightened wall, the novice Erasmus beheld an unknown maiden, as though she had stepped out of the wall. She was arrayed in white vestments, but here and there pink blossomed on the white, even as the sun stains on the wall.

'Who art thou?' Erasmus asked, his hands over his heart, which shuddered with fear and yet another, unknown trembling.

'My name is Mary,' replied the maid. 'I dwelt in Egypt, and I am sent to thee in answer to thy prayer.'

So overcome was he by the marvellous sign, that he forgot to cross himself again, but, falling on his knees before her, began at once to kiss the garment of the maid, first at her feet, then higher.

And he smelled an unknown smell, but one that seemed to have been ever in his heart before that hour. And everything rose in Erasmus and strove resistlessly towards the holy maid, even as grasses filled with the sap of spring stretch irresistibly towards the sun. Ashamed, Erasmus stepped away and, lowering his eyes, sought to arrange his garment so that the holy maid would not perceive his agitation.

But the maid called out his name, and her voice pierced his heart like a sweet sword, and she said to Erasmus: 'Wherefore, foolish youth, is thy heart confused? Draw near me. Hast thou forgotten the instruction of thy teacher Pamva, and why I have been sent here for a short hour?'

Then, mastering his confusion, Erasmus drew near the maid, untied her belt with trembling hands, and unfastened the clasp at her throat. Her white tunic fell to her waist, and Erasmus beheld the mystery of breasts, until then unknown to him. They were like two waves, rising high in a calm sea at the miraculous bidding of the Lord, and the sun, descending over the earth's rim, lit scarlet flames on the sharp summits of those waves. And Erasmus rejoiced in the Lord's wisdom that he was being taught to know, and, obedient to the instruction of the Elder, he began with zeal to study what had been revealed to him. Like the doubting apostle Thomas, he did not trust his eyes alone, but sank his fingers into the cool and tender waves, and every time he did so, the sweet sword went deeper into his heart, and he felt his life flow out of him in fiery drops as in a blessed death.

'But there is more that thou hast not yet come to know,' the maid said, smiling. 'Hasten, for I am sent to thee but briefly.'

And, trembling with the premonition of a mystery yet more tender and more beautiful, the young monk undid the lower clasp. But at the moment when the final mystery was ready to be revealed before him, he heard a faint ringing sound as of a thin glass vessel bursting, and the maid vanished from sight. And in the doorway of the cell, Erasmus saw the blessed Pamva. The Elder was wroth, his grey brows were raised like wings, and he was like a raging bird that rushes to defend her young. And in a loud voice Pamva asked him, saying: 'What wast thou doing, madman? And who was here with thee?'

Without concealment, Erasmus told the wise Elder all that had befallen: how he besought the Saint with tears to grant him knowledge of a woman's flesh, so that he might more fitly glorify her virtuous body, and how she had come in answer to his prayer, and how he had learned from her everything but a certain last mystery.

The blessed Pamva was greatly troubled by the tale told by Erasmus, for the Elder was not of firm faith that the vision had been sent of God, not of the devil. And in his wisdom, he said to Erasmus: 'Give thanks to Him who sent thee aid in thy labour for the glory of the Saint. But remember: the last mystery is not meet for a monk to know, nor dost thou need this mystery in thine art. Go then, and sleep in peace.'

But there was no peace in sleep for Erasmus. His bed was as coals, and until morning he suffered the unquenchable, unyielding striving towards the last mystery, and until morning he sank his fingers into the pearly waves miraculously risen on a calm sea. And in the morning, after the customary genuflection to the Elder, he washed his brushes and, remembering with trepidation that which had been revealed to him the evening before, he set himself to repairing the faults that had been shown him by his instructor in the art – the blessed Pamva.

Soon the icon was almost finished. The blessed Elder scanned it closely and saw that now the Saint was a woman among women not only in face, but also in body, and it even seemed to him that he could glimpse her breasts glowing with points of the lightest flame under her cloud-white raiment. But of this he said naught to Erasmus, thinking to himself that he was merely seeing, as was his wont, through female vestments as through glass. And, raising his brows, the Elder blessed Erasmus, saying: 'I perceive that thy soul is filled with burning for the Saint. Do not quench this burning until thou shalt complete thy work on the image.'

But even had he wished to, Erasmus could no longer put out this burning within himself. Soon after speaking these words, Pamva departed from the cloister, being summoned to the bedside of the prince of that land, who was ailing. As he went out of the gates of the cloister, the blessed Elder looked back for a last time at the golden cupolas of the church rising amongst the greenery, and saw a host of devils swaying in the branches of the ancient monastery lindens like swarming bees. And the Elder trembled with dark forebodings of new and hitherto unheard-of diabolic snares, but he dared not disobey the prince's will.

During Pamva's absence food was brought to Erasmus by the baker monk called Samson. Like Samson of old, he was great and powerful of body in every way, and he had no growth of hair either on his head or his face or any other place on his body, which made him look doubly naked. Therefore, as commanded by Pamva, he wore upon himself not less than three garments even in the heat of summer. As for women, their sight, not only in their natural being, but even in depictment, was wont to throw him into immeasurable rage. Fearing, therefore, this immeasurable rage, Erasmus received his food from the baker monk through a small opening in the door.

On that day a fiery heat flowed from the sun; in the great drought the grasses and the forests burned in the distance beyond the lake. And young Erasmus burned with the grasses without being consumed, and fiery images of the Saint's passionate life sprang one after the other on the smooth cypress wood.

He painted the doorway of a temple, and at the doorway a long line of youths and men of Alexandria, their lips blackened with the thirst for kisses – like unto a row of warriors with fire-hardened swords raised and waiting to rush at the enemy and pierce him with those swords to death. And below, framed in gold, was the temple itself, simple and white, for the Saint abode in poverty and took no payment for the beauty of her body. In the temple Erasmus depicted a humble and resplendent bed of grasses, and on the green jasper of the grasses – a golden fruit: the nakedness of the Saint, with four ripe crimson blooms stinging the eye of the beholder. As has been told, Erasmus already knew the mystery of lips and breasts. But the fourth and last mystery was still unknown to the young monk, and he composed this final mystery not of two but of three crimson petals, which gave it even greater power for the undoing of all who looked upon it. And in another frame of redgold, those flowers bloomed on a storm-tossed ship, and the sailors, forgetting the waves of the sea, rose and fell on other, fiery waves. And further on, in a scorched, straw-yellow desert, St Zosima met Mary and drew off his cloak in fear and threw it to her so that he might not be destroyed by the beauty of her nakedness. But the desert wind bore away the cloak, and Zosima stood with head bowed sorrowing to the ground, gazing at his own burning flesh. And so, until the holy death of the Saint, Erasmus depicted her whole passionate and hallowed life.

The sunset hour when Erasmus finished his task was imbrued

with sunny blood. At that hour, as was customary, Samson brought Erasmus his evening meal. And forgetting all caution, Erasmus cried to the monk, saying: 'Great is the hour when a journey is completed! Enter, Brother Samson, and tell me what thou thinkest.'

'It is dangerous for me, Brother,' Samson answered through the opening in the door.

'Enter, I say to thee,' Erasmus said in anger and impatience.

And, that he might not lead his brother into the sin of anger, Samson entered. And seeing, he swayed on his feet, as though his feet were suddenly weighed down with a great weight, and, bellowing in his rage, he cast himself upon his face and began to drill the cold earthen floor of the cell. Affrighted, Erasmus took the cup of water brought to him by Samson and poured the water on the raving monk. Then Samson arose and rent his garments, and, doubly naked, he cried: 'Woe is me, the accursed one. For my strength flows out in vain!'

And crashing through the door of the cell, he ran out. And night came, awful with signs and doings. Amid the smoky gloom, lighting their way with wax candles, the monks ran stumbling over gravestones. In the far corner, behind the bread cellar, a fiery window opened and shut again. There they bound the baker monk Samson in chains, to keep him from destroying the trees and utensils and the monastery buildings, for in his strength he could bring down everything in sight. And just above the roofs, where once the brethren had seen the cloud revealed to them by Pamva, they heard all through the night faint laughter as of someone being tickled, and a strange creaking, and all night there was a dripping of a terrible dew like unto white pitch.

The sun rose, scarlet through the smoke, and it was seen that in the night, as though by some marvellous dispensation, all trees and grasses had burst forth into bloom, opening wide their cups that were crimson and pink as bodies, and white as pearls, and giving off delightful fragrances. And everywhere – on trees, in the cups of the flowers, on the graveyard crosses and the window lattices, the vessels for drinking and the shoulders of the monks – everywhere there was a multitude of locusts with wings as of the heavenly rainbow, and they fluttered their wings, coupling in pairs.

Not hearing the customary morning bell, but the sounds rather of clamour and confusion, Erasmus came out to the brethren and said: 'Wherefore are ye troubled, brethren? Do not fear, but take from my cell the image of the Saint that had miraculously appeared before me, and I am of firm faith that she will heal you.'

And saying thus, Erasmus closed anew the door of his cell, remembering the penance laid upon him by the Elder. But the brethren did as Erasmus bade them and took the image of St Mary of Egypt which he had painted, and setting it up before the gates of the cloister, they built over it a canopy of flowers. But as they began the chanting of prayers and lifted up their eyes with hope to the holy icon, they beheld the four crimson flowers aflame on the recumbent golden body – the last, the fourth, composed, at the painter's will and through his ignorance, not of two but of three petals. And a passionate fire ran through each man, and all of them, young monks and aged elders, were like those youths and men of Alexandria at the temple gates, ready to pierce the beloved enemy with their swords.

And at that hour Samson, left without guard, had broken the strong chains that bound him and, ramming through everything that stood in his path, he appeared before the brethren, proclaiming with a loud voice and professing his lust. When the gatekeeper heard what he took to be the chanting of prayers, he opened the gates to the many lay women and maids and men who longed to enter. And all entered, and things unheard of came to pass everywhere – on the grasses, on the hitherto unsullied flagstones in the churchyard, on the steps of the cells and in the shadow of the shrubs that had burst into bloom the night before. And as at night, faint laughter, as of tickling, was heard over the roofs, and a strange creaking, and the grasses were washed with a terrible dew.

But Pamva alone, returning from the bedside of the prince of that land, could see, hovering over the cloister, clouds of devils, leaping and beating their wings for joy. Nor was this all: for none of the monks swayed by the devil saw the Elder's wrathful face or his brows raised like whips, and none heard his loud words of rebuke.

Then the Elder saw that the devils had won for a short hour, and he knew that until he had quenched the diabolic fire in young Erasmus, who, unknowing, wrought temptations – until that hour the devils would hold sway in the cloister.

And Pamva entered his cell, and from his cell, the cell of the novice Erasmus. And he saw Erasmus, who alone in the cloister lay without a woman. But his cheeks were burning with invisible fire, and with parched lips he drank of the unknown fourth mystery.

Closing the doors and windows so that his heart might not be offended by the whisperings and rustlings of the unholy frenzy raging outside, the blessed Pamva prayed long and fervently. And in answer to his prayer, understanding descended upon him, and he heard a voice as though within him, saying: 'Release the arrow, and the bowstring will slacken, and the bow will no longer be deadly.' And he said unto himself: 'Verily so.' And he prayed again, and the maid who had appeared unto Erasmus and who called herself Mary stood before him. The Elder took that maid by the hand and led her into the cell to Erasmus, and said unto him: 'Rise, Erasmus. The saintly maid has mercifully come to you once more. Take her, then, and learn the fourth and last mystery. For I see now: he who depicts creation must know all the mysteries of the Creator.'

And he beheld how Erasmus drew the raiment from the tender body, and after touching again the first three mysteries, sank moaning into the last.

And the sun sank into the waters of the lake behind the cloister, and on the innocent white vestments of the wall a stain appeared, as red as blood. And at that instant the bloom fell from the trees and grasses, the rainbow wings of the locusts scattered into dust, the devils melted away like wax, and the brethren, shamed, retired to their cells in the darkness. And the saintly Pamva went out into the courtyard and sent away the weary maids and women with a blessing, saying to them: 'Go in peace, for naught in this world is done without the will of the Creator, even sin, and everything is to the good.'

From that day forth it was as though the invisible diabolic flowers had dropped away from Erasmus, and he was cured of the possession that had worked in him. Without fear, the blessed Pamva gave him leave to abide with the rest of the brethren, and when Erasmus read in church, there was no longer temptation in his reading, and when he painted the images of saints, he painted like all others for the glory of the Lord, not of the devil. And the memory of the dark temptations of the devil and the terrible signs and extraordinary happenings was expunged by the prayers of the blessed Pamva even as spring snow is melted away by the sun.

And only I, the unworthy hermit Innocent, was blessed by the wise Elder to record all that befell for the edification and guidance of the priors of our cloister. As for the ordinary monks, the reading of this chronicle is forbidden to them.

[*1920, published 1922*]

IN OLD RUSSIA

Immemorial pine forest – trackless, primeval. Bears, the strong breath of mushrooms and pine resin, and hoary, shaggy mosses. The forest has seen the iron helmets of ancient princely warrior troops, the cowls of hermits of the old, true faith, the ragged caps of Stenka's freemen, and the frozen plumes of shivering Frenchmen. And all of this went by, as though it never was. And once again – blue winter days, great slabs of snow rustling down the branches, the dry, frosty snapping of twigs, the tapping of a woodpecker; then yellow summer days, wax candles in gnarled green hands, transparent honey-yellow tears creeping down rough trunks, and cuckoos counting the years.

But clouds bellied out in the sultry heat, the sky cracked open with a crimson gash, spewed flame – and the ancient forest began to smoke. By morning there was a mass of booming, fiery tongues, a hissing, crashing, howling all around, half the sky black with smoke, and the bloodied sun just barely visible. And what can little men do with their spades, ditches, and pails? The forest is no more, it was devoured by fire: stumps and ash. Perhaps illimitable fields will be ploughed here one day, perhaps some new, unheard-of wheat will ripen here and men from Arkansas with shaven faces will weigh in their palms the heavy golden grain. Or perhaps a city will grow up – alive with ringing sound and motion, all stone and crystal and iron – and winged men will come here flying over seas and mountains from all ends of the world. But never again the forest, never again the blue winter silence and the golden silence of summer. And only the tellers of tales will speak in many-coloured patterned words about what had been, about wolves and bears and stately green-coated century-old grandfathers, about old Russia; they will speak about all this to us who have seen it with our own eyes ten years – a hundred years! – ago, and to those others, the winged ones, who will come in a hundred years to listen and to marvel at it all as at a fairy tale.

These are not avenues laid out by Peter's measuring rod; no, that is Petersburg, Russia. Here we are in the ancient land – *Rus*. Narrow little streets, uphill and down, so that children can slide down in winter with shouts and whistles on flat slabs of ice. Alleys, dead ends, small fenced-in front gardens, fences and fences. Zamoskvorechye, with its immemorial, oak-carved names: Zatsepa, Ordynka, Balchug, Shabalovka, Babyegorod; on the outskirts of Moscow, Kolomna, and its iron fortress gates through which Prince Dmitry had gone out, crossing himself, to do battle on the Kulikovo Field; Vladimir's old town of Rzhev, still divided into the Prince Dmitry and Prince Fyodor districts, the residents of which may still, for all we know, be bloodying each other's noses in their famous bouts of fisticuffs; over the mirror-smooth Volga – Nizhny with its wide Makarievskaya, its steamboat races, sterlet, and taverns; and all along the Volga, the Yaroslavls, Romanovos, Kineshmas, Puchezhs – each with its city garden, its wooden sidewalks, its broad-hipped, squat, five-headed churches as tasty as communion bread; and all the black-earth-belt Yeletses and Lebedyans, with their horse fairs, gypsies, horses, brokers, hostels, pilgrims, and seers.

This is immemorial Russia – *Rus*. Just yesterday it teemed with all of these – and all of them can still be found here, preserved as in the sanctuary of the walled-in virgin forest of Belovezh: huge, bearlike, 'crush everything' merchants, inn-keepers like living samovars, wily Yaroslavl pedlars, sly-eyed self-styled 'princes' from Kazan hawking their wares. And in the midst of all of this you'll find a beauty, a real Russian beauty. Not one of your Petersburg wiggletail wasps, but like the Volga: stately, slow, broad, full-breasted; and, just as on the Volga – turn from mid-channel to the bank, into the shadow, and look out – a deep black whirlpool . . .

Take a walk in the town of Kustodiev (there is even a Cainsk –

can it be that there is no Kustodiev?), and you will see such a beauty: Darya, Darya Ivanovnă. Who hasn't known her parents? An old flour-merchant family, good stock. They would have lived and lived to this day if they hadn't gone out riding one day at Shrovetide. The horses weren't horses – tigers! And, the truth to tell, each horse had got a bottle of champagne mixed into his feed – for greater spirit. And so the sleigh and the riders and the coachman drove straight into a spring-thawed ice-hole. A fine end!

Ever since then Darya, ripening and filling up with sap like a crimson anise apple on a branch, has lived with Aunt Felicata, the prioress.

Side by side they walk along the convent garden home from church: Felicata with her rosary, all bundled up into her cowl and gown against the frost, and Darya, round, smooth, white. And bees seem to be humming in the sun, and the air is full of fragrance – is it of honey, or apples, or Darya?

'Well, Darya, it's marrying time, don't put it off. An apple must be picked in season, before the birds come down and peck it full of holes. Temptation doesn't wait!'

There was a time when Felicata lived out in the world; they used to call her Katya, Katyushenka – she knows and remembers.

Suitors come calling on Darya – and what suitors! Princes! Take Sazykin – one of the richest men in Kustodiev, second only to Vakhrameyev. His father, people say, had brought two *poods** of banknotes from Siberia inside frozen sturgeon and, they say, it wasn't all on the up and up. Still, money isn't marked. It's true, Sazykin isn't much on talk, and not in his first youth either; besides, there's something in him that reminds you of Yemelyan Pugachev,† but he's a smart trader; you don't find many merchants like him.

Vakhrameyev himself comes calling too. Mayor of the town, a widower after another wife. Pretends he's calling on Felicata (he had known her way back as Katya), but keeps bantering

---

* A *pood* is equal to about thirty-six pounds avoirdupois.

† Notorious brigand and leader of a peasant revolt during the reign of Catherine the Great.

mostly with Daryushka. He'll smooth out his beard – already grey now – sit down this way, with his feet apart, hands resting on his knees, ring glittering, and get going – he has pocketfuls of tales – you all but split your sides . . .

Her aunt meantime keeps urging Darya to hurry; her own days, she feels, are getting short: 'What's there to think about, Darya! In such things the mind will do you as much good as sugar on sturgeon. Write down their names on slips of paper and put them over here, under the icons, on the little shelf before the Holy Virgin. Whichever you take out, that's the one.'

Darya drew the slip with Vakhrameyev – and a load dropped off her heart. That other one, Sazykin, is a dark man, may God be with him. But Vakhrameyev is full of fun, and he had known her father – he'll be like a father to her.

When Felicata told Sazykin about the Holy Virgin's choice, he didn't say a word, but just kept looking down into the saucer with the jam. All he did was pull a fly out of the jam; it crawled off, squeaking, and he followed it for a long time with his eyes.

In the morning the town learned that he had driven his thousand-rouble trotter to death that night.

And Darya went to live in Vakhrameyev's two-storey mansion, the one that's near the town fire tower. And it was just as with an apple-tree when you transplant it – say, an apple-tree brought over from Lipetsk, from the famous Kozhin nurseries. It will droop a month or so, the leaves will curl up, while the gardener walks round it, watering, turning up the earth; and then, before you know it, it's taken to the new place, filled with sap, and once again it blooms and spreads its fragrance.

Vakhrameyev tends to Darya as though she were some special apple-tree, some precious Gold Naliv. He'll harness a pair of horses to a carpet-lined sleigh – the hooves churn up a snowstorm, fly like the wind, straight to his store: to show off his young bride to his 'lads'. The lads scrape and bow before her – all Darya has to do is walk over them! And should it seem to Vakhrameyev that some fiery gypsy eye has flashed a spark at her, he need but raise an eyebrow like a whip, and the gypsy eye will drop.

The fair came: to the fair with Darya. Epiphany frost, the trees wear coats of pale-blue snow fur, flags flutter on the poles. Booths, stalls, brightly decorated cakes of rye flour from Archangel, the shrilling of clay whistles, Yaroslavl pedlars hawking clusters of rainbow-coloured balloons, a carousel going round and round to music. And maybe Darya has no use at all for the Vakhrameyev trotters, snorting clouds of white steam; maybe she'd rather mount this wooden horse with its proud curved neck, holding onto someone – with the wind blowing up her dress, the icy air singeing her knees, and a hot spark flying from shoulder to close shoulder . . .

Saturdays were bath days, the same as with their fathers and their grandfathers. They'd walk out on foot – that was Vakhrameyev's custom; and from across the corner, from his own house, Sazykin – also to the baths. Vakhrameyev would shout some pleasantries at him across the street.

'Well, and how's God treating you? To the baths, eh? Good, good, wash off some mischief, wash on some goodness!'

Sazykin would be silent, his eyes black, his beard like pitch – a regular Pugachev.

And at the bathhouse they had their own 'Vakhrameyev entrance', and their own Vakhrameyev room all ready for them, filled with hot dry steam, and their own special soap from Kazan, and special silken besoms, made of young May birch. And there, throwing off her coat and shawl and dress, was Darya – satin smooth, opulent, pink, white, and round – emerging not out of sea foam, but out of hot clouds of bathhouse steam – a Russian Venus with a besom . . . And Vakhrameyev would grunt and shake his head and close his eyes . . .

Afterwards, as always, the dashing coachman Panteley would be waiting at the entrance – a button nose blue with the frost, teeth white as foam, a merry rogue's eye, hat at a rakish angle.

'Well, and a clean and steamy health to you! If you please!'

And then back home. The front apartments, with pictures, ancient silver wine-bowls, clocks and rarities of every kind under glass bells; intent blue windows shimmering with frost flowers; stairs; and then the squat, low bedchamber, the glinting haloes on the blessed icons, dark eyes with untold sorrow in their depths, and the double, down-filled feather-bed ...

And so life flows at an unhurried pace – and people stay rooted in their places all their lives like sturdy timber with roots deep in the earth. Days, evenings, nights, holidays, weekdays.

On weekdays Vakhrameyev goes first thing in the morning to his store in Merchants' Row. Teapots are brought in from the tavern, and well-browned rolls, and a five-pound jar of caviar from Sazykin's. In long-skirted frock coats, in fur greatcoats and bottle-shaped boots, with hair cut round like a cap, or straight across, in a manner handed down from father to son, the merchants play with millions around the tea-table, transfer wheat from Saratov to Petersburg, from Rostov to New York, and slyly, edging round and round about, try to bargain down an extra kopek from a friend, mopping their faces with checkered kerchiefs, swearing and making guarantees by all that's holy.

'This fellow won't believe himself unless he swears!' Vakhrameyev would quip about such guarantors, and they'd give in and keep their silence for a while. A quip in time is not the least of assets in trading.

But even at business Vakhrameyev does not forget about Darya. Every so often one of the lads from Vakhrameyev's shop will come with a bag of Crimean apples or nuts – walnuts from Greece, American filberts, cedar nuts, almonds.

'The master said to bring this to you.'

And a fiery ember of a gypsy eye will flash a spark at Dashenka, and she'll say thank you without lifting up her lashes. But later, forgetting the apple she has bitten into, she will stare long out of the window at the blue shadows of trees until the tight firm checkered silk will rustle on the high firm breast – a sigh.

Winter and winter without end. The snow makes everything seem soft: the houses with white hoary eyebrows over the windows; the round barking of dogs; the rosy smoke from chimneys in the sun; the shouting of boys, tobboganing somewhere far away. On holidays, when church-bells peal in all the forty churches, the pealing seems to carpet all the earth and sky with velvet. And one longs to run out in a sable coat and vari-coloured mittens across the smooth untrodden blue, so that each step will leave a mark for the rest of one's life; one longs to stand under the sorceress birch, all shaggy now with snow, and take a deep breath of the heady air, and let the cheeks grow pink with frost, or maybe with something else; the heart still feels so young, and there is something, surely there is something in the future – waiting, soon . . .

Lent. Ruts are turning yellow, as though filled with oil. Flocks of jackdaws are screaming in the sky, and it is no longer their winter cry. The ancient five-headed churches sing out in mournful unison as with a single bell. Tables are set with an-cient dishes, handed down from generation to generation: cab-bage soup with smelts, jellied oatmeal with honey water, pudding with pike, sturgeon roe in fish soup, bird-shaped rolls from the bakery with mustard sauce. Then comes Easter, sun-shine, the ringing of bells, as though the blood itself were ring-ing all day in the veins.

At Easter, as the custom is, the Vakhrameyev 'lads' come to the master's home with greetings, to exchange the three tra-ditional kisses with the master and the mistress. On their toes, their new boots creaking, their lips stretched out into an *o*, they come up one by one to touch their lips to Darya, as though she were the twelfth icon, and to receive from her hands the crim-son Easter egg with the golden letters *M. E.*

But suddenly one of them – or did it only seem? – one, beard-less, with gypsy eyes like embers, with dry lips, allows his trembling lips to rest on Darya's cheek for a mere smidgin of a second longer than the rest – as though Dashenka were not an icon to him, not an icon, but . . .

Is it his heart? No, not his heart but the Easter egg, red as his heart, slips out of his hands and rolls to someone's feet.

And Vakhrameyev's eyebrow goes up like a whip: 'Eh, butterfingers! Where's your head?'

A single night, and April broke out of its shell: the first dust, the first warmth. And just as in the winter-time the schoolboys know by the red flag on the fire tower that the frost is twenty degrees below and there will be no school, so now everybody knows that it is warm, for the trunk merchant Petrov has come out into the street with his wares. A variety of trunks with wrought and hammered fittings, gay with painted roses, are ranged before his doors. And I. S. Petrov himself is here, on a stool, with a newspaper, exposing his bald head to gather sunshine as a pail set out under a gutter gathers rainwater.

'What's new? What are they saying in the capital?'

And the trunk merchant – his spectacles astride his nose – looks over the spectacles and pronounces weightily: 'They've set up a leather dummy on Trubny Square in Moscow.'

'What kind of a dummy?'

'Oh, the kind you punch in the jaw, and it howls; the harder you punch, the harder it howls. For the encouragement of athletic strength, so to speak, and for testing. Yes.'

And so, for twenty years now, Merchants' Row has been learning from him about Moscow dummies, comets, wars – about everything going on out there, in far-off places to which the steamboats hurry, churning the water with their paddle-wheels.

Steamboats, clouds, months, days, birds – all of them going, flying. But here life seems to be anchored, swaying in a quiet harbour, and people are like sturdy timber with roots deep in the soil.

But the old folks say that once a year, when the new moon is being born in May and the night is dark – once a year even the trees, the flowers and grasses, all green souls are allowed to walk, just so that they return to their places by morning. And on their bare white feet filled with the sap of spring, with traces of the aromatic, rich earth still upon them, they wander off in a throng into the dark night, and then such things begin to happen that . . .

Hot. The days are yellow – heavy with the yellow ripeness of apples ready to drop if you but touch the tree, if you but look or blow. The lindens and the lilacs lean their breasts over the fence of Vakhrameyev's garden like those Russian beauties of Yaroslavl, Ryazan, Zamoskvorechye, who look out of their windows on sultry evenings, crushing their opulent bodies against the window-sills.

It is a week since all the merchants have gone off to the fair. In the wide apartments Darya is alone. A square of sunshine glides silently across the tile stove, breaks on the plinth, creeps over the waxed floor. In the wooden wall under the wallpaper something starts ticking softly – slower, slower, and dies out: as if the wood had suddenly acquired a heart. Darya is consumed with thirst; she takes another and another drink of iced *kvass*. Her lips are parched – can she be ailing? Or is it something else? Her dress seems to constrain her chest. In the evening she slips off her dress and falls to musing. Then she glides into the mirror – and quickly, quickly hurries to blow out the candle, to blow out her flaming cheeks.

In the morning an itinerant Kazan 'prince' came to her window – in a quilted fez, lop-eared, eyes needle-sharp, as though used to peeping into keyholes.

'Buy, lady, buy, fine silken shawls. Buy one, your sweetheart will love you more. Look, how fine!' he smacked his lips and held up the shawl before her. And leered, as though he had seen everything through the keyhole, as though he knew everything.

Darya dropped her eyes and scolded herself for it. She stepped out on the porch and angrily bought the first thing that came to hand – a lace handkerchief. Then she stood a while, following the 'prince' with her eyes, and looked up at a cloud that had separated, broken away from the flock. Once upon a time she had just such light and fluffy, innocent thoughts. She was already turning back when suddenly there was a rustling behind her at the garden fence, a creaking of the wooden side-walk, and a fiery gypsy eye looked out from around the corner.

'Darya Ivanovna . . .'

She stopped.

'Dasha' softly . . . 'Dashenka' in a whisper as dry as sand . . . 'Tonight – come to the garden . . . Will you come?'

. . . She stopped, to cut him short, to put an end at once to his impertinence. Yet God knows why the words did not come out, her tongue went limp. And so, silently, with her back to him, she heard him out to the end, and only the silk rustled tautly on her breast.

And at night she came out into the garden – on the dark May night when the new moon was being born, and all the trees, grasses, and flowers rustled, whispered, fluttered, their feet, full of the sap of spring, glowing whitely in the dark.

Then morning. The pink gold of the crosses over the blue cupolas, pink stones, windowpanes, fences, water. And everything is as it had been yesterday. Nothing has happened.

Vakhrameyev returned, gay as ever, full of jokes and banter, with a trunk full of presents. He opened the trunk before Darya. She took out the presents, looked at them, put them back, and sits without a smile.

'What is it, Darya? Did you swallow a fly with your *kvass* by chance?'

'Oh, nothing. I had a dream last night.'

But the dream came to pass. A day or two went by, when Vakhrameyev lay down after dinner for a nap, and never got up. It seems the cook had put a toadstool into his mushroom stew. That, it was given out, was what he died from. People said other things as well – but people will speak. One thing is known – he died as a Christian, and his last words to Darya were: 'Don't marry Sazykin. He palmed off dampened flour on me in Makarievo.'

That flour was Sazykin's undoing. It was not Sazykin the young Vakhrameyev widow married, but another – with the fiery gypsy eye. Rumour had it that Sazykin got himself blind drunk and ordered himself sewn into a bearskin. Then he went out into the yard to have the dogs – let off their chains – tear at him, so that he might not feel the pain tearing his heart. After that he took off for Siberia and was never heard of again.

Just so a stone dropped into sleepy waters will stir them up, send eddies running on the surface. The eddies spread, and nothing is left but gentle ripples, like the wrinkles in the corner of a smiling eye. And everything is still and smooth once more.

The eddies are gone – and once again life flows on, peaceful, quiet, like the muttering of the current against the bank. The abacus clicks on the counter and nimble hands roll the bolts of cloth, measuring out yard after yard. Leaning on a painted trunk with his newspaper, the trunk merchant I. S. Petrov bakes his pumpkin-bald head like a pumpkin in the sun. All in white the waiters bustle in the taverns, their embroidered towels and tasselled belts flying behind them like steam behind a locomotive. In his cubbyhole the signmaker Akimych, a steady customer at the tavern, hastily paints hams and sausages on a signboard, so that he may, at the usual hour, sit down with a decanter in his usual corner and weep for his wasted life.

And in the evening all the bells will swing in unison in the blue arches of forty bell-towers, and the brass velvet will spread over the city, the groves, the water, the fields, the pilgrims on the roads, the rich men and the drunkards, over the sin of humans and the innocence of grass – and everything will grow soft and quiet, will settle down like summer dust under the evening dew.

[*1923*]

A STORY ABOUT THE
MOST IMPORTANT THING

The world: a lilac bush – immense, eternal, boundless. In this world – I: a yellow and pink worm, *Rhopalocera*, with a horn on my tail. Tomorrow I must die into a chrysalis. My body is torn with pain, arched as a bridge – taut, quivering. And if I could scream – if I could! – everyone would hear. I am mute.

Another world: a river, mirror-smooth; a lacy, transparent bridge, made of iron and blue sky, with a tautly arched back; shots; clouds. On that side of the bridge are the Orlovka peasants, Soviet men in clay-coloured shirts; on this side is the enemy – the varicoloured peasants of Kelbuy. And this is I – both of Orlovka and Kelbuy; I shoot at myself; breathlessly I run across the bridge; I fall from the bridge – my arms spread out like wings – I scream . . .

And yet another world – far above the Earth, above the lilacs, oceans, *Rhopalocera,* clouds and shots. Above the Earth, rushing to meet it out of infinity, a still invisible, dark star. There, on the star, a faint red light illumines the ruins of walls, galleries, machines, and three frozen bodies – huddled close; my naked body. And the most important thing is to go faster, faster, to crash thundering into the earth, so that all this will burn up to dust, along with me, and burn to dust all the machines and walls on Earth. And then in scarlet flames – new fiery I's. And afterwards, in the white mist, still other, flowerlike new selves bound by slender stems to the new Earth. And when these human flowers ripen –

Over the Earth the clouds are like thoughts. Some – floating high, bright, joyous, pink like a young girl's summer dress; others – low, heavy, lumbering, cast-iron blue. Their shadow, like a quick dark wing, glides over the water, over the clay shirts, the faces, leaves. In the shadow, the *Rhopalocera* is tossing still more desperately, its head swaying right, left. In the shadow, the shots come thicker: without the dazzling sun it is easier to aim.

The worlds have crossed, and the worm *Rhopalocera* entered the world of Kukoverov, Talya, my world and yours. This happened on Whit Monday, 25 May, in the Kellbuy wood. In the wood there is a clearing, filled to the brim with the strongest, green, leaf-filtered sunny sap. In the middle of the clearing stands an enormous lilac bush, its branches bowed under the weight of flowers. Under the bush, sunk to its waist into the earth, a stone idol smiles its yellow, thousand-year-old smile. In a few moments five Kelbuy peasants will come to Kukoverov, to tell him when they will begin: the day after tomorrow, tomorrow, or perhaps even today. But there are still five minutes left to Talya and Kukoverov alone together here.

Kukoverov has no matches, and he catches sunlight with a magnifying glass – to light his cigarette. The hoary, curly ash silently grows on the cigarette; and Kukoverov's hair is like the ash, and under the ash . . .

It is intolerable to look at those curves in the corners of Talya's lips, and Kukoverov looks at the stone idol. But there are lips here, too, a smile, millennia. And he turns to Talya again: 'Once upon a time they smeared those lips with human blood. On a day like this.'

'Don't you all do it now?'

'Yes. But not only with the blood of others – with our own blood too. And, you know, perhaps . . .'

And to himself, very quietly: perhaps it will happen tomorrow, or the day after, and he must hurry and seize the sky – as much as he can hold – and this lilac bush, and the bee, burrowing into the flowers with its feet, and – and one more thing . . .

His fingers tremble lightly (one finger is yellow from tobacco), the grey, curly ash drops from his cigarette.

'You are eighteen, Talya, and I . . . It may be funny that I . . . after all, I know you only a week. However . . . Did it ever occur to you that the earth is turning a hundred times faster today, and every hour – everything – is a hundred times . . . and this is the only reason why no one seems to notice it? And so, you see, it may take only a day, or even a minute . . . Yes, a minute may be enough for you to know suddenly that somebody . . . that you . . .'

Dense lilac branches, bent under the weight of flowers. Under them, shadows, sun-embroidered here and there. In the shadows – Talya. Her thick lashes, bowed by the weight of unknown flowers.

Kukoverov no longer has any words, and for some reason he must bend a lilac branch, he must break it. The branch quivers – and the silken-yellow *Rhopalocera* falls straight down into Talya's lap, into the warm hollow of her sun-warmed, body-warmed dress. There it coils into an agonizingly tight ring – and if one could, if one could only cry out that tomorrow one must die!

Kukoverov is silent.

Talya: 'Yes? Go on! Yes?'

Lashes weighted down by the weight of flowers; a single tiny point in the corner of her lips. Kukoverov has no matches. He lights a cigarette with the magnifying glass, his fingers tremble, the point of concentrated sunlight trembles, intolerable to the eyes. And – yes, this is exactly it: the corner of her lips. As through a magnifying glass, it has gathered all of her, all that is young and feminine in her, all that . . .

'Shall I go on? You want me to go on, to say . . .?'

It is not Kukoverov's voice, it is dark, it comes from somewhere beneath . . . Talya raises her lashes, and catches unawares – his face, his blue wide-open eyes that seem to be saying everything aloud, the prison-furrowed wrinkles, the hair like ash, the tobacco-stained finger.

This lasts an instant. And Talya is back in the shadow of her lashes, of the lilacs. She bends lower and lower, and lightly strokes the back of the *Rhopalocera,* and utters a single word, inaudibly.

But it seems to Kukoverov that he has heard it, and his heart thumps painfully, as though it were not a heart, but a living child. And when he loudly breathes in the wood, the sky, the bee, the sun: 'How good ... after all!' Talya knows that he understood, and her heart, too, is like a living child.

And she speaks to Kukoverov, just above her, because it is impossible to be silent now: 'I've always ... When I was little, I used to raise them into butterflies. One hatched in winter, at Christmastime, the windows were covered with ice, it flew and flew ...'

Kukoverov – quietly: 'I also ...'

But what he 'also' did will never be said: five men are coming with bearlike gait, stepping heavily on bare heels, towards the stone idol, the god that had been nurtured on human blood. Talya quickly gets up from the shadows and walks away across the sunlight in her white, just faintly rosy dress, taking with her, somewhere deep within herself, the imprint of Kukoverov's eyes and, on her palm, the *Rhopalocera* that must die tomorrow.

Five peasants – one of them tall as a pine, as a wood goblin, head high as though atop a pole – tumble in all at once upon the still wide-open Kukoverov, and, in reply to his question, 'Well, fellows, what have you decided?' answer in chorus: 'Everything's ready! Our chairman, Filimoshka, is already under lock and key. Enough, the Soviet fellows have had their fun!'

The fuse is lit, and the spark is running towards the powder keg: the fuse may last hours, or days, but every minute brings the spark nearer – and soon, soon it will roar with flame and smoke and pieces of human hearts, my heart.

The same Whit Monday, in the city, with its white, never settling dust, its stones, tin-coloured clouds, red iron signs with golden letters, and iron men. There, on the outskirts, on a humpbacked street hens peck at the coarse grass that smells of radish – rumpled hens, as louse-ridden as the people. And there, tucked in behind the once-blue shutters, are sprays of birch-twigs. They were put there yesterday, before mass, by Dorda's mother, in celebration of Pentecost. From her antique silk headkerchief, her mushroomlike old woman's smell, from the birch-leaves curled in the sun, something flutters inside Dorda for a second, like a sun-scorched birch-leaf in the wind. But only for a second,

He takes out his revolver from the holster, and he himself is a revolver, in a black leather or perhaps even metal holster, with cold, loaded eyes. He says to his mother, loading his cartridge clip: 'So you've been to church again? Eh, you old woman! And she keeps saying, "I understand everything, I – I . . ." '

'Why, darling, Christ had all the working people with him – the shepherds, the magi, the angels. Sure. You can't say nothing against that.'

'How's this – working . . . angels?'

Sometimes the water suddenly bursts through the iron flanges of a pipe, sprays out upward and around, and the children dance. So now laughter burst out of Dorda, and the cartridge cannot find the clip. But grown-ups hurry over to chase away the children and plug up the water. And now Dorda is back in his holster – leather, or maybe metal; the cartridge clicks and slips into place.

The mother, angrily: 'What's all this? Loading up of a sudden, and on a holiday? Where to?'

'Oh, the peasants are kicking up in Kelbuy, that's where. They've had their fun. Enough now!'

Under the kerchief – wrinkles. The brown lips are stirring faintly, like birch-bark in fire, but nothing may be said aloud, and only the flap of the jacket is lifted up, to wipe the nose and eyes. And the eyes – the mother's eyes – try to remember all of him, to fill themselves with his dark, close-cropped head, that vein on his temple – so that on the day when they bring him . . .

His lips are tightly shut (always, nowadays), the entrance is bricked up and whitewashed – a wall. Then suddenly the mouth opens strangely, not where it seemed to be, but much higher – his upper lip is very short. And words: 'You'd better get me something for the road, instead of . . .'

Bowed over, she shuffles; her worn-down shoes rustle lightly. In the silence I hear . . . you know that funny human sound – with the nose – when nothing must be seen, when tears must be swallowed?

And, perhaps, Kukoverov is right – perhaps everything now rushes a hundred times faster. A minute, no longer, and Dorda is lying in a trench. In the trench there is moist clay. There is a small hollow under Dorda's elbow. His loaded eyes look through binoculars at the bridge, at the Kelbuy huts (their shutters are also blue). In the blue air – *whee-a-ow* – a whistling, a singing, a fall – a dying down – plop: a bullet. Lower and lower in the blue sky – a hawk, and now you can see: on the armless shoulders, the small head with its sharp eyes turns right, left. The eyes are aimed at Dorda, at the Orlovka peasants – some angry, some good-humoured, shaggy as bumble-bees – meat. One of them lies just beyond the trench. A moment ago he was I, and now he's simply meat, and thoroughbred, green flies crawl over his hand, his eyes, suck at the corner of his lips.

Near Dorda a pockmarked fellow, flat on his stomach in the clay, grumbles, good-humouredly clicking his bolt: 'What kind of a war is this? In wartime, I recall, it would come whacking down – your head would fly to Kostroma, your guts to Novgorod ... try and collect 'em ... That was something! Calling this a war!'

His clay-coloured shirt is buttoned wrong – one buttonhole was skipped and the gap reveals a yellow chest, covered with bumble-bee fur. And perhaps it is he, or perhaps somebody else like him, who speaks, slowly chewing black bread: 'Last year I bartered two roosters for a pound of nails – that was something! Comrade Dorda, a piece of bread?'

But Dorda does not hear: he is down on his knees, listening to his heart. One, two, three, like the chimes of a clock at night, when you cannot sleep. From somewhere: 'Christ had all the working people with him – shepherds, magi, angels ...' A black silk headkerchief. And Dorda commands harshly, like a revolver shot: 'Now – across the bridge! Singly! Run! Go!'

In the blue air – *whee-a-ow* – and the hawk. I – every I – know: this is for me – the hawk, the flies. The body arches into an agonizingly taut ring. And then, instead of I, we – and all of us bent on a single thing, the most important, the only thing in life: to get across the bridge, to break, to crush the others – sweep them off the road, off the earth – so they won't hinder ... What? Why, happiness, of course.

Somewhere above, in the hawk-soaring heights, between

heaven and earth, there is a bridge to happiness, boards and railings, Dorda, clay shirts. Through the iron lace – flying pieces of blue, of yellow straw roofs, grey ripples below. And the last thought: if you fall from here – it's high, a long, an endless flight.

Dorda does not yet know, he will not know for another two, three minutes whether he will fall or not. But on the dark star they know already: today is the last.

There it is night. On the Earth it's day, but there, on the star, it is night. In the black sky – two enormous, greenish-icy moons over rocks and deserts, serrated blue shadows from the rocks. Millennial silence. The moon climbs higher. And now the glass of galleries, walls, stairways, cupolas, reception halls glints dimly below – all of it greenish, translucent, made of the frozen light of two moons. Silence.

The moonlight grows brighter, and just as in a dream, when everything appears at once – carved out, momentary, clear – as in a dream – the four. Near the column, a man – no, a woman . . . Tall, motionless, waiting as marble waits. The stone slab has just been raised, the chain still sways over the hatch, and two lie on the floor, their fingers grasping the edge of the hatch so tightly that the nails have grown white. And at the side there stands a boy – deep, blind hollows where the eyes should be, a listening head – bent sideways, birdlike.

And through clenched teeth – a hard whisper, but every word comes clearly – as in a dream, when I live within, in everyone.

A whisper from the column (the woman, tall, knit brows, a deep cleft between them): 'Well – do you believe me now?'

A whisper over the hatch (two – a man and another woman, their lips trembling): 'Yes . . .' Louder, despairingly. 'No! The last? No!'

The last bottle of air. Here, on the star, there has been no air for a long time. It has been kept – like the most precious blue wine – in glass bottles for centuries. And now – the last bottle. And the last four – a tribe, a nation, a people.

One, tall – she is now standing near the column, and her

brows are tightly knit with pain – was once the mother of all three. When was it – a hundred, or a thousand circles back? It does not matter. This is the final circle, and the man is no longer her son; he is her husband. And the other woman is not her daughter; she is another woman.

The icy light is brighter, and there is only one thing now in the whole world: the raised arm, and the faintly glinting bluish bottle, pressed so hard by the fingers that the nails have turned white ... Not a single drop must be spilled. Every drop is a minute of my life. I am a man, I am strong, I will live. Stretching his neck, the boy feels about in the emptiness, stumbles, clutches at my hand ... Away, cripple!

But there, by the column, the brows are knit. One flash of the eyes – like a whip – and a man, his own eyes hiding under his brow, gives the blind one a sip. Then the three: with closed lids, heads tilted back, they drink, absorb, breathe. And the marble flushes rosy, the hearts ring out – to live! to live!

They are without clothing – like statues. When the younger woman drinks, you see the molten copper hair under her arm. Perhaps by accident the man's shoulder touches hers. No, it is not by accident. It has happened before. But now, when nothing matters and there is nothing more to fear – now he presses closer, still closer – and a smile passes from body to body; the shoulders smile, the knees, the thighs, breasts, lips, and there is no tomorrow, there is nothing – only now.

The older one, the Mother, looks on. The cleft between her eyes grows darker, deeper. She comes to him and presses his face, her husband's, between her palms. She forces herself into his eyes – down the slippery stairs, to the very bottom. There, on the bottom, she sees ...

Let them: but for one last time she will drink in this face, press it so hard that the pink flesh will bear the white marks of her fingers. And then her words – ordinary, simple, but each one must be torn out with the quick: 'I ... I will remain here. You two will bring some water. Go.'

They are gone. She stands by the column, alone, made of marble, the marble whiteness rising from her feet higher and higher. With closed eyes she sees what is taking place below, where the well is. There the bowls have been put down on the ground. The man's hand touches the slightly wiry copper hair of the woman, slips down her breast, her knees. One knee has a tiny white scar: do you remember? You fell, it bled . . . Do you want to – now?

Moonlit noon. Heavy, icy slabs of light. The boy with bird-like, motionless, blind eyes looks up, calls to the Mother: 'Water!' But she does not hear, because the door has opened, and those two come in. The woman's lips are moist; on one knee there is a white scar, and above it, on the thigh – a scarlet smear: the trace of blood. They are without clothing, like statues. Everything is naked, simple, final.

Taking the blind one by the hand, the Mother steps forward slowly to meet them, slow, marble white, like fate: 'Now, it is time. Follow me, do not fall back.'

'Where?'

'I know. There, in the lowest chambers, we shall still find a little, to breathe. And there . . .'

'What is there?'

She is silent. Clouds pass over her face: lowering clouds – in her last smile.

And – below, on Earth, where it is day now, where the clouds are heavy, metal-blue, and airy, flushing red, where spring rain slants across like flying sails, and then there is sun again – a thousand suns on blades of grass bent under sunny drops. If Kukoverov is right, and everything moves a hundred times faster, then this is the same endless, whirlwind-rushing day, and it is also weeks ago. There are still weeks of life for him who now lies as meat for the hawk on the yellow clay, and the *Rhopalocera* does not yet know that it must die tomorrow into a black chrysalis, and Dorda does not know, and the Kelbuy peasants have not yet arrested Filimoshka, and he is still just Filimoshka the pauper, and not the village chairman Filimon Yegorych.

A hut, rags stuffed in the holes of the windows – and black holes of broken teeth in Filimoshka's mouth. He puffs on a cigarette, leaning on the door jamb, waiting. On the road Fili-moshka's woman is coming home, stirring up the dust with her bare feet. In her arms there is a child – she borrowed one from a neighbour: when she has a child in her arms, Filimoshka does not beat her. But today he is different, today he would not beat her anyway.

'Come, woman, quick, you're going to the meeting with me. A paper came from town – it says the women should come too. Today, brother, it's strict!'

Before the porch of the meeting-house: backs, shirts blown out in the wind like bladders, necks tanned and toughened by the sun, a din and a racket. And suddenly – Heavenly Father! – Filimoshka steps out on the porch. Where to? What do you want?

'Comrades, quiet! Nowadays it's strict. No use wasting time – elect a secretary.'

Over the backs, over the heads, a mottled head seems raised up on a pole above the others – the same goblin-tall peasant, with a goblin's voice: 'You mean, we've got to buy a cart to fit the wheel? And what about a chairman, don't we need one?'

And Filimoshka: 'I'm chairman!' Chest out, one foot forward, big shot.

'And why you, if you don't mind telling?'

'Because the paper says: the poorest. And who's poorer than me? Come on, speak up! Well?'

The head on the pole turns this way and that. Hands scratching heads. According to the paper, it really seems to work out that way; no one's poorer than Filimoshka.

And so Filimoshka is chairman Filimon Yegorych. Now he is no longer living in his hut, but in the miller's house with Dutch tile stoves. He's got all of Kelbuy right here, in his fist – and he's squeezing the juices out of it: for his broken teeth, for all the holes, for thirty hungry years, for everything at once.

Slanting sails of rains, clouds, sun, nights, days – or only an hour, a second. And Whit Monday: on the threshold, in her headkerchief, her hand bent like a visor, Dorda's mother follows him with her eyes. And in Kelbuy, in the meeting-house, Filimoshka sits tied up under lock and key. Tow-headed kids are clustered round the window, their noses glued to the glass. At the door a shaggy peasant stands, planted firmly, with a gun.

A STORY ABOUT THE MOST IMPORTANT THING

The fuse is lit, the spark runs to the powder keg, and it seems to Kukoverov that he himself is filled with powder. It is both terrifying and good. Only everything must be hurried, faster, faster, to squeeze years into hours, to get everything done . . .

On the men's backs the shirts are blown up by the wind like bladders. Kukoverov, with his face towards me, towards you, is speaking from the porch, hair – faintly curling ash, and words . . . But what are words? If your heart had come alive today and thumped, like a living child – you strike the heart like a bell, and the response hums within everyone, and you've created everything: all these shaggy faces with child-like eyes, and the lilac branch over the fence etched in the sky, and the cloud of molten lead with the delicate pink edge like a girl's dress, and the restless, troubled swallows breasting the cloud.

Through all this, from afar – as though he were in a bell-tower, and the heads, arms, necks were far below – Kukoverov hears: 'Right! They've been pushing us around long enough! We've had it – we aren't kids!'

The sun is sinking behind the hill. In the doorways thin jets of milk spurt ringing against the tin walls of the pails; the cows kick over the pails – and this seems to be the end of everything. The women raise a howl; warm tears, warm milk. And on the porch of the meeting-house – a shaggy buzzing: Berdan rifles, double-barrelled bear hunters' guns dug up from their hiding-places pass from hand to hand. Like a tow-headed urchin pulling a wooden horse on wheels and looking back at it every second, as though he cannot get enough of it, the goblin-tall peasant pulls a machine-gun by a cord behind him through the dust. And in reply to admiring exclamations – 'Look at Fedka! Where'd you get that?' – he winks slyly: 'Oh, back in 'seventeen – from some soldiers. Got an army coat for two *poods* of grain, and this thing as a bonus . . .'

At twilight, when everything is made of glass, and bats are flinging themselves criss-cross silently over the street, Kukoverov enters the small garden. The lilac leaves are nearly black now, and Talya's dress, so white it almost hurts. Her face cannot be seen, she is bending down: 'Do you want to see? I brought him here from the woods . . . no, he's here, lower.'

185

'He' is the *Rhopalocera*, a shrivelled, motionless world, ready to die tomorrow. And because of this tomorrow, because of what had happened that morning in the woods, because of the faint tremor of Talya's voice, Kukoverov's heart is suddenly so wide open that he cannot breathe. And – foolishly, absurdly! – tears come to his eyes. He bends down silently, and a cool, dewy spray of lilacs brushes his cheek.

Later Kukoverov sits next to Talya in the hut, by the window. Through the window the cloud comes nearer and nearer, the swallows dart into the cloud. On the table there is a samovar. There is a smell of currant tea. The mistress of the house, Baranikha, is at the door – about to leave. And it is perhaps a little frightening that she will leave, and then they will remain alone. Perhaps to postpone it, Talya says: 'No, wait, tell us again how Filimoshka . . . that time, you know? . . .'

'Oh, you little sweetheart! You still remember, eh? Well, sure: he came to take the chickens – and it just came over me! "You so and so," I say, "may the holy Mother of God . . ." and so on and so forth. And he took offence: "I deprive you," he says, "of your voice for three days. Don't you dare to raise a peep for the next three days!" And what do you think? I went around for three days like a dumb one – that's the kind of son of a bitch he is! Well, drink your tea, God bless you, drink your tea . . .'

She slammed the door – and now there are only two of them, and they may no longer laugh; everything is now made of the thinnest glass, and even a single word . . . Somewhere in the street, thousands of miles away, a voice shouts – 'Va-si-ley! Va-si-ley!' And everything becomes even more glasslike, and both know that in a moment . . .

Talya: 'Your cigarette . . . You never . . . have matches . . . Do you want me to . . .'

But she cannot get up to go for the matches, and remains seated. And this seems to be the very last drop, are filled to the brim – it is impossible to bear it any longer. Swallowing air in gulps, Kukoverov takes her face into his palms. The world whirls slowly, blissfully, swaying a little. It will forever bear the imprint of a girl's lips, cool, like a spray of lilacs at dusk.

And immediately – a knocking at the window, a nose flattened against the glass.

'Hey, Ivanych, Kukoverov, you there?'

And when the window is opened, a voice is heard, with a trace of a merry shiver: 'Oh, brother, the fun is on: the Soviet fellows are coming over. Let's go.'

A bridge of blue sky and steel: *whee-a-oww*. Again. *T-ch-k* – into iron, and softly – into flesh. A man sinks like a sack onto the low railing of the bridge, the others rush past. The man cries out with his eyes: 'This is I, it's I!' They rush past him. Unhurriedly, the man keels over, and drops, head down. It's a long flight. Perhaps, still, somehow . . . Perhaps if he will only spread his arms this way, like wings . . .

Splash, a spray of drops, a rainbow for a second.

And Dorda: 'This is not I, it's not yet I. Faster!'

But the bridge lasts a lifetime – fifty years, compressed into terribly taut seconds. And from across, from the Kelbuy side – the chittering of a machine-gun. To stop on the bridge now is as impossible as stopping a hundred-verst train at top speed. Yet Dorda stops. He says to himself with rage: 'Oh, you! So that's how it is? "This is not I . . ." Scum!' He stops himself in mid-motion and stands with clenched teeth. The others rush past. *T-ch-k!* Again. Over there, that pockmarked peasant, breathless, with gasping mouth. Is he yelling something? Yes, he is yelling to Dorda: 'Hey, there! Did it smack you? No?'

A sweaty, pockmarked, shaggy smile. Charged with it, Dorda runs, and for some reason the pockmarked man reminds him of his mother: with her hand bent like a visor over her eyes, on the threshold (for a moment). Then nothing but pieces of blue flying by – the sky through the railing of the bridge. He had seen this before – sky and bars . . . when? And for a second – just as he had seen his mother – he sees clearly: a prison cell, an arch, a window. Dorda on a stool stands by the window with another – the other's head is grey like ash – and this makes Dorda still more . . .

A roaring, 'Hurrah!' The end of the bridge, everything disappears as from a screen when the light goes on – and only the

187

most important thing remains: to crush, to bend, to break those others. A log across the road. Over the log – Hurrah! A clay shirt prone, like a log, with arms going up, absurdly slowly, to the head, to cover it – jump over it, hurrah! – and down the gravel embankment – like hail, like battering rams, like logs, like a rushing storm . . .

Below, the storm suddenly dies down. Under the burning bush, under the lilacs, everyone drops down in the shadow without a single word of command. Dorda remains standing a moment longer, still taut as a spring, with loaded eyes – another second, and they'll shoot bullets at those who lay down without command.

At his very feet the pockmarked fellow is mopping his forehead with the edge of his clay-coloured sleeve held with two fingers; looking up with a sly, pockmarked smile. 'Two roosters for a pound of nails.' That's set, an article of faith, and nothing's to be done about it. Dorda breaks off a spray of dewy lilac and quickly bites off the bitter bloom, revolver in hand. The pockmarked peasant says to Dorda from below: 'Maybe we ought to go and have a talk with them? No point in shooting for nothing. They're Christians, after all. Eh, Comrade Dorda?'

'All right. It's all the same. Go, then, the two of you. Wait.'

Dorda writes something quickly in his notepad: the letters are straight, tall, sharp. The pockmarked peasant takes a handkerchief (once white) from his trouser pocket. A piece of bread is wrapped in it. He spills the crumbs into his palm and throws the handful into his mouth; the bread he puts back into his pocket. Then he ties the handkerchief to his bayonet, blowing away an insistent fly with his lower lip. On the sheet of paper from the pad the letters are already lined up in a row: 'Surrender arms immediately. Free the prisoners. Turn over the instigators – not less than five. Signed: Dorda.'

And now the two set out; over the shrubs the kerchief, once white, flutters. High above, the kite hangs darkly in the blue, head turning in his armless shoulders. And higher yet, the still invisible dark star over the Earth.

There, through the bluish ice of glass, motionless figures may be seen, as at the bottom of the sea: here and there solitary ones on the stairs, as though stopped suddenly in mid-motion; elsewhere clusters of tightly embracing bodies, likes sheaves. Sleeping. Perhaps sleeping. Who knows?

And four, walking alone empty, echoing, bare halls. In front — she, tall, upright, marble, and the boy with the listening head, cocked sideways, in the manner of a bird; he shivers and clings to her thigh. The icy-blue vaults of the ceilings are ever lower, heavier. She walks without stopping. Now, in mid-stride, she glanced back over her shoulder, and I can see: her brows are darkly, tightly knit. She alone knows what the other three do not know; she has lived long, she always knows — and she has decided. What her decision is is still unclear, it is like the distant smell of burning, like the black hole of the gun barrel sensed by the beast. And yet it is inescapable, it comes nearer and nearer with every step.

Stairs leading down. On the stairs someone lies prone, his right hand flung out palm upward, as though he had been running. Is he asleep? O silent, springy feet, like an animal, the man steals up . . . pounces — grasps the sleeper by the waist, lifts him up, and lets him go at once. The body rolls down the stairs, the palm swings up and drops with a wooden sound, again and again. This body is cold, it is different from me and can do nothing to me. I am a man, I know it; yet for some reason I must quickly have the living shoulder next to mine — hers — young, warm, just recently mine. Then the trembling stops and I can open the door, I open it, I – a man.

Behind the door – the glitter of wheels, of spokes: machines – round, many-legged, angular like spiders – the dead bodies of machines. And just as motionless and cold, human bodies, clutching one another, one upon another in a spasm, like a man and a woman. In their hands, knives, cooling in the icy light.

'I won't go any further – we do not want to, we will not go!'

But she, the tall one, walking ahead, she who a thousand circles ago was Mother, goes on without stopping, and I, the man, obediently follow her. Men, machines, mute hordes of books, painted images on walls – faces, gold, red – millennia rush through me with a silent, deafening roar – and I have no more power.

Evening. Huge moons are bowing low over the ground, the shadows are long. Four bodies crushed by the last, stony sleep. Hours, minutes – it makes no difference.

And then a movement. The younger woman rises slightly on her elbow, her face turned this way, towards me, towards you. Her eyes are green, they glow in the dusk like water slashed by an oar – and the dense icy rays are like water. She puts her hand on the man's breast; he starts, answers her eyes, 'Yes, in a moment,' and crawls away somewhere on all fours. Suddenly he halts and draws his head into his shoulders like a turtle. No, it only seemed to him . . . The Mother is fast asleep. There!

He returns. The bottle is raised, gleaming, before the green eyes of the woman. Two tilted heads. They drink, their bodies glow pink. The woman's breasts are warm, sharp, and sweet, she is fragrant, she whispers to me. And with all my tense muscles, with my skin, lips, body I know that this is so, it is just: I must live, I and she, and there is still air at the bottom of the bottle. It is for me and for her, and for no one else – no one else must live.

To take the knife . . . But it is tightly clutched in someone's fingers, and the fingers are ice cold. The man's hand recoils. His upper lip, with the barely noticeable hollow over it, quivers. He glances back and sees: the green eyes watch intently his every movement. Closing his eyes, with shivers running through him, he pulls away the knife from the dead fingers and crawls with it – years, a lifetime.

A long, birdlike neck bent to one side. The blind one sleeps face down, his nose pressed into his palm. It must be aimed here, to the right, where the vein bulges like a tiny column. The man's hand is raised. In his hand – the knife blade, chilly in the icy light. And in a moment, on the dark star, for the thousandth, the billionth, the last time, somebody's blood will be spilled for the sake of . . .

Over the Earth the sun is tossing in its last anguish, the clouds swell and thicken with blood, scarlet rivulets stream down the gilded spires and white walls, drip down the mirrorlike windowpanes of palaces. And red drops scatter here, too, on the green Maytime meadow grasses.

The meadow before Kelbuy. Over the meadow rise the gloomy frames of barns, with narrow loophole windows under the eaves. These are towers and battlements – it is an ancient fortress town. Just yesterday, just the day before yesterday, the native tribes of old had built such outposts in the green steppe to meet Prince Oleg's banded troops, to shower them with arrows from the battlements, to pour down pitch.

And here is the ancient council: a shaggy circle, axes, rifles, somebody's head raised high as though on a pole over the rest. And Kukoverov's head – like faintly curling ash. Before Kukoverov stand two from over there, from the Soviet side: one grey, an everyman, one of thousands, an ant; the other, with a ruddy, pockmarked grin, a white rag on his bayonet, a message. And Kukoverov has to read the signature once more, and still once more – and turn it so, towards the light.

'Dorda? Dorda ... Wait, what does he look like?' Wrinkles run over Kukoverov's face, clouds – dark, light.

'He? Oh ... well, he's smallish, kind of like a peg. But his eyes ... Oho!'

'Shaved? But, of course, it's he!' and for a short taut second Kukoverov sees: a blue patch of sky through a grating, a stool by the window, and on the stool ...

Over the barn, turning its head on armless shoulders, the hawk comes lower, lower. Below, on the grass sprayed by red dew, there lies a man, one who just recently had been a man. Now he lies prone, as though he had fallen while running; his right hand is flung out, palm upward, with yellow calluses. And next to him – I, of Orlovka, pockmarked, with a kerchief on my bayonet; and I, of Kelbuy, with a machine-gun and a head as though on a pole. Both of us look at our dead self – down there, in the grass.

'Come on, you pockmarked devil, rub your eyes, take a good look: a fine job, eh? The fellow left three kids behind him, and a wife with a belly. Sons of bitches!'

'And you, there, with your machine-gun – you're not a son of a bitch? How many of our men did you cut down on the bridge? Who's talking! You'd do better to keep your mouth shut! At least, we're fighting for our government, and you? Who are you fighting for?'

'Go-vern-ment! You ought to get your nose poked in our Filimoshka – like a cat in shit . . . Then you'd . . .'

'Go on, just try and poke! I'll give you such a poke, brother!' The bayonet with the white kerchief is levelled, ready; eyes bristle round the circle. With angry buzzing the circle closes in, the axes gleam. The ancients had a custom: they bent two trees and tied one foot to each, head down, then they let go . . .

In Kukoverov's hands the cigarette trembles, Dorda's letter trembles . . . shaved, yes, yes, of course. Well, so we shall meet again, we'll talk about old times, how we had . . .

For some reason he takes out his watch. Without looking, he begins to wind it, tighter, tighter – now! – the spring snaps, the hands whirl madly, ever faster – or perhaps this is happening inside, in Kukoverov?

When the watch stops, he puts it back into his pocket, rises, gathers up all eyes as in a fist, and tightens the reins. He speaks: 'Well, then – this letter. We're asked to surrender, to give up five men, the ringleaders, and all our arms, and to free our prisoner. That's it. It's your decision.'

The circle, the ancient council. In the centre, on the grass – the prone body. The green flies hum. Silence. Then a voice, from behind the backs: 'The fellows kept saying – we've got a machine-gun, a machine-gun. But look at them – they've swung across the bridge without a by-your-leave. They did, all right. If that's how it goes . . .'

The rest are silent. Kukoverov tightens the reins: 'It's up to you. Who has the keys to the meeting-house? You, Sidor? All right, then, go ahead, let Filimoshka out, bring him here. And tell him . . .'

The tempers rise: 'Filimoshka? Oh, no! The devil! We'll kick them all the way to hell! Have Filimoshka over us again? Oh, no!'

Kukoverov suddenly feels tired, he must sit down. He sits down and tears up the letter. The pockmarked fellow pulls off his pancake-cap, blows his nose into it and clamps it on again, hard, down to his ears: 'So-o, that's how it is. Well, then, good-bye to you. Too bad, though. Whatever way you look at it, we're still, all of us, Christians . . .'

From the fort the two walk slowly away across the ancient steppe. One of them – everyman, one of thousands, an ant. The other, with a pockmarked face, a white rag on his bayonet. The hawk hangs low: you can see its head turning right, left on armless shoulders. Through field-glasses, with loaded eyes, Dorda watches them come.

And when the messengers already feel the damp, the smell of lilacs and tobacco from the bushes, an almost silent shot comes from the barn, from the Kelbuy side. The pockmarked peasant doubles over and dashes, looping, rabbit-like, into the shrubbery. The other, the grey one, the one of thousands, the ant, sways a little and topples over, flat on his back – and no one now will ever know what his name had been.

Dorda jumps up. Perhaps he waited for this, even wanted it. He jumps up, all of him loaded like a revolver, eyes shooting bullets – at one, at another, at each of the grey everymen, men of thousands.

'Well? Have you seen? Maybe you want to send more men for talks?'

Someone's shaggy grunt. Silence. So a felled tree grunts as it drops – catches at something with gnarled paws, a moment of silence – then a crash. Shouts, fists, teeth, beards, oaths – in a single burst. The hundred-headed bear roars, crashing through the shrubbery, mouths are open wide, but no one hears, blood on the grass, but it makes no difference: over stones, over logs, over men, over oneself. Only to run, to reach the goal, and there, in twos, in threes, embracing tightly – like man and woman – just as it happened somewhere before . . .

Circling, with a long bird-cry, the sun is falling – and it will rise again only tomorrow, or perhaps it will not rise at all. On the porch of the meeting-house Dorda stands firmly as though bolted to the ground, in a leather or maybe even a metal holster. The revolver is held so tightly in the hand that the nails have turned white. Next to him is Filimoshka, chest out, one

foot forward – big shot. And Kukoverov – in the midst of bay-
onets, hatless, a quiver running through his cigarette, his smile.
From behind the fence across the street – a faint fragrance of
lilacs.

'Put this one under guard, until dawn . . .' Dorda looks somewhere above the hair, grey as ash, and curling faintly like ash.
'And these five – now.'

And these five – in the meadow, near the gloomy, ancient
towers. Red gashes in the green sky, the bridge arched tautly in
a spasm, mist over the river – for the last time. Just overhead
the bats dart silently, criss-cross. And five dark backs, forever
etched in the glass sky, five heads – one raised above the others,
as on a pole.

'Hey you, long noodle! Get down on your knees. The others
will get it in the head, and you – in the ass? It won't be right.'

This is said by the pockmarked peasant in the clay-coloured
shirt. He says it simply, with good humour. There, in front, the
long one drops down to his knees. Five dark figures etched into
the green immobile sky . . .

From the hand raised with the knife a blue, cast-iron shadow
falls on the neck, the back of the blind one. Perhaps he senses
the cold of the shadow. He starts, raises himself on folded legs,
sits up with his back to me, to you, his head just slightly to the
side, birdlike. He feels around him – where is Mother? In a
moment the blind fingers will touch her shoulder and she will
awaken.

The knife gleams above him – here, on the right, where the
vein stands out like a tiny column by the ear. And the thin neck
wilts. Without a cry, he slumps down, face into his knees, and
bowed over, sits motionless. I, the man, look at him, with
round, wide-open eyes.

Now I must wipe the cold drops of sweat from my forehead –
with my left hand; the right is spattered. And then, only another
step . . . Trembling – clutch the knife more tightly! – only one
step, to her who had once been Mother, and now . . . and
now . . .

Eyes. Her eyes look up. She lies ready, on her back, but her eyes are open, and it is impossible – when one human being looks the other in the eyes. One must quickly hide under one's brows, into the farthest corner, and from there . . .

Two icy moons sway on the very edge. In just a moment they will break off and plunge downward. Her lips, the Mother's lips, are coiled into a taut ring, like the *Rhopalocera* that is dying into a chrysalis. She lies there, throwing her head back. There is a dark shadow here, in the small hollow under her throat. A strained, flat voice: 'Well? Here – right here!' she points her finger to her neck.

The knife falls ringing to the floor. She rises, slowly, a marble figure. Her shadow grows huge, breaks on the wall, climbs to the cupola – still higher. She looks from afar, from above, at the machines congealed in their last movement, at the motionless bodies which had once killed one another, at the small thin body, its head buried immobile in its knees – it is already merging with the thousands of others, faintly darker against the greenish icy sky.

She goes to the boy, raises his head, kisses the still warm mouth, and the head falls once again upon the knees. Then she approaches the other one, the man: his cheekbones quiver, and his nostrils, and his upper lip with the faint hollow. He is human. If she could also lift his head and kiss those lips, still warm and alive . . . but she merely passes her hand over his face. And now hurry, hurry, while there is still strength to finish . . . If only one were not human – if one were free of pity!

The door is opened to the final chamber. Two intent, wild moons, resting their snouts on the floor. A huge circle on the floor, marked off with subdivisions. Yes, it will happen here.

She, the tall one, steps into the circle. For a second she stands immobile, marble white, like fate. Now she bends down, and now . . .

The moon, our own, earthly moon is bitterly lonely, because it is alone in the sky, always alone, and there is no one to turn to, no one to turn to it. All it can do is ache across the weightless airy ice, across thousands of versts, towards those who are equally lonely on earth, and listen to the endless howling of dogs.

Talya – alone in the garden. There is no one. Now under the moon the iron leaves of the lilacs are almost black. The lilac branches are bowed under the weight of the flowers: blooming is hard, and the most important thing is – to bloom. Talya bends down – sinks her face into the cold flowers. Her face is wet, and the lilacs are wet with dew. Over there, still lower, on the iron leaf just slightly curled and wrapped in a web is the dead body of the *Rhopalocera* turned into a chrysalis. From out of this tiny immobile body, as from a pebble thrown into water, rapid quivering circles are running, spreading wider and wider. Talya's eyes are fixed, wide open, like the doors of a house where somebody is dead, and for the first time she sees everything, clearly: another such immobile body, bent fingers – one yellow from tobacco smoke. And this is unthinkable, impossible, and one must, one must do something quickly, one cannot stand here any longer and listen to the interminable howling.

In the house, the landlady, up on a stool, is lighting the lamp before the icon. Her upraised arms flash and go out in the red light. The house is filled with the most ordinary smell, the smell of freshly baked bread, but this . . .

'Timofeyevna, darling, I cannot . . . how can it be, how can it? Tomorrow – grass and sun, and everybody around will take bread and eat – and he? And he?'

'What can you do, my child. If we're alive and well, we'll all, God willing, die some day. You'll also die – what do you think? An hour sooner, an hour later – it's all the same.'

But maybe Kukoverov is right. Perhaps a minute, a year are both the same. Perhaps sometimes an hour is all of life. Talya sits on the bench, white in the quivering red light, her eyes still staring, open wide, her hands between her knees. A minute, an hour, a year.

She rises. Quickly, as in a fever, she runs to the mirror. Heavy lashes, bent by the weight of flowers, and shadows. She must wipe her face with something wet, with a towel, to wipe away the traces. And now her coat . . .

'Where are you off to – are you mad? They'll grab you in the street, and that'll be the end of you!'

'Perhaps I want them to grab me?'

A STORY ABOUT THE MOST IMPORTANT THING

White dust under the moon. Over the fence – a black sharp branch against the sky. The silence, piled like rocks, makes the dogs howl. A familiar porch. Carved, pinched-in columns. On the steps a guard, his rifle between his knees, sitting just as the other guard, the Kelbuy one, had sat the other day. Could he be dozing? Talya takes another step.

The guard jumps up, his eyes wide open like his mouth, and shouts with his mouth, with his bulging eyes: 'Where to, where do you think you're going? I'll crack you on the head with the butt, then . . . Don't you know the orders – to stay in?'

But she has nothing in her hands. She ducks her head a little and covers it with empty hands. The pockmarked face under the cap relaxes, quiets down. Without taking his eyes off – who knows? . . . you can never tell! – the guard knocks at the window. The frame is a dark cross against the red light, and inside . . .

Another one in a clay shirt comes out on to the steps – one of thousands, an ant with a rifle. The guard says to him: 'Look here, will you take over for a while? I want to get this woman to the chief.'

Dogs, moon, dust. A bitter, wormwood wind blows from the pasture, dries the lips.

'Eh, listen to them howl . . . What's eating them? . . . You . . . what's your name?'

'Natalya.'

'Na-h! The devil! My wife's Natalya too. Isn't that something! Hey, hey, look where you're going. A cow passed along here – you'll get your little feet messed up . . . Some cows they've got here! Around here, for a pound of nails . . . There's places – generally! Did you come here with salt, or with cloth, to exchange?'

'No, I am here to teach the children – in the school.'

'Good Lord! Then you can tell him straight out: such and such, you see, I teach the children. Nothing will happen to you – take my word. Don't fear, even if he's . . .'

'I am not afraid.'

And now the door is open, and the breath comes hard, through the thinnest crack between clenched teeth. Within the

door-frame, in the wavering circle of candlelight, this face forever: loaded eyes, sharp cheekbones, and the lips: there are no
lips, no pink line. None, and there will never be any words.

Silently, with his eyes. Then suddenly the slit of his mouth
opens – not where you expected, but much higher, and the
upper lip is very short. Words: 'You knew the orders?'

'I did.'

'Then why?'

'To make them bring me to you.'

The candle crackles faintly as it gutters. Shadows beneath the
cheekbones. On the table, on the papers – a revolver. And, like
two revolver muzzles, the eyes.

'Any weapons?'

Breath coming through the thinnest slit. A clenched 'None'.
He rises from behind the table, the flame of the candle flutters.
One moment, silently. Then, with a practised movement, lightly,
he passes his hands down her body, pressing faintly along
the hips, where arms might be hidden in the folds. It sems
to Talya that his hand quivers – or is it her own trembling?
– her lips are dry, and for a second, needle-sharp, the thought:
'That? With him?' and she answers herself: 'Yes, anything
– if only . . .'

Without raising her lashes, bent under the weight of flowers,
tripping, licking her dry lips: 'I . . . no . . . you are wrong. I
came . . . because you have . . . I know: you want to . . . it's
about him . . . you want to – tomorrow morning . . .'

'Him? Whom?'

'Kukoverov. I – I cannot let him . . . I'll do anything. I'm
ready – all of myself – anything you want! I'll be grateful for
the rest of my life . . . I love him – you understand?'

Silence. The candle crackles as it burns. Now the line of the
lips is clearly visible on his face; the upper lip is very short and
trembles slightly – perhaps from the shadow of the candle.

'I . . . love him too.'

Talya's eyes are huge, wide open: 'You?'

'Yes, I. We sat a year together in prison. We lived together.
Such things are not forgotten.'

'So you . . . will not . . .'

'Tomorrow I will shoot him. Not I – but that is all the same.'

Gasping for breath, the gutted candle sways, the floor sways, and the walls. Talya must hold on to the table, bend her eyes lower to the other eyes. Her eyes are winged – wide open.

Dorda gets up – firmly, all of him encased in a holster. He takes the revolver from the papers on the table.

'I am going to him now. Wait for me here.'

And once again his voice, from the distance, from behind the door, to the guard: 'Wait here with her till I return.'

Silence. The wick is a black hook, like a hawk's beak. Above, the ceiling weighs a thousand tons, and further up – the sky, wastes, glaciers, the dark star.

Machines and men congealed in the last movement, and mute hordes of books, and centuries – with a silent, deafening roar: all this, in order that in the end the three last humans on the star may be cast up here, on the naked shore.

A naked, empty chamber. Nothing but a huge circle on the floor, with some mysterious divisions, and the still immobile black arrow. It is very simple, there is nothing to it at all. And yet, they are like a beast who, trembling, senses the black hole of the pointed gun.

The two face this way. The light of the moon is below and behind them. Their faces are in shadow. Two profiles are etched against the greenish, icy sky: the man, scowling from under his brow, his chin pressed to his chest, muscles knotted beneath his shoulder, and the young woman – sharp line of eyelashes, lips that have just spoken and are not yet closed.

And now she, the older one, who had been Mother a thousand circles back, bends down. Her hand is on the arrow; it is marble-white, and from the hand the marble rises higher and higher; and it seems as if the hand will never be moved from its place. Eyebrows, teeth, all of her – tighter, tighter, till something snaps! A movement. With a creaking sound, the arrow slowly begins to crawl around the circle.

It is simple, there is nothing to it at all. I, the man, know. Press yourself to me, so that your shoulder ... don't be afraid, don't look there, do not look. The arrow crawls, creaking, reaches a certain figure – yes, here ... it stops. That is all.

She, the Mother stands – upright, tall. Over her face the clouds sweep like a storm – about everything at once: about the dead boy, about them, about herself, about millennia, about this – last – second, and about that which is to happen now.

Tightening more and more, the finest hairspring snaps – and there is an enormous, hollow rumbling somewhere below. Everything shakes. With an absurd bounce and a final flash, the two moons tumble down. In the next chamber – the clattering of chains and clanging of collapsing machines. Through all this crashing – a scream. And – sudden darkness, night on the dark star.

Dorda looks into the blue wide-open eyes, he looks at Kukoverov's moving lips, his finger – tobacco-yellowed on the side, below the nail. This is a man, a living man. And to know ... precisely – to *know* – that tomorrow ...

Yes. And now it is as though, if Dorda makes the slightest movement, if he as much as moves this pencil on the paper, it will happen – not tomorrow, but now, here, for Kukoverov is made of the thinnest, of paper-thin, glass. And Dorda is motionless – a statue cast in dark, shiny metal.

'Give me a cigarette ...' Kukoverov's voice comes with difficulty through dry lips.

With the cigarette he bends over the glass shade of the iron lamp (he has no matches). The red tongue in the glass leaps up, smokes.

'Remember, Dorda, that time in the cell, without tobacco? There was one cigarette – I wanted you to take it, and you wanted me to. And then we nailed it to the wall – as a memento ... as a ...'

It is as though the third whistle has been blown on the platform, the train is just about to pull out, and one must hurry, one must hurry, there is still so much to say – about this and that ... fragments. Kukoverov smokes greedily. Grey, faintly curling ash grows on the cigarette, and in his head the watch-hands whirl madly.

'And then: you and I – at the window, on the stool. The sky, and something else ... Oh, yes: the ringing of the trolleys, and they sounded to us like ... like ... And now – you and I ... Funny! I kept thinking ... This tin cup, with water – see, all the dirt on top under the seam? You understand – I looked at it and thought: tomorrow it will be exactly the same ... And there – perhaps a total vacuum, emptiness, nothing ... And, you know, I thought: what if I should suddenly see this cup *there*, and this dirt on it? It might be such incredible joy – such ... Or to see – a worm crawl. Nothing more – a worm.'

Dorda sits, resting his head firmly on his hand. He has no lips. With the pencil he draws a cross on the paper, makes it bigger – there is not enough room, he must move the revolver from the paper. But as he touches the revolver, a thought occurs. He hears: one, two, three! – his heart beats like a clock on a sleepless night. Yes, perhaps this ...

He gets up, walks slowly to the window. Stops. And with his back – somewhere right there, between his shoulder blades – he even wants to touch the spot, which prickles just a little now – with his back, Dorda sees clearly: Kukoverov takes the revolver he left lying on the table, now he picks it up. Through the window – the sky, wastes, glaciers, a huge, blue star. Beneath them, a cloud is rising from behind the roofs like a cast-iron wall. For an instant – who knows why? – he sees his mother on the threshold, hand held up like a visor over her eyes ... Dorda waits a minute, another minute.

Nothing. He turns quickly. Kukoverov, bending over the lamp, is lighting a new cigarette. The revolver lies on the table as before. In the shadow, under Dorda's sharp cheekbone, a dark thread twitches, like a worm. Dorda walks to the table, takes the revolver from the paper. Red lips are suddenly slit open in his face, not where you would expect, but higher, the upper lip is very short. And words: 'You're an idiot, an intellectual! I always said it to you ...'

'I remember ...' A smile. Ash – grey, faintly curling – in a moment it will drop and scatter.

'I would have taken it and fired. You may be sure of that.

Tomorrow I will fire at you – well, not I, but it is all the same.'

'Tomorrow – yes. But now you . . .'

'That'll do, you're talking nonsense! You don't imagine that I left it there for you on purpose? Idiot!'

'All right. But maybe, for this single minute, I . . . you . . . But listen, don't you understand that the most important thing . . .'

The broken watch whirls madly – an hour, a second. There are no people, and therefore the two are people, and now, as after the third whistle, they must hurry, there is something else that they must say, and something else. The chipped wood of the table is littered with the white small corpses of cigarettes, curling ash. Wrinkles fan out on Kukoverov's temples as he smiles: his eyes shine.

'You know, Dorda? I'm sorry for you – just simply . . . Perhaps it's only now – perhaps tomorrow I'll . . .'

Suddenly, this simple . . . The tomorrow of both of them: still invisible, it is rolling somewhere now in a huge light wave – ever nearer. In the shadow under Dorda's sharp cheekbone a dying worm seems to toss. Both are silent, and this seems very long. Then Dorda says quietly, looking down at the pencil: 'I've had a visit from your . . . I don't know who. She said all sorts of . . . Well, that she loves you, and other things – I don't remember what. It's unimportant. In fact, this is why I've come.'

Dorda looks down on the cross – drawn on the paper with a pencil – and hears Kukoverov's breath, slow, tight, as if all air had suddenly hardened for him into lumps. Kukoverov is silent.

'Well? Why don't you say something, d-damn it!'

Dorda jumps up, goes to the window. The star is no longer there, the whole sky is cloud, cast-iron. Back to the table, where Kukoverov is silent.

'Maybe it's stupid, and forbidden – but anyway: if you want it – she'll come here to you? I'll tell the guard. Well? Do you?'

The air – like stinging lumps. There are no words. On Kukoverov's face – a smile, clouds, bright and dark; they say that this is – like a day or like . . . – and that it is impossible, unbearable. And yet, the faintest nod: Yes, I do.

When Dorda gets up to go, Kukoverov's voice comes with difficulty, forced through the teeth: 'Leave me some cigarettes – I have none left. Thanks. Generally.'

Once, long ago – the last cigarette was nailed to the wall. That was how it was.

Tomorrow is still hidden by an iron, rumbling curtain of clouds – just as the dead, suddenly shaken star is hidden – from Dorda, from Kukoverov, from people, from the Earth. On the star everything is black; night. But only for a short minute, and now the sky is breaking through. Not of green ice, as yesterday and the day before: now it flashes red – like a young girl who sees, who feels for the first time – her cheeks flush hot, and her heart, humming with blood, rushes out to meet – to burn, to be burnt to ash.

One more division, a hair's breadth, and instead of two moons, a new unknown moon is rising slowly, hugely, pressing its nose to the window: a red, shaggy, pockmarked, cruel, merry, indifferent, curious face. The walls flush red with translucent blood, the red line on the younger woman's breast is like a crack in a chalice, and there are red scars on the man's shoulder.

His nostrils quiver – like the nostrils of an animal that senses a distant, still inexplicable smell and backs away, bristling. Without taking his eyes from the terrifying new moon, he takes a step back, another – puts out a hand to shield himself. Then suddenly he bolts to the door – to get out, quickly, not to see, not to . . .

But there is no longer any door, it is blocked off outside with pieces of broken walls, huge lumps, piles, mountains of glass ice sparkling red. It is impossible to go back, only – forward. Where?

I alone – I, the Mother, have lived a thousand circles. I alone know where. I hear how, whistling madly, a hundred times faster, we rush, spinning, to meet the Earth. And for the sake of this, everything. For the sake of this, I have doomed these last two, the man and the woman: they are still alive, they are still humans.

And I am human. If only one were not human, if . . . But this must not be said aloud, and I know: in a moment I shall smile to him. Now! I smiled.

With both hands, he clutches his raging head, his eyes are round – like the eyes of a child, of an animal. Quietly, he says to her, to the Mother: 'What did you do? What is this – red – there?'

'It is the Earth. I turned towards the Earth, so that we . . . No, no, listen: there, on Earth, there is air, there are people, men and women, and they breathe all day, all night – as much as they want, and there it is no longer necessary to kill, and there . . .'

His lips are moving – he is repeating her words, like a prayer. On his upper lip there is a faintly visible hollow. And to know beforhand how this lip will snarl in the last smile, how his teeth . . .

Aloud: 'And you . . . you will breathe – day and night, always, as much as you wish!'

The man closes his eyes. It is impossible to believe this at once, his heart is hammering. And immediately he opens his eyes, so that he may believe – so that he may stretch out his hands to the shaggy, splendid, terrifying Earth – to shout a welcome to it, like an animal at dawn – to seize the other woman in drunken joy, to press her roughly, cruelly, tenderly.

Circling and trembling, the Earth waits to be pierced to her dark depths – so that impatient, boiling scarlet lava will burst out – so that she may be burned up, so that she may burn up to ash. Trembling, she wraps her nakedness in clouds, pours forth rain that scalds like tears – may it come faster, faster, may it never come: it is blinding, it hurts.

From the roof, drops fall on to the stone window-sill, and in the whole world two – Kukoverov and Talya – hear every drop. A lamp, a wooden table, on the table – the small corpses of cigarettes. The lashes bent by the weight of blooming are lowered – to Kukoverov. He is on the floor, his face in the warm hollow between Talya's knees, where the worm *Rhopalo-cera* was tossing recently . . . And in the silence, drops; from one drop to another – centuries.

Kukoverov raises his face, his closed eyes, his smile.

'Drops – do you hear them? How huge a drop seems – or, perhaps, that isn't it, but you understand? I know: I shall hear them always – all my . . .'

He wanted to say 'all my life' – and tripped. His smile whitens, he stands on his knees silently, rubbing his forehead, here over the right eyebrow – one finger is yellow from tobacco.

Talya's heart turns within her like a living child with such pain that she must scream, she must . . . all of herself – the most impossible, the most difficult – so that this hour, these two hours may be to him . . .

Kukoverov opens his eyes, blue, astonished – because he suddenly hears her laughter.

'Listen – but how stupid I am! I forgot the most important thing . . . I just spoke to him, to Dorda, he says that tomorrow . . . that, generally, you will not . . . I don't remember . . . I was in a hurry – he said you will be taken to the city – he will see to it that . . .'

Kukoverov's eyes – round, like a child's – grow wider, more blue.

'But . . . he has just said – something altogether different . . . We have just . . .'

'No, no! Perhaps because I asked him . . . I don't know – he said so, I tell you!'

A cigarette. There are no matches. The red tongue in the lamp quivers and stretches upwards. In Kukoverov's head the thoughts rush madly, buzzing like the watch with a snapped spring. Words, bursting from the cage, tumble over one another: 'Yes, yes, Dorda and I had once . . . He is very . . . These are his cigarettes – you understand? And if . . . And then you and I will go away somewhere . . . It's very simple: the name can be . . . Funny – where is this from? There was a man called Panteley Pupynin – you know? And the man applied to change his name to "Robespierre" – Panteley Robespierre! Really, really – Panteley Robespierre!'

Talya must laugh along with Kukoverov, because if she does not laugh . . . A single, empty, breathless second, then laughter – in lumps, in pieces – altogether dry, scattering immediately into dust. Kukoverov starts again about the same thing – how they will together . . . Will? And she has no more strength, she cries: 'Don't! Be silent! I cannot!'

Silence. Drops on stone. Kukoverov is on his knees, his head in Talya's hands . . . To press this head, like this, with both hands, hard, and look without breathing, more, and more – so that she will remember for the rest of her days.

The girl's young lips, cool as lilacs at twilight, imprint themselves in Kukoverov forever – until tomorrow. And when he kisses her afterwards through the silk, Talya – spinning and trembling, her hands grown chill and trembling – must – all of herself, something utterly unthinkable – she quickly undoes her dress and takes out her left breast – she would take it out so for her child – and offers it to Kukoverov: 'Here . . . do you want . . .?'

The drops, a thousand versts away. With his hot cheek, his lips, Kukoverov hears all of her – and her words, slipping out in confusion: 'When he was searching me – I thought . . . I thought that I could – yes, I could have! I want you – I want you to . . . I want you to leave yourself in me, so that . . . No, no, no, this isn't because I think that tomorrow . . . no! I tell you: he said to me – I tell you he did! But is it necessary to eat together and go walking together all one's life? The most important thing, after all . . .'

Drops on stone, huge in the silence. And hugely, easily, like the Earth, Kukoverov suddenly understands all. And he understands: yes, this is so, this is necessary. And he understands: there is no death.

He goes to the door and listens, then slips on the hook. His memory will hold forever – until tomorrow: the half circle in the wood under the hook, etched by the hook where it has swung for hours, years, centuries. And one more thing: the window has already turned pale, the black cross of the frame, clouds, a huge, distant, hollow rumble, coming nearer and nearer

A STORY ABOUT THE MOST IMPORTANT THING

Through millions of miles of airy ice, whirling ever more furiously, a star hurtles, whistling – to be burnt up, to burn up – nearer and nearer. And on it – the last three. Illuminated by the new, red, last light, they greedily, recklessly drink the remaining air. Intoxicated, they breathe as men had breathed here, on this star, long ago, thousands of circles back. Oh, once in their life – without thought, without care – with the body, mouth, breast!

The man and woman are embracing closely: two are one. And the other one, the older one, the Mother – is over them, over everything. Her profile is etched against the red glow of the sky, her brows and lips are tightly knit, she is marble like fate, her shoulders are just faintly bowed under some burden. She stands, waiting. And now, the floor under her feet is rising like a living body. Cracks, glowing red, open up in the thousand-year-old walls . . . the ringing of glass spray . . .

Silence. Serrated shadows of overturned cliffs in the deserts. Jumbled icy masses of glass afire with scarlet sparks, and under them – as at the bottom of the sea through ice – the dark heaps of machines, books, bodies, three instantly frozen bodies pressed close to one another.

In the silence – drops on stone. From drop to drop – centuries, seconds. At some appointed second – the clouds suddenly collapse. Against the blinding whiteness – the black cross of the window-frame, columns of lightnings, and above – stones, crashing, flame.

From the houses, shifting, lumbering, rearing up like bears, humans come leaping out – the men of Kelbuy and Orlovka – and all of them run wildly somewhere, fall into fiery cracks. The Earth is opening her womb wider – still wider – all of herself – in order to conceive, in order that new fiery creatures may come forth in the scarlet light, and then, in white warm mist – still newer, flowerlike forms bound to the new Earth only by the slenderest stem. And when these human flowers ripen . . .

[*1923, published 1924*]

THE MIRACLE OF ASH WEDNESDAY

This story is about the miracle that took place on Ash Wednesday, and also about Canon Simplicius and Doctor Voychek.

For it was Canon Simplicius through whom this miracle was wrought. And Doctor Voychek was the only man in the world who witnessed it all from beginning to end.

If you take a miracle that happened long ago, to someone else – that's somehow easier to accept. I could believe in it, and so could you. But just imagine – if it should happen now, if it happened yesterday, to you – yes, precisely, to you! And therefore, whenever Doctor Voychek dropped in to spend an evening with the canon and they were settling down to their game of dominoes, the canon never failed to repeat his timid inquiry: 'But still . . . still, have you found nothing, nothing at all in your books? Perhaps another case – perhaps in antiquity?'

Doctor Voychek's greenish goat's eyes would narrow and his lips would stretch, frightening Canon Simplicius with their smile. And so, for a minute or two. Then Voychek would begin to twist the red hair over his forehead, as his habit was, until two small red horns stood up on either side, and Voychek would shrug and spread his hands: 'No. What can you do, my friend? It is a miracle. I'd be just as happy as you if all of this could somehow be . . . But what can I tell you, when I saw it with my own eyes? Saw it! – felt it with this very pair of hands . . . But what's the good! Oh, well . . . and how's your . . .'

Canon Simplicius knew what was coming next. For a moment he was a side of venison on a spit over a slow fire: the doctor was unhurriedly lighting a cigarette.

'. . . how's your Archbishop? In good health, I hope?'

'Thank you, thank you. I paid him a call yesterday – he is feeling fine.'

Many people knew of the special favour in which Archbishop Benedict held the canon, and no one wondered at it: whose heart would fail to throw its gates wide open to the knocking of the canon's eyes – those two astonished babes with their thumbs in their mouths? And yet, perhaps it was not even the eyes; perhaps it was the dimples in the canon's cheeks; yes, indeed, it must have been the dimples. As for Archbishop Benedict – well, after all, he was human too.

And now Doctor Voychek was speaking, very seriously, with just the faintest stirring of a horned smile: 'My dear friend, if you are troubled by the thought of the next world, of retribution and all that – which is understandable – I can put your mind at ease: in any case, it will not be so soon. There is a sure-fire method of prolonging life to any point you choose.'

'What do you mean? How?'

'Quite simply. You remember, the Archbishop told you he had to turn his watch more than an hour back when he came to Rome? That means an additional hour of life. You understand? Now, if you go to London, you will add two hours to your life; if you go to New York, you add more than six hours; and so on. In short, if you keep travelling west from here, you will be adding days, weeks and years to your life – as much as you like. It's a foolproof method!'

Dimples. Babes sucking their pink thumbs in wonder. It seems strange, but, then, it seems to be right. There's no arguing with figures. Generally, of course, Canon Simplicius was quite accustomed to this: every evening, at departure, Doctor Voychek left some such thorny point stuck in the canon's head. Afterwards the canon twisted and tossed in bed, thinking and thinking, turning the matter this way and that: no, Voychek is right; Voychek is a man of extraordinary intelligence. And, naturally, to whom would he have turned if not to Doctor Voychek when *that* began to happen?

It began on August first, during Mass, on the Feast of the Apostle Peter's Chains. A week before that the canon had called on Archbishop Benedict. The Archbishop, just back from Rome, was especially benevolent and treated him to prickly Asti, the slow, thick wine of the Benedictine Brothers, and to

Roman lobster, pink as a baby. Later the canon told Doctor Voychek about all this and many other things, without concealing anything, as at confession – although it might be that the evening at the Archbishop's had no connection whatsoever with the events that followed. At any rate, during Mass on the Feast of the Apostle Peter's Chains, Canon Simplicius felt for the first time that he might not be entirely well: he felt dizzy, and there was a strange heaviness in his stomach.

August first was a yellow, hot day; the church was filled with people, the air was dense and it was difficult to breathe. When the cannon raised the Host, which gleamed with golden rays, and intoned '*Corpus Domini Nostri custodiat . . .*', he noticed that a woman who had evidently turned faint was being taken to the door. At the same instant, the stone floor under his feet became as soft as cotton, the organ was somewhere a thousand versts away, and cobwebs swam before his eyes. It was only by biting his lips until they bled that the canon kept himself from falling like that woman, and managed to complete the Mass.

The days were like amber rosary beads, one like the other, transparent, yellow. Then came a rosary of cool autumn crystal, and a rosary of snow-white ivory. And through them all, the same heaviness – customary now – and within it, a light, even perhaps a somewhat pleasant pain. In every other way, the canon was entirely well; people had even remarked that he was gaining weight.

One evening, over the dominoes, Doctor Voychek fixed the canon more intently than usual with his green goat's eyes: 'You know, I don't like your looks, my friend. You are pale. What's wrong?'

The canon told him about the Mass, about his faintness and the pain in his stomach.

'Take off your clothes. Come, take them off, I tell you! Such precious modesty! I'll bet when you . . .'

'No, no – I will, one moment.'

And then his body: there are such chairs in women's bedrooms, upholstered in pink satin, full of warm folds and dimples, alive – you'd almost think they're ready to replace their mistresses. Doctor Voychek twisted his red horns till they were even sharper and the familiar smile crept to his ears. But a moment later he was serious. Bending down, he laid his ear to the pink satin-covered body and felt the stomach.

'Hm-m ... Now, why didn't you say a word about it till now?'

'Well, I somehow ... People have even told me I was gaining weight. What is it?'

'What! We'll have to cut you up.'

Dimples; frightened babes with thumbs in their mouths.

'But why? What do I have? In the name of Holy Mary?'

'I am afraid it's ... However, I'll tell you when I open you.'

'But, doctor, is it serious?'

'What can I say? When a woman's belly swells up it isn't serious, but when yours or mine does, it's no joke ... Tell me, have you had it long?'

The canon thought back: yes, yes, it was since August – there was the Feast of the Apostle Peter's Chains – Archbishop Benedict's return from Rome – and ... well, just about then, soon after that.

Doctor Voychek's horns stirred faintly; a shadow of a smile.

'I see, I see ... Well? Today is Monday? Come to see me at the hospital on Wednesday.'

And it was on Wednesday, Ash Wednesday, the first day of Lent, that it all happened. February. In the still-wintry sky everything seemed to fly – the vividly blue window-panes, the wind. The room was quiet, with eerily white walls, doors, and benches, as if it were no longer here, on earth, where everything is varicoloured, noisy, where black and white are always intermingled. In the white room Canon Simplicius waited, numb with anxiety, side by side with a woman who looked like a spider: a huge belly under grey calico, and everything else – arms, legs, head and small white eyes – arranged around the belly.

For a long time they sat silently, each with his own thoughts. Then the spider woman stretched a leg from out of her belly, and the canon saw a worn, misshapen shoe with a loose flap. The woman sighed a tight, round sigh with her belly, and rested

one of her numerous arms on the belly, as though it were something external to her, as though it were a table.

'My third baby – and every time they have to cut me open ...
Mother of God! They'll slaughter me, and what will Stas and
Yanek and Franz do without me? You're here to see the doctor
too?'

'Yes, I am also here to see Doctor Voychek.'

'What is it to you! But when I think – my eldest is only eight
... It's lucky the doctor has a kind heart – he doesn't charge me
anything.'

Who knows, perhaps Canon Simplicius will soon be sitting
with this woman, not here, in this white room, but in some
other, vast and silent chambers, waiting for an hour still more
awesome ... And it would not be amiss if the woman said a
kind word about him then ... Canon Simplicius took out his
purse, emptied it, and gave everything that was there to the
woman. And at the moment when she was tucking it all into her
huge, taut belly, Doctor Voychek came in. He narrowed his
eyes and slowly advanced upon the canon, frightening him with
his smile.

'Storing up good deeds for the road? Counting your sins?
Don't worry, don't worry, my friend: three weeks from now
you'll be eating lobster with the Archbishop again. Come ...'

After that – whiteness, steel, a table. Trembling. From far
away, from earth – the enormous, echoing voice of Doctor
Voychek: 'Count aloud: one, two, three ... Well? Do you hear
me?'

And then there was no longer any tongue; no body – nothing,
the end ...

But for Canon Simplicius it was only the beginning. For the
spider woman it was the end: she lay motionless, covered with
white. Her rusty shoes were tied into a bundle with her dress,
and the bundle had a note pinned to it. And in one of the white
rooms a red infant screamed – an infant with a huge, wise
brow.

Canon Simplicius unglued his eyelids: bending over him he
saw a pair of horns and narrowed goat's eyes. Nevertheless, this

demon was unquestionably Doctor Voychek, and the canon was obviously still here, on earth . . .

'And that woman – the one who . . .' The canon lost his voice, he had no strength to go on, but Doctor Voychek twisted his horns so hard that they hurt.

'You were luckier than she was, my friend: she is already reporting your good deeds to the appropriate authorities.'

And immediately there was a strange, pitiful whimper behind the canon. The canon wanted to turn, but Doctor Voychek shouted angrily: 'Have you gone mad? Lie still!'

He stepped away somewhere and returned after a moment to the white centre of the room with a wrinkled infant, its knees gathered up under its belly.

Canon Simplicius stared at Doctor Voychek, at the infant, his eyes widening and becoming rounder and rounder.

'What's this? . . . Where from?'

Doctor Voychek was silent for a long while, squinting at the canon with his goat's eyes, looking right into him, deeper and deeper, to the very bottom. Suddenly, that creeping, frightening smile – who knows what he was smiling at! At last he said, very seriously: 'In any case, I would have to tell you sooner or later . . . It might as well be now. This child is yours.'

Frozen dimples; open-mouthed, frightened babes.

'You mean . . . What do you mean, mine?'

'Very simply – yours.'

'But I . . . Holy Virgin! But I'm, after all, a man!'

'My friend, I know it as well as you. Nevertheless . . . You understand, I am a doctor, it's much more difficult for me to believe in a miracle than it is for you – a priest. And yet, it can't be helped! I must believe. Accept it as a test – a special token of favour from on high.'

'But doctor, but this is . . . but it's inconceivable!'

'And what about the resurrection of the dead – is that conceivable? Or do you mean to tell me that you don't believe in it?'

'Oh, no, no – I do believe . . . But why me? Why just me?'

'Perhaps it is intended as a punishment for some sin you have committed? How would I know? Or perhaps it is that heaven selects the simple-hearted as its instruments, and you are, fortunately, as simple and pure in heart as a babe. But calm down, calm down, it isn't good for you . . . This is a son, a boy.'

Was there anything left to Canon Simplicius when even Doctor Voychek – Voychek himself! – believed in the miracle? The canon submitted to it and bore it as meekly as the Apostle Peter bore his iron chains. It even seemed to him that he knew why heaven had so punished and rewarded him. And only at times, in the evenings, when he was sitting down with the doctor for a game of dominoes, the canon would ask timidly: 'But still . . . still . . . perhaps you've found something in your books?'

But the reply was always the same: 'Nothing. What can you do, my friend? It is a miracle.'

Doctor Voychek faithfully kept the secret of the miracle that had occurred on Ash Wednesday. He told many people that the canon, out of the goodness of his heart, had adopted the son of a poor woman who had died in labour, and the canon's fame grew, and the boy Felix grew.

When Felix called the canon 'Papa', the canon would turn a delicate, satiny pink.

'Don't call me that, Felix. I am not your father.'

The boy would wrinkle his high, clever forehead and fall silent. Then he would ask: 'And my mamma? Who is my mamma?'

The canon would become even silkier, even more pink: 'That is a secret. I will reveal it to you only on the day when I'm about to close my eyes forever.'

This day, by the will of fate, was also in February, like that first Ash Wednesday – with the same clouds, and the same vividly blue widow-panes in the still-wintry sky. A dark cross – the shadow of the window-frame – flowed slowly and with incredible speed along the wall before the canon. Holding fast to this cross, Canon Simplicius clenched his teeth and nodded to Felix: 'Now, Felix . . . No, doctor, do not go. You know it anyway, and you will tell him that it was exactly as I say. You must have thought, Felix, that I am your father. Well, I am not – I am your mother. Your father was the late Archbishop Benedict.'

For the last time the canon saw Felix's high forehead, just

like the Archbishop's, the doctor's red horns, and something bright – like tears – in his goat's eyes. And, strangely, it seemed to the canon that Doctor Voychek was laughing through his tears. However, all this came to him mistily, from far away, as in a dream: the babe was already going off to sleep.

[*1924, published 1926*]

X

The principal lines in the spectrum of this story are gold, red, and lilac, since the town is full of cupolas, revolution, and lilacs. Both the revolution and the lilacs are in full bloom, from which we may conclude with a certain degree of authenticity that the year is 1919, and the month is May.

This particular May morning begins with the appearance of a procession on the corner of Pancake and Rosa Luxemburg Streets. The procession is evidently religious: it consists of eight clerical personages, well known to the entire town. But instead of censers, the clerical personages are swinging brooms, which transfers the entire action from the plane of religion to the plane of revolution. These personages are now simply unproductive elements of society performing their labour duty for the benefit of the people. Instead of prayers golden clouds of dust rise to the heavens. The people on the sidewalks sneeze, cough, and hurry through the dust. It is just past nine o'clock, and work begins at ten, but today for some reason everyone is out early, and the crowd hums like a swarm of bees.

On this day (20 May 1919), all citizens between the ages of eighteen and fifty, with the exception of the most unregenerate bourgeois, were in government service, and today there was something for everyone from eighteen to fifty in the various U.E.P.O., U.E.K.O., and U.O.N.O.* The main thing in all this was that this mysterious 'something' was an unknown – an 'X', and human nature is so constituted that it is most attracted to Xs (this is put to excellent use in algebra and in fiction). In the

---

* These were the initials of the various cooperative and government organizations for the distribution of consumer goods, established after the abolition of private enterprise.

given case the X proceeded from the repentant Deacon Indi-koplev.

Deacon Indikoplev, who had publicly confessed to having fooled the people for ten years, now quite naturally enjoyed the confidence of both the people and the authorities. He even went fishing on occasion with Comrade Sterlingov of the District Executive Committee – as indeed he had done the night before. The two had gazed at the floats and at the red and gold and lilac water, and talked about carp, the leaders of the revolution, sugar-beet molasses, the escape of the Socialist-Revolutionary Perepechko from prison, and imperialist sharks. At this point, quite inapropos, the deacon remarked, shyly covering his face with his hand: 'If you will pardon me, Comrade Sterlingov . . . your trousers . . . in the back, I mean . . . Not that they're al-together . . . but sort of . . . you know . . .'

Comrade Sterlingov merely scratched the fur on his face: 'Oh, well, they'll last till tomorrow! Tomorrow they'll be issu-ing special clothing to every worker – a paper just came from the centre. But mind you, keep it under your hat . . .'

On his way home with three perch the deacon naturally knocked on the window of the telegraph clerk Alyoshka and told him about it – in strict confidence, of course. And the telegraph clerk Alyoshka, as you know, is a poet. He's already written eight pounds of verse; they're stored in his trunk, over there. As a poet, he did not feel that he had the right to keep secrets locked up in his heart. It is the poet's vocation to open his heart for everybody's benefit. And so by morning everybody from eighteen to fifty knew about the special clothing.

But nobody knew what this 'special clothing' was. One thing was clear, though: special clothing was something that de-scended from the fig-leaf. In other words, it was something that covered Adam's nakedness and adorned the nakedness of Eve. In 1919, moreover, the total area of nakedness was considerably greater than the area of fig-leaves. So much so, in fact that the telegraph clerk Alyoshka, to take one instance, had long been going to work in his underpants, transformed with the aid of

217

drying oil, soot, and red lead into a pair of waterproof trousers – grey, with a red stripe.

Naturally, therefore, in Alyoshka's mind, special clothing assumed the shape of trousers; in the imagination of the beauteous Martha it blossomed into a pink spring hat; in the mind's eye of the ex-deacon it consolidated into a pair of boots, and so on. In short, special clothing was clearly something akin to protoplasm, to the primary substance out of which everything evolved: baobabs, lambs, tigers, hats, Socialist-Revolutionaries, boots, proletarians, unregenerate bourgeois, and the repentant Deacon Indikoplev.

If you will now hazard taking a dive with me into the dust-clouds on Luxemburg Street, you will hear through all the sneezing and coughing the same things I hear: 'The deacon ... With the deacon ... Where is the deacon? Have you seen the deacon?' The deacon alone, experienced fisherman that he is, could pull out this hook, this X, with its bait of special clothing, which has caught everyone. But the deacon is not here. The deacon must be sought at this moment not along the red line of the spectrum, but along the lilac line – the line of love and Maytime. And this line does not run along Rosa Luxemburg; it runs along Pancake Street.

The repentant deacon is standing at the very end of Pancake Street, near the house painted in the most tender rose and lilac hues. Now he knocks at the gate. In a moment we shall hear Martha's rosy voice in the yard: 'Kuzma Ivanych, is that you?' And the gate will open. While he waits, the deacon examines the physiognomy painted on the gate; it is adorned with a villainous moustache, and has the legend BE IT SO written under it. Nobody knows what it means, but the deacon instantly recalls that he is now clean-shaven. Ever since he repented of religion and shaved off his clerical beard and moustache, he has had the constant feeling that he has taken off his trousers, and that his nose protrudes altogether indecently and must at all cost be covered. It's sheer torment!

With one hand over his nose, the deacon knocks again and again. No one responds. And yet Martha is home; the gate is locked from within. And that means – what? It means that she is with someone else ... The deacon punctuates the scene inwardly with the three dots we have graphically depicted just above, and, tripping over them at every second step, he proceeds to Rosa Luxemburg Street.

A few minutes later, we see the telegraph clerk and poet Alyoshka on the same spot, near that most delicately pink house. He also knocks at the gate, contemplates the moustachioed physiognomy, and waits. He stands with his back to us: we can see only the dark back of his head and his ears, which stick out with a sort of comfortable hospitality, like the handles of a samovar.

Suddenly all of Alyoshka becomes a mere superfluous appendage to his own right ear: only the ear is alive – it drinks in the whispers, the rustling, and the sound of footsteps in the yard. A poet must know everything and see everything. He dashes to the fence, grasps the edge, heaves himself up, tears his sleeve – and catches a momentary glimpse of something in the yard, under the barn.

Perhaps it is not worth our while to tear our sleeves climbing the fence after the poet: sooner or later we shall learn what Alyoshka saw there. In the meantime, we may draw our own conclusions from his face: with his wide-open mouth and round eyes Alyoshka looked at that moment like the unfortunate perch mercilessly strung on a cord and dangling in the deacon's hand before Alyoshka's window the previous evening. Alyoshka stood there in this perchlike state precisely long enough to find a word to rhyme with what he had seen (the word, which rhymed only approximately, was 'latch-key'). Then he broke off the cord that fate had strung him on, and darted off towards Rosa Luxemburg.

There a catastrophe was in the making: a clash – within a certain human point of intersection – between two warring lines of the spectrum, the red and the gold – the lines of revolution and of cupolas.

This human point of conflict was the deacon. He was dressed in wine-red trousers and an equally red Tolstoy blouse made of his former holiday cassock, and could be seen from afar like a flag or a conflagration. From the moment his glowing image became visible in the clouds of dust, the whole of Rosa Lux-emburg converged around him: dozens of questions, hands, and eyes glued themselves to him. The deacon stood in an invisible pulpit, and from this pulpit he dispensed pronouncements to everyone: 'Yes, special clothing ... Yes, yes, a paper from the centre.'

'What paper? Bluff some more!'

'What do you mean – "Bluff some more"?'

'That's what – it's plain enough.'

'You don't believe me? I'll swear to it by the holy cross – there!' And in order to retain his place up above, in the pulpit, the repentant deacon forgot that he had repented and actually made the sign of the cross. Then he flushed dark red – a reflex from another line of the spectrum – and (invisibly) tumbled from his eminence.

This catastrophe was caused by the fact that a hand-rolled cigarette set in the middle of a furry face was suddenly dis-cerned staring at the deacon out of the neighbouring dust-cloud. Sterlingov, of the District Executive Committee. And, of course, he had seen the deacon crossing himself.

The deacon became agonizingly aware of his naked nose, covered it with his hand, and pressed the other hand to his heart.

'Comrade Sterlingov ... Comrade Sterlingov, forgive me, for Christ's sa ...' And, turning a still deeper red, he froze mo-tionless.

Sterlingov removed the butt from his mouth, evidently in-tending to say something. But he did not say it – and that was still more terrifying. He only gave the deacon a silent glance and walked away. The deacon, still pressing his hand to his heart, like a creature demented, followed him.

Given another five or ten lines of our story, the deacon surely would have thought of something to say and would thus have saved himself. But at this moment Alyoshka shot out from around the corner. He bounded up to Sterlingov and, instead of the word he needed, he blurted out the rhyme: 'Latchkey! I mean ... I want to talk to you ...'

He fell silent, glancing behind him and shifting from foot to foot, his waterproof trousers rattling like the bulls' bladders that boys use to learn swimming. Sterlingov angrily spat out his cigarette.

'Well? What about?'

'A . . . about a secret matter,' Alyoshka whispered.

Dozens of ears floated around them in the dust waves; the whisper was heard, and it ran on like a spark along a gunpowder wick. Alyoshka's secret message, the mysterious special clothing, the deacon's catastrophe – all this was too much. The atmosphere was charged with thousands of volts, and something was needed to discharge the electricity, to clear the air.

And indeed the discharge took place: there was a sudden downpour. Everybody from eighteen to fifty dashed into gateways and vestibules, and watched from these safe shelters the dense, rustling curtain of glass beads. It's all right, let it come down – this rain is equally necessary both for the republic's grain harvest and for the subsequent events in our story. The rain will make it easier for the pursuers at dusk to hunt down a certain fleeing X by his tracks in the moist earth.

Everybody who has ever seen the deacon, and even those who have just caught sight of him on Rosa Luxemburg Street, know that he is a strapping giant of a man. So that I may be running the risk of unpleasantness if I should chance to meet him in another story or novel. Nevertheless, I consider it my duty to expose him here to the very end.

After he had repented and shaved off his beard, Deacon Indikoplev published a bull to his former flock in the *Izvestia* of the District Executive Committee. Printed in bold pica, the bull was posted to the local fences, and all and sundry learned from it that the deacon had repented of religion after hearing a talk on Marxism by a visitor from Moscow. It was true that the talk had produced a great impression generally – so much so that the next lecture at the club, devoted to astronomy, was announced under the following title: 'The Planet Marx and Its Inhabitants.' Nevertheless, I have authentic knowledge of the true reason for the revolution in the deacon's mind, and it was not Marxism but Marthism.

X

The originator of this teaching (which is entirely outside the philosophy of the class struggle), until now merely glimpsed between the lines, had gone down one fine morning to the river for a swim. She undressed, hung up her clothing on a willow branch, and, standing on a stone, she dipped the toes of her right foot into the water – how was it this morning? She splashed once, twice . . . A yard or so to the left of her the naked (and as yet unrepentant) Deacon Indikoplev sat under a bush, pulling up the lobster-trap he had set out for the night. His expert fisherman's ear caught the splashing sounds. 'Must be a whopper!' He looked up . . . and was undone.

Martha moved her shoulders (the water was chilly), and began to arrange her braid in a crown around her head. Her hair was ripe, rich, tawny blonde, and all of her was ripe and rich. Ah, if the deacon could only paint like Kustodiev! The picture of her against the dark greenery, her hand raised to her head, a hairpin in her teeth, the teeth like sugar, so white it had a faintly bluish tinge, and a little green enamel cross on a black cord between her breasts! . . .

Being naked, the deacon could not very well get up and leave at once. As for getting dressed, his underwear was a disgrace. Willy-nilly, he had to endure it all to the end – until Martha had her fill of swimming, came out of the water (the sight of the drops rolling off those tips!), and dressed unhurriedly. The deacon endured it, but from that day on he became a confirmed Marthist.

In essence, Marthism was much nearer to the Holy Scriptures than to Marxism. Thus, for example, Martha's first commandment was unquestionably 'Love thy neighbour'. For her neighbour's sake she was ever ready to obey the Gospel and take off her last shirt. 'Oh, you poor darling, what am I to do with you? Come on, then, honey, come over here to me!' She said this to the Socialist-Revolutionary Perepechko ('the poor dear has been in prison'), to Khaskin of the Communist cell ('the poor dear, such a scrawny neck, just like a chicken!'), to the telegraph clerk Alyoshka ('the poor dear – sits there and writes the livelong day!') . . .

And here that accursed relic of capitalism awakened in the

deacon – the instinct of private property. And the deacon said, 'I want you to be mine, and no one else's! If I . . . if you . . . I can't . . . you know what I mean?'

'My poor dear! Of course, I know, I kno-w! But what can I do when they beg and plead in the name of Christ? I haven't got a heart of stone, I feel so sorry for them!'

This conversation took place on a quiet revolutionary evening, on a bench in Martha's garden. A machine-gun tick-tocked tenderly somewhere in the distance, calling its mate. A cow sighed bitterly in the barn behind the fence. And in the garden the deacon was sighing still more bitterly. And so it would have gone on if destiny had not brought red into the tale – the colour of all upheavals in history.

One day, instead of sugar, the store issued to the local citizens containers of red lead dissolved in oil. All that day the deacon clattered barefoot on the iron roof of his house, painting it copper-red. And in the evening, as soon as it turned dark, the deaconess (her neighbours had long been whispering to her about the deacon) made her way across the backyards to Martha's garden. In her hands she carried a bundle, and in the bundle there was something round – perhaps a bomb, perhaps a chopped-off head, or perhaps a pot with something in it. Ten minutes later the deaconess climbed out of the garden, wiped her hands on the wide burdock leaves (were they bloody?), and returned home. Later it was as always: stars, the machine-gun, the cow sighing in the barn, and the deacon sighing on the bench in the garden. He sighed once, twice, and swore: 'What the d-devil! Even here it stinks of paint. Can't get away from it anywhere – soaked in it through and through, painting all day!'

Fortunately, a spray of lilac was pinned to Martha's bosom. My dear comrades, are you familiar with this superstructure on the tenderest of bases – in full accordance with the teaching of Marthism? If you are familiar with it, you will easily understand the deacon who very quickly forgot about paint and everything else in the world.

No wonder he could barely get his eyes open in the morning for early Mass. He must get dressed in a hurry. He picked up his trousers . . . Mother of God! It wasn't a pair of trousers; it was straight material evidence: everything was smeared with red. The seat of his grey tunic was also red, and the flaps were red ... The bench had been freshly painted the other night! So that's what it was! No wonder he had smelled paint!

The deacon rushed to his wardrobe to get another pair of trousers, without such a graphic diagram of his crime. But the wardrobe was empty: the deaconess had hidden everything.

'No, Grishka,* no, Rasputin that you are, go as you are!' screeched the deaconess. 'Go, go, let all good people see what you're up to! Oh, no, I won't, I won't, I won't give them to you, go as you are!'

And he went – as once the Prophet Yelisey had gone – with a mob of howling urchins behind him.

Nobody has ever succeeded in giving a true depiction of a simoom, an earthquake, childbirth, a bad hangover. It is impossible to convey what went on inside the deacon while he was celebrating that Mass. One thing is important: by the end of the Mass the deacon had arrived at a full appreciation of the achievements of the revolution, and particularly of the fact that the revolution had demolished the prison of bourgeois marriage.

On the following day the deacon took his holiday cassock to the tailor. And two days later, dressed in a wine-red Tolstoy blouse, clean-shaven, shyly covering with his hand his shamelessly upstart nose, he paid a call on Martha, to declare to her that for her sake he had decided to ruin his immortal soul, repudiate everything, divorce his deaconess, and marry her, Martha.

'Oh, my poor darling! Come on, come over here to me ... But what's the matter with your eyes, they look so queer?'

Eyes! A man is lucky nowadays if he can keep his brains from getting scrambled, with all the goings-on.

And the deacon's brains were indeed getting scrambled: just as he had once sat at the seminary cramming his texts, so he was now cramming Marx and attending classes at the study circles every evening. But behind the deacon's Marxism there was

* Diminutive of Grigory, Rasputin's first name.

nothing but the purest Marthism: after my impartial testimony this should be entirely clear to the court of history. Besides, citizen judges of history, haven't you just seen this allegedly repentant ecclesiastic publicly crossing himself? It was seen by the entire Rosa Luxemburg, including our esteemed Comrade Sterlingov of the District Executive Committee, and isn't that proof enough?

At this moment the entire Rosa Luxemburg is a theatre: the glass-bead curtain of rain has been drawn aside, the gateway-loges are full of spectators, hundreds of eyes are glued to the stage. The stage consists of two platforms, in true constructivist style – à la Meyerhold: namely, two entranceways under protective awnings at the doors to the Perelygin Haberdashery Shop (the doors are, naturally, boarded up; the year is 1919). The action develops simultaneously on both platforms. On the right are Sterlingov and the telegraph clerk Alyoshka; on the left the Marthist deacon and Martha.

Alyoshka is as pale as Pierrot, and only his ears, projecting at either side, are made up red. With obvious effort (the spectators can see it) Alyoshka finally brings out a certain word. Sterlingov's cigarette drops to the ground, and his hand flies to the holster of his revolver. Then he raises both hands to Alyoshka's head, as if to seize it by the handles, like a samovar, and take it off his shoulders. The head remains on the shoulders, but it is clear that Sterlingov is saying something on the order of, 'Look out, if you're lying I'll have your head!' Then both actors walk off or, rather run off the scene, Sterlingov dragging Alyoshka by the sleeve somewhere backstage.

On the left-hand platform a lovers' dialogue is obviously in progress. The deacon begins it in severely restrained style, without gestures, but in the pocket of his Tolstoy blouse something jumps and tosses like a cat in a sack: it is the deacon's furiously clenched fist. We may be sure that the deacon is asking Martha: 'Why didn't you open the gate this morning? Who was with you? You'd better tell me – who? Do you hear?' Martha raises her eyebrows and stretches out her lips – as when you say to a baby, 'a-goo, a-goo-goo'. But this no longer works with the deacon. His brains have obviously jumped the track, the cat may any moment leap out of his pocket. But the presence of the audience in the loges constrains him. He says (the text is approximate), 'All right, just wait!' and walks away with a firm resolve (the fist in the pocket grows rigid like a rock): he will hide in Martha's garden in the evening and spy out his rival.

The show is over. Martha remains alone on the stage and bows to the audience. The audience still lingers: the rain has gathered strength again, and none will brave getting drenched to the bone but those who, by the will of fate, are drawn into the principal threads of the plot – such as Sterlingov and the telegraph clerk Alyoshka.

Dripping wet, they were already at this point entering the building of an institution which in those days bore a far sharper and more metallic name than it does today.* A pockmarked soldier indifferently impaled Alyoshka's pass on his bayonet, where a dozen other Alyoshkas, transformed into scraps of paper, were fluttering. Then – an endless corridor, some fugitive, almost transparent faces made of human gelatin, and finally, behind a table at the door to a certain office, a young lady of the secretary breed (a special variety of spaniel).

Sterlingov's voice, huskily, through the fur on his face (or was it hoarse with agitation?), 'Is Papalagi in?'

The spaniel slipped into the office, out again, and waved her tail to Sterlingov, 'Go in, please'.

A moment later the telegraph clerk Alyoshka was already standing in the presence of Comrade Papalagi himself. On the table before Papalagi stood a plate with the most ordinary millet gruel, and it was a marvel to see him eating it in the most ordinary manner, like everybody else. But the moustache on Papalagi's face was huge, black, pointed – Greek, or what have you . . .

'Well, citizen . . . your name? Ah? Go on. Well?'

Alyoshka's knees were trembling so violently that he could hear his waterproof trousers rattling like bulls' bladders. Stuttering, with periods and semicolons after every word, Alyoshka reported that, on that very morning, in the courtyard of citizen

* The reference is to the Cheka, or political police.

Martha Izhboldina, he had seen the Socialist-Revolutionary Perepechko, which Socialist-Revolutionary had obviously spent the night on a pallet in the barn.

'All the better: so he's coming into the trap himself! We'll have a ready welcome for him.' His sharp moustache was like a pair of horns ready to gore. 'All the better, all the better . . .'

Papalagi pressed the bell; a gelatin face appeared in the doorway. 'Remember, tonight on Pancake Street . . . But we shall talk later. You can go now. You can also go.' This to Alyoshka, and Alyoshka rustles stiffly out of the office.

Silence. Millet gruel. The horns are aimed at Sterlingov.

'Hell! You understand, the staff demands an issue of special clothing . . . What will they think up next in Moscow? Listen, Sterlingov, isn't there anything left in the stores that we might requisition and distribute?'

Sterlingov burrows in his furs, staring at the millet gruel.

'Hm . . . We might still dig something up at Perelygin's . . . Nowhere else . . .'

'All right, then, make it Perelygin's. But make it fast, tell them to bring it here. At such a moment, you understand . . . That son of a bitch Perepechko . . .'

Gruel. Silence. The tapping of rain outside the open window. The smell of lilacs, penetrating even here – without any passes. In the gateway-loges on Rosa Luxemburg Street the public is still waiting for even the briefest dry intermission.

But instead of an intermission the show suddenly resumes: three militiamen (extras, silent parts) and a man in a white shaggy jacket made of a bath towel walk onto one of the stage platforms. The white man is instantly recognized and causes a stir: 'Susin! Susin of the District Food Supply Committee! Susin!'

A slight wave of the hand from the great Susin, the sound of boards being ripped from the doorway – and the militiamen are already dragging some cardboard boxes from the store and piling them into the former mayor's droshky.

The rain stopped suddenly, like a spoiled brat who stops squalling when he sees that no one pays him any more attention. The black oilcloth hood of the droshky, still wet, gleamed in the sun. The sparrows shouted something to the people from the roof. The people, from eighteen to fifty, shouted to the actors on the stage: 'Hey, comrades! What have you got there?'

The militiamen, who were not given any lines by the author, were silent. Susin paused long enough, then carelessly, over his shoulder, as you might throw away a match after lighting a cigarette, he threw out the words, 'Special clothing'.

And Susin's match immediately ignited all of Rosa Luxemburg, from eighteen to fifty.

'Special clothing? Where? For whom? Oh-h, so that's what you're up to, and we're to get a fig? Citizens, working people, hold them! Citizens!'

Susin jumped into the droshky, with the militiamen close behind him. One of them began to whip the horse as if it were the class enemy himself (indeed, the 'as if' may even be superfluous – the horse had formerly belonged to a merchant). The grey class enemy broke into a gallop, carrying away with it the secret of the special clothing.

Half an hour later the telephone in Papalagi's office rang to report that there was unrest in the street on account of the special clothing. To pacify the citizens, everyone from eighteen to fifty was issued an additional food coupon. And matches: one matchbox to every three men. The people from eighteen to fifty buzzed still more violently, like swarming bees. Swarms of events were in the air, though at the moment it was still unclear where they would settle, where they would come to hang in a tangled, dark, winged cluster.

The repentant Deacon Indikoplev lived in a rented room. His house, the deaconess, his children, his money, and his sofa – everything firm and solid – had been left behind, and the deacon was now living in the midst of swirling chaos: photographs of Marx and Martha, a bed without sheets, pamphlets and cigarette butts. When the deacon returned here at twilight and hid his naked nose in the dirty pillow, all those things began to turn around him; his bed swayed and cast off with the deacon from the shores of reality.

At once his hands, feet, fingers were a hundred versts away, and at the same time right there – as distant and as near as the dots and circles of cities on a map. The deacon leaped through himself along a curious spiral and took up a position in the corner, from which he could see everything. And it was quite clear that the spot where the deacon's naked nose was resting was Moscow, buried in the soured feathers of the pillow. To keep from suffocating, it was essential to lift a hand, to free Moscow from the feathers. But the house, the deaconess, the children, and the sofa crushed him with their weight. It was the end! If he could only cross himself – but that was forbidden. From his corner the deacon saw that he was dressed in a wine-red Tolstoy blouse instead of a cassock, and on the wall above him was a furry Marx, who looked like Sterlingov ...

Sterlingov's name pricked his stomach like a knitting needle. The prone, hundred-verst-long deacon and the tiny deacon in the corner merged into one, and this one jumped up and opened the window. From the cemetery came the sound of bells ringing for vespers. Around the corner, soldiers were singing the 'Internationale'. And it was impossible for all this to be together. He must disentangle it right away, he must seek out Sterlingov at once and explain to him that, by God, there is no God, but there is ... there is ... That, well – there is ... what?

The deacon despairingly waved his hand and hurried off to the District Executive Committee. There he was told that Sterlingov must be in the club upstairs. The deacon climbed the staircase, opened the door covered with torn oilcloth, and entered.

In the huge hall – way down, a hundred versts away – a kerosene lamp blinked in a blur of smoke. A little old woman at a piano was playing a mignon. Militiamen in blouses made of sacks were stepping backwards, bumping into one another with loud peals of laughter. A class in ballet and dramatics for militiamen. The rank stench of a hospital train.

The deacon shouted, 'Is Comrade Sterlingov here?'

The mignon froze in mid-step, the old woman took out a handkerchief and either blew her nose or cried. The deacon covered his naked nose with his hand and said to somebody's merry teeth holding a cigarette, suspended in a cloud of smoke, without a face: 'I must see Comrade Sterlingov, I have to explain to him that God ... I ... It's urgent business. Can't I see him now? Find out, please.'

'Oh, all right ...' and the militiaman, backing away with mincing dance-steps, vanished in a dark corner.

A short, three-eighths' pause, filled with a medley of tolling bells and the 'Internationale' (the window was open). After the three-eighths were gone, the deacon heard through the smoke, from a hundred versts away: 'He can't be seen now. He said to detain you. Sit down here for the time being.'

The deacon sat down obediently. After a final sob the little old woman resumed her playing. The militiamen floated once more in the smoke, stepping backwards. And it was only then that the word 'detain' reached the deacon across the vast distance. Detain! He was lost! They would come after him with guns and take him away ... On its way down his heart stopped in his feet; his feet became independent, logical, thinking creatures. In the space of a second they made their decision and cautiously raised the deacon; stepping backward in time to the music, like everybody else, he edged towards the door. There, filling his lungs with all the air they would hold, he tumbled headlong down the stairs, dashed out into the street, and ran.

It was like being in a train – telegraph poles, black squares of windows, tiny pinhead lights, a samovar on a table. And suddenly, a bright slanting shaft of light, heads sharply outlined against the darkness, shoulders, noses, a crowd. The way forward was blocked. Turning back was unthinkable. The deacon squeezed himself into a brick niche in a gateway, closed his eyes tightly, and waited: in a moment they would come after him.

And indeed somebody came up and shouted right into the deacon's ear: 'It's finished! They gave it all away!'

Who gave it away? It made no difference. He must run. The deacon threw himself forward and opened his eyes.

In front of him stood the telegraph clerk Alyoshka, his arms stretched out before him, clasping a piece of black bread tightly between cupped palms, like a bird that might fly off.

'They gave it out,' he cried, 'instead of special clothing! I was the last to get it, there's no more left.'

The deacon let all the air out of his lungs with a long hissing sound like the cow in the barn. And all at once he realized that he was hungry, he hadn't eaten anything since morning. At home he had some gruel in the cupboard. He must go home! But Alyoshka seized him by the sleeve, 'Look, look, look! But look!'

In the strip of light slanting from a window, he saw Susin in his shaggy white coat on the porch across the street. Next to him was the pockmarked Puzyrev, the one who had been missing in action for two years and then came back from a German prisoner-of-war camp. Puzyrev poked Susin with two fingers as though he was pronging a cucumber with a fork. 'So there's no more bread? In that case, will you tell me, for example, what I was missing in action for, for two long years? Fellow citizens, get him, let him have it!'

Everything tilted in the slanting light. Susin fell, and the crowd piled up on him in a dense, swarming mass. For a moment Susin's hand clutching a key stood out clearly ...

Several lines seem blotted out here. Or perhaps the deacon had really forgotten how he got back to his room, how he ate the cold gruel. After he had finished he wanted to cover the saucepan with a Trotsky pamphlet, but then he changed his mind: he knew that he would never return here, because the end of the story had to be tragic. To fulfil this end, he picked up the iron cleaver that he used for splitting kindling for his samovar, and went out to meet the inevitable.

Branches of lilac hung over the fence next to his house. At this hour the lilacs were iron-black. Two figures sat embracing under the lilacs; a stocking and a bare knee gleamed whitely in the dark. The two were kissing loudly. This seemed to turn on a switch inside the deacon, lighting up a room (inside the deacon) where Martha was kissing somebody. Everything else went dark, and the deacon now remembered only one thing: he must hurry to Martha's house, to spy him out.

There, in the house on Pancake Street, one window was bright, and a shadow moved against the white curtain. Now she raised her arms to her head: she had evidently just undressed, and now she was coiling her braid like a wreath around her

head – as she had done that first time, by the river. The thought
scalded the deacon as though he had swallowed a glass of un-
diluted alcohol. He began to tiptoe to the window, intending to
raise the curtain, when someone sneezed behind him. The
deacon started, turned, and saw *him* at Martha's gate. The face
was indistinct. All he could see was the turned-up collar and a
dandyish white sailor hat like a plate pulled low over the eyes.

In his pocket – far, far, a hundred versts away – the deacon
felt the cleaver with trembling fingers. No, later! Let *him* climb
into the garden first! And he went on, past the lighted window,
past the ruins of the Perelygin house. Then he glanced back: the
sailor hat was turning round the corner, to where the garden
gate opened on the alleyway. Martha's window went dark; it
meant that she expected a visitor . . .

The deacon delayed a moment – like the bombs in Leo Tolstoy which delay exploding but spin around and around again.
He pulled out the cleaver, wiped it for some reason with his
coat-tail, then, vaulting over the fence into the garden, he shot
like a bomb through the wet, swishing lilacs toward the bench,
to finish off both *him* and this story with a single blow.

We have long become overgrown with calluses; we no
longer hear people being killed. Nobody heard the deacon cry
as he swung the cleaver. Everyone from eighteen to fifty was
busy with the peaceful revolutionary work of preparing supper:
herring cutlets, herring ragout, herring dessert. Somewhere in
the street lay Susin with a key clutched in his hand. The
fragrance of lilacs wafted in through open windows. Comrade
Papalagi was interrogating five men arrested near the bread
store and inquiring by telephone about the outcome of the
affair of Pancake Street.

But the affair of Pancake Street was not yet over. The bomb
was spinning still more madly. The deacon found no one on the
bench. Scratched, wet, flaming red, he rushed to Pancake Street.
On the corner he halted, still spinning, and caught sight again of
the white sailor hat among the Maytime lilacs, floating quickly
towards him.

Instantly the room devoted to Marthism turned dark (inside
the deacon), and the light was switched on in another room –

the room with Marx, Sterlingov, and other dreaded furry men. For it was, of course, the furry Sterlingov–Marx who had sent the sailor hat to detain the deacon. This became as clear as daylight in the darkness. He must run – anywhere, to any place his feet will take him!

The deacon – huge – sped down Pancake Street, and saw his own swinging arms. But it was not really he: he himself, tiny as a dot, stood in the middle of the street and watched the other one running. And suddenly fear pricked his stomach. He noticed that the other, the huge one, was running backwards, like the militiamen stepping backwards in the dance . . . and now . . . now he was backing up past the charred walls of the Perelygin house. He must stop, he must make some sense of what was happening. The deacon dived into a bare, doorless opening in the wall and crouched down, breathing hard.

There was a dense dank odour – as in all the empty houses that year. From above, through the black rectangle, the stars looked down indifferently on Russia, like foreigners. In a single instant the deacon heard loud breathing, the tolling of bells from the cemetery (for the third time!), and shots. And, of course, it was impossible for one man at the same moment to hear all that, to see the stars, to smell the stench. Hence, the deacon was not one, but . . .

Flat, plopping footsteps behind the wall. Slowly, unfolding himself joint by joint like a folding ruler, the deacon raised himself, looked out through the opening in the wall, and gasped: the man in the sailor hat had doubled himself, and now – double, in two sailor hats – he was squatting and striking a match, examining the deacon's footprints in the damp earth. The deacon could endure it no longer: screaming, jumping over logs, stoves, bricks, he plunged across the Perelygin house. He heard *him* trip and stumble, swearing in two voices, falling behind.

The deacon ran through empty alleys stuffed with black cotton wool until he reached the cemetery; it started immediately after Pancake Street. There he huddled by the fence, where the cemetery dropped into the ravine and where the dead were buried in mass graves that year. Salty, acrid drops crept from his forehead into his eyes. The deacon wiped his face and sat down on a gravestone. A breathless red moon climbed out, and the deacon saw a marble tablet with golden letters: DOCTOR I. I. PHENOMENOV. VISITING HOURS, 10 TO 2. The tablet had formerly hung on the doctor's door, and when the doctor had moved to the cemetery, it was bolted onto his gravestone. The deacon understood very clearly that something was wrong with his head. He really ought to have a talk with the doctor, and he decided to wait for the beginning of Phenomenov's visiting hours.

But he was not destined to see the doctor. *He,* of the white sailor hat, reappeared over the graveyard fence. And he multiplied himself with terrifying speed: now he was no longer two, but five – in five white sailor hats. The deacon knew this was the end, there was no way out, and he shouted, 'I give up! I give up!'

When the captive was brought in, Papalagi turned the green lampshade so as to throw the full light on him and asked: 'Name?'

'Indikoplev', said the deacon.

'Ah, In-di-ko-plev! I see! Social origin? Parents?'

Somewhere far, a hundred versts away, the deacon knew that it would not do, it would not do at all to say that his progenitor had been a priest. He covered his naked nose with his hand and mumbled uncertainly through his hand, 'I . . . they . . . there were . . . no parents.'

Papalagi aimed his terrifying black moustache at him – like a pair of horns. 'Quit fooling around! Confess!'

The deacon was impaled. So everything was known! It was all the same now.

'I confess,' he said. 'I crossed myself. Though I'd given up religion. I crossed myself publicly, I confess.'

Papalagi turned to someone in the corner. 'What's the matter with him? Is he trying to play the idiot? All right, just let him try!' Papalagi pressed a button.

And then *he* entered – an indeterminate, gelatin face, with a raised collar and a sailor hat. The deacon blanched and began to mutter, backing away, 'That's him . . . five hats – the same . . .

Please, don't. For the sake of Chri ... I mean, no, no, not for the sake!'

Papalagi glanced at the hat and his moustache bristled angrily. Then he pointed at the captured Socialist-Revolutionary who was pretending to be mad: 'Take him to cell number ten. And report back to me at once!'

The deacon was taken away. Afterwards, when all the five in the elegant sailor hats stood lined up in the office, Papalagi shouted, 'What's this masquerade? What sort of hats, what nonsense? Whose idea was it?'

The one nearest the desk took his hands from his pockets, removed his hat and turned it in his hands.

'You see, Comrade Papalagi ... It's the special clothing they issued, you see ... to be worn ... I mean, according to orders ...'

'Off with them at once! Do you hear me?'

And the five articles of special clothing obediently lay down in a neat pile on the desk.

Such was the end of the myth concerning special clothing. And, evidently, this is the end of our story as well, since there are no more Xs left and, moreover, since vice has already received its due punishment. As for the moral (every tale must have a moral), it is entirely clear: never trust priests, even when they supposedly repent.

[*1926*]

COMRADE CHURYGIN HAS
THE FLOOR

My most esteemed citizens – and also lady citizens, who are giggling, way in the back, in disrespect to the moment that is an evening of recollections about the revolution – I ask you, citizens: do you desire to join my recollections to yourselves as well? In that case, I will beg you to sit without any giggles and refrain from interfering with the preceding orator.

First of all, maybe I ought to apologize that my recollections, as against all the rest, are an honest-to-goodness bitter fact. Because everything that was said here was as smooth as writing, but my story isn't writing, but just as it naturally happened in our village of Kuyman, in the Izbishchensk district, which is my beloved homeland.

Our whole nature out there is situated in a solid forest; there is nothing like a more-or-less provincial town in the distance, and the life that goes on in those parts is dark and ignorant – like, you might say, among the zebras or some such tribe. Myself, of course, included – without social consciousness up to the age of sixteen, and even believing in religion. But now, of course, all that is quit and finished, and amen. My brother Stepka – may his soul rest in paradise! – was about twenty-five, and long-grown in height besides, though somewhat literate. Aside from Stepka, we had another hero – the cooper's son Yegor, who'd also shed his life's blood at the front.

But as all of this existed at the moment of capitalism, there was also the enemy class three versts away, in the person of the former spider – I mean, the landowner Tarantayev – who naturally sucked our blood and brought back home from foreign lands all sorts of things, like, for example, naked statues. And these statues were set out in his garden, just like

236

that, especially one with a spear, some sort of a god – not our own Christian Orthodox one, but a god all the same. And there were parties in the garden, with songs and lanterns, and our peasant women used to stand and gape behind the fence, and Stepka, too.

Stepka, he wasn't nuts or anything, but queer somehow, and he had something damaged inside, so they never even took him in the army, and he remained like an unemployed member of our household life. Everybody envied him, front and back, and he sat sighing and reading books. And what kind of books, I ask you, did we have at that Tsarist moment? Not books, but, if one may say so, dregs of society or, to make it short, fertilizer. And the whole public library, if you allow me, was in the form of the lay nun Agafya, forty-three years old, who read the Psalter over the dead.

Well, naturally, Stepka filled himself up on those books and started playing the fool. At night, sometimes, I'd wake and look down from the bunk, and there he was, all white, before the icon, hissing through his teeth, 'Do-o-st hear-r me? Do-s-s-st hear?' Once, just for fun, I say to him, 'I hear, I hear.' And he gives a start and jumps this high! But then I couldn't hold it any more, with laughter bursting out of my nose. He gave me such a shaking, my lungs and my liver didn't know which was which – took me a good long while to catch my breath.

Then in the morning, Stepka bowed low to our father's feet. 'Let me go into a monastery,' he begged. 'I can't live daily like the rest of you, for there's an unknown dream stuck in my breast.' And Daddy said to him, 'Stepka,' he said, 'you're a practical fool and nothing else. Tomorrow you're going to the city, to work with Uncle Artamon.' Stepka began to argue, saying all sorts of words out of the Holy Writ. But our daddy, he wasn't no man's fool, and with a streak of cunning besides. So he said to Stepka, 'And what does it say in your Writ? That every son of a bitch must listen to his mother and his father. Them are the true holy words.' And so he wiped Stepka's organ of the nose with the Holy Writ himself, and Stepka gave in and went off at dawn to Uncle Artamon, who was working as a retired watchman in a factory.

And here, as they say, is a bird's-eye picture of life for you: here, for example, is a factory turning full steam, and somewhere on the African border there are impossible cliffs of mountains and a frightful battle going on, but we in our woods see nothing; the women bawl like calves without their men, and on top of it all there's a bitter frost.

In the course of time, the cooper's daughter-in-law got a letter from her husband Yegor at the front that he was made a hero, first class, with the Cross of St George, and she was to expect him home any day now. Naturally, the woman rejoiced and put on clean stockings. One afternoon, it was St Nicholas' Eve, my daddy and I came out to look, and there was Yegorka, the cooper's son, in a sleigh, waving his hand and saying words we couldn't catch, steam pouring out in clouds from his mouth in view of the cold frost.

I was, naturally, all excited to see the hero, but my daddy says to me, 'We'll bide a while, give him a chance to make a junction with his woman first.' And just as he said it, Yegor's woman bursts into our house herself. Her eyes white, terrible, her hands shaking, and she cries in a black voice, 'Help me, in God's name, help me manage with Yegor!' Well, we think, he must have trounced her – we've got to stick up for a female creature. So we washed our hands and went with her.

We come in and take a look: the samovar is boiling, the bed is made up on the bunk, everything right and proper, and Yegor himself is standing quietly by the trunk. Except he isn't standing: he's propped against the trunk like he was a sack of oats, and his head is level with the trunk. As for his legs, there's not a stump left – cut off clean under the belly.

We were stunned and just stood there without any consequences. After a while, Yegor began to laugh in a queer, ugly way – it set my teeth on edge to hear him – and he says to us, 'Well? A fine hero, first class? Got your eyeful? Now lift me up on top of the woman, with your help.' And so his woman lay down on the bed, and we lifted up Yegor from the floor and laid him down in the proper way. After which we went out, and I banged the door and caught this here finger in it, but didn't even feel no pain to speak of: I walk and keep on seeing in my eyes the imagination of Yegor against the trunk.

In the evening, of course, the village gathered in Yegor's house, every man and woman of us. Yegor was on the bench under the icons, either standing against the wall or sitting, whichever way you'd put it. And everybody who came in shook his head at the fright of it and kept silent, and he kept silent and smoked. And I stood there by the stove and could hear the roaches crawl out and rustle on the wall.

Luckily now, the cooper came, the father, and took out a bottle of vodka from his pocket. Yegor, naturally, drank down a glass and just began to pour another when somebody's kid bounced in from the street, yelling happily, 'The *barin*! The *barin*!' We look, and it's a fact: the *barin* Tarantayev comes in the door. All shaven, with a fine, luxurious smell around him – you could tell he was accustomed to light food. He just nodded to us and turned straight to Yegor. 'Well,' he says, 'congratulations to you, Yegor, congratulations.' And Yegor grinned with his face on one side, unpleasant-like, and said, 'And may I take the liberty, just what do you congratulate me for?' The *barin* says to him in reply, 'In view as you're our pride and a hero who has suffered for the homeland.' And he lifts up the sacking around Yegor's lower parts and bends down with his nose to look.

At that moment, Yegor's face got twisted, he scrunched his teeth, and whacked him on the neck, once and again. The *barin* got so flustered with excitement, he poked Yegor, who keeled over on his side like a sack and couldn't get up, but just yelled, 'Get him! Get him!' I jumped up to the *barin* with the rest, my heart shaking like a rabbit's tail, and there was nothing in the world I needed except to grab him by the throat. In short – the class war. *Barin* Tarantayev, red-faced, opened his mouth to speak, but tripped against our hateful eyes as if he'd stepped into a bed of nettles – and dashed double-quick for the door.

Under the impact of this victory, the peasants quieted down and told Yegor he was sure a hero, first class. Yegor naturally tossed off another glass and gradually made a speech that how was he a hero when he'd squatted down at the front into a hole to do his rude necessity, when it came down from above, smack on his feet? 'But we shall soon', he says, 'make an end to all this deception of the people's vision in the form of war. Because', he says, 'we know without contradiction that now we've got one of our own, a muzhik, at the Tsar's court, Grigory Yefimych by name.* He's over all the ministers, and he'll show them where the hell they get off.' When our peasants heard this, well, they were all moved with feeling and yelled with rejoicing that now, of course, both the war and the gentry were done for, finished, and we all relied our hopes on Grigory Yefimych, being he was in power and our own muzhik. And I'll tell you, fellow citizens, that now, of course, I understand everything quite expediently about this Grigory Yefimych, but at that time the news just sent my blood into a pulse.

And now, the rest of it. Namely, after Yegor insulted the *barin* on the neck, there was a strained rupture between us and that spider. He'd even posted a purebred Circassian at his gate, with a dagger for the prevention of entry. Before that, we used to go to the estate for newspapers and such, but now we lived in total woods, like zebras, and knew nothing at all about the course of events on the distant globe of the earth, like, for example, in Petersburg.

By and by, the former Christmas came around, then Shrovetide, frost, and thaw. And on Shrovetide my daddy receives a sudden letter from Stepka in the city. As we had no liquidation of literacy to speak of at that time, and the only reading man, as you might say, was Yegor, a peck of folks piled up at his house to hear Stepka's letter. And Stepka wrote that it was now inconvertibly known at his factory that all the business about God was nothing but a superstitious fact; as against it, there was a book called Marx. Also, he said, a certain important killing had taken place in the capital city of Petersburg, and, therefore, he said, wait and see what big things happen next in the near future. As for the wages at the factory, they were as miserable as could be, only nine and a half a month, and he was soon arriving in his own person.

* The reference is to Rasputin.

Yegor stood on the bench, propped up against the window-sill, and he added with his hands, 'You see,' he yelled, 'what did I tell you about Grigory Yefimych? It's all his work, don't have no doubt about that!'

Although the letter was unclear about the killing and kind of incomplete about God in the matter of prejudice, we had a feeling in our bones that all these things weren't to no purpose, and so we actually waited. We had no idea what we were waiting for, but, if you know what I mean, it was like a brute dog – pardon the expression – worrying before a fire. That's how we were. And besides, there was a terrible frost, everything quiet, and a woodpecker tap-tapping in the woods. And all of us, just like the woodpecker, harping on one thing – Grigory Yefimych.

In due time, a day or two went by; then it was dusk, and we see a mounted messenger on a black horse galloping straight for the Tarantayev estate and, over behind the estate, the setting sun, all swollen from the cold, and red. Yegor is, naturally, our general in chief, and he says, 'It's starting. Keep an eye on the estate without cease and bring me back reports.'

Just to be sure, we posted up two sentries: myself and another fellow, the hunchbacked Mitka. So we sit in the bushes, blowing on our fingers to keep them warm, and we can hear every nervous noise in the manor yard, and the dogs barking, and we're shaking. After a while, we look: without an evil word, the gates fling open and a crazy sled pops out, with the lady Tarantayev and her girl, both of them bawling, and after them the mounted fellow on his black horse, yelling at the lady like she was a dog, '*Alé!*' And then the sled goes one way, and the horseman the other – straight at us. The hunchbacked Mitka tried to pull me into the bushes, but my blood boiled up all of a sudden, as if I'd filled myself with alcoholic fumes and didn't know what I was doing. I waved my arms and ran straight at the horseman. Naturally, he stopped and says, 'What's happened?' and his horse snorts in my face. And I say right out, 'Nothing here, but what is happening out there, with you people?' 'That,' he says, 'ain't nothing to do with you. *Alé!*' But I stare him in the eye and say with expression, 'And how,' I say, about Grigory Yefimych? Does that have anything to do with you?' And he answers with a certain little laugh, 'Your Grigory Yefimych is done for. Thank God, he was bumped off a long time ago!' And he gallops off in the direction.

So I rushed full speed to Yegor. His house is chock-full of peasants, everybody in tense expectation. As I started to report, my innocent heart of a sixteen-year-old got into my throat, and I cry bitterly for the lost happy dream in the form of Grigory Yefimych, and I see that everybody else sits with a sigh, stunned-like. And in conclusion of this sad intermission, Yegor announces his orders: everybody is to disperse home till morning for various natural necessities, like food and soporific rest.

Then gradually comes this significant morning when you in Petersburg see the triumph and the jubilee of the revolution, with flags and all, but in our parts there wasn't nothing like it at all. Still, as a man might say, the things that happened were, of course, the distant thunder in full connection, and on top of everything there was this frightful frost. So we gathered in front of Yegor's house in felt boots, and we lifted up Yegor into a basket filled with hay, like in a manner of speaking, on a platform, and put him into a sled. After which Yegor announced from the basket that the hours were struck and we couldn't take it any longer, so we'd storm the Tarantayev manor in force. Let the *barin* give us a full accounting of how they'd killed our defender Gregory Yefimych, and, maybe, God willing, he was still alive. Naturally, we all unanimously marched along the snow, and the snow was so blue in the sun it made your eyes water, and inside of us everything boiled wild as in a dog that sat ten years tied to a chain and suddenly broke loose and went off on a rampage.

The moment Tarantayev's purebred Circassian saw us in full numbers, he shut the gate and raised a row and all sorts of excitements inside, including the voice of the *barin* Tarantayev telling us that unusual events were going on in the capital and so we'd best go home without grievous consequences and wait for speedy developments. And Yegor shouted to him from his basket that we'd waited enough, we'd eaten two barrelfuls of waiting, and now we were obliged to find out the facts, and let him open up the gates at once, because we'd break them down anyway.

Then we heard a silence and a whispering, after which the gates creaked, and we saw the pleasant view with the pines along the road, and in the sight of all, the statue with a spear, which still had a useful role before it in coming events. Naturally, we marched inside in solid ranks. Namely, Yegor in front in his basket, and the rest of us behind, bunched up any which way. And the *barin* leading with his hind back to us, sprinting at top speed to the goal of his house. Suddenly, there's a revolver from out of nowhere in Yegor's hand, and he yells, aiming at the *barin*, 'Halt!' As soon as this offal of society saw the revolver, he stopped without another word next to the god with the spear, himself stiff like an alleged statue. Then he says to us, 'You're simply making a mistake. I am myself a man out of the people's freedom.' And Yegor says to him sternly, 'So you're at one with Grigory Yefimych? Speak up!' To which the *barin* answers in trembling words, 'Why, no,' he says, 'how can you say that? We're all very happy that this scoundrel Grishka was killed off.' At this, Yegor saw red and yelled to every side, 'You hear him, fellows? The "scoundrel", he says! "Very happy", he says! You so and so!' and so on, with all sorts of swearing remarks. 'And now,' he says, 'we'll pop you off your own self with this revolver.'

Naturally, being he was a specialist, Yegor was a trained hand at every military killing and didn't give a spitting damn. But we still had a certain shade of feeling inside – it was kind of against the grain to do in a fully living man. And while we were, so to speak, exchanging opinions, the *barin* Tarantayev, he stands there without a sign, like a total corpse. Only once, I remember, he wiped the dripping of his nose.

And here a new fact appeared on the road outside the gate, in the form of a man running towards us full speed and waving his hands. Gradually, as we look, it turns out to be Stepka from the city, in accordance with his foregoing letter. His face shines, a tear is creeping down from his eye, and he waves his arms like they were wings, like he would any moment fly up on the will of the air, like a certain bird. And he keeps yelling, 'Brothers, brothers, we've had an overthrow and a revolution, and my heart is just about to crack from impossible freedom, and hurrah!'

We couldn't tell what it was all about, only we felt that Stepka was exploding, as they say, from an overflow of soul, and even his yelling sent goose pimples up and down our backs, so there was general hurrah and an elemental excitement, like at the superstition of Easter. And Stepka gradually clambered up a bench next to the statue, wiping his tears with his mitten and saying, in addition, that the Tsar in the form of Nicholas was retired and that all the rotten palaces should be wiped off to the foundation from the face of the earth, and let there be no more rich men, but let us all live like a poor proletariat according to the former Holy Writ, but nowadays, however, all this was coming to pass according to the science of our dear Marx.

Then every man of us confirms this in the form of 'Hurrah!' and Yegor yells from his basket, at the top of his voice, 'We thank you, our hero Stepka, from our Orthodox Christian hearts! With God's blessing – smash their whole luxurious budget!'

And Stepka grabbed an axe from one of our peasants, jumped up to the statue, the one with the spear, and swung at it from the fullness of his soul to smash it. But at this moment, the *barin* Tarantayev seemed to wake up from out of his corpse and cried, 'This is a precious statue, innocent of any guilt, and maybe that I brought it overland all the way from Rome itself, as it's a countless, costly image, by the name of Mars.'

And we see Stepka's hand drop without consequences, and he says with expression, 'Brothers! Just as I pronounced to you this dear name, suddenly we find his true image right before us in the form of a statue. I take this as an omen from on high and propose that we all bare our hats.'

I ask you, fellow citizens, to take into account that we were then an altogether dark and ignorant people – as you might say, plain Hindus. In consequence of which, we all unanimously pulled off our hats, and so, without our hats, we grabbed this dear image under the backside and hoisted it into the sled next to the basket in which Yegor existed. And Stepka adopted a resolution: to let the *barin* Tarantayev go harmless for the good service that he revealed to us this image; but as a lesson against riches, let him watch how we exterminate his budget. Every man of us confirms this again in the form of 'Hurrah!' – with pleasure that a programme is shaping up without the spilling of a live man. But all the same, sad fate came out contrary to our expectations.

Namely, we advance on the house, with our vanguard in the form of the sled with the statue and Yegor in the basket, and walking alongside of it, our Stepka and the *barin*, with his arms tied up. And the windows glitter at us like suspicious eyes, and I particularly remember one, the attic window under the very roof, with a pleasant-looking pigeon sitting up there. And Stepka turns back his beautiful smile of happiness and yells from out of his soul, 'Brothers, it's more than I can stand! What an extraordinary first and last day of the new life we're having this day!'

And just as he says it, we see the pigeon flutter up, and from the attic window comes an insignificant puff of smoke. And then, maybe in just another tenth moment of a second, there is a terrible crash in the form of a shot, and our Stepka with the foregoing smile drops nose down into a snowdrift.

We stand there like stunned posts and have no time to get our wits back, when another shot knocks off the statue's fingers, and then Yegor, with a frightful shout of profanity, sends two bullets from his revolver into the attic window and one back into the *barin* Tarantayev, who lies down next to Stepka in his dead form. And Yegor, in a hateful state of feeling, fires three more shots at him, with the addition of words: 'And this is for Stepka! And this for Grigory Yefimych! And this for everything!'

And then, of course, there was general hollering and the final merciless degree of events – or, to make it short, total extermination. And you could see all over that innocent snow pieces of broken glass and other utensils, like a sofa that gave up the ghost with its feet up in the air, and the broken corpse of Tarantayev's purebred Circassian, as it was naturally he that fired from the attic, and he was cut down by a bullet from Yegor's military hand. And also I remember, up on a twig, a gilded cage, and an unknown aristocratic bird jumping up and down in it and squealing with its last voice.

In the course of time and according to nature comes the night and the well-known system of stars, looking as though nothing had happened, and only a premature red dawn rises from the darkness – or, in short, the last flames of the former manor house. And with all that, there is a total silence in the village, and all the dogs howling; and in the community house, Stepka lies under the icons in the form of a victim with a smile, and next to him the statue, and the nun Agafya, forty-three years old, reading the Psalter, and the village folks with various tears.

And that's the end of our diversified dark events as in a dream, and after it comes the dawn of an entirely class-conscious day. Namely, a visit from an actual orator. And then we learned in the right and proper manner about the whole current moment, and that Grigory Yefimych, or, in short, Grishka, was no hero, but even on the contrary, and that this statue of ours occurred by reason of a mistake of sound.

And in conclusion, I see that the lady citizens which first sat with a look of laughter, they now have the opposite look, and I support it entirely, seeing as all this is the bitter fact of our dark culture, which, thank the Lord, today exists on the background of the past. And here I will put a dot in the form of a sign and retire, my dear fellow citizens, into your unknown ranks.

[*1926 published 1927*]

THE FLOOD

Around Vasilievsky Island the world lay spread out like a distant sea: out in the world there had been a war, then a revolution. But in the boiler-room where Trofim Ivanovich worked the boiler hummed as usual, and the manometer indicated the same nine atmospheres. Only the coal was different: formerly it had come from Cardiff; now it came from the Donetsk Basin. The new coal was brittle; it crumbled, and the black dust penetrated everywhere. Nothing could wash it off. And it was as though this black dust had imperceptibly coated everything at home as well. Outwardly, nothing was changed. Trofim Ivanovich and Sofya continued to live as they always had, without children. Sofya, though almost forty, was still as light and strict of body as a bird. Her lips, which seemed forever tightly shut to everyone, still opened to Trofim Ivanovich at night. And yet, things weren't the same. The difference was not yet clear, had not yet hardened into words. The words came much later, in the fall, and Sofya remembered: it was on a Saturday night; there was a high wind; the water in the Neva was rising.

That day the water gauge in the boiler-room had burst. Trofim Ivanych had had to go to the repair shop store-room for a spare. He had not been to the workshop for some time, and when he entered, it seemed to him that he had come to the wrong place. Formerly, everything here stirred, tinkled, buzzed, sang – as though a wind were playing with steel leaves in a steel forest. Now it was autumn in this forest. The transmission belts flapped idly, only three or four machines were turning sleepily, a washer squeaked monotonously somewhere. It gave him a turn, like coming to an empty pit, dug for some unknown purpose, and he hurried back to his boiler-room.

In the evening he came home, still heartsick. He ate his

dinner and lay down for a rest. When he awakened, the feeling was gone, forgotten. But he was troubled, as though he had had a dream or lost a key and could not remember what the dream had been about, or what the key was from. It was only at night that he remembered.

All night the wind blew from the sea, beating at the windows. The window-panes rang out. The water in the Neva was rising. And, as if bound with the Neva by underground veins, the blood seemed to be rising too. Sofya did not sleep. Trofim Ivanych found her knee with his hand in the dark, and they were together for a long time. And again it was all wrong, again there was that strange empty pit.

He lay still, the window-pane tinkled monotonously under the pressure of the wind. And suddenly he remembered: the washer, the workshop, the idling belt . . .

'That's it,' Trofim Ivanych said aloud.

'What?' asked Sofya.

'You have no children, that's what.'

And Sofya understood: yes, that was it. And she knew: if there were no child, Trofim Ivanych would go, would imperceptibly trickle out of her drop by drop, like water from a dried-out barrel. Such a barrel stood in their passageway, behind the door. Trofim Ivanych had long been planning to repair it with new hoops, but he had never found the time.

That night – it must have been already close to morning – the door swung open and crashed into the barrel. Sofya ran out into the street. She knew it was the end, there was no way back. Sobbing loudly, she ran towards the Smolensk Field, where somebody was lighting matches in the dark. She tripped and fell, her hands striking something wet. Then it turned light, and she saw that her hands were covered with blood.

'Wake up, why are you screaming?' Trofim Ivanych asked her. Sofya awakened. There was indeed blood, but it was her usual, female blood.

Formerly, those had been simply days when walking was uncomfortable, when her thighs felt cold, unclean. Now she seemed to face a judgement every month, and she waited for the sentence. When the date approached, she could not sleep, both fearful and impatient: perhaps this time it would not come, perhaps she'd turn out to be ... But nothing happened. Inside her there was only emptiness – a pit. Several times she noticed: at night, when she timidly whispered his name, hoping that he would turn towards her, he pretended that he was asleep. And then Sofya would dream again that she was running to the Smolensk Field alone at night. She cried out, and in the morning her lips were shut more tightly than ever.

In the daytime the sun endlessly circled the earth like a bird. The earth lay bare. At twilight the whole Smolensk Field steamed like an overheated horse. One April day the walls became so thin that Sofya could hear distinctly the children in the yard, shouting: 'Catch her, catch her!' Sofya knew that 'she' was the carpenter's girl Ganka. The carpenter lived upstairs, and he lay ill – probably with typhus.

Sofya went down into the yard. Ganka, with her head thrown back, rushed straight at her, chased by four neighbourhood boys. When Ganka saw Sofya, she shouted something over her shoulder to the boys and slowed down, approaching Sofya sedately. Ganka exuded heat, she was breathing fast, her upper lip with the small black birthmark quivered. 'How old is she?' thought Sofya. 'Twelve, thirteen? ...' That was exactly how long Sofya had been married; Ganka could have been her daughter. But she was someone else's, she had been stolen from her ...

Something contracted suddenly in Sofya's stomach and rose to her heart. She hated Ganka's smell and her faintly quivering lip with the black birthmark. 'A lady doctor came to see Papa; he's unconscious,' said Ganka. Sofya saw Ganka's lips tremble. The girl lowered her head; she was evidently trying to suppress her tears. And Sofya immediately ached with shame and pity. She took Ganka's head and pressed it to her breast. Ganka broke away with a sob and ran off to the darkest corner of the yard. The boys dashed after her.

With a sharp pain lodged somewhere inside her like a broken needle, Sofya entered the carpenter's rooms. To the right of the door, the lady doctor was washing her hands over the washstand. She was high-breasted, snub-nosed, in pince-nez.

'How is he?' asked Sofya.

'He'll last until tomorrow,' the doctor answered cheerfully. 'And then you and I will have more work.'

'Work? . . . What work?'

'What work? There will be one man less, so we shall have to have more children. How many do you have?' One of the buttons across the doctor's breast was undone; she tried to button it, but the blouse wouldn't meet. She laughed.

'I . . . I have none, Sofya said after a while, opening her lips with an effort.

The carpenter died on the following day. He had been a widower, without relatives. Some neighbouring women came in and stood at the door, whispering among themselves. Then one, wrapped in a warm shawl, said: 'Well, my dears, what's the good of standing here?' And she began to remove her shawl, holding the pin in her teeth. Ganka sat on her bed silently, hunched over, her legs thin, pathetic, bare. On her knees lay an untouched slice of black bread.

Sofya went down to her own apartment; she had to get dinner ready – Trofim Ivanych would soon be home. When she had finished everything and began to set the table, the sky was already turning dark, brittle, pierced by a single desolate star. The doors were slammed upstairs: the neighbours must have done their work and were now leaving, while Ganka still sat motionless with the slice of bread in her lap.

Trofim Ivanych came home. He stood near the table, broad, short-legged – as though his feet were rooted in the earth up to his ankles.

'The carpenter, he died,' said Sofya.

'Oh-h, he died?' Trofim Ivanych asked absently. He was taking a loaf of bread out of a bag; bread was more unusual and rare nowadays than death. Bending over it, he began to slice it carefully, and Sofya suddenly – as though for the first time in all those years – saw his reddened, ravaged face, his gypsy head, thickly sprinkled with grey as with salt.

'No, there won't be any, there won't be any children!' Sofya's heart cried desperately, dropping. And when Trofim Ivanych picked up a slice of bread, Sofya was instantly upstairs, where

Ganka sat alone on the bed with the bread on her lap, while an April star, sharp as the point of a needle, looked into the window. The grey hair, Ganka, the bread, the solitary star in the empty sky – all this was fused into a single whole, incomprehensibly interlinked, and Sofya said, unexpectedly even to herself: 'Trofim Ivanych, let's take Ganka, let her live with us ...' She could not go on.

Trofim Ivanych looked up at her, surprised, and then the words reached into him through the coal dust, went deeper, and he began to smile – slowly, as slowly as he had untied the bag with the bread. When he untied the smile all the way, his teeth gleamed, and with a new face he said: 'You're all right, Sofya! Bring her here, we'll have enough bread for three.'

That night Ganka slept in their kitchen. Lying in bed, Sofya listened to the girl settling down on her bunk, and later to her even breathing. Sofya thought to herself, 'Now everything will be well,' and fell asleep.

2

The children in the yard were now playing new games. The latest was 'kolchak'. The one who was 'kolchak' hid himself; the others looked for him, then shot him with their sticks to the accompaniment of drums and songs. The real Kolchak* had also been shot. No one ate horsemeat any longer. The stores were now selling sugar, galoshes, flour. The boiler at the plant was still heated with Donetsk coal, but Trofim Ivanych now shaved his beard, and the coal dust washed off easily. He used to shave his face many years ago, before his marriage; now he seemed to have returned to those years. Sometimes he even laughed in the old way, his teeth flashing white like accordion keys.

This usually happened on Sundays, when he was home and Ganka was home. She was just finishing school. Trofim Ivanych made her read the newspaper aloud. Ganka read rapidly and

* A. V. Kolchak was a Tsarist admiral and a leader in the early counter-revolutionary struggle. He was captured and shot by the Bolsheviks in 1920.

fluently, but she garbled all the new words: 'molbization', 'Central Sense Administration'.

'What, what?' Trofim Ivanych would ask, simmering with laughter.

'Central Sense', Ganka would repeat calmly. Then she spoke about a new teacher who had come to her school the other day and told them that there were bodies on earth and also bodies in the sky.

'What bodies?' Trofim Ivanych asked, barely able to contain his laughter.

'Um, what bodies! Like this!' Ganka poked her finger at her breast, small and sharp under her dress.

And Trofim Ivanych could no longer suppress his laughter; it burst out of his nose and mouth like steam out of the safety valves of a boiler under pressure.

Sofya sat alone, apart. Central Science Administration, heavenly bodies, Ganka with a newspaper – all this was equally remote and incomprehensible to her. Ganka spoke and laughed only with Trofim Ivanych. When she remained alone with Sofya, she was silent; she made the stove, washed dishes, spoke to the cat. Only at times her green eyes slowly, intently turned on Sofya, clearly thinking something about her, but what? It is thus that cats stare at your face, thinking their own thoughts – and suddenly you feel uneasy under the scrutiny of those green eyes, with their incomprehensible, feline thoughts. Sofya would slip into her jacket, throw her thick shawl over her head and go out somewhere – to the store, to church, or simply out into the dark of Maly Prospect – just to avoid remaining alone with Ganka. She walked past the still unfrozen, black ditches, past fences made of roofing iron, and felt nothing but a wintry emptiness. On Maly, across from the church, there was just such an empty house with windows that seemed to have crumbled away. Sofya knew: nobody would ever live there again, it would never know the sound of merry childish voices.

One evening in December she chanced to pass this house. As always, she hurried to get past without looking at it. But fleetingly, out of the corner of her eye, as a bird in flight might see it, she caught the glimmer of a light in one of the empty

windows. She stopped: it couldn't be! Retracing her steps, she
glanced into the gaping square. Inside, amidst a litter of broken
bricks, a fire was burning and around it were four ragged
urchins. One of them, facing Sofya, black-eyed – he must have
been a gypsy – was dancing up and down; a silver cross
bounced on his chest, his teeth glittered.

The empty house had come alive. The gypsy boy somehow
resembled Trofim Ivanych. Sofya felt suddenly that she was also
alive, that everything could still change.

Excitedly, she entered the church across the street. She had
not been there since 1918, when Trofim Ivanych, with other
workers from the factory, was leaving for the front. The service
was conducted by the same moss-grown, grey-haired little
priest. The singing filled her with warmth, the ice was melting,
the winter within was going; in the darkness before her someone
was lighting candles.

When Sofya returned home, she had a strong desire to tell
Trofim Ivanych about everything. But what exactly was this
'everything'? She no longer knew it herself, and merely said that
she had been to church. Trofim Ivanych laughed: 'Going to the
old church! If you'd at least go to the Living Church – their
God still has some sort of a Party card.' He winked to Ganka.
With that winking eye, beardless, his face was mischievous like
the gypsy boy's – with teeth, gay and greedy. Ganka sat with a
flushed face; she hid her eyes and only threw a quick, sidelong
glance at Sofya.

After that Sofya often went to church, until one day when a
Living Church priest appeared at Mass time, with a crowd of
his followers. The new priest was a red-haired giant in a short
cassock and looked like a masquerading soldier. The grey little
old priest shrieked, 'I won't, I won't let you,' and flung himself
at him; the two rolled out onto the porch; fists began to flash
over the crowd like banners. Sofya left and never returned
there. She began to take the trolley to Okhta, where the cobbler
Fyodor, with a bald yellow skull, preached the 'Third Tes-
tament'.

Spring was late that year. By Whit Monday the trees were just
beginning to come into leaf; the buds quivered with a tremor

invisible to the eye and burst open. Evenings were bright and brittle, with swallows darting about restlessly. The cobbler Fyodor preached the imminent coming of the Last Judgement. Large drops of sweat rolled down his bald yellow skull, his frenzied blue eyes glittered so that one could not look away. 'Not from heaven, no! From here, from here, from here!' Trembling with his whole body, the cobbler struck his breast again and again and tore his white shirt, exposing his yellow, crumpled body. He clutched at himself, trying to tear his skin as he had torn his shirt. He could not breathe. With a desperate, gasping cry, he dropped to the floor in a fit of epilepsy. Two women remained with him; everyone else left quickly without waiting for the end of the meeting.

All in a fever from the cobbler's insane eyes, bursting with tension like the buds on the trees, Sofya returned home. There was no key in the door; the door was locked. Trofim Ivanych and Ganka must have gone out somewhere and would not be back until eleven – she had told them not to expect her before eleven. Sofya thought of going upstairs for a while, to wait for their return.

The apartment upstairs was now occupied by Pelageya and her husband, a coachman. Through the open window Sofya heard her talking to her child: 'Agoo-agoo-agoonyushki ... There, there!' No, she had no strength now to see the woman and her child. Sofya sat down on the clay steps. The sun was still high, the sky glittered like the cobbler's eyes. From somewhere came a smell of hot black bread. Sofya remembered: the bolt on the kitchen window was broken, and Ganka had probably forgotten to fasten the window; she always forgot. It might be possible to open the window and climb in.

Sofya went to the back of the house. The window was not fastened. Sofya easily opened it and climbed into the kitchen. She thought: anybody could have gotten in – perhaps someone had? Something seemed to rustle in the living-room. Sofya stopped. The house was quiet, only the clock ticked on the wall, and inside Sofya, and everywhere. Without knowing why, Sofya walked on tiptoe. Her dress caught at the ironing board that leaned against the door; the board crashed to the floor.

Immediately, there was a padding of bare feet in the room. Sofya gasped and began to back toward the window – to jump out – to call for help . . .

But there was no time for anything: the door was opened by Ganka, barefoot, in nothing but a crumpled pink shift. Ganka stood petrified, her mouth and eyes staring roundly at Sofya. Then she shrank like a cat when someone lifts an arm to strike it, cried out, 'Trofim Ivanych!' and dashed back into the room.

Sofya raised the board, put it back in its place, and sat down. She had nothing – no hands, no feet, nothing but a heart, and the heart was tumbling like a bird, falling, falling, falling.

Almost immediately, Trofim Ivanych came in. He was dressed. Apparently, he had not taken off his clothes. He stood in the middle of the kitchen, large-headed, short-legged – as though sunk into the ground up to his knees. 'You . . . How come you're back so early today?' he asked, and wondered at himself: why had he said it, how could he have said it?

Sofya did not hear. Her lips were twitching like the skin on milk when it is cooling. 'But what is this, what is this, what is this?' Sofya brought out with difficulty, without looking at Trofim Ivanych.

Trofim Ivanych shrivelled up, huddled into some corner inside himself and stood so for a moment silently. Then he pulled his feet up out of the ground, slowly, with the root, and walked away into the other room, where Ganka was already pattering with her shoes, all dressed.

Everything in the world went on, unchanged, and one had to go on living. Sofya prepared supper. As always, the plates were served by Ganka. As she brought in the bread, Trofim Ivanych turned, his head struck it and the bread fell into his lap. Ganka shrieked with laughter. Sofya looked at her; their eyes collided, and for a moment they stared at one another in an altogether new way. Sofya felt something rising within her, roundly, slowly from the pit of her stomach, then faster, hotter, higher. Her breath came fast. She could no longer look at the blond bangs over Ganka's forehead, the black birthmark on her lip. She felt that she must scream like the cobbler Fyodor, that she must do something at once. Sofya lowered her eyes. Ganka grinned.

After supper Sofya washed the dishes. Ganka stood near her with the towel, drying them. This went on endlessly; it was, perhaps, the most difficult thing that evening. Then Ganka retired to her cot in the kitchen. Sofya began to make the bed; everything within her was burning and she shook as with a fever. Turning away, Trofim Ivanych said, 'Make my bed on the bench by the window. 'She made his bed on the bench. At night, when she stopped tossing, she heard Trofim Ivanych get up and go to Ganka in the kitchen.

3

On Sofya's window-sill stood a glass jar, turned upside down. A fly had somehow gotten into the jar. It had no way of escape, yet it crawled and crawled about all day. The sun made the air under the jar thick with slow, indifferent, impenetrable heat. The same heat hung over the entire Vasilievsky Island. Yet Sofya moved about all day, forever doing something. Often during the day the clouds gathered, hung low and heavy, and it seemed that in another moment the green glass overhead would crack, bursting at last into a downpour. But the clouds silently melted away. By night-time the glass became still thicker, still more stifling and impenetrable. Nobody heard the different breathing of three people at night: one, buried in the pillow, trying not to hear anything; and two – through clenched teeth, greedily, hotly, like a boiler sprayer.

In the mornings Trofim Ivanych went to the factory. Ganka, who had finished school, remained alone with Sofya. But she was very far away from Sofya: Ganka, Trofim Ivanych, everything around was now seen and heard by Sofya as from an immense distance. From this distance, she would tell Ganka without opening her lips: sweep out the kitchen, wash the millet, chop some firewood. Ganka swept, washed, chopped. Sofya heard the blows of the axe and knew that it was Ganka, that girl Ganka, but it was all far, far away, she could not see any of it.

Ganka always chopped firewood squatting down, with her round knees spread wide apart. One day Sofya suddenly saw those knees, the slightly frizzled lock of hair over the forehead. There was a hammering at her temples; she quickly turned away and said to Ganka without looking: 'I'll do it myself ... Go out into the street.' Ganka gaily shook her bangs and ran out, returning only at dinnertime, just before Trofim Ivanych was to come home.

She began to run out every morning. Pelageya, the woman who lived upstairs, warned Sofya: 'Your Ganka keeps running to the empty house with the boys. You ought to watch her, before she gets herself in trouble.'

Sofya thought, 'Trofim Ivanych ought to be told ...' But when he came, she felt that she could not utter that name aloud. She said nothing to him.

The summer passed in this glassy, tearless way, crushing everything with the weight of its dry clouds. Autumn was coming, just as dry. One blue and unseasonably warm day the wind began to blow from the sea. Through the closed window, Sofya heard a muffled, cottony thud. Soon it was followed by another, and a third. The water in the Neva was probably rising. Sofya was alone. Neither Ganka nor Trofim Ivanych were home. Again the cannon shot thumped softly at the window; the window-panes rang out in the wind. Pelageya came running from upstairs, breathless, her clothes flying, all of her wide open. She cried to Sofya: 'Have you gone mad – why are you sitting here? The Neva is spilling over, in a moment it will flood everything.'

Sofya ran out after her into the yard. At once, the whistling wind wrapped her around tightly as with a sheet of linen. She heard doors banging somewhere, and a woman's voice screaming: 'The chicks, get the chicks together, quick!' Overhead, a large bird, its wings spread wide, was swept aslant across the yard on a blast of wind. Sofya suddenly felt great relief, as if all this was just what she had needed – just such a wind, to overwhelm, to sweep away, to drown everything. She turned to face it, her lips opening wide; the wind burst, singing, into her mouth, her teeth felt blissfully cold.

Together with Pelageya, Sofya quickly moved the bedding, the clothes, the food and the chairs upstairs. The kitchen was already empty, except for the trunk in the corner, adorned with painted flowers. 'And that?' asked Pelageya.

'That's . . . hers,' said Sofya.

'Whose, hers? Ganka's, you mean? So why'd you leave it?' Pelageya lifted the trunk and, balancing it with her stomach, carried it up the stairs.

At two, the wind smashed one of the window-panes. Pelageya ran to stuff the opening with a pillow. Suddenly she wailed, 'We're lost . . . Good God, we're lost!' and rushed to pick up her baby. Sofya looked out of the window: where the street had been, there was a rapid torrent of green water, pitted by the wind. Somebody's table floated past, turning slowly; a white and yellow cat sat on it; it's mouth was open, it must have been meowing. Without naming Ganka, Sofya thought about her, and her heart beat faster.

Pelageya was making the stove. She ran from the stove to the baby, then to the window where Sofya stood. A transom was open in a ground-floor window across the street, and they could see it rocking in the water. The water was rising steadily. Boards, logs, hay swept past. Then something round flashed by; it might have been a head.

'Who knows, my Andrey and your Trofim Ivanych may already be . . .' Pelageya did not finish the sentence. Her tears rolled down – her feelings wide open, large and simple.

Sofya wondered at herself: how was it that she seemed to have forgotten Trofim Ivanych and had been thinking all this time about one thing only, only about that . . . Ganka?

All at once both of them – Pelageya and Sofya – heard voices somewhere in the yard. They ran to the kitchen, to the windows. Pushing through the floating firewood, a rowboat moved across the yard. In it were two strangers and Trofim Ivanych, hatless. Over his quilted vest he wore a blue blouse; the wind pressed it close to his body on one side and billowed it out on the other, so that he looked broken in the middle. The two men asked him something, then the boat swung around the corner of the house, and the wood, colliding, floated after it.

Wet to his waist, Trofim Ivanych ran into the kitchen. The water ran off him, but he did not seem to notice. 'Where ... where is she?' he asked Sofya.

'She went out in the morning,' said Sofya.

Pelageya also understood his question. 'I've been telling Sofya for a long time ... Always running around. She's got hers now, floating somewhere ...'

Trofim Ivanych turned to the wall and began to trace something on it with his finger. He stood so for a long time, the water running down his clothes; he did not feel it.

In the evening, when the water receded, Pelageya's husband came home. His strong, ripe, bald skull gleamed under the hanging lamp as he told them about a gentleman with a briefcase who paddled to his house astride a floating tree, about ladies running and lifting their skirts higher and higher.

'Were many people drowned?' asked Sofya without looking.

'A frightful lot! Thousands!' the cab driver screwed up his eyes.

Trofim Ivanych got up. 'I'll go now,' he said. But he did not go anywhere: the door swung open and Ganka stood in the doorway. Her dress clung to her breast and her knees, she was muddy and dripping, but her eyes glittered. Trofim Ivanych's face twisted into a strange, slow, ugly smile; he seemed to be smiling only with his teeth. He stepped over to Ganka, seized her by the hand and led her away into the kitchen, closing the door tightly after him. They heard him say something to Ganka through his teeth, then he began to beat her. Ganka sobbed. Then she splashed herself with water for a long time, and returned to the room merry again, shaking the bangs on her forehead.

Pelageya put her to sleep in the pantry behind the partition, and made a bed for Trofim Ivanych and Sofya on the bench in the kitchen. They remained alone. Trofim Ivanych put out the lamp. The window became pale; the moon trembled in a thin shift of clouds. Dimly white, Sofya undressed; then Trofim Ivanych took off his clothes.

Lying in bed, Sofya thought of one thing only: he must not notice how she trembled. She lay stretched out, as though covered from head to toe with the thinnest crust of ice: such immaculate sheets of ice sometimes coat the branches of trees on autumn mornings; then, at the first touch of the wind, they scatter into dust.

Trofim Ivanych did not move. She did not hear him. But Sofya knew that he was not asleep: in sleep he always smacked his lips like a suckling baby. And she knew why he did not sleep. Here he could not go to Ganka. Sofya closed her eyes, shut her lips tightly, gathered in all of herself – she must not think about anything.

Suddenly, as if coming to some decision, Trofim Ivanych turned quickly to Sofya. Her blood seemed to stop in mid-course, her legs went numb, she waited. Behind the window, the moon trembled for a minute, two minutes, wrapping itself in a blanket. Trofim Ivanych raised his head, looked at the window, then carefully, trying not to touch Sofya, turned with his back to her again.

When he finally began to breathe evenly, smacking his lips in his sleep like a child, Sofya opened her eyes. She quietly bent over Trofim Ivanych, so near that she could see a long black hair coming down from his eyebrow over his eye. His lips moved. Sofya looked, and she no longer remembered anything about him. She felt only pity. She put out her hand – and drew it back at once: she wanted to stroke him like a child, but she could not, did not dare . . .

And so it was every night for three weeks, while the downstairs apartment was drying out. Every morning, before going to work, Trofim Ivanych went down for a half hour and mended one thing or another. One day he came back in high spirits and bantered with Pelageya, but Sofya saw his eyes following Ganka: Ganka, bent over, was sweeping the room. As he was leaving, Trofim Ivanych said to Sofya: 'Well, start moving down, it's time, everything is ready.' Then to Ganka, 'Make a good fire today, don't stint on wood, we want to get the house warm by evening.'

Sofya knew that he meant night, not evening. She said nothing and did not raise her eyes, only her lips twitched faintly like the skin on milk when it is cooling.

4

The cabman, Pelageya's husband, did not drive out to work until the afternoon that day. Until then, together with Sofya and Ganka, he quickly brought all their belongings downstairs. 'Well, what shall I wish you now? Good luck in your new-old home, I guess?' he said to Sofya.

Quickly, with a few wide wingbeats, like a large bird, Sofya swept the room with her eyes. Everything had returned to its old place: the chairs, the dim mirror, the clock on the wall, the bed where Sofya would be alone at night again. Suddenly, the weeks upstairs seemed happy to her: there, she had heard him breathe at night; he had not been with the other one, he had been no one's. But now, today, that very day . . .

Ganka was out; she had gone to bring some wood. Sofya stood leaning her forehead against the window. The panes rang out under the onslaughts of the wind. Grey, low, stony, city clouds rushed in the sky overhead. It seemed to Sofya that the stifling clouds of last summer, which had never once burst through into a rainstorm, were coming back. She felt as though these clouds were not outside the window, but in herself; for many months they had been piling up inside her like heavy rocks. If they were not to suffocate her now, she must smash something, or run from here, or scream out in a frenzy as the cobbler had screamed, announcing Judgement Day.

Sofya heard Ganka come in and shake the wood out of the sack onto the floor. Then she began to feed it into the stove. The window throbbed as though a heart had knocked against it from without. It was the cannon: the wind was driving the water again, swelling out the blue veins of the Neva. Sofya continued to stand as she was, without turning back, so as not to see Ganka.

Suddenly Ganka began to hum something quietly, under her nose – this never happened before. Sofya glanced back. Ganka had put down the axe and squatted on the floor, splitting some kindling with a knife. Her knees, spread wide apart, quivered under her dress; the lock on her forehead bobbed up and down.

Sofya wanted to take away her eyes and could not. Slowly, heavily, like a barge drawn by a cable to the shore against the current – the cable quivering, almost breaking – Sofya approached Ganka. Ganka was flushed with the work. The hot, sweetish odour of her sweat struck Sofya's nostrils. She must have smelled like that at night.

And at the first whiff of this smell, something rose up in Sofya from below, from the pit of her stomach, whipped across her heart, flooded all of her. She wanted to seize hold of something, but she was swept along just as the logs of wood and the cat on the table had been swept along the street that first day by the torrent. Without thinking, caught up by the wave, she lifted the axe from the floor, herself not knowing why she did it. The huge heart of the cannon thumped once more against the window. Sofya suddenly saw with her eyes that she had the axe in her hand. 'Oh Lord, oh Lord, what is this?' one Sofya cried desperately within her, but at that instant the other Sofya struck with the butt end of the axe at Ganka's temple, straight at that lock of hair.

Ganka did not cry out; her head dropped forward into her lap, and then she softly keeled over to the side from her squatting position. Quickly and greedily, Sofya struck at her head again and again with the sharp of the axe. Blood spurted out on the sheet of iron before the stove. And it was as though this blood were flowing from herself, from Sofya, as though some festering abscess in her had burst at last, and the disease poured out, dripped out, every drop increasing her relief. She threw down the axe and took a deep, free breath, as if she had never breathed before, as if she were just taking her first great gulp of air. No fear, no shame – nothing but a sense of newness, lightness all through her body, as after a long illness.

Afterwards, it was as though Sofya's hands, quite independently of her, thought and did all that was necessary, while she herself was blissfully resting somewhere on the side, and only once in a while her eyes opened and she began to see, and then she looked at everything with astonishment.

Ganka's slippers, her brown dress and shift, doused with kerosene, were already burning in the stove. Ganka herself, all naked, pink, fresh as new milk, lay face down on the floor, and a fly crawled over her unhurriedly, confidently. Sofya saw the fly and shooed it off. Sofya's alien hands easily, calmly chopped the body in half – otherwise it would be impossible to carry it away. Sofya in the meantime was thinking of the potatoes on the kitchen table; Ganka had not finished peeling them. They'll have to be cooked for dinner. She went to the kitchen, fastened the hook on the door, and made the oven.

When she returned to the room, she saw that the new piece of oilcloth, grey, with a marble pattern, had been taken out of the drawer and was lying on the floor, torn into two pieces. Sofya wondered: who could have torn it? what for? But she immediately remembered, spread the oilcloth at the bottom of a sack and put one half of the pink body into it. The same fly insistently kept settling on her hands, clinging to them; Sofya chased it away, but it came back again and again. Once Sofya saw it quite near: its legs were thin as though made of black thread from the spool. Afterwards the fly and everything else disappeared, and there was only one thing – someone's knocking on the kitchen door.

Sofya tiptoed to the threshold and waited. The knocking started again, louder and louder. Sofya watched the hook quiver from the blows – no, she did not even watch it, she felt it; the hook was now a part of her, like her eyes, her heart, her suddenly numbed feet. A seemingly familiar voice cried from behind the door, 'Sofya!' She was silent, and somebody's feet stamped noisily down the stairs. Sofya began to breathe; she looked out of the window. It was Pelageya; the wind whipped at the dress behind her, so that it clung tightly to her body and it seemed that she was walking with bent knees.

Again, for a long time, there were only Sofya's hands, while she herself was absent. Suddenly she found herself at the edge of a ditch. The water in the ditch was lilac, glassy with sunset, and the whole world, the sky, the madly tumbling lilac clouds were there, as though someone had thrown them into the ditch. On her back, Sofya carried a heavy sack, and her hand was holding up something under her coat. She could not understand what it could be. Then the hand remembered that it was a spade, and everything became simple again. She crossed the ditch and glanced around only with her eyes, quite independently of herself. There was no one in sight. She was alone on the Smolensk Field. It was swiftly turning dark. She dug a pit and threw into it everything that had been in the sack.

When it was quite dark, she returned there with another full sack. Then she filled the pit and started out for home. She walked along the black, uneven, swollen earth, the wind whipped cold, taut towels against her legs. Sofya stumbled. She fell, her hand struck something wet, and she walked on with a wet hand, afraid to wipe it. Far away – it must have been on the seashore – light blinked, glowing and disappearing; or perhaps it was somewhere quite near – perhaps somebody was lighting a cigarette in the wind.

At home, Sofya quickly scrubbed the floor, washed herself in the basin in the kitchen and put on everything fresh, as after confession on the eve of a holiday. The wood kindled by Ganka had long burned down, but the last blue flames still flickered over the coals. Sofya threw in the sack, the oilcloth, all the remaining trash. The fire flared up and everything was burned; now the room was altogether clean. And all the trash had also burned out in Sofya, and everything within her became clean and quiet.

She sat down on the bench. All the knots in her were loosened, untied, and she felt suddenly more tired than she had ever been in all her life. She put her head down on her arms on the table, and fell asleep instantly – deeply, fully, happily, with all of herself.

5

The pendulum on the wall tossed like a bird in a cage under a cat's intent stare. Sofya slept. This may have lasted an hour or only the instant between one swing of the pendulum and the next. When she raised her head, Trofim Ivanych stood before her, his feet rooted in the earth.

His collar constrained him and he unbuttoned it. 'Where is she?' he asked, bending down to Sofya. He smelled of wine; a taut, tense heat came from his body. 'Where's Ganka?' he repeated.

'Yes, where is she now?' thought Sofya, and answered aloud, 'I don't know'.

'Ah-h . . . You don't know?' Trofim Ivanych said crookedly, slowly.

Sofya saw his eyes quite near; they were like bared teeth. He had never struck her, but now it seemed to her that he would strike her. But he only looked at her and turned away. It might have been easier if he had hit her.

They sat down to dinner. Sofya was alone. She felt that Trofim Ivanych did not see her; it was not at her that he was looking. He swallowed a spoonful of cabbage soup and stopped, gripping the spoon tightly in his fist. Suddenly he took a deep, loud breath and banged his fist on the table. The cabbage flew out of the spoon into his lap. He picked it up and did not know what to do with it; the tablecloth was clean, and he held the cabbage in his hand with an absurd, confused air like a child – like that gypsy boy Sofya had seen in the empty house. She felt warm with pity and held out her own, already empty plate. Trofim Ivanych threw the cabbage into it without looking and got up.

When he returned, he had a bottle of madeira in his hand. Sofya understood that it had been bought for the other one; her heart immediately froze, she was again alone. Trofim Ivanych poured the wine into a glass and drank.

After dinner he silently moved the lamp nearer and picked up a newspaper, but Sofya saw that he was reading the same line over and over. She saw the newspaper tremble: the boards creaked in the hallway . . . No, it was not to them; someone went up the stairs. Again it became quiet, and only the pendulum tossed on the wall like a bird. Upstairs they were moving something heavy; they were probably going to bed.

Ganka was still out. Trofim Ivanych walked past Sofya to the clothes rack, put on his hat, stood a while, then tore it off as though he wanted to tear off his head along with it – to be rid of his thoughts. Then he lay down on the bench, with his face to the wall. 'Wait, let me put down the bedding,' said Sofya. He rose, looked at her, and his eyes went through her like a draught.

She made his bed and went to the door to hook it shut. She had already stretched her hand, then stopped: what if Trofim Ivanych asked her how she knew that Ganka would not return? She knew she must not, but she glanced back.

Trofim Ivanych watched her, watched her hand, stretched out and not daring to touch the hook. 'Well, why did you stop?' he asked and grinned crookedly, with half of his face.

'He knows everything . . .' thought Sofya. The pendulum swung once before her and froze. Trofim Ivanych was slowly, silently turning red. He pushed away the table. Something fell – it was in Sofya, inside her. Now, this very moment, he will say everything . . .

Pulling his feet out of the earth with great effort, he was moving towards Sofya. A blue vein, swollen like the Neva, stood out on his forehead. 'Well? What's the matter with you?' he shouted. Everything stopped in the room. 'Lock up! Let her sleep anywhere she wants to, with anyone she likes – in the street, under a fence, with the dogs! Lock up, do you hear?'

'What . . . what?' Sofya mumbled, still not believing.

'That's what!' Trofim Ivanych snapped at her and turned away. Sofya slipped on the hook.

For a long time she lay shivering under the blanket until she warmed up at last, until she finally believed that Trofim Ivanych could not, did not know. The clock above her pecked loudly at the wall as with a beak. Trofim Ivanych began to turn on his bunk, breathing greedily through clenched teeth. Sofya heard him clearly, as though he were saying everything aloud, in words. She saw before her the hateful blond curls on that forehead – and in the same instant they vanished: Sofya remembered that they were gone, and never would return. 'Thank God . . .' she said to herself, and caught herself immediately: ' "Thank God" for what? Oh, Lord!'

Trofim Ivanych began to toss and turn again. Sofya thought that he was, really, gone too, he too would never return; she would always be alone now, out in the draught. What was the good, then, of all that had happened that day? With an effort, step by climbing step, she began to draw air into her lungs; it was as though she had to raise a heavy stone with her breath, as with a rope, from somewhere at the very bottom. Then, just as it reached the surface, the stone broke away, and Sofya felt that she could breathe. She sighed and slowly began to sink into sleep, as into deep, warm water.

When she was almost at the bottom, she heard bare feet step down on the floor. She started and instantly swam up to the surface. The floor creaked, Trofim Ivanych was cautiously going somewhere. It was like this that he would go to Ganka in the kitchen at night. Sofya would always gather herself into a tight knot, to keep from breathing, from crying out. Now, too, she shrank into herself. She knew: he was drawn there; perhaps he'll seize and crush her pillow, or simply stand there, before Ganka's empty bed ...

The boards creaked, then they were silent. Trofim Ivanych had stopped. Sofya opened her eyes a crack: Trofim Ivanych, dimly white, stood halfway between his bench and the bed where she was lying. And Sofya suddenly was pierced through with the knowledge that he was not going to the kitchen, he was coming to her – to her! A wave of heat swept over her, her teeth began to chatter, she tightly shut her eyes.

'Sofya ...' Trofim Ivanych said quietly, then still more quietly, 'Sofya.' She recognized his special, night voice; her heart dropped from its branch and, tumbling wildly, like a bird, began to fall. Not with her mind, with something else – with her knees, clenched together so tightly that they hurt, with every fold of her body – Sofya understood that it would be simpler, easier for him if she did not reply, and she lay breathless, silent.

Trofim Ivanych bent over her; she heard his breath quite near, he must be looking at her. This lasted only a second, but Sofya was afraid she would not endure it. She cried out soundlessly, 'Lord, Lord!' From above, from thousands of versts away, where the clouds were rushing madly now, came the faint sound of Pelageya's laughter. A hot, dry hand touched Sofya's legs. She slowly opened her lips, she opened to her husband all of herself, to the very end – for the first time in her life. He crushed her mercilessly, as if trying to avenge on her all of his greedy anger at the other one. Sofya heard his gritting teeth, she heard again the low laughter of Pelageya upstairs – then she remembered nothing.

6

The morning was frosty. The windows seemed made of rock candy. A blue and yellow spot of reflected sunlight crawled across the white wall. Sofya went down into the yard. Everything had quietened down during the night; the air was calm and transparent; smoke rose to the sky in upright, rosy shafts.

Pelageya was also out in the yard. She said to Sofya, 'So your Ganka ran off? A waste to feed that kind!' Sofya looked at her with light, transparent eyes, made of that morning; she tried to remember yesterday, and could not. All of that was very far away; most probably it never happened. Pelageya said that Trofim Ivanych had come up in the morning before going to work to ask if they had seen Ganka. Sofya laughed. 'What is it?' Pelageya glanced at her, surprised.

'Oh, nothing ...' said Sofya, looking at the straight pink column of smoke. She remembered just such smoke in her home village, from which Trofim Ivanych had taken her. They must be chopping cabbage out there now. She thought of the cabbage stalks – cool, white, crisp. It seemed to her that all of this had been but yesterday, and that she herself was just the same as she had been then, when she ate cabbage stalks.

When he returned from the factory, Trofim Ivanych only asked: 'Well? Not back?'

Sofya knew what he meant; she calmly answered, 'No.'

Trofim Ivanych ate his supper and went out somewhere. He came back late, scowling. He must have looked for her, asking everybody, everywhere. At night he came to Sofya again – as silently, angrily, greedily as the night before.

On the following day Trofim Ivanych reported Ganka's disappearance to the militia. Sofya, Pelageya, her husband and other neighbours were called in. Behind the table sat a young fellow in a cap. On his nose there was an earnest, rimless pince-nez, and his face was small and pockmarked. He looked like a half-grown chick, and on the table before him lay some slices of dry black bread, covered with papers. All the witnesses told him the same thing: they had seen Ganka running around with some fellows – not local boys, strangers, from the Petersburg side. Pelageya recalled that Ganka had told her one day that she would run away, she was fed up with everything here. The fellow in the cap wrote it all down. Sofya looked at his pock-marked face, his pince-nez, the slices of dry bread, and she felt sorry for him.

On the way home, Sofya asked Trofim Ivanych to buy a new axe: the old one must have been stolen, or had been mislaid somewhere – she could not find it. Sofya did not think about Ganka any more; Trofim Ivanych never said a word about her either. At times, though, he sat staring endlessly at the same line in his newspaper, and Sofya knew what he was silent about. Just as silently, he would raise his coal-black, gypsy eyes at her, and heavily, silently follow her with his eyes. It unnerved her: what if he should say something suddenly? But he said nothing.

The days continued clear and crisp, but were becoming shorter and shorter. It seemed that soon, before one knew it – if not today, then tomorrow – they would flare up for the last time like a burnt-down candle, and then – darkness, the end of everything. But tomorrow came, and the end was not yet. Nonetheless something began to go amiss with Sofya. She did not sleep one night, then another, and a third. Dark circles appeared under her eyes; the eyes sank. Just so the snow darkens, settles, sinks in springtime, and suddenly patches of earth appear beneath it. But spring was still far off.

In the evening Sofya poured kerosene into the lamp through a tin funnel. Trofim Ivanych cried: 'Look out, look what you're doing: it's over the brim!'

It was only then that Sofya saw that the lamp was full, and the kerosene must have been spilling over on the table for a long time. 'Over the brim . . .' Sofya repeated, bemused. Her lips, always tightly shut, were parted as at night. She looked at Trofim Ivanych, and it seemed to him that she wanted to say something else.

'Well, what is it?' he asked.

Sofya turned away.

'Is it ... something about her ... about Ganka?' his voice came through clenched, white gypsy teeth.

She did not answer.

When she served supper, she dropped the plate of buck-wheat gruel on the floor. Trofim Ivanych looked up and saw her strange, unfamiliar eyes, sunken like snow in spring, and it gave him a turn to look at her: it was not she. 'What's wrong with you, Sofya?' And again she said nothing.

That night he came to her; he had not been with her since those two nights. When she heard his old night voice saying, 'Sofya, tell me, I know you have something to tell me,' she broke down; everything brimmed over, and she burst into tears. They were warm – Trofim Ivanych felt them with his cheek and they frightened him. 'But what is it? It doesn't matter – just say it!' Then Sofya said, 'I ... I'm going to ... have a child ...' This happened in the dark, it could not be seen. Trofim Ivanych passed a hot, dry hand over her face – to see. His fingers trembled, they discovered that Sofya's lips were parted wide and smiling. He only said, 'So-of-ka!' He had not called her that for a long time, for at least ten years. She laughed blissfully, fully. 'When did it happen?' asked Trofim Ivanych. It had happened during one of those two nights, immediately after Ganka's dis-appearance.

'You remember – Pelageya, upstairs ... And I thought then that I, too, would have ... like Pelageya ... But no, I'm lying. I didn't think anything then, it's only now ... But even now I don't believe ... no, I do believe!' she ran on confusedly, and her tears flowed easily like rivulets of melted snow on the ground. Trofim Ivanych put his hand on her stomach and cautiously, timidly passed his fingers over it, from below upward. Her stomach was round, it was the earth. In the earth, deep down invisible to anyone, lay Ganka, and in the earth, invisible to anyone, seeds burrowed with white roots. This was at night. Then came the day, and evening once again.

In the evening Trofim Ivanych brought a bottle of madeira to supper. Sofya had already seen such a bottle once before: it would have been better if he had brought something else this time. But Sofya did not even think this – she merely registered it in passing with her eyes; it did not enter her. Her whole body smiled, it was full to the brim, there was no room in it for anything else. It merely frightened her that the days were getting shorter and shorter. Any day now they might burn out altogether, and then – the end. And she must hurry, she must still say or do something before the end.

One evening Trofim Ivanych came home later than usual. He stopped on the threshold, broad, deeply planted in the earth with his feet, his face covered with coal-dust. He said to Sofya, 'Oh, they called me in again.'

Sofya instantly understood where and what for; inside her, the pendulum stopped again and missed – one, two, three beats. She sat down. 'Yes?' she asked Trofim Ivanych.

'Well: they said the case was closed, they didn't find her. She ran off somewhere with her tramp – and the devil take her! If only she doesn't show up again . . .'

Sofya's heart revived: it was not yet the end.

And immediately something stirred and came to life within her, a little lower, like another, a second heart. She gasped aloud and caught her stomach with her hands.

'What is it?' Trofim Ivanych ran up to her.

'It's . . . moving . . .' Sofya whispered.

Trofim Ivanych shook his head, caught Sofya and lifted her up; she was light as a bird.

'Let go,' she said.

He set her down on the floor, his teeth gleaming white like accordion keys; he laughed with all the keys at once. This was the first time since Ganka, and he must have realized it himself. He said to Sofya, 'Now, listen, Sofya. Remember – if she turns up now, I'll . . .'

There was a knocking at the door, and they both turned quickly. Sofya heard Trofim Ivanych think almost aloud, 'Ganka.' The same thought flashed through Sofya's head. She knew it could not be – yet here it was.

'Shall I open?' asked Trofim Ivanych.

'Open,' Sofya answered in a white voice.

Trofim Ivanych opened, and Pelageya entered – loud-voiced,

all of her unlatched, wide open. 'What is this – why are you so white?' she said to Sofya. 'You have to eat more now, woman.' Pelageya had already given birth twice. She began to talk about it to Sofya, and all of Sofya's body began to smile again; she forgot Ganka.

At night, when she was already sinking to the depths, falling asleep, Ganka suddenly flashed again before her, as though she were lying somewhere in those nocturnal depths. Sofya shook and opened her eyes. Bright spots played on the ceiling. She heard the driving wind outside the window; the panes rang out faintly just as they had that day. She tried to remember how it all happened, but could not remember anything, and for a long time she lay awake. Then, as though entirely unconnected, quite separately, she saw a piece of marbled oilcloth on the floor and a fly crawling on a rosy back. She clearly distinguished the fly's legs – thin, made of black thread. 'But who, who did it? She – this is she – I . . . Here is Trofim Ivanych, next to me, and I will have a child – and it was I?' All the hair on her head became alive. She seized Trofim Ivanych by the shoulder and began to shake him: he must tell her at once that it had not happened, that it wasn't she who had done it.

'Who . . . who? Is that you, Sofka?' Trofim Ivanych pulled his eyes open with an effort.

'It wasn't I, not I, not I!' cried Sofya and stopped: she realized she could not, must not say any more, and never would – because . . . 'Oh, Lord . . . If only the baby would come soon!' she said aloud.

Trofim Ivanych laughed: 'You silly! There's time!' and soon began to smack his lips again in sleep.

Sofya did not sleep. She stopped sleeping at night. But, then, there were almost no nights now; behind the window, bright, heavy water seemed to be heaving all the time, and summer flies buzzed ceaselessly.

7

Before going to work one morning, Trofim Ivanych told Sofya that a flywheel had caught one of the oilers the previous day and kept turning with him for a long time; when he was taken off, he felt his head, asked, 'Where's my hat?' and died.

The winter window had already been removed. Sofya polished the panes with a rag and thought about the oiler, about death; it seemed to her that it would be quite simple – just like the sun setting: darkness, then day again. She climbed up on the bench to wipe the upper panes – and suddenly the flywheel caught her, she dropped the rag and screamed. Pelageya came running, and this was all that Sofya remembered. After that there was nothing; everything turned and turned, everything rushed past, and she was screaming. Once she very clearly heard the distant clanging of a streetcar and the voices of children in the yard. Then everything stopped in mid-flight. The silence weighed a ton, and Sofya felt blood gushing and gushing from her. This was how it must have been with the oiler when he was taken off the wheel.

'It's over now,' said Pelageya. It was not over, but Sofya knew that only minutes were left before the end, and she must hurry, hurry . . . 'Hurry!' she said.

'Hurry what?' asked Pelageya's voice.

'The girl . . . show her to me.'

'How did you know it is a girl?' Pelageya asked with astonishment and showed her the red living piece torn out of Sofya: the tiny toes on the feet drawn up under the belly stirred, and Sofya looked and looked. 'All right, then, take her,' said Pelageya. She put the baby down on Sofya's bed and went away to the kitchen.

Sofya unbuttoned her shift and brought the baby to her breast. She knew that this should not be done until the second day, but she could not wait, everything had to be done quickly, quickly. Blindly, still awkwardly, swallowing the wrong way, the baby began to suckle. Sofya felt everything flowing out of her – warm tears, warm milk, warm blood. All of her was open wide and running over with juices. She lay there, warm, blessed, moist, resting, like the earth: it was for this one moment that she had lived all her life, everything that went before had been just for the sake of this.

'I'll run upstairs for a moment – you don't need anything else?' asked Pelageya.

Sofya merely moved her lips, but Pelageya understood that she needed nothing more now.

Afterwards Sofya seemed to doze off. It was very hot under the blanket. She heard the ringing of the streetcars and the children in the yard shouting, 'Catch her!' But all of this was very far away, it came to her through a thick blanket. 'Her? Whom now?' thought Sofya and opened her eyes. Far away, as though on the other bank, Trofim Ivanych was lighting the lamp. A dense rain was falling; it made a darkness all around, and the lamp was tiny as a pinhead. Sofya saw the white teeth like a keyboard. Trofim Ivanych must have been smiling, saying something to her, but she did not catch it – she was being drawn to the bottom.

Through her sleep, Sofya was constantly aware of the lamp: tiny as a pinhead, it was now somewhere inside her, in her stomach. Trofim Ivanych said in his night voice, 'Ah, you, my Sofka!' The lamp began to burn her so badly that she called Pelageya. Pelageya dozed sitting near the bed; she jerked her head up like a horse.

'The lamp . . .' Sofya brought out with difficulty, her tongue like a stiff mitten.

'Shall I put it out?' Pelageya hurried to the lamp. Then Sofya woke up completely and told Pelageya that she had a burning in her stomach, all the way down.

At dawn Trofim Ivanych ran to get the doctor. Sofya recognized her: the same buxom one, in pince-nez, who had come to see the carpenter before he died. The doctor looked at Sofya. 'Yes . . . good . . . very good . . . Does it hurt here? Yes, yes, yes . . .' Then she turned her snub nose cheerfully to Trofim Ivanych: 'Well, we must get her to the hospital, quick.' Trofim Ivanych's teeth disappeared, his hand, with its coal-darkened lines, gripped the foot of Sofya's bed.

'What's wrong with her?' he asked.

'I don't know yet. Looks like childbed fever,' the doctor said cheerfully and went out into the kitchen to wash her hands.

Sofya was lifted on to a stretcher and was being turned towards the door. Everything she had lived with moved past her: the window, the wall clock, the stove. It was as though a boat were casting off, and all the familiar things on the shore were floating away. The pendulum on the wall tossed one way, the other – and could be seen no more. It seemed to Sofya that there was something that still had to be done in this room one last time. When the ambulance door had already swung open, Sofya remembered what it was. She quickly undid her shift and took out her breast, but no one understood what she wanted; the orderlies laughed.

For a while there was nothing. Then the lamp appeared again; now it was overhead, under the white ceiling. Sofya saw white walls, white women in beds. Very near a fly was crawling on something white; it had thin legs made of black spool thread. Sofya screamed and, waving it away, began to slide down from the bed onto the floor.

'Where are you going? Lie still!' said the nurse, and caught her up. The fly was gone. Sofya calmly closed her eyes.

Ganka came in – with a sackful of wood. She squatted down, spreading her knees wide, glanced at Sofya, and shook her fair bangs, grinning. Sofya's heart beat fast, she struck her with an axe and opened her eyes. A snub-nosed face with pince-nez was bending over her, thick lips were saying rapidly, 'Yes, yes, yes . . .' The pince-nez glittered, and Sofya shut her eyes tightly. Immediately, Ganka came in with the wood and squatted down. Sofya hit her with the axe again, and again the doctor shook her head, saying, 'Yes, yes, yes . . .' Ganka's head dropped forward into her lap, and Sofya struck her another time. 'Yes, yes, yes . . . Good,' said the doctor. 'Is her husband here? Call him in, quickly.'

'Hurry, hurry!' cried Sofya. She understood that this was the end, she was dying and must hurry with all her strength. The nurse ran out, slamming the door. Somewhere very near the cannon boomed; the wind was wildly beating at the window. 'A flood?' asked Sofya, opening her eyes wide.

'Just a moment, one moment . . . Lie still,' said the doctor.

The cannon boomed, the wind rushed in her ears, the water was rising higher and higher – in a moment it would flood and sweep everything away. She must hurry, quick, quick . . . Yesterday's familiar pain tore her in half. Sofya opened her thighs.

'I must give birth . . . I must give birth quickly!' she seized the doctor by the sleeve.

'Quiet, quiet. You've had your baby already – whom else do you want?' Sofya knew whom, but she could not utter her name, and the water was rising, higher and higher, she must hurry . . .

Ganka, with her head in her lap, sat crouching by the stove. Trofim Ivanych came near her and shut her out. 'It wasn't I – not I, not I!' Sofya wanted to say. This happened once before. She remembered that night and immediately understood what she must do; everything in her was suddenly white and clear. She jumped up on her knees in bed and cried to Trofim Ivanych: 'It was I, I! She was making the stove – I hit her with the axe . . .'

'She is delirious . . . she doesn't know what she's . . .' Trofim Ivanych began.

'Keep quiet!' Sofya cried. He fell silent. Huge waves swept out of her and washed over him, over everyone. The room was suddenly still, there was nothing in it but eyes. 'I killed her,' Sofya said heavily, solidly. 'I hit her with the axe. She lived with us, she lived with him, I killed her, I wanted to have a . . .'

'She is d-d-del . . . d-del-lirious,' Trofim Ivanych's lips shook, he could not pronounce the word.

Sofya became terrified that they might not believe her. She gathered everything that still remained in her, she strained her memory to the utmost and said: 'No, I know. I threw the axe under the stove, it is still there . . .'

Everything around was white and very silent, as in winter. Trofim Ivanych did not speak. Sofya saw that they believed her. Slowly, like a bird, she sank back on the bed. Now everything was good, blissful, she was finished, all of her had poured out.

Trofim Ivanych was the first to recover. He rushed to Sofya and clutched at the bed; he must hold her back, he must not let her go. 'She's dead!' he cried out.

The women jumped off their beds, came running, craning their heads. 'Go away, go away! Get back to bed!' the nurse waved at them, but they would not leave.

The doctor lifted Sofya's hand, held it a moment, then said cheerfully, 'She's sleeping.'

In the evening the whiteness turned faintly greenish like still water, and like the sky behind the window. The buxom doctor stood again near Sofya's bed. Next to her were Trofim Ivanych and a young man with a scar on his cheek. The scar made it seem that his face hurt all the time, yet he smiled continually.

The doctor took her stethoscope and listened to Sofya's heart: it was beating evenly, calmly, and her breath was calm and even. 'Yes, yes, yes . . .' The doctor thought for a moment. 'By God, she'll make it, after all. She'll live!' She put on her pince-nez, and her eyes became like the eyes of children when they look at fire.

'Well, then, let's begin!' said the young man with the shaven face and took out a sheet of paper. He was in pain, but he smiled with his scar.

'No, let her sleep, not now,' said the doctor. 'You'll have to come back tomorrow, my dear comrade.'

'Very well. It's all the same to me.'

'And it is certainly all the same to her; you can do anything you want with her now!' The doctor's pince-nez glittered. The young man, smiling through his pain, went out.

The doctor continued to stand, looking at the woman: she slept, breathing evenly, quietly, blissfully, her lips parted wide.

[*1929*]

THE LION

It all began with an utterly fantastic event: the lion, that magnificent king of the beasts, got stinking drunk. He stumbled on all four paws and kept keeling over on his side. It was a complete catastrophe.

The lion attended Leningrad University and at the same time worked as an extra at the ballet theatre. In today's performance he was to stand on a cliff, dressed in a lion skin, and wait to be struck by the spear thrown by the heroine. Then the dead lion would fall from the cliff on to a mattress backstage. Everything went excellently during rehearsals; then suddenly, on the day of the premiere, a half hour before curtain time, the lion played such a swinish trick! There were no substitute extras. And the show could not be cancelled: it was to be attended by a People's Commissar who had just arrived from Moscow. An emergency meeting was called at the 'Red Director's' office.

There was a knock at the door, and the theatre fireman, Petya Zherebyakin, entered the room. The 'Red Director' (he was actually red at this moment – with chagrin) shouted at him: 'Well, what is it, what do you want? I have no time now! Get the hell out!'

'I . . . comrade director . . . I mean – about the lion,' said the fireman.

'Well, what about the lion?'

'I mean, as our lion is plastered, maybe I could play the lion, comrade director . . .'

I don't know whether there are bears with freckles and blue eyes. If there are such bears, then the hulking Zherebyakin in his huge cast-iron boots was much more like a bear than a lion. But maybe he could, by some miracle, be made into a lion? He

278

swore he could, he swore that he had watched all the rehearsals from the wings, and that back in his soldier days he had played in *The Emperor Maximilian*. And mostly to spite the *régisseur*, who had permitted himself a crooked grin, the director ordered Zherebyakin to dress up instantly and try for the part.

A few moments later the musicians on the stage were already playing the 'lion's march'. The lion Petya Zherebyakin stepped out in the lionskin as though he had been born in the Libyan desert instead of a village in Ryazan. But at the last moment, when he had to fall from the cliff, he looked down – and stood petrified.

'Fall, you devil . . . go on, fall!' the *régisseur* hissed at him in a furious whisper.

The lion obediently plopped down. He fell heavily on his back, and lay there, unable to get up. Wouldn't he get up? Was there to be another catastrophe – at the very last moment?

He was helped up. He climbed out of the skin and stood there, pale, holding on to his back and smiling in confusion. One of his upper teeth was missing, and this made his smile pathetic and childlike (but then, there is always something childlike about bears, isn't there?).

Fortunately, there were apparently no serious injuries. He asked for water. The director ordered a glass of tea to be brought from his office. After Petya had drunk the tea, the director began to exhort him: 'All right, my friend, you've called yourself a lion – climb into the skin! Go on, climb, brother, quick, we're starting soon!'

Somebody obligingly hurried over with the skin, but the lion refused to climb into it. He declared that he must leave the theatre for a moment, refusing to explain this urgent need but merely grinning with embarrassment. The director flew into a temper. He tried to order him, he reminded Zherebyakin that he was a candidate for Party membership, that he was a shock worker, but the shock worker-lion stubbornly persisted. They had to give in. Beaming with his toothless smile, Petya Zherebyakin rushed somewhere out of the theatre.

'Where the devil is he off to?' the director asked everybody, turning red with rage all over again. 'What's all this mystery?'

Nobody could enlighten the Red Director. The only one who knew the answer was Petya Zherebyakin – and, of course, the author of this story. And while Petya Zherebyakin is hurrying through the Petersburg autumn rain, we can slip away for a moment to that June night when the mystery was born.

That night there was no night: it was day, alertly dozing off for a second, like a soldier during a campaign, still marching, and hovering between dream and reality. In the rosy glass of the canals, the upside-down trees, windows, columns – Petersburg – dozed lightly. And suddenly, there was the faintest breeze, and Petersburg vanished. Instead, there was Leningrad, with the red flag over the Winter Palace wakened by the wind, and a militiaman with a rifle standing near the wrought-iron fence of the Alexandrovsky Garden.

The militiaman was surrounded by a band of night workers waiting for the trolley. From behind their backs, Petya Zherebyakin could see only the militiaman's face – round and smooth like a Ryazan honey apple. Something very strange was taking place: the men were pawing at the militiaman's hands and shoulders, and finally one of the workers, stretching out his lips, tenderly smacked him on the cheek. The militiaman turned purple and furiously blew his whistle. The workers scattered. Petya Zherebyakin remained alone face to face with the militiaman – and then the militiaman vanished just as suddenly as the mirrored Petersburg, ruffled by the wind. Before Zherebyakin stood a girl in a militia uniform and cap – the first militiawoman posted by the revolution on Nevsky Prospect. Her black eyebrows met angrily over her nose, and sparks flew from her eyes. 'Shame on you, comrade!' That was all she said to Petya Zherebyakin, but how she said it!

He was unnerved and muttered guiltily: 'I swear to God, it wasn't me! I was just going home . . .'

'You . . . A worker, too!' the militiawoman looked at him. But how she looked!

If there had been a trap door in the pavement, as on the stage, Zherebyakin would have dropped into it, and that would have been a blessing. Instead, he had to walk off slowly, feeling on his back the eyes that burned him through and through.

THE LION

The next night was again a white night, and again comrade Zherebyakin walked home from his job at the theatre, and again the militiawoman stood at her post by the gate of the Alexandrovsky Garden. Zherebyakin wanted to slip by, but he noticed her looking at him, and greeted her with guilty confusion. She nodded. The dawn gleamed on the mirror-black steel of her rifle, and the steel seemed pink. And Zherebyakin trembled before this pink rifle more than he had ever trembled before all the rifles that had fired at him for five years on the various fronts.

It was only a week later that he dared to address the militiawoman. It turned out that she was also from the Ryazan province, and still remembered the honey apples of their native Ryazan. Sure: sweet, with just a touch of bitterness. There were no such apples here . . .

Every night, on his way home, Zherebyakin stopped at the Alexandrovsky Garden. The white nights had gone altogether mad, and the green, rose, and copper sky never darkened for a second. In the Garden embracing couples sought the shade as in the daytime to escape being seen.

It was on such a night that Zherebyakin asked the militiawoman, clumsily, in bearlike fashion: 'And tell me, for example, are you militiawomen allowed to get married during the performance of duty? I mean, not during actual performance, but generally – seeing as your service is military, sort of . . .'

'Why "get married"?' Katya the militiawoman asked, leaning on her rifle. 'We're now – like men: if we want to, we love, just the same . . .' Her rifle was rose-coloured. The militiawoman raised her face to the feverishly flaming sky, then looked off somewhere past Zherebyakin, and added: 'For example, if there was such a man as wrote poems . . . Or an actor, who'd come out – and the whole theatre would clap . . .'

A honey apple – bittersweet. Petya Zherebyakin understood that he had better go and never return again: he was finished . . .

But no, he wasn't! There are miracles on earth! And when the incredible event took place, and the lion, by the dispensation of

281

the Lord, had gotten himself stewed – Petya Zherebyakin had a mighty inspiration, and rushed to the director's study . . .

However, all this was now a matter of the past. Now he was speeding through the autumn rain to Glinka Street. Luckily, it was right around the corner from the theatre, and luckily, he found Katya the militiawoman at home. At this moment, however, she was not a militiawoman, but simply Katya. With rolled-up sleeves, she was laundering a white blouse in a basin. There were dewdrops on her nose and forehead – and she had never seemed more desirable than now, as her simple, domestic self.

When Zherebyakin put the pass before her and told her that he was playing in the show that night, she did not believe him. Then she became interested. Then, for some reason, she turned shy and rolled down her sleeves. Then she looked at him (but how she looked!) and said that she would come, without fail.

The bell for the curtain was already shrilling in the smoking room, the corridors, and the foyer of the theatre. The bald-headed People's Commissar was squinting through his pince-nez in the loge. On the stage, behind the still lowered curtain, the ballerinas were smoothing out their tutus with the gesture of swans preening their wings as they lower themselves into the water. And behind the cliff, near the lion, the *régisseur* and the director were frenzied with anxiety.

'Remember: you're a shock worker! Remember, don't mess it up!' the director whispered into the lion's ear.

The curtain began to rise, and beyond the blazing line of footlights the lion saw the dark hall, filled to the top with the white blurs of faces. Long ago, when he had still been Zherebyakin, he had climbed out of a trench; shells were exploding around him – he'd start each time and cross himself by old peasant habit – and nevertheless he kept running forward. Now it seemed to him that he could not make a single step. But the *régisseur* gave him a push from behind, and, dragging with enormous difficulty his suddenly alien hands and feet, he slowly climbed on to the cliff.

On the summit of the cliff the lion raised his head – and saw, quite near him, in the second-tier loge, the militiawoman Katya leaning over the banister: she was looking straight at him. The lion heart thumped loudly once, twice! and stopped. He shivered: his fate hung in the balance, and the spear was already flying at him. Wham! – and it struck his side. Now he must fall. But what if he falls wrongly again and spoils everything? He was more terrified than ever in his life – much more than when he climbed out of the trench . . .

In the audience, they had already noticed that something was wrong on the stage: the mortally wounded lion stood motionless on the cliff, looking down. Those in the front rows heard the *régisseur*'s desperate whisper: 'Fall, you devil, fall!' And then came something altogether fantastic: the lion raised his right paw, rapidly crossed himself – and dropped from the cliff like a stone . . .

A moment of stunned silence, and then, like a deadly shell, wild laughter exploded in the hall. Tears of laughter ran down the cheeks of Katya the militiawoman. The stricken lion sobbed, hiding his muzzle in his paws.

[*1935*]

MORE ABOUT PENGUINS
AND PELICANS

Penguinews, which appears every month, contains details of all the new books issued by Penguins as they are published. From time to time it is supplemented by *Penguins in Print*, which is a complete list of all titles available. (There are some five thousand of these.)

A specimen copy of *Penguinews* will be sent to you free on request. For a year's issues (including the complete lists) please send 50p if you live in the British Isles, or 75p if you live elsewhere. Just write to Dept EP, Penguin Books Ltd, Harmondsworth, Middlesex, enclosing a cheque or postal order, and your name will be added to the mailing list.

In the U.S.A.: For a complete list of books available from Penguin in the United States write to Dept CS, Penguin Books Inc., 7110 Ambassador Road, Baltimore, Maryland 21207.

In Canada: For a complete list of books available from Penguin in Canada write to Penguin Books Canada Ltd, 41 Steelcase Road West, Markham, Ontario.

YEVGENY ZAMYATIN IN PENGUINS

WE

We tells of persons known as numbers living in the One State. All numbers live by a rigid timetable, performing exactly the same motions in time with one another in their all-glass environment.

We is the story of D-503, who is aroused from acceptance of the system by a strange woman, E-330. His transformation from conformity to radical action, his revolt against the state, and his eventual defeat are vividly chronicled in his diary.

Not for sale in the U.S.A. or Canada

ISAAC BASHEVIS SINGER IN PENGUINS

THE SÉANCE

Isaac Bashevis Singer is a master story-teller of our time. *The Séance*, one of his finest collections, is set in the terrain of the imagination, a world of shadows inhabited by saints and sinners, the quick and the dead, angels and demons. The scene is largely the Old World, yet the characters and the truths they illustrate are universal.

The stories range from the ironic and poignant title story in which an old man regularly visits a Central Park West medium who 'more than once . . . emerged from her trance to discuss stocks, bonds and dividends' to perhaps the masterpiece of the collection, 'Cockadoodledoo', an allegory in the classic fable tradition, a monologue delivered by a rooster who speaks in terms of the Jewish and human experience.

'In finely wrought simple language, and with controlled feeling and clarity these tales have both beauty and humanity' – Geoffrey Watkins.

Also available

The Slave